ANNICE PAUSED FOR A MINUTE ON THE EDGE OF THE CLIFF....

To her surprise, she spotted a vessel bobbing around in a small circle almost at the mouth of the bay.

The sudden appearance of a pair of kigh very nearly flung her a disastrous step forward. Heart racing, she staggered, fighting for balance. The long pale fingers of the two agitated kigh continued to tug at her, and she drew a breath to whistle them away. Then the message got through.

She snatched up her flute and threw herself down the path to the village, Singing as she ran. Twice she stumbled and the kigh caught her. Once, the earth rearranged itself under her feet. By the time she reached the first cottage, people were running to meet her. She pushed through the crowd, still Singing. If the kigh were right, she had almost no time.

Finally she reached the water's edge. She raised the flute to her lips. The first note was so sharp it hurt, but forcing herself to ___ e normally, she found the second an___ d on the boat, threw everythin___ e Call.

The fish___ of water and began ___ ter of kigh benea___ shore. With the bo___ turned the Song to a gra___ flowed out from underneath it, ___ the sea.

Annice ___ gered back against a solid chest.

"I've got you, child." Arms wrapped around her, and she gratefully sagged against their strength, her vision swimming. Annice saw blurry figures rush forward and lift a small body out over the stern of the boat.

Someone yelled, "Get him to old Emils!"

Then the world tilted and went away....

SING
THE FOUR
QUARTERS
TANYA HUFF

DAW BOOKS, INC.
DONALD A. WOLLHEIM, FOUNDER
375 Hudson Street, New York, NY 10014

ELIZABETH R. WOLLHEIM
SHEILA E. GILBERT
PUBLISHERS

First Printing, December 1994
3   4   5   6   7   8   9

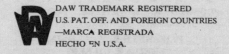

For Daniel,
whose timing couldn't have been better.

And for his mother, who shared.

CHAPTER ONE

"Was it something I said?" The innkeeper laughed as the young woman continued her headlong dash out the door, ignoring him completely. Lifting a slab of fried ham off the grill and onto an already full plate, he slid the pile of food across to his other overnight guest. "Kids these days. You just can't make 'em understand that if you sit up all night drinkin' you pay for it in the morning."

The burly wool merchant lowered his tankard, wiped the ale foam off his mustache, and dug into his breakfast with enthusiasm. "Used to be," he said around a mouthful of fried potatoes, "I could empty a good half barrel on my own and never feel it. But these days ..." He sighed and speared a pickled onion. "I remember when my youngest brother got joined; the hangover nearly killed me. I was seeing cross-eyed for three days."

"Wine," declared the innkeeper sagely. "Don't get that kind of a hangover on ale."

The merchant snorted. "Depends on how much you drink."

The story that followed probably contained as much wishful thinking as accuracy, but it was well enough told that the innkeeper rested his forearms on the counter and settled in to enjoy it. No point fixing more food when the only person around to eat it was still dumping her evening into the privy.

Annice spit the last of the bile out of her mouth and straightened, brushing damp strands of short, dark-blonde hair up off her forehead with the back of one hand. Her face felt clammy.

"No surprise," she muttered, sagging sideways against the rough plank wall. "All things considered."

Perfectly willing to pay for a night's excess, she considered it entirely outside the Circle to be so sick when she'd only had water and a little soft cider to drink. She hadn't overindulged—*Overindulged? I haven't even indulged!*—for about a month now because the smell of anything containing alcohol was enough to send her racing from the room.

In fact, the memory of the smell. . . .

Stomach heaving, she bent over the hole again.

A few moments of painful dry retching later, she lifted her head.

"All right," she panted, stepping back. "If I don't shake this bug by the end of the week, I *promise* I'll see a healer." With a shaking hand, she dumped a dipper of ash into the privy and fumbled at the door latch.

A cold wind roared across the courtyard and ripped the door out of her grasp. Reluctantly stepping out into the weather—she'd thrown on barely enough clothes for decency and not nearly enough for warmth—she grabbed the door with both hands and fought to close it behind her. The wind fought back. Frowning, Annice peered around the edge.

A thin and sharply pointed face, stormy gray eyes the most well-defined point in the shifting features, hung in the air over the wind-sketched outline of an elongated body. A wide, nearly lipless mouth opened in silent laughter as long, pale fingers clung to the boards.

"Kigh," Annice muttered. "Just what I needed." Running her tongue over cracked lips, she whistled a series of four piercing notes.

Its expression clearly stating, *I didn't want to stay longer anyway,* the kigh let go of the door and rode the wind out of sight.

The privy door, now pulled in only one direction, slammed shut.

"Shit!" Sucking on her pinched finger and wrapping the other arm around her for warmth, Annice staggered toward the inn. *I remember when I used to like mornings. . . .*

A wet fall, hanging on long past its time and leaving the roads a muddy quagmire, combined with the expectation of the river finally freezing had put a damper on traveling and given Annice not only the Bard's corner but the entire dormitory to herself. Leaning against the lingering warmth of the huge stone chimney, she tucked in her linen shirt and struggled to close the carved wooden button at her waist.

"I suspect," she grunted, as she finally forced the button through and reached for her sweater, "that the cloth for these breeches wasn't as preshrunk as the weaver insisted."

Somewhat to her surprise, as the inn was only a day's walk from the Bardic Hall in Vidor, a heavy fleece overcoat, very nearly her size, had been left in the closet. Although she'd already switched to fleece-lined boots, she decided not to take it. It wasn't so cold that her oilcloth jacket wouldn't do and any bards walking the Final Quarter might need it more. Although she hated being wet with a cat's passion, the cold hadn't actually had much effect on her this year. Placing the folded blankets up onto the shelves, she tossed in the pair of heavy socks she'd just finished knitting and Sang the closet locked.

Checking that both her instruments were secure, she heaved her pack up onto her shoulders and headed for the stairs.

"Down for breakfast, then?" the innkeeper called as she descended into the common room.

Annice smiled tightly and let her pack slide down onto the floor by the bar. "No. Thank you." As she breathed in the odors of the grill still hanging in the air, she could feel the nausea returning. "Just my journey food, please."

The innkeeper laughed, picked a heel of bread off the counter, and handed it to her. "Here, gnaw on this while I fetch your bundle. It'll help."

Although dubious, Annice obediently nibbled at the edge of the crust. It couldn't hurt and if there was any chance it *might* help. . . .

The wool merchant watched her over the rim of his tankard. When he finally lowered it, empty, to the bar, he nodded at her pack. "Heading to Elbasan, then?"

"Yes."

"You finishing a Walk?"

He'd been in the common room the night before while

she'd been singing, so he knew she was on her way home. Annice considered pointing that out but decided it might be safer to continue repeating words of one syllable. "Yes."

"I'm going that way myself. I was late leaving Vidor on account of that fire at the Weavers' Guild. I suppose you heard about that?"

Annice forced down a gummy mouthful of well-chewed bread. "I'm carrying a follow-up," she told him with little enthusiasm, hoping he wouldn't want a recall. Every moment she stayed inside, inhaling the bouquet of greasy smoke and stale ale, increased the odds of another dash to the privy. Given the inn's nearness to the source, most of the story still sat on the surface of her memory, but she strongly suspected—from the tightening in her throat and the churning behind her belt— that even recalling it without trance would take *much* too long.

"Terrible thing." He dusted crumbs out of his beard. "Anyway, I found a pilot willing to risk freeze-up and take me into Riverton. You want a lift? It's a short walk into Elbasan from there and you'll be home in plenty of time for Final Quarter Festival."

Five days, weighed against eight, maybe ten walking. *Maybe more if whatever I've got doesn't let go.* As well as the nausea, she'd found herself tiring easily this last little while which meant more frequent stops and less distance traveled and not arriving home in time for the Festival which was when she was expected. Although she shuddered to think what the motion of the river would do to her stomach, it really wasn't a difficult choice.

"I'd love a lift. Thank you."

"Good, good. And maybe you could convince the kigh to get us there a little faster?"

Annice frowned. "You *know* we're not permitted to Sing you an advantage."

"An advantage?" The wool merchant's teeth flashed white in the depths of his beard. "Hardly that when everyone else is already downriver."

"You have a point. . . ."

"And you *are* allowed to Sing boats out of freeze-up, I saw it done once."

"And you're splitting hairs." She sighed. "Still, if you're determined to go, then the faster you travel the less likely you'll get caught in freeze-up and have to hire a Song to get you free. So I suppose it would actually be doing a sort of public service if I helped."

His grin broadened.

You can rationalize anything if you want to do it badly enough. "I'll do what I can, but the kigh decide."

"Good enough." He held out his fist. "Jonukas i'Evicka. Everyone calls me Jon."

Annice touched his fist lightly with hers. "Annice," she told him. Bards, like priests, used neither matronym or patronym, and after ten years her name alone was seldom enough to provoke a reaction.

The riverboat rode low in the water by the inn's dock, the pilot waiting impatiently on the stern deck by the sweep oar.

"What did you get hung up on?" she snarled as they approached. "And who's she?"

Jon leaped aboard, timing it expertly between swells. "She's a bard. Name's Annice. She'll be traveling with us."

The pilot's snort was nonverbal but expressive for all of that. "You payin' her weight?"

Annice swallowed another mouthful of the bread. To her grateful surprise, it seemed to be settling things. "I've offered to Sing. To help you reach Riverton before freeze-up."

"You a water?" Her tone seemed to indicate she considered it doubtful.

"I Sing all four quarters."

The pilot's brows disappeared under the edge of her knit cap. "Well, la de sink it da. You know the river?"

"I thought that was *your* job." The tone had been finely tuned to land just this side of insult.

The two women measured each other for a moment, then the pilot snickered. "Get on," she said, jerking her head at the tiny covered cockpit up in the bow. "River's runnin' too fast to need you today, but the Circle'll bring tomorrow around soon enough. Folk call me Sarlo. That's i'Gerda or a'Edko if you wanna do a song about me later. Make it romantic, I like them best. Now move yer butt."

More than willing to move her butt out of a wind that stroked icy fingers over any exposed skin, Annice took a deep breath and stepped across onto the narrow deck. Safely on board, she spat over the side and muttered, "We give to the river. The river gives back."

Sarlo started. "You know the rituals?"

Annice smiled up at her. "I'm a bard. Knowing the rituals is part of what we do."

One corner of the older woman's mouth twisted up. "Think highly of yerself, don't you?"

Annice's smile broadened. "I'd float with rocks in my pockets," she said.

Lashing her pack to the cargo stays, she wrestled herself, her instrument case, and the day's journey food into the tiny bullhide shelter tucked in between the cargo and the bow. When Jon and two bundles joined her a moment later, it got distinctly crowded.

"I hope you don't mind riding with the front curtain up." He tied it back as he spoke. "But I like to see where I'm going."

"Actually, right at the moment, I appreciate the fresh air." Between the smell of the hide and the lingering smell of tar clinging to the boat, Annice was beginning to regret the piece of bread.

"Still a bit queasy?" he asked, sitting down and managing to squeeze his shoulders in beside hers.

"No. I'm fine," Annice said. But she said it through clenched teeth.

Back on the stern deck, the pilot yelled a command and a pair of rope-soled boots under oilskin clad legs pounded into view.

"Sarlo's youngest, Avram," Jon explained as Annice craned around the edge of the shelter for a better look. "I think he's got a love in Riverton. Didn't take much convincing when his mother decided to take my cloth."

Late teens or early twenties, the bard decided, watching Avram expertly work the side paddle. He was short and slight like most of the Riverfolk, but the hands wrapped around the paddle's polished shaft gave an instant impression of capable strength and seemed almost out of proportion to the rest of his body.

As though he felt her scrutiny, he half-turned, flicked

a shock of dusty black hair up out of dark eyes, and grinned down at her.

In spite of the lingering nausea, Annice grinned back. *Good teeth and great hands, I do enjoy the scenery on the river.*

At another command from the stern, he rounded the bow and moved out of sight. With only the bare branches of trees blowing about on the far shore remaining to look at, Annice stifled a sigh and settled back.

Jon propped his feet up on the bow deck and pulled a ball of gray wool and four horn needles out from a small pack tucked under the seat. "I can't sit with empty hands," he explained. "And it takes most of my travel time just to keep myself in socks. I hate having wet feet."

"As a matter of fact ..." Shifting her weight against the motion of the river, Annice got comfortable in the other corner and slipped an almost identical setup out of a pocket on the side of her instrument case. The fresh air seemed to be canceling out the rocking of the boat so, while she wasn't feeling any better, at least she wasn't feeling any worse. Remembering the alternative, she decided she could live with that. "... I know exactly what you mean."

They sat knitting in companionable silence for a time, watching gray sky slide by above darker gray water, listening to the occasional profanity drifting up from the stern, when suddenly a gust of wind dove into the shelter, ripped the front curtains from the tiebacks, and belled the hide out above them.

"Bugger it!" Jon grabbed the flapping hide in one beefy hand and dragged it back against the wind.

Annice twisted around and glared up at the two kigh who were pushing against the roof of the shelter. Pursing her lips, she twice repeated the series of four notes she'd whistled at the kigh by the privy. The smaller of the two shot her a haughty glance, twisted back on itself, and ran its fingers through Jon's beard as it left. The larger circled the inside of the small area twice, then squeezed itself out the space between Annice and the curved wooden frame, lifting the ball of wool off her lap and taking it along.

She grabbed for it but not in time.

"Kigh?" Jon asked, retying the curtains.

"Kigh," Annice repeated, pulling her dripping wool back on board.

"You usually have this much trouble with air?"

"It's usually my best Song. I can't understand why they're being such a pain lately."

"I've heard," Jon said as he smoothed his ruffled beard, "that across the border in Cemandia there're those that say the kigh aren't in the Circle at all. And there're some people even here in Shkoder that say the bards should have nothing to do with the kigh."

Annice snorted. "Have these people got a way to convince the kigh to have nothing to do with bards?" There'd been enough lanolin in the wool to prevent much water from being absorbed, but it was still too wet to use. "Because if they do, I'd love to hear it."

Jon spread his hands. "Just repeating what I heard."

"Sorry." Annice felt herself flush. She'd had no call to snap at the merchant, especially not when he was passing on exactly the kind of things that bards were expected to listen for. As the crown's conduit to the people, it could be vitally important that they hear what *some people say.* "They weren't saying it when I was in Vidor . . ." She let the end of the sentence trail off; not quite a question but definitely an invitation to talk.

"I'm not actually in Vidor much," Jon admitted. "I spend the late spring and summer collecting fleece from the small holders in Ohrid and Sibiu—mountain fleece can toss lowland fleece right out of the Circle as far as I'm concerned."

"You do the traveling yourself?" While she wanted to know, it was more interesting to learn that Cemandian ideas seemed to have crossed into at least two of the mountain principalities.

He laughed. "I don't trade for anything I can't touch and I probably travel as much as you do. My family lives in Marienka, at the head of the lake. We weave for the local trade, but every fall I bring our extra fleece to the Weavers' Guild in Vidor, pick up the fabric from last year's extra, *minus* their percentage . . ."

Annice made a mental note to have the Guild's percentage checked into. While traders traditionally complained about the percentages they had to pay in order to deal with the larger guilds, the Council had asked that bards keep an eye out for price gouging.

". . . and then I continue—usually a little farther from freeze-up—downriver to Elbasan."

Merchants said that in Elbasan they could trade for the world. As a child, Annice had loved to be taken to the harbor to watch ships unload strange and exotic goods. While the captains had entertained one or another of her older siblings, she'd run about the docks poking her nose into odd corners and driving her nurse to distraction. As an adult, she often thought about petitioning for what the bards called a Walk on Water but had never gone so far as to actually make the request.

Warming to his subject, Jon leaned forward and began sketching trade possibilities in the air. Annice, not really interested in the cycle of wool cloth for exotica for linen back in Vidor, slid into the light trance that would ensure memory as he expanded on his season. She had no idea if the information would ever be of use, but under the bardic adage, *wasted knowledge is wasted lives,* better to have it than not.

". . . and if that trader from Cemandia's still up in Ohrid, I might be able to unload some on him."

That roused her. She'd run into a pair of Cemandian traders in Ohrid and another in Adjud. She'd even seen a small cluster of them in the market in Vidor. In fact, she'd seen more on this latest Walk than she had in all her previous travels combined.

Jon laughed when she mentioned it. "There's always been some trade across the border. Ohrid's never quite managed to close the pass." Then he was off again on an unlikely tale of how he'd bested a Cemandian in an impossible deal.

Annice slid back into trance; all Jon seemed to need was an audience and she was more than willing to oblige. Few people realized that bards spent half their training time learning to listen. *And half of that,* Annice mused as the story slid from unlikely to improbable, *learning to sleep with our eyes open.*

"All right, Bard. This is where you float yer weight." Sarlo hooked the sweep oar into one armpit and gestured ahead with her free hand. "Got a whole stretch of river here where the current spreads out and ain't worth shit. Not to mention wind's comin' northwest and'll keep tryin' to blow us onto the far shore. We get through it slow and sure as a rule, but since I don't want to end up with my butt caught in ice, it's all yers."

Fingers clamped not quite white around the oar support, Annice peered off the stern. The fantail following the riverboat was a deep gray-green; not exactly friendly-looking water. Watching the bubbles slipping away upstream induced a sudden wave of vertigo. Annice swallowed hard and sat down, legs crossed for maximum support and eyes closed. Thanks to the innkeeper's well-timed hunk of bread, she'd discovered that small, bland meals at frequent intervals both remained down and damped the nausea to merely an unpleasant background sensation. Unfortunately, during the two days on the river, she'd found all sort of new ways to make herself sick.

"You okay?"

Annice opened her eyes and decided she could cope. "I'm fine."

"You seen a healer yet?"

"I'll see one after I get to Elbasan."

Sarlo snorted. "Yer business."

Reaching under her jacket and sweater, Annice pulled out her flute, the ironwood warmed almost to body temperature. When the kigh arrived she'd Sing, but first she had to get their attention.

"They're gonna be deep with freeze-up so close," Sarlo observed.

Annice ignored her, setting her fingers and checking the movement of the single key. She took a deep breath and slowly released it, then lifted the flute to her mouth.

The kigh took their time responding to the call, but eventually three distinct shapes became visible just below the surface.

Three would have to be enough.

Shoving chilled fingers and flute between her legs, Annice Sang. Some bards argued that as long as the music was right and the desire strong, words were unimportant; that the kigh didn't understand the words anyway, so why tie rhyme and rhythm into knots in what was probably an unnecessary attempt to Sing a specific request.

Personally, Annice preferred to repeat variations of short phrases over and over. It occasionally got tedious, but it usually got results.

The kigh listened for a few moments, one lifting a swell two feet into the air the better to stare intently at the source of the Song, then suddenly all three dove and the boat jerked forward.

"Whoa!" Sarlo took a steadying step and braced herself against the sweep as Annice let the Song fade to silence. "This'll make us some time. How long do you figger they'll push for?"

Annice slumped forward. "Hard to say," she admitted. "I haven't actually asked for much, so we might make it out of the slow stretch before they get bored."

"Then what?"

"Then I'll play them a gratitude and we're back on our own."

"They won't hang around and cause trouble?"

"Probably not...." A sudden gust of wind lifted the top off a wave and flung it up over the high stern deck of the riverboat and into Annice's face. The air kigh flicked the last few drops off its fingers at her, then sped away.

"More kigh?" Sarlo asked.

"More kigh," Annice sighed and pulled the sleeve of her sweater down to wipe at the freezing water. "I've always been strongest in air, so they get jealous when I Sing the others."

"Sort of like being followed around by a bunch of obnoxious kids."

"Worse."

The pilot snorted. "You were never stuck on a riverboat with my right-out-of-the-Circle three."

"Why didn't you leave them with their father?"

"Couldn't. He was my crew till he got knocked off and drowned."

"I'm sorry."

"Why? You weren't the one what pushed him in."

Annice didn't care how unbardlike it was; she wasn't going to ask, she didn't want to know.

They were a day out of Riverton, buildings frequently visible on shore through the slanting rain, when Jon cast off a completed sock and said, "I figured out who you remind me of."

Annice felt her shoulders stiffen.

"I was watching you last night at the inn, while you sang in the common room," he continued. "Firelight was flickering on your profile, turning it kind of goldlike, and it suddenly hit me." He reached under his clothes and pulled out a coin.

In spite of herself, Annice leaned over and looked. Most of the sharp definition had worn away over the years, but it was still easy to see that the profile of the last king, not the current one, lay cradled in his palm. *He would have a Mikus not a Theron,* she sighed. The gold coins were struck only once, at the beginning of a reign and named for the likeness of the king they bore.

Jon tucked the old coin safely away. "You look like your father."

"Only from that side."

"My youngest brother knows all twenty-seven verses to 'The Princess-Bard' and still sings it."

The only response she could think of was too rude to say, so she clamped her teeth shut.

"Not a lot of songs stay popular for ten years, but this one's got a real catchy tune." He started to hum but abruptly broke off when he caught sight of her expression. "I, uh, I guess you're tired of hearing it."

"You might say that. Yes."

"Sorry. It's just—well, the Princess-Bard crammed in right here beside me."

"It's the same person who was crammed in beside you yesterday."

"But yesterday, I didn't know you were the Princess-Bard."

If he said it again, she was going to slug him.

"Do you ever miss it? Being royal?"

"No. Never."

And because she'd been trained to use her voice, he believed the lie. Annice had been fourteen when she left the palace for the Bardic Hall in Elbasan and while she never regretted the decision, she did occasionally wish that some things could've been different.

Given the chance to live it over, would she make the same choice?"

Yes.

"King Mikus is near death."

The whisper had scurried around the palace for days. The king had been dying for months, but this new phrasing had finally gained enough conviction to be repeated as a certainty in the city. Goldsmiths who had the royal charter were making ready to cast the new coins. Bards were working on eulogies while criers memorized the highlights of the old king's rule. Priests prayed for the dying man's peace. The more pragmatic visited Centers to pray for a peaceful transition of power.

Deep in the palace, King Mikus' family gathered about him. Neither Prince Rihard, now joined to the Heir Apparent of Petrokia, nor Princess Irenka, now, by joining, Lady of the Havakeen Empire, could be present, but enough remained to pack the small bedchamber uncomfortably full.

Tucked back against the wall, Annice watched her relatives and waited, more or less patiently, for her chance.

Prince Theron, as Heir, stood close by the pillows on the right of the bed. His wife, heavy with their third child, sat in a padded chair by his side. The king had taken leave of his two older grandchildren earlier, in private, but tradition insisted that both Heir and Heir's Consort remain until the end. Theron had attempted to have his wife excused because of her advanced pregnancy, but Lilyana had sternly told him not to be an idiot and had her favorite chair carried in from her solar. As a political joining it hadn't been without its difficulties, but over the years they'd developed a relationship that appeared to work although Annice had never understood quite how.

Her sister, the Princess Milena, seemed to lean on the Duc of Marienka's bulk. Joined for only a year, a joining deliberately arranged to tie his lands more tightly to the crown, they were disgustingly happy. Each made it obvious they considered the other the center of the Circle. Annice figured they were making the best of a bad situation and left it at that.

Prince Tomelis, the king's youngest and only surviving brother, stood quietly, arms folded, his partner, Lukas i'Johanka a silent strength by his side as he had been for the last thirty years. Now that Rihard was gone and Milena had lost her mind and Theron had gotten so difficult, Annice

considered Uncle Tomelis to be her favorite relative. Not
only because he'd refused an advantageous political joining
with a prince of the Empire and followed his heart, but also
because she'd heard him say that he'd rather have his teeth
pulled than spend more time than necessary trapped within
the walls of the palace. It was a sentiment with which she
heartily agreed.

Her Aunt Giti, the Princess Gituska, supported by both
her son and daughter, sniveled into a lace-edged handker-
chief. Annice had no use for those particular cousins, the
only ones who remained in the Elbasan area. Two years
ago at a First Quarter Festival, *she'd* got stinking drunk and
embarrassed the family by having to be carried home and
he'd thought the whole thing was funny. Her aunt's grief,
Annice would allow, however, was genuine.

The king's personal healer stood opposite the Heir at the
head of the bed, arms folded, hands tucked into her
sleeves, her face struggling to come to terms with the
knowledge there was nothing more she could do. Two
members of the Governing Council watched from the foot
of the bed and the current Captain of the Bardic Hall in
Elbasan waited about halfway up the left side beside the
droning priest—positions all demanded by the ceremony accompanying the passing of a king. A fire of wood soaked
in aromatic oils blazed on the hearth. A low table held a
basin of water and one of earth.

And as long as we're breathing, we can't keep air out.
Annice tried not to fidget. *Why don't they get on with it?*

One after another, the king's family approached the bed
for the formal farewell; first the cousins—*A nonrepresenta-
tive sample at best,* Annice snorted silently—then the aunt,
then the uncle and his partner. As youngest child, Annice
should've gone next, but somehow Milena and the duc
ended up by the bed.

Annice was proud of the subtle manipulation she'd per-
formed in order to move her sister up a place in line—a bit
of shy hanging back combined with a silent plea to the
sister for rescue—until she caught the Bardic Captain
watching her. Flushing slightly, she quickly schooled her
features.

Finally, it was her turn.

The growth just under the edge of her father's ribs had
been killing him slowly for the last two quarters. Here, at

the end, he was a physical caricature of himself, flesh long melted away, skin hanging loose on the bone, gray hair dull and brittle. Only his eyes remained unchanged even sunk as they were deep below saffron-tinted cheeks.

Annice dropped gracefully to one knee, took a deep breath, and caught up the limp hand lying against the embroidered coverlet in both of hers. "Most gracious and regal Majesty, I request a boon."

The corners of his mouth twitched slightly. "Go on."

"I do request that rather than be promised to the Heir of Cemandia, to be joined for political expedience when we are of an age, I be permitted to enter the Bardic Hall of Elbasan."

Within her grip his fingers moved. "Who promises you to Cemandia's Heir?"

"Theron."

The old king's eyes blazed. "Theron," he said in a stronger voice than any had heard from him in days, "does not rule yet."

Theron leaned forward. "Lord Juraj, the ambassador, only spoke of it, Majesty."

"Yet neither you nor he saw fit to speak with the king."

"We did not wish to tire you over mere speculation."

"You passed this speculation to your sister."

"Only to see if she would be willing."

The dying man jerked out a dry laugh. "Obviously, she is not."

Go ahead, Annice thought, *tell him that I never told you I didn't want to go along with your premature little power play and I'll call you a liar to your face. Go ahead, Your Royal Highness, Heir of Shkoder, I dare you.*

She could feel the heat of Theron's glare, but all he said was, "I would not force her."

"You *cannot* force her." The king paused, fighting for breath, but Annice could feel the pressure of his fingers against hers and knew he wasn't finished. After a moment, he turned his head toward the Bardic Captain. "You have been after her for some time."

It had been an open secret in the palace for very nearly a year. Annice had no idea why her father hadn't agreed and realized she was attempting to force his hand as much as her brother's.

"Her Highness has both talent and skill," the captain allowed diplomatically. "If you give your permission and she is willing to take the oath, the Hall will accept her for training."

"Did you know of this . . . boon?"

Captain Liene's eyes never left the king's face. "No, Majesty. I did not."

"Very well." The king lay quietly for another moment. When he spoke again, his voice held the ringing tone of proclamation. "I, Mikus, King of Shkoder, High Captain of the Broken Islands, Lord over the Mountain Principalities of Sibiu, Ohrid, Ajud, Bicaz, and Somes, do on this day grant the boon of my youngest daughter that she should be permitted to enter the Bardic Hall of Elbasan. Witness?"

As the only bard present, the captain nodded. "I so witness."

Annice released a breath she couldn't remember holding. "Thank you, Majesty." Then she stood to take a formal farewell of her king. Her father.

After the words, which were words only, as her lips pressed a kiss against his cheek, he whispered, "Well played."

Later, after the death had been witnessed and they were waiting for priest and bard and the new king to leave the bedchamber, Milena cornered her in the king's solar and hissed, "Just what's wrong with the Heir of Cemandia?"

"Nothing." Annice jerked her arm out of her sister's grip. "I just don't want to be joined with anyone. I want to be a bard."

"And you always get what you want, don't you? Did you even consider your family obligations? Of course you didn't. There's a price to be paid for good food and warm clothes and a lifetime of servants saying 'yes, Highness, and no, Highness.' " Milena tossed her braid back over her shoulder. "But I always said Theron spoiled you."

"He did not!" He'd just always been there when their mother had been interested only in the beautiful Irenka or their father had been too busy being the king, which was most of the time. Theron had brought her the news of their mother's accident and she'd clutched his hand when they'd buried her, not understanding why the healers couldn't fix her. She'd been the first after the proud parents to hold Theron's baby girl. That wasn't being spoiled. "Look, Milena, you're happy. Why can't I be?"

"I found happiness on the path of duty. Obviously, that's

not good enough for you." Having said what she'd come to say, Milena spun on her heel and returned to her partner's side. After a moment, their heads moved so close together a feather wouldn't fit between them.

Annice felt her lip curl watching them, so she propped one leg on the window ledge and glanced around the room. Everyone seemed to be staying as far away from her as they could get, as if afraid physical proximity might implicate them in her plan. *Well, Theron had been pretty angry and was likely to stay that way for some time.* Only Tomelis would meet her eyes. *Why does he look so sad?* she wondered. Just for an instant, she wondered if she might have made a tactical error. How could she at fourteen actually outmaneuver a man nineteen years her senior?

But I've done it. With everyone else joined before Theron takes the throne, he's already let me know that I'm too strong a game piece for him to lose from the board. Even if I didn't join with Prince Rajmund, he'd never let me become a bard.

He couldn't stop her now.

The door to the bedchamber opened and the men and women in the solar dropped to one knee as the new king emerged. Expecting him to walk right on through, Annice was startled when he stopped before her.

"By the will of the late King Mikus," he said, "you have permission to enter Bardic Hall. I, Theron, King of Shkoder, High Captain of the Broken Islands, Lord over the Mountain Principalities of Sibiu, Ohrid, Adjud, Bicaz, and Somes, do on this day declare that by doing so you forfeit all rights of royalty, that you shall surrender all titles and incomes, that all save your personal possessions shall revert to the crown. Furthermore, for the stability of the realm, you may neither join nor bear children without the express permission of the crown. To do so will be considered a treasonous act and will be punished as such."

Annice thought she heard a deep voice murmur a protest, quickly hushed. Eyes narrowed, she glared up at her brother, her new king.

"Do you understand?" he asked, his lips pulled tight against his teeth. To be convicted of an act of treason was to face a Death Judgment.

He thought she'd back down. Well, he was wrong. "I understand."

"Witness!"

Behind him, the Bardic Captain sighed. "Witnessed."

Annice thought she saw something that might have been regret flicker for a moment in Theron's eyes then he turned away from her and said, "Done."

Done. Annice pulled off her mitten and rubbed the back of her hand under her nose. *Sometimes Bardic Memory stinks.* She didn't know whether she'd seen regret that afternoon or just imagined it. She'd never spoken to Theron, to any of them, again. Not once in ten years. She wasn't even sure if *that* was his idea or hers.

"Annice?" Jon laid his huge hand lightly on her shoulder. "Are you all right?"

"Yeah. I'm fine."

"I didn't mean your stomach."

She sighed and let it go with the breath. "I know."

He sat back, still watching her, worry creasing his face. "I'm sorry I brought it up." He offered her a tentative smile. "I'll forget it if you like."

"Will you forget that unenclosed song, too?"

"I'll even pound it out of my brother's head."

Annice grinned and held out her fist. "Done," she said.

CHAPTER TWO

"You want yer weight carried back upriver in the spring, Bard, you whistle me up." Sarlo smacked her fist into the top of Annice's with enthusiasm. The kigh had got them to Riverton one full day faster than average. "Pity I couldn't use yer help in the races."

"Wouldn't you rather win because of your skill not because of a push from the kigh?"

Sarlo snorted. "I'd rather win."

Grinning, Annice bent to pick up her pack but found Jon already holding it. "Thank you." She slipped her arms behind the leather straps, settled the familiar weight on her shoulders, and turned to face him. "And thank you for offering the ride. Considering the weather, and the way I'm feeling, I'd have been lucky to get home by First Quarter Festival, let alone Fourth."

A smile gleamed in the depths of his beard. "I was glad of the company. You sure you're going to be okay for this last little distance?"

"I just spent two quarters walking to Ohrid and back," she reminded him. "I think I can manage." She held out her fist. "Good trading, Jonukas i'Evicka."

"Good music, Annice." He let his fist rest against hers for a moment. "And see a healer. All that puking isn't natural."

She nodded. "The moment I get home. Or maybe first thing tomorrow," she amended, glancing at the rapidly darkening sky.

"Witness?"

"Jon, I can't witness for myself."

"Then promise."

"Oh, all right." Shaking her head, she traced the sign of the Circle over her heart. "I promise." She waved at Avram, who waved back from his perch on top of the cargo cover, and regretted one last time that she hadn't felt well enough, long enough, to try to get to know him better. Picking her way carefully along the wet rocks, she started up the dock toward home.

"Annice?"

Hand against the hull of a riverboat already out of the water for the season, Annice half twisted around.

"May I tell my brother?"

The brother who knew all twenty-seven verses to "The Princess-Bard." She laughed ruefully. "Why not?"

The rain held off and in spite of the road, a muddy mess from previous downpours that somehow seemed more resilient under her boots than it should, Annice reached the bridge over the new canal before full dark.

The East Keeper lumbered out of his tiny shelter and held out a massive hand.

"Bards don't pay toll," Annice reminded him and started to go around.

He blocked her path.

And most of the rest of the bridge, she realized. *Big boy.*

"How do I know you're a bard?"

"You could take my word for it." It wasn't healthy to lie about being a bard. Bards who found out tended not to take it very well.

"No, I can't." Crossing meaty arms over a barrel chest, the keeper scowled down at her. "Sing for me."

"What?"

"I want you to Sing me your name."

That she'd be expected to identify herself in order to enter the city used up about all the patience she had remaining. Taking a deep breath, she looked him in the eye and said, **"Get out of my way."**

He responded to her Command with the gratifying promptness shown by most petty tyrants and others of like personality. Resisting the urge to tell him to jump in the canal and realizing she was teetering just beyond the edge of her oath as it was, Annice stomped up and over the arch and into Elbasan.

Her mood lightened as she followed River Road into the heart of the city. Evenings were long at the dark end of the Third Quarter, so taverns and soup shops were doing their best business of the year. Annice briefly considered stopping for supper before she headed up the hill, but smells, individual and combined, from a thousand different sources changed her mind. She was *not* going to throw up in the gutter like a common drunk.

At least she hoped she wasn't.

Hill Street to the Citadel seemed steeper than it had when she'd left. She felt ready to collapse when she reached the wall and sagged panting against the stone by the gate. *You'd think that after walking for two quarters I'd be in better shape.* Nothing hurt, she just felt drained. As she stood there, trying to catch her breath, the clouds that had been threatening finally made good on their promise of rain. *Shit.*

Dragging up her hood, she decided she was too exhausted to Sing the Bard's Door open and staggered in under the arch of the main gate. She didn't know the guard on duty, but the bard had been a fledgling with her.

"Annice. Bard. Going to the Bardic Hall."

Jazep peered up under her hood. "Witnessed," he said. "You look like you've fallen out of the Circle, Nees." His deep voice rumbled with concern. "Rough Walk?"

"Long Walk," she told him, already moving. "I'll see you later."

The rain came down in icy sheets as she made her way diagonally across Citadel Square. A dry route existed through barracks and stables and storerooms, but she wasn't up to negotiating her way past their occupants. It was faster and easier to get wet.

Eventually, putting one foot in front of the other, she arrived at the main entrance to the hall. Lifting her head, she blew a drop of water off the end of her nose, pulled the door open, and went inside.

The bard sitting duty in the main hall glanced up from her book. "You're dripping."

"It's raining."

"Annice?"

Annice shook her hood back, spraying the immediate area with a fine patina of water.

"Well, I guess the Circle does hold everything. Welcome home, Annice." The older woman rested her forearms on the desk and leaned forward, frowning. "You look awful."

"Thank you." If one more person told her that tonight, she was going to puke on their shoes. "If you'll record that I'm back, Ceci, I'm going up to bed. I don't even want to think about recall until morning."

"Do you want me to have the kitchen send something up?"

No. Except that she was starving. "Soup and bread. Thanks."

Ceci turned to watch as she started toward the stairs. "You going to make it all the way to your rooms?" she asked dubiously.

"Of course I am. I'm fine. I'm just a little tired. It's my punishment for sitting on my ass all the way from Vidor."

"Riverboat?"

"What else."

"You push?"

"A little."

"Captain won't like that."

"Extenuating circumstances."

Ceci laughed. "They always are. Stasya's out in the city."

"Good for her."

"When she comes in, shall I tell her you're back or let her find out for herself?"

Annice thought about it for a moment, then called down from the top of the stairs. "You'd better tell her. You know how she hates surprises."

"You're the one who wanted to be on the fourth floor," she reminded herself a few moments later, resting on the third floor landing. "And you're the one who wanted rooms at the back of the building not the front. You've got no one to blame for this final effort but yourself."

The soup and bread very nearly made it to her rooms before she did. She'd barely Sung the lamp alight and checked to see that the kigh dancing on the wick was safely contained when the server arrived.

"Just set the tray here," she said, lifting a jumbled heap of slates off a round table and searching desperately for a place to put them. As usual, Stasya had left their common room looking like a storm had recently passed through. Finally, as it seemed to be the only clear space remaining, she stuffed the slates under a chair, stood her instrument case against the wall, and shrugged her pack off to crash to the floor.

The older man clicked his tongue—at the noise or the mess, Annice wasn't sure which—and nudged a pile of colored chalks aside with the edge of the tray. "I brought you some cheese," he said, straightening. "Need more than just bread and soup after a Long Walk."

"I only walked in from Riverton today, Leonas," Annice pointed out, removing a half-strung harp and a pair of torn breeches from her favorite chair. "Not all the way from Ohrid."

Leonas ignored her. "Probably haven't had any decent food for the whole two quarters."

"I actually ate quite well."

He snorted and looked her over. "Gained a little weight, did you?"

Annice sighed. She couldn't win. "Good night, Leonas."

"Good night, Princess."

"Leo . . ."

"If I can call my Giz *Cupcake* when she never was one," he interrupted, glaring back at her from the threshold, "I can call you Princess when you aren't one no more. Get some sleep. You look terrible." Jerking the door closed behind him, he left Annice no room to argue.

Leonas had already been serving at the Bardic Hall for thirty years when the fourteen-year-old Annice arrived. Determined not to let it show, lest word get back to her brother, she was hurt and confused and had no idea of how not to act like a princess. Leonas had gruffly taken her under his wing, explaining little things it had never occurred to the bards that she wouldn't know, easing the transition as much as he could. Over the years, he'd slid into the role of trusted retainer and if he wanted to call her "Princess," she supposed he'd earned the right. She tried to discourage it, though; she'd long left that life behind.

Stripping off her wet clothes and letting them lie where they fell, she pulled a heavy woolen robe and sheepskin slippers from the wardrobe in her bedroom, shuffled down the hall to use the necessity—fortunately running into no one with whom she'd have to make conversation—then finally sat down to eat.

The soup was excellent, big chunks of tender clam in a thick vegetable stock. Not entirely trusting her stomach, Annice saved the bread and cheese for later.

She thought about lighting a fire, but—in spite of the rain slapping against the shutters—it just wasn't cold enough to justify making the effort. Besides, once in bed with the curtains closed, she'd be plenty warm enough. Setting thought to action, she picked up the lamp and shuffled into the bedroom.

Blankets and sheets were heaped in a tangled pile. The down comforter trailed on the floor, evidence of a hasty departure, and all but one of the four pillows had been thrown to the foot of the bed.

"I can't believe she can sleep in this," Annice muttered, tugging the mess into some semblance of order. "And I don't even want to know how she tore that corner of the curtain." Bed finally tidied, she Sang the kigh in the lamp a gratitude and, in the dark, slipped off her robe and slid naked between the sheets. Just as they began to warm around her body, her bladder decided to get her up again.

"I just went!" she told it.

It didn't seem to matter.

"If it isn't one end lately, it's the other," she complained, groping for her slippers. "I am really getting tired of this."

"Nees? Are you asleep?"

Annice roused enough to murmur an affirmative, then gasped as a cold body wrapped around hers. "Stasya, you're freezing!"

"You're not. You're nice and warm."

"I *was* nice and warm."

"Oh, hush. I'll warm up in a minute and you won't even know that I'm here."

"Not likely." Annice squirmed as the other woman began chewing on her ear. "Stop it, Stas. I'm tired."

"I missed you. . . ."

"I missed you, too, but I'm *tired*."

"Can I welcome you home in the morning?"

"You can do what you want in the morning," Annice muttered, "if you'll just let me sleep now."

When she woke again, weak light shone through the space between the bedcurtains, enough to illuminate the woman propped on one elbow and staring down at her.

"Hi."

"Hi yourself." Stasya smiled and waggled dark brows. "It's morning. Welcome home. Remember what you promised?"

She remembered a cold body very clearly, but the rest only vaguely. "Stas . . ."

"Stas . . ." The other woman mocked and leaned forward. "It was witnessed by a bard," she whispered, breath tickling Annice's lips.

"Stasya." Annice shoved her aside as her stomach rose to greet the day. "Get out of my way. Now!"

"How long has this been going on?"

"I don't know." Panting, Annice sat back on her heels, steadying herself against the toilet. A while now."

Stasya leaned against the open door of the cubicle and frowned. "What do the healers say?"

"I haven't seen one."

"You are *such* an idiot. Why not?"

"I figured I'd see one when I got home."

"Fine. You're home. Are you finished?" Stasya stepped forward, bent, and helped Annice to her feet. "You can go see one right now."

"But I haven't talked to the captain yet."

"So?"

Yanking the chain that flushed water through the pipes with one hand, Annice secured her robe with the other. "In case you've forgotten, I just got back from a Long Walk; I'll be in recall all morning."

"Healers take precedence."

"But I'll likely have to sit around the Hall for hours before they can see me."

"Not at this time of the morning." Fingers locked around Annice's arm just above the elbow, Stasya propelled her down the corridor and into their rooms. "Get dressed," she commanded. "You're going to see a healer if I have to drag you, so you might just as well go comfortably on your own two feet."

Realizing that Stasya had made up her mind and resistance was therefore futile, Annice sighed and surrendered. "It's going to be a waste of time," she muttered. "They won't know what it is. They never know...."

"When was the last time you had your flows?"

"My flows?" Annice frowned as she shrugged back into her clothing. "Oh, come on, Elica, I can't remember that."

The healer rolled her eyes. "You're a bard. You can remember if you want to."

"Well...." The frown smoothed out as Annice slid into a light recall. "I was between Adjud and Ohrid. Four days out of Adjud and thirteen from Ohrid."

"How long ago were you in Ohrid?"

"Nine weeks."

"So you've missed two, almost three cycles." Elica pushed a carved wooden box out of the way and sat on the edge of her table. "Didn't you ever wonder about that?"

"I was on a Long Walk. I had other things on my mind."

"You shouldn't have."

"Why?" Annice's head came up and her tone sharpened defensively. "What have I caught?"

"You haven't caught anything," the healer sighed. "You're pregnant."

"You're WHAT?"

"Keep your voice down," Annice hissed, pushing past her. "Do you want the whole Citadel to know?"

Stasya hurried to catch up as Annice stomped down the corridor of the Healers' Hall. "You're kidding, right?"

"No."

"Well, how did it happen?"

"How the empty Circle do you think? The *usual* way."

"What about the teas the healers gave you?"

"I gave them to a woman who'd had seven babies in six years. She seemed to need them more."

"Very commendable, I'm sure, but none of her babies

were committing treason in the womb." Together they pounded out of the Healers' Hall and across the courtyard. "Annice! Slow down. Where are you going?"

"I've got to talk to the captain."

"I'll say. Can you get rid of it, or has it gone too far?"

"I can. But I'm not going to. That's why I have to talk to the captain."

"This," Stasya said with feeling, as they raced up the stairs to the captain's chambers, "is what comes of sleeping with men."

Liene stared up at the young woman standing on the other side of her desk. *Why me?* she asked the Circle silently. *Or more to the point, why her?* "You're positive?"

"Healer Elica is."

Wonderful. The Bardic Captain closed her eyes and heard King Mikus ask in memory if she had known about his youngest daughter's boon. It had been a fair question. The old scoundrel had bloody well known she'd been after his permission to recruit Annice for almost a year. Practically every time the child opened her mouth, kigh flocked around her. Allowing that kind of talent to remain untrained would have been criminal. Even more so considering how badly Annice had wanted to be a bard.

Eyes still closed, Liene rewitnessed the old king's declaration and the new king's conditions. She'd strongly disapproved of those conditions, but the king had refused to listen to her counsel. The child had been only fourteen, so she'd decided to deal with both conditions and king later. As Annice threw herself into her studies, becoming less the princess and more the bard, *later* moved farther and farther away.

Later, Liene sighed silently, *seems to have come home to roost.*

The Bardic Oath stressed the responsibilities of power but mentioned nothing about celibacy, and Annice was not the first bard to conceive. While it didn't happen often—the healers thought it had something to do with Singing the kigh—babies had been raised in Bardic Halls before. Bards had even occasionally left to raise babies with nonbardic partners. Babies happened. Sometimes, they even happened on purpose. Personally, the captain rather liked having children around, although not to the extent that she'd ever thought of having her own.

She could hear the young woman fidgeting and reluctantly opened her eyes to meet a cautiously defiant gaze. "You do realize that, considering the king's edict, what you did was, to say the least, irresponsible?"

Annice tossed her head. "I didn't do it on purpose."

Liene leaned back and slowly lifted one brow. "My point," she said, "exactly." When understanding registered, she sighed and leaned forward again. "I realize why you gave away the tea, Annice, although, as we've been importing it from the south at ridiculous prices to prevent exactly this situation, I'm sure *you* realize that I wish you'd never met the woman. The deed being done, however, didn't it occur to you to temper later actions?"

A blush stained Annice's cheeks deeply pink in spite of color left by two quarters on the road. "It only happened the once. There just weren't any alternatives handy, and . . ."

"Never mind." A chronicle of spontaneous passion was more than Liene felt up to at the moment. "You're certain about the father?"

"Yes, Captain."

"And it's none of my business. Succinctly put. Annice's voice control was a credit to her training. "Do you feel any obligation to let him know?"

"No, Captain. It was a casual encounter. He'll have no interest in a child from it."

Because a difficult situation would be marginally less difficult if the father never knew, Liene was willing to go along with Annice's assessment. "And you're determined to continue the pregnancy?"

"Yes."

"Why?"

"Why?" Annice repeated, looking confused.

"You're still within the healer's limits. Why continue when, considering His Majesty's edict, it would be easier—not to mention less dangerous—to terminate?"

Annice paced the length of the room and back, then bent over and placed her palms very precisely on the edge of the captain's desk. "Look, Captain, I'm twenty-four years old. I'm in excellent health. I haven't got a family anymore and I suddenly find that I want one now I've got this chance."

"I thought the bards had become your family, Annice."

She caught the older woman's gaze and held it. "Have they?"

Liene recognized the challenge. One family had turned their backs on this young woman already. Would a second? "If I support you in this, it is my treason, a bardic treason, as much as it is yours."

"I know that."

"The king would be within his rights to have everyone who knew and who didn't tell him put to the sword."

Annice almost smiled. "Then tell everyone."

"Your point," Liene acknowledged. "As he certainly can't execute us all, we're safe enough. But, considering it objectively, you're probably just as safe. You don't honestly believe that His Majesty would have you put to death over this matter, do you?"

"I can't afford not to believe it. I have my baby's life to consider."

"Then you should go into hiding."

"Where would be safer than Bardic Hall?"

Just about anywhere farther than a stone's throw from the palace, Liene thought but she kept that opinion to herself as she recognized the expression on Annice's face. Nothing she could say would change the younger bard's mind at this point and, as she herself didn't believe there was any great danger, she decided not to make it an order. His Majesty would find out about the baby in due time and then things would get interesting. Bards appreciated that. Still. . . .

"I think you should tell him," she said finally.

"I'm a bard." Annice straightened, brown eyes narrowing. "Why should a bard have to tell the king she's having a baby?"

"He's your brother."

"He proclaimed me out of the family. He shouldn't be able to have it both ways."

Liene drummed her fingers on her desk as she considered the options, one hand beating counterpoint to the other. It didn't seem worth mentioning that, as the king, he could have it any way he wanted it. "Very well, Annice." The rhythms merged and stopped. "The Bardic

Hall will support your choice as it would any other bard's."

"Thank you."

She saw Annice's shoulders visibly relax and allowed her tone to soften as she realized just how worried the young bard had been. "I suggest, however, that we work out a way for you to keep a low profile. There's no point rubbing King Theron's nose in your decision." *Again,* she added silently. While the maneuver that had gotten Annice into the Bardic Hall originally had been ingenious—the deathbed promise of the old king could hardly be disallowed by the new, regardless of his personal plans—it had been significantly lacking in tact. "When are you due?"

"Uh ..." A quick calculation got chewed out of her lower lip. "Just into Second Quarter."

"How do you feel?"

"Nauseous mostly."

"I've heard that should stop soon. I'll have a word with the healer—Elica was it?—before I schedule you in for even Short Walks this coming quarter."

"I'm fine. Really."

"If you don't mind, I'll check with the healer anyway. Now then ..." fingers laced together, Liene allowed herself a smile, "as long as you're here, did anything *else* of interest happen during the two quarters you were away?"

Again the blush. "There were more Cemandian traders around than usual."

"You're not the first to mention it. Anything else?"

"Actually, there is. Cemandian superstitions seem to be growing stronger in the mountain provinces. Although most people seemed glad enough to see me, I caught an extraordinary number of these ..." Annice flicked her fingers out in the Cemandian sign against the kigh. "... thrown in my direction."

That was not good news and would have to be dealt with the moment the weather allowed bards back into the mountains. A greater amount of intolerance seemed to be accompanying the greater number of traders. Liene wondered, for a moment, if it were an intentional import. "Any overt hostility?"

"No. Fortunately, it doesn't seem to mean much yet.

But it's spreading enough so that even a wool trader from Marienka noticed it."

"And the rest of the Walk?"

Although she tried to remember the highlights, it soon became apparent Annice was having trouble concentrating on the details of the last two quarters. Under the circumstances, Liene could hardly blame her and dismissed her early. At least in recall she'd be able to report her observations without the emotional interference caused by this new knowledge of her condition.

Sighing deeply as the door closed behind the young bard, the captain tipped her chair back and swung her feet up on the desk, wincing with the movement. Every year after fifty seemed to drive the damp deeper into her bones.

It had been an interesting morning and looked as though it would get more interesting still.

"Treason, my ass." Liene rubbed at her temples. Overreacting to his youngest sister's coup, King Theron had hit back as hard as he'd been able to with the limited weapons Annice had left him.

It was long past time for a reconciliation. This would force it. The king, while an admirable man in every other way, was deaf to counsel concerning his youngest sister, and Annice had a stubborn streak that bordered on pigheaded. Neither could be brought to see that they were equally at fault.

Had Theron not been king, the situation would have resolved itself long ago, but not even the Bardic Captain dared tell the king what he should and should not feel, and there were few things more extreme than royal pride. Annice had not helped when, in her second year of training, she'd rejected her brother's one attempt at compromise. Liene hadn't been surprised; had His Majesty been trying to further alienate his sister, he could not have done a better job.

While she'd meant what she'd said about not rubbing King Theron's nose in Annice's pregnancy, only a fool would doubt that eventually he'd discover it.

Bards were terrible at keeping secrets. They insisted on putting them to music.

"Can you hear me, Annice?"

"I hear you."

Slane picked up his first pen. "Begin recall."

Deeply in trance, Annice started to speak, each word carefully enunciated. "I left Elbasan in early morning, one day after Second Quarter Festival. . . ."

The two quarter scroll began to fill with bardic shorthand and Slane let the greater part of his mind wander. Some bards never quite got the hang of editing out their personal lives, but Annice, no matter how deep she went, had never let a salacious detail slip.

Observant, Slane acknowledged. *But boring.* With any luck, he'd be on recall when Tadeus came in. Now there was a bard who knew how to party.

A baby. Shoulders braced on the stone chimney, Annice slid down until she settled on the roof of Bardic Hall. She was going to have a baby. Between her discussion with the captain and the rest of the day spent in recall, this was the first chance she'd really had to just think about it.

At least the weaver hadn't lied about the wool for her breeches being preshrunk.

A baby.

She let her head fall back against the masonry hard enough to snap her teeth together. "What in the Circle do I think I'm doing?"

Having a baby.

"I don't know anything about babies!"

But she knew she wanted it. Had wanted it from the moment Elica had told her. Or perhaps a little after that, when she'd calmed down and stopped demanding to see a healer who knew what she was doing.

A cold wind off the harbor moved her around to sit on the palace side of the chimney. In a little while, when the lamps were lit inside, she'd be able to see her old suite. It wouldn't take much to discover who was living there now—she could Sing a kigh over to the windows in a couple of minutes—but she didn't want to know. Hadn't ever wanted to know. She went into the palace to take her turn witnessing in the courts but that was it. She'd never been asked to play at any function and she'd never attended any that were within her rights as a bard to attend.

Although Bardic Hall and the palace were both within the Citadel walls, there was no chance of an accidental meeting with His Gracious Majesty, King Theron. He lived surrounded by insulating layers of people and protocol and moved in circles far from those of a lowly Bard. Even while growing up with the full rights and privileges of a princess, she'd gone for months without seeing her father.

But Theron *could* have called for her at any time. Their father had often spoken with the bards just returned from Walks rather than relying solely on the records. Apparently, it hadn't occurred to him that a bard who'd spent the first fourteen years of her life learning politics and protocol might make useful observations.

It didn't take Bardic Memory to recall the message that had accompanied the invitation to her cousin's joining—Theron had added a pompous declaration of forgiveness for the mistakes of her youth. Well, *he'd* been the one who'd cut her off from everything she'd known and *she* hadn't forgiven *him*. She'd said as much in the message that had gone back to the palace. All she'd wanted was for him to say that he was sorry for the way he'd hurt her. He never had.

It didn't matter. As the captain had said, the bards were her family now.

Annice slid one hand inside her jacket and pressed it against her waist. She remembered how Theron had looked when he'd laid his heir in her arms. He'd stared down at his daughter as though she was the most amazing creature he'd ever seen, as though she was the only baby ever born.

Annice tilted her head to watch the sky as lights began to break up the block of shadow dusk had wrapped around the palace. *I want to feel what Theron felt when he looked down at Onele. I want something I can love that much.*

A gust of wind, cold across her ear, brought her head around in time to see a kigh disappear below the eaves. So much for quiet contemplation; she wouldn't be alone for much longer.

"Although, come to think of it, I haven't exactly been alone for about nine weeks."

* * *

Stasya Sang the kigh a gratitude and beat her head lightly against the casement. Annice was on the roof again, sitting at the base of one of the chimneys where the ridge of slate flattened out for about a foot all around. It wasn't actually as dangerous as it seemed, or the captain would've put a stop to it years ago, but it was a habit that drove Stasya crazy.

If she wants to be alone, why doesn't she just close the bedroom door? Stasya hadn't gotten an answer to that question at any time over the last ten years and wasn't expecting one any time soon.

"Nees?" She directed her voice up and over the edge of the eaves. "Nees, you're going to freeze or fall off or something. Why don't you come down?"

Annice's voice, equally directed, drifted back. "Why don't you come up?"

"Because I don't have a death wish."

"Chicken."

She's going to cluck in a minute. Stasya tucked the ends of her scarf into her jacket, and stepped out onto the small balcony just as the henhouse noises began. *Considering that she never even saw a chicken that wasn't covered in some kind of sauce until she was fifteen, she's not bad.*

The steeply pitched roof of Bardic Hall almost met the floor of the balcony. Bolted down beside the gabled window, a narrow metal ladder—intended for use by the chimney sweeps who descended on the Hall once a quarter—stretched up to Annice's perch. Stasya peered up at the dark on dark silhouette against the late afternoon sky, blew on her fingers to warm them, and began to climb. Having spent her childhood clambering about the rigging of her parents' ship, she had no problem with either the physical effort or the distance from the ground, but she couldn't get her head around the concept.

"Why the roof?" she asked, as she'd asked a hundred times, sitting down beside Annice with a heavy sigh.

"I think better up here. With nothing around me but sky ..."

"... your mind is unfettered. I've heard you sing the song, Annice. I've sung it myself. I just keep hoping you'll come up with a reason that isn't such a bardic cliché." She sat back and swept her gaze over the view. "Palace looks a lot smaller from up here."

"Last time you said it looked bigger."

"That was then. This is now. Nees, are you sure you're not having this baby just to get the king's attention?"

Annice twisted around to stare at her. "Are you nuts? Stas, if he finds out, I'm dead. And so is the baby."

"You don't really believe that."

"I have to."

"You don't."

"Stasya." Annice made the name a warning.

"All right." She threw up her hands. "I think you want a reconciliation, but you're just too stubborn to make the first move and you've finally come up with something he can't ignore. But you don't have to listen to me."

"I'm not."

"I also think that's a really bad reason to have a baby."

Annice glared at her for a moment, then pointedly looked away. The brittle silence that followed stretched into an uncomfortable length of time.

"Nees?"

"You're wrong."

"About what?"

"Everything."

Then why didn't you have the captain tuck you away out of sight? Stasya asked silently. But all she said aloud was, "All right. It was an accident. Then why *are* you keeping it?"

"Why does everyone keep asking me that?"

"Maybe because we all want to know."

"I'll tell you the same thing I told the captain. I want a family. I lost the one I had and now I have a chance to start another."

"Babies don't love unconditionally, Annice. I helped raise four younger brothers and you wouldn't believe how self-centered the little shitheads can be."

"Maybe I want someone *I* can love unconditionally."

"What am I, fish guts?"

"It's not the same."

"I should hope not."

"Stasya, when I think about this baby, I feel the way

I feel when I Sing; that sense of everything snapping into place and being, if only for a little while, absolutely right."

"Oh." Stasya reached out and laced her fingers through the other woman's. "Why didn't you say so?" She still believed Annice was making a deliberate attempt to attract King Theron's attention, but she was willing to allow for the rise of stronger feelings. "It might be kind of nice to have a baby around."

"So you don't want to move out? Find a new set of rooms?"

"Not unless you start going all esoteric Mother-goddess on me."

Annice snorted. "Hard to be an esoteric Mother-goddess and puke your guts out at the same time."

"Good point. What did Slane say about it when he took your recall?"

"It didn't come up. Unlike certain other bards, I don't kiss and tell, even under trance. Besides, I found out this morning and the Walk ended last night."

"Another good point. Nees, I can't feel my butt any more. Can we go in now?"

"Sure." Annice stood and had to make a sudden grab for Stasya's shoulder as a kigh whipped around the chimney and almost sent her off the roof. Heart in her throat, she watched it disappear into the clouds, eyes so wide they hurt. "Did you see that?"

"Yeah. I saw. Let's get inside. Now."

"I'm sorry, Annice. I should have warned you. Your pregnancy is affecting your orientation to the kigh."

"What do you mean? Air kigh don't like babies?"

"No, but they're jealous. You always Sang strongest in air and they can feel that changing."

"To what?"

"Earth."

"Oh, great."

"It shouldn't be too much of a difference for you, you've Sung earth before."

"Not often. There isn't anything you can do with earth. Except maybe grow things."

"I warned you about that Mother-goddess shit," Stasya snickered.

"Shut up, Stas! Captain, there's got to be something I can do."

"Bit late in the cycle for gardening."

"Shut *up,* Stas!"

Liene bit down on a smile. "Well, to begin with, I suggest that you stay off the roof. And then, you should ask Terezka some questions. Her Bernardas is just two; she should still remember what she went through. Don't ask anything of Edite, she hasn't forgiven Dasa for choosing to live with her father."

"But that happened five years ago."

"I know."

Annice shook her head. At least she wouldn't have to worry about *that.*

"Sarlote just left to spend Fourth Quarter with her family—Hard to believe that Ondro's almost ten, isn't it?—but she'll be back before you're due and you can talk to her then. Speak with Taska and Ales if you want, but they're grandmothers now and I'm pretty sure their memories of the experience have been gentled by time."

Stasya made a face. "Oh, I can't see why. Puking and pains are memories *I'd* want to hang on to."

Smiling sweetly, Annice kicked her in the shin. "Good," she said. "Remember that."

"They know, don't they?"

"What are you talking about?" Stasya asked, mopping up gravy with a thick slice of bread. "Who knows what?"

"The fledglings, at the end of the other table. They're looking at me."

Stasya swiveled around on the bench and the three youngsters immediately became interested only in their dinners. Sighing theatrically, she turned back and shook her head at Annice. "Of course they're watching you. They got here while you were Walking and now you're back they're checking to see if you match the songs. Every new kid for the last ten years has done the same thing. I thought you were used to it by now."

"You're sure that's all it is?"

"Yes, I'm sure." She shot another glance over her shoulder. "And with any luck that blonde'll grow into her nose."

"Stas ..."

"She looks like she should be wearing a hood and jesses."

"Stasya!"

"What?"

"You are being *really* cruel."

Stasya grinned. "And you are *really* being an idiot."

Annice pushed a boiled bit of something around on her plate. "I know. I'm sorry." She put down her knife, picked it up again, and stabbed at a piece of meat. "It's just that when I walked into the dining room, I felt ..."

"Sick?"

"Exposed. Like I had a purple 'p' painted on my forehead or something."

"No one knows but me and the captain, Nees, but you've got to get used to the fact that they're all going to find out."

"All of them? Why all of them?"

She looked so startled that Stasya reached for her hand. "Nees, sweetie, you're going to get—how can I put this delicately?—bigger. Bards are trained to observe. They'll notice."

"I hadn't thought of that."

You haven't thought of much, Stasya realized, but she kept it to herself. "I can't believe I haven't asked you this yet, but who's the father?"

"This isn't to go into any songs."

"I swear. I'll have it witnessed if you like." She pitched the word "witness" to carry.

Of the nine other bards in the dining room, only Terezka, busy picking bits of carrot out of her son's hair, didn't turn.

Teeth clenched, Annice waved them back to their meals. "Don't be such a jerk," she muttered.

"You're the one who cast aspersions on my discretion." Stasya bracketed her plate with her elbows, cupped her chin in her hands, and leaned forward. "So tell."

"Pjerin a'Stasiek."

"Never heard of him."

"He's the Duc of Ohrid." Stasya continued to look blank so she added, "Remember 'Darkling Lover'?"

"*That* Duc of Ohrid? You're kidding."

Annice flushed. "Why would I kid about something like that?"

Stasya shrugged. "I don't know. Why would you sleep with the Duc of Ohrid?"

"Well, for one thing, the song's right—he's absolutely gorgeous. And for another ..." Annice frowned as she remembered violet eyes and a thick fall of ebony hair and a night that very nearly blew the roof off the keep. "Actually," she said thoughtfully, "there isn't another. Pjerin a'Stasiek is the kind of man you don't mind going to bed with ..."

"*You* don't mind going to bed with," Stasya corrected acerbically.

"... but you wouldn't look forward to facing over breakfast the next morning."

CHAPTER THREE

Pjerin a'Stasiek, sixth Duc of Ohrid, slid his grip up the smooth wood of the haft, drew in a deep lungful of cold air, and slammed the maul down. The split round of ash exploded away from the chopping block, one of the pieces slamming into an outbuilding just as a small, dark-haired boy ran around the corner. The child cried out and fell.

"Gerek!" Throwing the maul aside, Pjerin dove toward his four-year-old son.

Scowling at the wedge of wood, Gerek scrambled to his feet. "I'm okay, Papa," he insisted, kicking indignantly at a rock sticking up through the snow. "I just jumped back from the noise and that tripped me."

Pjerin checked anyway, his hands engulfing the skinny, wool-covered shoulders as he turned the protesting boy around. There didn't appear to be any damage, so he brushed off a snow-covered bottom and stared seriously down into eyes the same dark violet as his own. "Ger, you know better than to come around the shed like that. What have I told you to do when someone's at the woodpile?"

"Go 'round by the other side so they can see you and stop chopping." Gerek managed to repeat the entire instruction on one long-suffering sigh. "But Bohdan sent me to get you. 'Cause that man is with Aunty Olina again."

"You're certain this will work?"

"Not entirely, no." Albek took a sip of mulled wine and peered at Olina over the edge of the thick pottery mug. "But anything worth achieving carries with it a certain amount of risk. Don't you agree?"

Olina smiled tightly at him and turned to kick at a

smoldering log with one booted foot. "That depends on how much risk you consider *a certain amount* to be. As much as I despise the current situation, I have no intention of losing my head."

"Far too beautiful a head to lose," Albek agreed with polished sincerity.

"Don't change the subject." Nails tapped out her impatience on the mantelpiece. "How great is the risk?"

He set the mug down on the round table drawn up beside his chair. "We now know, thanks to record keeping that borders on the compulsive, that what we plan has either never been attempted or the attempt has never been discovered. It doesn't really matter which as both will serve us equally well. We also know that in the eight generations since Prince Shkoder sailed from the north and founded the country that so originally bears his name, high court procedures have not changed. Our plan will use the court's own formula against it."

"It still seems too simple."

"All the best plans are."

"Don't be facetious, Albek," she warned. "To use a bardic skill ..."

"A skill that bards make use of," the Cemandian corrected, spreading his hands and smiling reassuringly up at her. "Not a talent, not an innate ability, just a skill. A skill that in Shkoder is confined to bards and to healers but in my country is used by anyone with enough interest to learn." While that wasn't the entire truth, it was close enough to be believed.

Olina frowned, brows sketching an ebony vee against pale skin. "And the bards can't detect it?"

"Of course they can. If it occurs to them to look for it." Albek leaned back, stretching his feet toward the fire, and reaching again for his mug. "But it won't occur to them. Especially when everything they discover will match exactly with the information they'll already have from young Leksik."

"Leksik? *Who* is Leksik?"

"The fanatic I told you of. Quite frankly, he makes such an unbelievable trader, I'm amazed they haven't picked him up yet. When he's finished ranting and raving, you'll have King Theron's men camped on your doorstep in no time."

"So you've already used this layered trance thing on him?"

Albek shook his head, the rubies in his ears flashing like drops of captured fire. "Remember simplicity. Why risk tampering with his memories when lying serves as well?"

In three long strides she crossed to bend over him, the fingers of one hand clamped tightly around his jaw. "And how well does lying serve?" she asked softly.

In spite of her grip, his lips curved into a smile. "I have never," he said, staring up into ice-blue eyes, his chest beginning to rise and fall a little more quickly, his voice leaving no room for doubt, "lied to you."

"Am I interrupting something?"

Olina slowly straightened, fingertips caressing the marks left on Albek's face as her hand fell away. Twitching her embroidered velvet vest back over her hips, she turned to face the door. "Pjerin," she said, exhibiting no surprise at his sudden arrival, "do come in. I thought you were out playing woodsman."

"I was." Pjerin circled around his father's sister and went to stand by the window. The pale winter light shining through the tiny glass panes touched his eyes with frost. Weight forward on the balls of his feet, he crossed his arms and glowered. "Bohdan told me Albek had returned."

"With no intention to keep you from your work, Your Grace," Albek protested. Although he and Olina had been speaking Shkoden, he now switched to Cemandian. He always spoke Cemandian with the duc. "I'm on my way home and as this is the western end of the pass . . ."

"On your way home *now?*" Pjerin interrupted. Fluent in both languages—although he spoke neither most of the time, preferring the Cemandian-derived mountain dialect of the region—he didn't care which the trader used as long as it soon included a variation on *"Good-bye."* "You're cutting it fine. Other years, the pass has been snowed in by Fourth Quarter Festival."

"But not this year. I've been keeping a very close eye on the weather, I assure you. If I leave first thing tomorrow, I should have the time I need." He traced a sign of the Circle over his heart. "All things being enclosed."

"Festival's day after tomorrow." Pjerin paused, then ground out, "You're welcome to stay until after."

Such a gracious invitation. Albek thought, but all he said was. "No, thank you. I can't risk the weather."

Grunting an agreement, Pjerin tried, unsuccessfully, not to appear relieved. "What about your packs?"

"Yes, uh, well, I admit I was a little overly optimistic about the amount I could move this year." The trader dropped his eyes and appeared fascinated by the pattern woven into the thick nap of the carpet. "I was hoping you could continue to store them for me. The lighter I travel, the faster I travel, and the less chance I'll be caught in the mountains. I mean . . ." His gesture somehow encompassed not only the room they were in but the great, stone bulk of the keep it was so small a part of. ". . . it's not as if you don't have the space."

"Oh, plenty of space." Pjerin spread his arms and scowled. "What about your mules? Shall we store those, too? Next spring, why not bring an army of traders through with you and we'll billet the lot of them in the Great Hall. We're not using it for anything."

"Pjerin." Olina made his name a warning. "Don't be an ass just because you can."

He turned, smile gone. "Don't push me, Olina. I will not have my home become a tollbooth or marketplace to suit your plans to exploit the pass. Nor will I have my son exposed to . . ."

"Exposed to what? To new ideas? To the possibility that the seventh Duc of Ohrid might actually be in a position of power instead of a hewer of wood and a drawer of water like his father and his father before him?"

Albek stood. "You'll excuse me, I've caused unintentional strife between you, I'll just . . ."

"Sit," Olina snarled.

He sat, smoothing the wide legs of his trousers and hiding a smile. Glancing up through his lashes, he studied first Pjerin than Olina. The duc, in his late twenties, was a powerfully built man whose height made him appear deceptively slender. His aunt, eleven years older, was a slender woman who radiated power. He wore his thick black hair tied back at the nape of his neck with a bit of leather. She wore hers in one heavy braid wrapped

around her head like an ebony crown. He smoldered.
She flamed. They were both tall, and dark, and beautiful,
and Albek loved to watch them fight.

"Ohrid controls the pass. Therefore, we control what
passes through it." Olina advanced on her nephew. "We
could become the linchpin between two great nations."

"Increased trade with Cemandia," Pjerin growled, "is
a betrayal of everything this family stands for!"

"Because generations ago our ancestor was chased out
of Cemandia?" Her posture changed from aggressive to
mocking. "The first Duc of Ohrid, fleeing from oppres-
sion, building a keep at the head of what he so romanti-
cally named Defiance Pass to protect his people from
pursuit. He built this keep in order that he and his entire
household not be dragged back to face a charge of treason. You, of course, are happy to huddle in this pile of
rock, trying desperately to keep warm, holding tight to
tradition when we could use what we have to become
rich and powerful. To better the lives of everyone in
Ohrid."

"None of my people are fool enough to believe Cemandian promises. We increase trade and Cemandia will
do everything in its power to crush Ohrid's
independence."

She moved closer. Pjerin stepped back, one step, then
his shoulders folded the heavy tapestry against the wall
and she closed the distance between them. He tossed his
head like a horse fighting the bit. "If you're not happy
here, Olina, go somewhere else."

"Like your mother did?" She spread the fingers of
one hand on his chest and smiled with satisfaction as he
tried unsuccessfully to flinch away. "Maybe if your father
had been a little more open to change, she wouldn't
have gone. Wouldn't have run off with that Cemandian
trader. Wouldn't have caused your father so much trouble trying to get you back."

"Stop it!"

Olina waited long enough for it to become obvious
she moved only because she wanted to, then she turned
on one heel and strode back toward the fireplace. "It
occurs to me," she said thoughtfully, "I should be speaking to King Theron, not to you."

"What are you talking about?" He jerked away from

the wall and shoved at a lock of hair that had fallen forward out of the tie.

"Well . . ." She bent and threw another piece of wood on the fire. ". . . if King Theron were to tell you to open the pass to expanded trade, you'd have no choice."

"King Theron?"

"He is your liege lord," she reminded him dryly. "You do remember that great-grandfather, *your* great-great-grandfather, surrendered Ohrid's ever so valued independence to Shkoder. If King Theron says jump, my dear Pjerin, you ask how high on the way up."

A muscle twitched in Pjerin's jaw. "I don't give a rat's ass about *King* Theron. *I* am Duc of Ohrid and *I* will not allow increased trade with Cemandia." Hands curled into fists he charged toward the door, whirled, and glared down at the Cemandian trader. "See you that remember it, Albek!"

"I will, Your Grace. Oh, and I was sorry to hear about your dogs." His sincerity was undeniable. "To lose them both at once must have been very upsetting."

Pjerin stared at the Cemandian, conflicting emotions twisting his face. Unable to find an answer, he snarled what might have been a wordless agreement and slammed out of the room.

"Well, that bit of unexpected sympathy certainly confused him," Olina observed. "Which I'm sure was your intention."

"If he doesn't think of me personally as an enemy, it will make things easier tonight." Albek sighed and stretched his feet back toward the fire. "Besides, I *was* sorry to hear about his dogs. I had a dog once myself."

"Spare me."

"You play him very well."

Olina snorted. "It isn't difficult. He's too arrogant to see past what I dangle in front of him. It never even occurs to him that I have as little desire to run a tollgate between Shkoder and Cemandia as he does, that I want a part of something bigger."

"That you want to control a part of something bigger."

"That goes without saying."

"I liked the bit about King Theron. A nice touch. I can use it."

"Of course you can."

"But you still seem hesitant."

"I'm still considering your *certain amount of risk*," she told him dryly.

"Olina." Albek shook his head. "I've studied every possibility and this leaves us with the greatest chance of success. Consider," he raised a finger, "the accidental death of the duc would require a full investigation before the title could go to his son. The bards would not only question us but the kigh as well, and *that* risk is far too great. While the kigh are not always around, we can't take the chance they won't be watching." He closed his eyes for an instant as fear beaten into him his entire life threatened to break through his control, then he raised a second finger. "Assassination, the same result. But . . ." A third finger lifted to join the other two. ". . . if he condemns himself by his own mouth, there will be no further investigation, there never is. You will be left to regent for the child with a shocked and saddened people behind you."

"And it will all be over."

"Oh, no. It will just be beginning." He dropped his hand and laced his fingers in his lap, adding with no change of expression in either face or voice, "You've bedded him."

"Yes." It wasn't a question, but she chose to answer it anyway. "Was it that obvious?"

Albek smiled, wondering why she'd chosen to let him know, fully aware she did nothing without a reason. "Wasn't it intended to be?"

"Perhaps." Pushing herself away from the mantle, she advanced on the trader. "At nineteen he was an enthusiastic partner, but as he got older . . ."

"He insisted on retaining control?"

"Essentially."

"And the boy, Gerek?"

"What? Do you suddenly think he's my son as well? Don't be a fool." Amusement and disdain were equally mixed in her tone. "Gerek is exactly what we say he is; the legally witnessed child of a woman who had her eye on timber rights. Pjerin, in turn, wanted an heir but had no interest in being joined; not after the mess his father made of it. She got her favor. He got his heir. I thought you spoke to Gerek's mother? You told me that, in your not so humble opinion, as long as her son was safe and happy she would be no problem."

"I did." Albek brushed a honey-colored curl back off his face and let both shoulders rise and fall in a graceful shrug. "But I had to explore the possibility. You understand."

"Yes, I understand." Her voice held an edge. She straddled his outstretched legs, and slowly, deliberately, stroked her gaze down the length of his body and back.

He shifted in the chair. "I do have to go, as I said, tomorrow morning."

"Of course you do. The pass doesn't defy the weather and won't remain open much longer."

"And tonight ..." He tried to look away, found he couldn't, and wet his lips. "Tonight, I must concentrate on Pjerin."

"How pleasant for you both." Olina bent forward. Her eyes still holding Albek's, she grasped both arms of the chair and made him a prisoner beneath the arch of her body. Her smile became decidedly feral. "All things considered then, I suggest that we don't waste the afternoon."

"Papa, why don't you like Aunty Olina's friend?"

"Because I think he'd sell his own mother if the price was right." Pjerin lifted his son out of the bath and set him on the hearth, wrapping him in the towel that had been warming in front of the nursery fire.

"Oh." The piping voice came out a little muffled through the enveloping fabric. "How much does a mother cost?"

"Why? Do you want one?"

Gerek's head emerged, hair sticking out in damp black spikes, expression indignant. "I got one," he reminded his father. His mother came to visit sometimes and sometimes, although he didn't like it as much—because his grandpapa was very old and didn't care much for small boys even when they tried hard to be quiet—he went to visit her. "And I got you, and Nurse Jany, and Aunty Olina, and Bohdan, and Rezka, and Urmi, and Kaspar, and Brencis ..."

"Wait a minute." Bohdan was his elderly steward;

Rezka ruled the kitchens, and Urmi, her partner, was
the stablemaster; Kaspar was Gerek's pony. Pjerin made
a point of knowing the names of all his people, high or
low, and occasionally four-legged. "Who's Brencis?"

"A goat." Gerek shrugged at his father's ignorance
and obediently turned to have his back dried. "Aunty
Olina likes him."

"Who? Brencis?"

"No! Albek!" Standing naked in the firelight, he
scratched the back of one leg with the other foot. "If
you don't like him, how come you let him stay around.
You could make him go if you wanted to."

"Your Aunt Olina likes him. And this is her home,
too."

"Oh. Bohdan doesn't like him neither. Bohdan says
that Albek is so slippery even the Circle couldn't hold
him."

"Arms up."

Gerek raised his arms and poked them through the
sleeves of his nightshirt. "Does that make him a bad
man, Papa? I thought everything was in the Circle?"

Pjerin made a mental note to speak to Bohdan about
his choice of words. *And then he can explain theology to
a four-year-old.* Maybe it *was* time they had a priest at
the keep. "Everything is in the Circle, even Albek."

"But Bohdan said . . ."

"Never mind what Bohdan said."

Gerek peered up at his father from under his lashes.
Ever?"

"Never mind what he said about Albek, you terror.
You still mind what he says the rest of the time." The
next few moments degenerated into a wild free-for-all
that ended with Pjerin flat on his back and Gerek
perched on his chest demanding his surrender.

"You win. I surrender."

"Kiss my finger."

"Is that part of the surrender?"

"No. It got bit by a chicken."

"What were you doing in the henhouse?"

"Helping." At Pjerin's frown he hastily added, "Really helping. Not like last time."

Pjerin raised his head off the floor and kissed the prof-
fered finger. Then he continued the motion, scooping

Gerek into his arms and rising lithely to his feet. With
the boy cradled against his chest, he stepped around the
pair of servants removing the bath and settled down into
the only piece of furniture in the room large enough to
hold his weight.

Gerek squirmed around until he was sitting half on
his father's lap and half beside him tucked into the angle
of the big chair. Stretching his bare toes out toward the
fire, he said, "Can I stay with you for vigil this year?"

"Of course you can."

"Can I have my own candle?" His voice was hopeful,
but he obviously didn't expect a positive answer.

"Yes."

"Really? Truly?"

Pjerin hid a smile at the tone. Last year, Gerek's candle had very nearly set the keep on fire when he'd fallen
asleep and it had dropped to the floor but not gone out.
Fortunately, the burning tapestry had smelled so bad
that he and Olina had been able to put it out with only
a handbreadth of damage done. This year, they'd be
more alert. "Really. Truly."

With a satisfied sigh, the boy leaned his head against
Pjerin's chest. "Nees sang me a song about the sun coming back," he said.

"Is Nees another goat?"

"No! Nees the bard!"

"Nees?" Pjerin frowned. He couldn't remember a
bard named Nees and, with Ohrid right on the border,
they didn't get many walking out so far.

"You know, Papa, the one who was here when it
rained so much and she sang me stories and she kept
making Aunty Olina mad by smiling at her."

Then he remembered. Olina had been in a mood; at
her most challenging and ready to remove the evening
from the Circle altogether. The bard had said quietly, *I
wouldn't. You'll lose.* To his surprise, Olina had studied
the younger woman for a long moment, nodded, and
blunted the edge of her tongue. He'd been the only one
close enough to hear the exchange but—if even Gerek
had picked up on it—the results had obviously been noticed by the rest of the keep. That wasn't likely to make
Olina happy if she found out. "You mean, Annice, Ger."

"Yeah. Nees."

Frankly, the bard hadn't looked like the sort who could give Olina a run for her money. Although she'd worn the same annoying air of cocky independence that marked every bard he'd ever seen, the expression in her eyes had been contemplative rather than combative. Hazel eyes, the kind that turned almost green when ... He shook himself free of the memory. It had ended up an interesting night all around. "So the bard sang you new stories, did she?"

"Uh-huh."

"Well, maybe you should tell me a story tonight."

"No." Gerek snuggled into Pjerin's side, fingers playing with a damp spot caused by a spout of bathwater accidentally rising to meet a shirt. "*You* tell *me* about the dragon who wanted to be a boy."

"But you've heard that one a thousand times, Ger."

"So?"

Pjerin smiled, inhaled the clean scent of his child, and began. "Once upon a time, there was a dragon who wanted to be a boy ..."

The knock on the heavy oak door of the tiny room he used for a study was so faint, Pjerin thought at first he'd imagined it. When it sounded again, he threw his hair back over his shoulder and turned to face it, calling, "Come." He hated ciphering and anything would be a relief from the columns of figures Bohdan had insisted he go over tonight.

Almost anything, he amended a moment later. "What do you want?"

Albek stepped apologetically into the room, a pottery carafe in one hand, two heavy mugs in the other. "I saw you were still up. I thought we might ..."

"Have a drink together? Don't be an ass." He dragged the chair around to face the other man and scowled. "What my aunt does is her own business, but I don't drink with Cemandians. Get out!"

"I was hoping, that is, I hoped that until Olina went to sleep ..."

Pjerin's scowl deepened. "I thought you *got along* with Olina?"

"I do." Albek's smile had picked up a slight twist of

desperation. "But I can't . . . get along with her . . . again. Not so soon."

"You're limping."

"Nothing permanent. I assure you I can still leave in the morning."

"Good." Pjerin exhaled noisily and shook his head. It wasn't pity, exactly. It was just that Albek wore an expression he'd seen in his mirror more than once before he'd finally found the strength to tell her no and make it stick. "She'll go exactly as far as you let her, you know."

"I know." The Cemandian trader's tone was distinctly tart.

In spite of himself, Pjerin almost smiled. "She won't look for you in here."

Albek shifted his weight and winced slightly. "My thought as well."

"What's in the jug?"

"Mulled wine. Your cook has a very fine touch with it."

"I know. How old are you?"

The question seemed to take the other man by surprise. "Twenty-six."

Pjerin glanced down at his accounts and then jerked his head at the other chair. "Sit. If you can. I suppose we can find something to talk about that won't have us at each other's throats."

"Is it done?"

"It is." Albek closed and latched the door. He pulled the tapestry back down into place, his fingers lightly caressing the stag as it fell beneath the hounds, then he turned and walked briskly across the room to Olina's bed.

Clothed only in shadows and the thick, black fall of her hair, the firelight licking golden highlights on her skin, she watched him approach. "I'm amazed he even let you in. He doesn't like you, you know."

"I know. But I gave us something in common."

"What?"

"You," he told her, pausing on the hearth, close enough to the bed to read her features but more than an arm's length away. The heat of the blazing fire was uncomfortably hot on his legs but, until he had her reaction, it posed the lesser danger of being burned.

To his surprise, she began to laugh. "Were you hiding from me, then? Taking refuge with someone who would understand?"

"Why ..." he began, and stopped as it suddenly became clear. "That was why you let me know about the two of you."

"I thought you might be able to make use of it. Was it enough for him to open his door to you?"

"Not quite. I also lied about my age. As soon as he saw me as younger than himself ..." Albek spread his hands and, now that he knew it was safe, moved to the side of the bed.

"You became someone to protect, if only for a short while." She slid her legs to one side so he could sit. "Very clever. And the drug?"

"Already in the mug. Once it relaxed him, I had no trouble."

Olina rubbed her bare thigh against his side, and studied him through half closed eyes. "And did you take advantage while you had the opportunity? He *is* very beautiful."

"My tastes do not lean toward taking advantage." His fingers lingered on the curve of her hip. Blocked from the heat of the fire by the rest of her body, the skin was smooth and cool like silk. He had seen a rope made of silk once; it had been far stronger than any made of a coarser, more common fiber. "As you very well know." The oblivion he needed had been too long conditioned. "But may I ask you something?"

She looked amused. "Ask."

It wasn't a question he should be asking, but he found he couldn't help himself. "The duc is your blood, your family; doesn't it bother you that we've just arranged to have him executed?"

"This from the man who brought me the way to be rid of him? Who said he could recognize waste when he saw it and that he had a way to help me to the life I desired?" Her eyes narrowed. "Why do you want to know?"

Why indeed. "My Queen would not be happy if you were suddenly overcome with remorse." Which was true.

Olina laughed. "When I finally have a chance to hold real power? Don't be ridiculous, Albek."

He inclined her head, acknowledging her point. "I was deep in his memories. Sometimes, it's unsettling."

"And now it's my turn?"

"There *are* still a few loose ends that must be tucked neatly out of the way." Albek leaned forward and picked a pewter goblet off the pedestal table beside her bed; its contents prepared before he left to find Pjerin. "And as you are as little likely to voluntarily surrender control as your nephew . . ." He offered her the wine.

She wrapped her fingers around his, trapping them within her grip as she drank. Then she held them a moment longer just to prove she could. "So." Releasing his hand, she reached out further and laid her palm against his cheek, turning his head slightly so that she could catch his gaze with hers. "Once again I will be in your complete control." Beneath the rough stubble of whiskers, she could feel the heat of blood rising in his face. "*Don't* abuse the privilege."

Albek swallowed. "I wouldn't," he said, with complete sincerity, "dream of it."

Lilyana glanced up as the door to her solar opened. When she saw who moved wearily into the warmth of the small room, she motioned for her attendant to leave them alone.

The younger woman nodded, rose, bowed to the king and slipped around him, quietly closing the door behind her. She could be counted on to ensure that king and consort were not disturbed.

"You look like you had a tiring meeting," Lilyana observed, allowing the book she'd been reading to fall closed on her lap, her fingers resting lightly on the carved wood of the cover. "Are you hungry? Do you want me to call for something?"

"Thank you. But no." Theron dropped into the other chair by the fire, letting the heat bake the chill from his bones. From the middle of Third Quarter on, the larger of the two audience rooms became perpetually cold and damp and he had no idea why he'd used it today. Well, actually, yes, he did. He had no wish to see the Cemandian ambassador in any kind of an intimate situation.

"I really can't stand that son of a bitch. I wish you'd been there."

She smiled. "When I offered to attend, you told me there was no reason for us both to suffer. So, what did the ambassador say when you confronted him with the bardic reports on the traders?"

"For the most part, more of the usual. That his queen wished to establish a trade route to the sea and that the traders were merely finding the best corridor through Shkoder. Then he said that as I had raised no objection to the first he couldn't understand why I would object to the second."

"And you told him?"

"That he was a slimy little eel and I should have sent him packing before the pass closed."

"Theron." She reached out and prodded him in the calf with the toe of her fleece slipper.

He sighed and unfastened the throat of his heavy brocade overtunic, catching himself before he could roll the embossed gold button between his fingers. It was a habit he was trying to break and, besides, his valet would be unbearable if he lost another one. "Well, that's what I wanted to tell him. Instead, I informed the slimy little eel that agreeing in principle to an expressed desire did not mean that I had agreed to a small army of traders poking their noses where they don't belong. That if a corridor is to be laid out, *I* will say where it goes."

Lilyana nodded. "And he said?"

"That his people were just trying to help." He began to grow annoyed again, remembering, and his tone sharpened. "That all information would, in time, have been brought to me in order that I could come to a decision."

"And you said?"

"Lilyana, there was a bard there. The whole conversation was witnessed. If you want me to repeat it back to you, word for word, it would be easier to ask for a recall."

"But you're here now," she told him, "and I'm asking you."

The king glared at his consort, who met his gaze levelly, her expression clearly stating she depended on him, and only on him. He sighed again, not the least taken in, and undid another button. "I didn't lose my temper, if that's what you're afraid of. The little sea slug isn't worth it. I told him that I would express my displeasure to Her Majesty the moment the pass cleared and a messenger could be sent. Whereupon," he raised a hand to forestall her next question, "he then went on about how the pressure of the Empire against both our borders suggests that we would have much to gain from closer ties, and then he mentioned, as he always does, that we haven't chosen partners for either of our daughters and that the Heir of Cemandia is still unjoined. I reminded him that Onele is my Heir and he replied with . . ."

"The line about our grandchild ruling two great countries combined. He's so predictable." Lilyana drummed her fingers against the tooled leather covering the arm of her chair. "As if the two countries could combine without Cemandia trying to roll right over Shkoder to the sea."

Theron grunted his agreement. "Then, I pointed out that Brigita is, at ten, fifteen years younger than Prince Rajmund, and still too young to be considered as a partner for anyone. Which ended that topic yet again."

"He'll keep bringing it up."

"Of course he will. It's his job. All things being enclosed, I'm thankful there isn't a female member of the Cemandian royal family around the right age or he'd be nagging me about Antavas, too." He rubbed at his temples where the headache that always accompanied the ambassador still pounded. "Rajmund and Annice were of an age. This could have all been settled so easily years ago."

Lilyana's eyes widened slightly, her only reaction to the surprising introduction of a topic never discussed.

"They could have found happiness together," Theron continued. "They could have built the first span in a bridge between Shkoder and Cemandia, given me a foundation of family to build on." He frowned at the mixed metaphor and locked up at his consort. "*You* found happiness, didn't you?"

"Don't be ridiculous," she said complacently, "you know I did." She'd been sixteen when they'd been formally betrothed, nineteen when they were joined. They'd spent maybe five months of those three years together. But from the beginning they'd both been willing to make the best of the situation and, over time, tolerance had become trust, had become friendship, had become. . . . She was no longer able to imagine life without him and knew how much he depended on her. If she had to put a name to it, Lilyana supposed that love was as good a one as any.

She studied his face. He was six years her senior and there were new lines around his eyes and mouth, and the gray at his temples had begun to spread through the soft brown curls. At least he still had his hair; her family tended toward baldness, something Antavas would not thank her for later. Almost half her life spent reading nuances off a face schooled to hiding expressions behind political dissembling told her Theron was honestly worried. She also realized that her happiness—while he did care about it—was not the issue bothering him now. Stroking the rope of pearls he'd given her when Onele was born, she added thoughtfully, "But I never had another life pulling at me. Annice did."

When Theron's frown twisted into a scowl, she met it with a neutral expression and blandly pointed out, "You mentioned her first."

The wood and leather chair creaked a protest as Theron shifted his weight. "She didn't even give it a chance," he growled. "Didn't even consider what it might mean to Shkoder."

"She was fourteen. She overreacted." Lilyana had thought at the time that if Annice had tried to find the worst possible way to handle the situation, to handle Theron, she couldn't have found anything better. *If only she'd come to me.* But the adored youngest princess had been jealous of her brother's new loyalties and, to be honest, Lilyana had never blamed her for that. That Theron, nineteen years Annice's senior, had also overreacted had only made things worse. They'd hurt each other very badly and pride had kept the wounds from healing.

It hadn't helped that when Theron had decided to meet Annice halfway, Annice had refused to be met. Lilyana had tried to explain how Annice felt, had tried to get Theron to apologize—for she knew that in his heart he *was* sorry—but without success. *"I am the* king!" he had snarled, his sister's message crushed in his fist. *"I held out my hand and she not only ignored it but dared to tell me what I should have done. What kind of a king surrenders to the whims of a spoiled child!"*

Pride and temper—in this Annice and Theron were too much alike. Lilyana had mentioned that at the time, endured the storm produced, and never mentioned it again.

"A diamond for your thoughts?"

"A diamond?" Lilyana smiled at him. "I doubt they're worth so much. I was just thinking that Annice and you might . . ."

Theron chopped at the air with his left hand. The royal signet flashed in the afternoon sun slanting through the tiny panes of the window behind him. The gesture very clearly said he no longer wished to talk about it.

It isn't Annice that worries you, although this new trouble evokes the older one. Lilyana waited.

Conscious of her steady gaze, Theron stared in turn at the fire. For seventeen, almost eighteen years, Lilyana had been, as she was now, a quiet sounding board for his fears. She'd stood serene against his temper and from the maelstrom pulled, nearly every time, the true reason for his anger. Even when he hadn't been sure of it himself. He'd been a better king with her beside him. Probably a better person. Had he ever told her that? He glanced up from the flames, caught her eye, and realized she knew. For a moment, there was only the two of them, then the moment passed and he sighed.

"Queen Jirina badly wants a route to the sea, but why stop at that. Why settle for a trade corridor when she can try for the entire country? In her position, I'd certainly be considering it. I've had reports out of the Empire about mercenary troops crossing the border into Cemandia. She could easily be building an army."

"What does the ambassador say to that?"

"He denies even the possibility, of course. My guess is, Jirina's deliberately keeping him in the dark. What he doesn't know, he can't give away. Anyway, I spoke to the Bardic Captain this morning. Cemandian traders remaining on this side of the border over Fourth Quarter will be gently questioned."

Lilyana's brows rose but all she said was, "Why *gently?*"

Theron half laughed. "Because if it happens that she isn't considering invading, I don't want to give her ideas." He quickly sobered. "All things being enclosed, I'd give almost anything to have a bard on the other side of those mountains."

It was a hollow wish, and they both knew it. In Cemandia the kigh were considered outside the Circle and the bards, therefore, outside as well. The last bard who had crossed into Cemandia had been stoned to death, the crowd too large for him to defend himself although he Sang until the end. The kigh had brought his Song back to Shkoder and the bards, though they traveled north to Petrokia and south into the Havakeen Empire, now went no farther east than Ohrid.

"If we must defend ourselves," Theron continued, "at least there's only the one pass she could bring an army through."

"Defiance Pass. In Ohrid." Lilyana's fingers toyed with the book on her lap. "And how secure is Ohrid?"

"If you're asking about the keep, it's as secure as a paranoid man and a horde of stonemasons could make it. You know its history?" When she nodded, he went on. "Whoever controls the keep controls the pass. If you're asking about the man who controls the keep, well, you must remember Pjerin from the Oath of Fealty. He stood out."

"Theron, I was eight months pregnant, with two small children, and my partner had just become king. I had a lot on my mind."

"Tall. Long black hair. Physically powerful, even considering he was only nineteen. He's the one that overheated bard wrote 'Darkling Lover' for."

"Oh." She stared into the past and slowly smiled. "Now I remember."

"I thought you might."

"He threw the Duc of Vidor's cousin—that overbearing, pompous cretin—into a pile of horse manure. He was like a breath of fresh air."

"More like a bloody gale. By all reports, he hasn't changed. If anyone can hold Defiance Pass, he can."

"So the next logical question becomes, will he?"

Theron sighed. "I like to think so. He seemed to take his oaths seriously enough. Still, he's never attended a Full Council, always sends a proxy. I didn't care much either way, but now I wish I'd gotten to know the duc better. The mountain provinces are poor, far from Elbasan, and, if you ignore the obstacle of the mountains, Ohrid is considerably closer to Cemandia." He shifted again in the chair, as though the edges of potential trouble kept prodding him. "According to the captain, a bard's just returned from there and they're transcribing the recall now. I told her to send it over the instant it's readable." His voice changed slightly, picking up a speculative tone. "The duc has a son."

"How old?"

"Four."

"Brigita's ten, Theron. Four years until she's old enough to consult and ten until the boy is. It doesn't sound like we have that kind of time." Lilyana stood and shook out the heavy velvet folds of her skirt, "It sounds to me that you've done all you can. Further decisions will have to wait on more information."

The king snorted. "I don't wait well."

"Nonsense. You just don't enjoy it much." She moved around his chair and placed her hands on his shoulders. "And as Brigita is far from old enough to be consulted about joining anyone, why worry about *that* now?"

His shoulders rose and fell beneath her touch. "I don't know."

"Because you love her." She bent and lightly kissed the top of his head. "The father wars with the king; the demands of the heart with the demands of the crown." Her fingers tightened for an instant. "Now, if you will excuse me, I have things to ready for tonight's vigil and tomorrow's festival."

Theron sat for a while longer after she left, sat while a servant stoked the fire, sat while the sunlight faded. He didn't often have the opportunity to just sit. And think.

This could have all been solved ten years ago.

How many times had he left meetings with a succession of Cemandian ambassadors and thought that? A thousand. A hundred thousand.

Solved but at what cost?

He'd only just started to work at that. And every time

he considered a joining for one of his children, he got closer to an answer.

I never wanted her to be unhappy.

She made me look like a fool. Like a tyrant. As though I couldn't be reasoned with.

But I never wanted her to be unhappy.

"Annice? Are you in there? It's almost sunset, we're going to be late."

Annice came out of the privy, adjusting her robe. "All things being enclosed, it's a good thing water's the closest quarter to the door."

"All things being enclosed," Stasya repeated wryly as they hurried toward the Center. "When was the last time you Sang water at a vigil?"

"Two years ago," Annice told her smugly. "I was on a Walk and I ended up perched on a stool in a shepherd's cottage, surrounded by about a dozen more people than the place could hold, three orphaned lambs, two cats, and seven kittens. I Sang all four quarters in rotation throughout the night. By dawn, I was so hoarse I Sang the sun back as a bass-baritone."

"Show off."

"I have a feeling tonight pays for expediting my trip downriver. When the captain gave me the assignment, she said, *After all, you've had practice Singing water lately.* The word practice dripped with double meaning."

Stasya laughed at the impersonation—Annice had the captain's acerbic tone down pat—but sobered quickly. "Maybe she just wanted you where I could keep an eye on you. Are you sure you're going to be able to do this?"

"I slept most of the day, I've got dried fruit and a flask of water in my pouch, and I only have to stand while I Sing." Annie followed Stasya through the Bard's Door and waited while she Sang it closed. From the outside of the building the door would now appear to be part of a wall of unbroken stone—symbolism insisted that Centers have only four entrances. "As long as I can run off to pee in between solos," she continued as they started up the spiral staircase, "I'll be fine."

"Yeah, but . . ."

"Stas! Don't fuss. This baby and I walked all the way

back from Ohrid, didn't we? I think I can manage a vigil."

As Stasya had reached the gallery, she could only turn and silently glare.

Rolling her eyes, Annice climbed the last few steps, and set her mouth against her lover's ear. "I'll be fine," she whispered, added a kiss, and pushed the other bard toward her own position. She watched Stasya's robe— the pale gray-blue of a winter's sky—until it disappeared into the shadows, then stepped through the curtain and out onto the small semicircular balcony where she'd be spending the night.

Down below, the choir was gathered around the altar and crowds of people were standing more-or-less quietly, waiting. Directly beneath her at the south door, eddies of movement marked latecomers racing sunset. Across the great round chamber, a baby began to fuss. Annice wasn't sure if there were a greater number of children present than usual or if she were merely more aware of them.

She watched an obvious family group rearrange itself around a young woman carrying a squirming toddler, and found herself suddenly remembering the horrified expression on Theron's face when an infant Onele had started to scream the moment one of the priests began to invoke the vigil. Lilyana had calmly rearranged her mantle, lifted her shrieking daughter out of Theron's arms, and put her to the breast. The Annice of memory had somehow managed not to giggle.

Tonight, the king and his family would be in the Center at the Citadel. The captain would be Singing there with the three of the senior bards and the fledglings. Fledglings always Sang at the Citadel during their training as it helped to emphasize their duty to Shkoder. Annice had only been able to get through those years, pointedly ignored by her family, by immersing herself completely in the Song.

She shifted, her chest tight, forcing her attention back to the here and now. Closing her hands around the polished wood of the balcony rail, she turned, and with the crowds below, watched the light begin to fade from the west windows. As the colors dulled in the intricate patterns of stained glass arcing up into the vault of the ceiling, the choir began to sing the farewell to the sun.

Annice shivered.

When the last note slid into silence, the last of the light went with it, plunging the Center into darkness.

Somewhere in the crowd, a priest called out, "From light into darkness into light again."

The people answered, "The Circle encloses us all."

From balconies in the four quarters of the chamber, the bards began to Sing. First, air; Stasya's powerful soprano rose to open the shutters in the vault. Leaning into the rush of wind, Annice called water into the Song and heard the fountain on the altar leap into life. The next instant, her body thrummed with the stones of the Center as Jazep's resonant bass evoked earth. The three of them wove a melody for a dozen heartbeats, then paused for a dozen more as an achingly pure tenor Sang fire.

The darkness vanished as a burst of flame crowned the four great candles as well as the hundreds of smaller ones held carefully by the crowd.

Annice felt the hair on the back of her neck lift as the elements united into one glorious, all-encompassing whole and it became impossible for that moment to tell if she were singer or part of the Song. Then, just as the paean trembled on the edge of what flesh and blood could bear, the choir took up the melody. Panting, fingers laced across her abdomen, Annice staggered and sat down heavily on the narrow bench, listening as Stasya Sang the first of the solos that would continue until dawn.

Final Quarter vigil had begun. Throughout Shkoder—in Centers, in their homes, out under the stars—people kept the light alive, waiting on this the longest night of the year for the return of the sun.

CHAPTER FOUR

"Elica?" Annice brushed a dangling bit of vine out of her way and stepped down into the warm, moist air of the small, glass-enclosed room that jutted off the back of the Healers' Hall. "Are you in here?"

What had appeared to be a bundle of cloth on the far side of a tiny, central hearth straightened out and became the healer. Her hands full of dried plants, she stared at Annice in disbelief. "Oh, no. Is it that late already?"

"Later. I've been waiting in your chambers. When one of the apprentices told me that you were in the growing room, I came searching." Stepping over a pile of earth, Annice walked slowly down the narrow aisle, staring around her in amazement. On either side, five graded shelves covered in plants rose in staggered ranks from the floor to about hip high. Above the shelves, walls and ceiling were constructed of glass—more clear glass than Annice had ever seen in one place in her life. Outside, although the sun shone, the temperature had dipped below freezing, and a cold wind danced swirls of yesterday's snow against the glass. Inside, summer reigned. And the closer she got to the hearth, the more summerlike it grew. "What *is* this place?"

"In simple terms, a Fourth Quarter herb garden." Gathering up her apron, Elica dropped what she carried into the fold and secured the bundle at her waist, leaving her hands free to sketch theories in the air. "The glass concentrates the sunlight for the plants and also heats the room."

"But the hearth ..."

"The hearth keeps the temperature constant after dark."

Dressed for the cold, Annice could feel sweat trickling

down her sides. "Okay, so that's what it is. But what's it for?"

"We're trying to grow some of the healing plants we import from the south. Most of them are so expensive. But . . ." She spread her hands triumphantly and smiled. ". . . if we can grow them ourselves, we can lower the cost and use them for more people. Like the teas you were taking to prevent pregnancy."

Annice decided to ignore the implied sarcasm. "What an absolutely brilliant idea." She added just enough Voice so that the healer would know how much she meant it and realized it must have been Elica's idea when the other woman flushed with pleasure. "Really, truly brilliant. But how did you afford all this glass?" Some of the small panes were quite green and a number showed bubbling or other obvious flaws, but, considering what glass of a similar quality had cost her and Stasya for the two windows in their sitting room, the sheer quantity present represented a considerable expenditure by the Healers' Hall. Not even the palace could afford glass windows in every room.

"The Matriarch of the Glassmakers' Guild donated most of it and bullied some of the other members into donating the rest. She's very interested in developing a local source for those teas. Her daughter died in childbirth, you see, and—" Suddenly remembering Annice's condition, Elica winced. "I'm sorry. I didn't mean. . . ."

"Don't worry about it." Annice shrugged and one hand came around to rest on the slight curve of her belly. "I've heard more horror stories about being pregnant and having babies in the four weeks since the vigil than I had in the entire twenty-four years before that. Every bard in the Hall seems to know someone who had a terrible time and they're *sure* I should hear their recall about it."

Elica smiled at her tone but continued to look worried. "Are these stories bothering you?"

"Not really." Sometimes they crawled into her dreams and filled the darkness when she lay awake at night. During the last two nights, since Stasya had left on a Walk and she no longer had the rhythm of the other woman's breathing in the bed beside her, they'd bothered her more. But, as far as Annice was concerned, what went on in her head wasn't the healer's business. Physically, she was fine. "Stories are my trade, remember. I can spot exaggeration when I hear it." She waved a hand about as though to clear the subject from the air. "So, how's it working?"

"What? Growing the teas? Not very well, I'm afraid." The healer shot a disappointed glance down at the contents of her apron. "I just don't know what we're doing wrong."

Annice took another look around the room and frowned. Now that she took the time to study them, leaves were curling, or missing, and many plants appeared as much yellow as green. "Have you asked someone to Sing earth?"

"Inside?"

"Why not? We do it in the Centers."

"They're specially constructed," Elica pointed out, shaking her head. "This isn't."

"The altar's just a big hole in the floor," Annice corrected, snatching up a metal poker from beside the hearth and dropping to her knees. "What's under here?"

The healer looked down and shrugged. "Dirt."

"Great." She dug the point of the poker into a crack and leaned back on it. "Let's get one of these boards up." A moment later, the smell of damp earth rose up through a hole about a handbreadth square. "Sorry about that." Annice sheepishly pushed the splintered piece of wood under a shelf and rushed on with an explanation before the scowling healer could speak. "Most of the earth kigh are asleep right now, waiting for First Quarter, but with all the heat in here and nothing under the floor...." Taking a deep breath, she Sang.

Nothing happened. Wishing she had her flute, Annice Sang louder.

All at once, the floor rippled; shelves, plants, walls, rose and fell behind the crest. Elica cried out as the wave surged by beneath her and grabbed wildly for support. Shattering glass laid a descant on the Song.

Annice toppled back as the squat brown shape of a kigh bulged through the opening she'd made, ripping the rest of the broken plank aside as it came. Ignoring both bard and healer, it glanced around, exploded into a dozen smaller versions of itself, and disappeared into the mass of upended plant pots.

Training got Annice through the gratitude, but only just.

"I don't usually Sing earth," she said, getting slowly to her feet and looking around at the chaos. "I wasn't expecting that."

"Good." Elica's tone was dry enough to ignite. "And just what did we get in return for our six broken panes and one out of the Circle mess?"

"A kigh in every pot." Annice offered the information as an apology. "If you leave the hole so it ... they can come and go, I think you'll have a lot better luck with your plants."

"You think?"

"I'm pretty sure. You might ask the captain if Jazep can come by occasionally. He Sings earth, so he's assigned to the Hall until spring."

"I'm not sure we could afford more Singing."

Annice felt her face grow hot. The healer was acting as if she'd *intended* to break the windows.

"Never mind, Annice." Elica raised a calming hand. "All things being enclosed, if the kigh make the difference, the rest doesn't matter. How are you feeling?"

Calmed in spite of herself, Annice sighed. "I'm fine." Lately, Singing air left her feeling both faint and exhausted. She managed water marginally better, but fire had become even more capricious than usual. Earth, on the other hand, seemed to use no energy at all. "By the time the baby's born, I'll only be good for making mud pies."

"Well, there isn't any reason why you shouldn't Walk, but I'm still not sure I approve." Elica stepped back from the couch, brows drawn in. "Can't you stay at the Hall?"

"For the next five months?" Annice sat up and reached for her clothes. "First of all, I'd go crazy. Secondly, although I've pretty much stopped throwing up, I'd like to get away from the smells of the city for a while just in case. Third, I'll only be gone for three weeks."

"But it's Fourth Quarter, the weather ..."

"Will be clear for the next few days, according to the kigh. That's why I want to leave as soon as possible. Clear and cold makes for wonderful walking weather. Besides, I'm going up coast where you can't spit without hitting a fishing village. At the very most, I'll never be more than half a day away from shelter."

"Half a day can make a dangerous difference," Elica insisted. "In case you've forgotten, you're going to have a baby."

"No?" After a speaking glance that took in the expanding shelf of her breasts and the dark line of skin curving down from her swelling navel, Annice shrugged into her shirt. "I guess that explains the stretch mark.'

"Just one?"

"So far." She paused, pants half on and twisted until she could see the slightly indented pink streak that had appeared the week before, radiating in from her hip. "Can you *do* something about this?"

"No. But maybe it'll help if you think of it not as a disfigurement but as a medal of motherhood." Elica burst into laughter at the bard's expression, and managed to add a choked, "Maybe not."

"Medal of motherhood," Annice muttered, shoving her head through the neck of her sweater and bending for her boots. "Spare me."

Winter winds roaring in off the sea had scrubbed the air over Elbasan to a purity that caught in the back of the throat and tasted like the promise of snow. Standing in the Citadel Gate and staring down at the city as it sloped toward the docks, Annice drew in a deep, satisfied breath.

"I can't believe you're actually happy to be Walking in Final Quarter," Jazep said, shaking his head. A heavyset man at the best of times, he was so bundled against the cold that he appeared to be as wide as he was tall. "And you *know* what the storms are like along the coast at this time of the year."

She turned an unworried smile at him. "I found one of my best songs in a storm." Pulling off her mitten, she patted the bit of ruddy cheek visible between his hat and scarf. "Don't worry, Jaz, I've still got enough contact with air to know the weather."

"Not enough to control it."

"So I'll duck out of the way, just like everyone else has to."

He snorted disapprovingly. "Petrelis should be going."

"Petrelis has a fledgling to teach—what's his name, Ziven, he needs instruction in air and water. And don't say that I could do it," she cautioned as Jazep opened his mouth to speak, "because you know I couldn't. I'm so up and down right now, I'd tie the poor kid's abilities in knots. Besides, I'll be working on memory trances with all three of them when I get back." She couldn't decide if she was looking forward to that or not. "So, if you could lift my pack for me, I'll be on my way."

Looking unconvinced, Jazep hefted Annice's travel pack and jiggled it thoughtfully. "You sure this isn't too heavy?"

Annice rolled her eyes as she pushed her arms through the straps. "Trust me, Leonas spent so much time fussing over what I'm carrying and how much it weighs, he could've outfitted an army."

"He's worried."

"I'm fine." She pitched her voice for Jazep's ears alone. "You'd think that no one's ever had a baby before the way he's acting, the way Stasya's acting, the way the whole lot of you are acting."

Jazep's slow smile crinkled the corners of his eyes. "Every baby born is the first baby born in the world," he told her, speaking as she had, voice to ear. "You wait. You'll see."

She snorted and shifted back to broader tones. "I've got to get out of here or I'll never make the fort by lunch. Good music, Jazep."

"Good music, Annice." He pulled her into a brief hug. "Circle hold you and Walk safely."

Returning the pressure of his arms, Annice fought to breathe against the sudden tightening of her chest. When he released her, she turned quickly, blinking the moisture from her eyes, and waved a cheery hand at the gate guard. "Good vigilance, Corporal Agniya."

The guard, who'd been leaning into the curve of the arch and yawning, straightened. "Good music," she began, then stopped and looked confused.

"Annice."

"How . . ."

"Did I know your name?" Annice shot a rakish look back over her shoulder as she stepped away from the gate, out onto Hill Street. "I'm a bard. We know everything."

"Nothing as yet, Majesty."

"Nothing?"

Liene barely managed not to bridle at the king's tone. For reasons that were never discussed, the crown and the Bardic Hall had maintained a more distant relationship than was usual over the ten years of King Theron's reign. Not so distant that it affected the smooth running of the country, Theron was too good a king for that, but enough so that he could easily avoid meeting with the young bard who'd defied him. "Nothing more than rumor and innuendo," she told him levelly.

"Which were investigated?"

"Yes, sire."

Theron leaned forward on his desk and looked up at the Bardic Captain. "And your opinion?"

"There's definitely something going on—with this much smoke there has to be a fire somewhere—but we haven't yet found the person—or people—directly involved."

"No mention of Ohrid?"

"Only as concerns the business of the pass."

"And the duc?"

"He objects to being Shkoder's gatekeeper." The king started and Liene hastened to explain. "According to the traders, it's collecting the tolls he objects to, Majesty, not holding the pass."

His expression thoughtful, Theron nodded and slowly sat back. "I remember reading something about that in the recall. Also that he cares for his people a great deal and thinks we should be moving a little faster toward ending the isolation of the principalities."

"Our numbers are limited, Majesty, and Ohrid is a long walk. . . ."

"I'm not accusing you of anything, Captain. I *am* aware of both your numbers and how much country your people have to cover. But I think I'd like to talk to that bard, the one who was lately in Ohrid."

Although he read the recalls, King Theron never spoke to the bards and not the best control in the world could keep that thought from showing, for an instant, on Liene's face. *Well, isn't that a bit of unenclosed luck. First time in ten years I've had a chance to throw those two together—and on the king's command yet—and the fates conspire against us all.* "She left on a Walk three days ago, sire, heading north up the coast. Shall I have the kigh tell her to return?"

Theron stared up at the Bardic Captain, weighing her momentary lapse against the expression she now wore. Just for a moment, Liene thought she saw him reaching for the opportunity, then his eyes narrowed, and he said, "No. It's important that contact be maintained up the coast, especially in Fourth Quarter when isolation can so quickly set in. After all, the whole point of recall is that it includes a complete observation."

No name had been spoken, but the identity of the bard filled the space between them.

Annice paused for a moment on the edge of the cliff and looked down at the village tucked between sea and rock. From this angle, all she could see were the snow-dusted tops of cottages staggered up the hillside and the outside crescent of beach being rhythmically pounded by waves. Although she spotted a number of fishing boats pulled up on the gravel out of the sea's possessive reach, to her surprise a single vessel bobbed around in a small circle almost at the mouth of the bay. It seemed a little crazy to her, considering that puddles of ice reflected the sun all along the shore, but then small boats on summer seas seemed a little crazy to her, too, so she supposed she was unqualified to judge.

The sudden appearance of a pair of kigh very nearly flung her a disastrous step forward. Heart racing, she staggered and fought for balance, the weight of her pack dragging at her shoulders finally pulling her back onto solid ground. While the long, pale fingers of the two agitated kigh continued to tug at her clothing, she drew a deep breath to whistle them away. Far away.

Then the message got through.

She dropped her pack so hard it bounced, snatched up her flute, and threw herself down the path to the village, Singing as she ran. Twice she stumbled and the kigh caught her. Once, the earth rearranged itself under her feet. By the time she reached the first cottage, a group of astonished people were running out to meet her, calling out questions she had no time to answer, the village dogs barking hysterically around their feet. She pushed her way through the crowd, still Singing. If the kigh were right, she had almost no time at all.

Finally she reached the water's edge. Throwing the case to one side, she shoved the halves of her flute together and raised the mouthpiece to her lips. The first note was so sharp it hurt, but, forcing herself to breathe normally, she found the second and, eyes locked on the boat, threw everything she had left into the Call.

Behind her, she heard the villagers exclaim as the fishing boat lifted on a column of water and began to rush toward the shore. Soon a stooped figure could be seen bending over something in the stern. As the boat came closer, the figure turned, became a woman, a sun-bleached fringe of blonde hair framing an expression part worry, part relief. Her mouth moved, but her voice was lost under the sound of the waves and the Song of the flute.

The cluster of kigh beneath the boat continued up onto the shore. The villagers cried out and scattered. With the bow almost upon her, Annice turned the Song to a gratitude and the kigh flowed out from underneath it, returning to the sea. The bottom of the boat dropped onto the gravel, exactly at the high water mark.

Annice let the flute drop away from her mouth and staggered back against a solid chest.

"I've got you, child." Arms wrapped around her, holding her on her feet, and she gratefully sagged against their strength, her vision swimming.

In the babble of voices that followed, Annice heard the woman cry out a name, then saw blurry figures rush forward and lift a small body out over the low stern.

Someone yelled, "Get him to old Emils!"

Then the world tilted and went away.

Annice woke staring up at the low, beamed ceiling of a fisher cottage. She struggled to sit, but a large hand pushed her back against the mattress.

"Emils says you're fine, your baby's fine, and you're an idiot."

Considering the way she felt, Annice decided not to argue with that last statement. Squinting to see in the dim light that came through the small, leather-covered window, she watched a heavyset, middle-aged woman with close-cropped gray hair cross the room to a pitcher, fill a clay mug with water, and return.

"Taska, isn't it?"

The woman smiled, pleating her face into a map of her life, and held the mug to Annice's mouth. "Imagine you remembering that. It must be three years since you Walked this way. Drink slowly, Annice. I don't want you choking to death after carrying you up those unenclosed stairs."

"That was you? The one who caught me?"

"None other." She hooked a stubby-legged, driftwood chair with her foot and dragged it across the uneven floor to the bed. "Now then." The chair groaned as she sat. "Tell me what brought you flying down the cliff just in time to rescue young Jurgis."

Jurgis. So that was the child's name. "How is he?"

"He's a tough kiddie and Emils hates to lose a patient. Takes it personal. He'll be all right after a while."

"The woman?" She tried to keep her tone neutral and didn't quite manage.

Taska's brows dipped slightly. "Nadina i'Gituska. His mother. She's outside making a nuisance of herself, along with most of the village. Refuses to leave until she's sure her kiddie's okay."

"Who's his father?"

"Who knows."

"Are you still Head?"

The brows dipped slightly lower. It wasn't a full frown, but it was close. "Wouldn't be here if I wasn't."

"The kigh came for me. They said she was killing the boy."

To her surprise, Taska only nodded slowly. "Thought there was more to it than her story of him slipping on a bit of gut and going over." At the bard's questioning look, she added, "Water in the bay felt wrong."

Annice nodded slowly in turn. With training, Taska could have Sung water, but she'd had no interest in becoming a bard. According to the recall of the bard who'd found her some forty years before, nothing—not appealing to her sense of adventure, nor her sense of duty, nor just plain pleading—had shaken her from her polite reply. *"No, thank you. I'd rather fish."*

One hand wrapped protectively around her belly, Annice threw back the rough wool blanket and carefully sat up. "Let's get this over with."

"Are you crazy, Bard? Me hurt Jurgis?" Nadina looked as though she'd just been hit. Her left hand even rose to cup her cheek. "He's all I live for."

A concurring murmur ran through the surrounding crowd.

Leaning against the door of the healer's house, Annice dragged her tongue across her lips. She hoped she had the energy left for this. "Is there a quorum of villagers present?"

Beside her, Taska finished counting. "There is."

Annice straightened. **"Nadina i'Gituska, step forward."**

Red-rimmed eyes welling with tears under nearly white brows, Nadina had no choice but to do exactly as she was commanded. The semicircle of villagers shifted nervously.

Holding the other woman's gaze with her own, Annice spoke the second of the two ritual phrases. **"Nadina i'Gituska, you will speak only the truth."** Now that the command had been given, the questions themselves could be asked in a normal voice. "What were you doing to the child, Jurgis, out on the bay this afternoon?"

Above the salt-stained collar of her jacket, Nadina's throat worked, fighting the compulsion. Finally, she sniffed and rubbed her nose on her sleeve. "I was trying to get him to Sing."

There was no mistaking the bardic emphasis. Annice blinked and wondered if she looked as astonished as everyone else. "To Sing? Why?"

"Because I'm tired of working so hard. Tired of watching *her* ..." A weather-cracked finger jabbed toward Taska. "... bring in catch after catch while my lines run empty, and my nets tangle." Nadina tossed her hair back off her face and, unable to turn, appealed to the crowd behind her with a gesture. "Why should *she* be the only one to benefit from the kigh? That's not fair, is it? So ..." Her tones slid from injured to self-satisfied. "... six years ago I got me a baby off a bard who Sings water and today I took him out to Sing some fish into my nets."

"But boys never Sing until after their voices change." Annice was so startled she lost eye contact.

It didn't matter. "That's what I thought, too, but I heard him this morning. And I know when water acts like it ain't supposed to. I figured the Circle moved in my favor, seeing as how he wasn't the girl he was supposed to be. So why should I wait any longer? He can Sing all right. He just wouldn't." She ground out the last word between clenched teeth.

Feeling slightly sick, Annice rephrased the first question, "What did you do to him?"

"I shook him." Her chin went up as though she were daring anyone to deny her right. "And I shook him. He made me so angry. All he had to do was Sing and he wouldn't. Then he made this noise and the boat started to in circles and he kept saying he didn't know what I wanted, but the boat wouldn't stop ..."

In memory, Annice again looked down from the cliff top at a boat making circles in the bay.

"... so I hit him, and I hit him ..." Her hands were clenched on air and slammed an invisible burden up and down. "But the boat still wouldn't stop, so I thought, if he thinks so much more of the kigh than me, he can just go to the kigh."

"You threw him overboard?" This from one of the men in the crowd.

Nadina turned on him. "No! I just held him under the water. I pulled him in as soon as the boat straightened out. As soon as we started heading for shore." She was panting, moving back and forth between her neighbors. "He wouldn't Sing. I knew he could, but he wouldn't do it. And after I waited so all those years. Six years watching her bring in more fish than the rest of us combined. Then he called the kigh on me. On me. His own mother. I had to do something. Look at my hands! I almost froze my hands."

A teenaged girl stepped back, away from her. "You almost drowned your son!"

"Well, he's *mine!* Mine, no one else's."

"Not any more."

Taska's voice drew Nadina around. "What are you talking about, old woman? I bore him. Me. I raised him. He's *mine.*"

Annice stepped back as Taska stepped forward.

"You do not own your children," the village Head told Nadina, her voice harsh. "Their lives are their own. By bearing them, the Circle grants you the right to guide them and to love them and raise them to be the future of us all, but nothing else. By your actions, you have proved yourself unfit for this responsibility."

"Unfit? He owes me! He wouldn't even have a life without me!"

Taska ignored her. "Do I have four witnesses from those who know them both?"

After a moment's shuffling, two men, an elderly woman, and the teenage girl who'd accused her of almost drowning her son, stepped out of the crowd.

"Nadina i'Gituska, as of this moment, we take the child Jurgis from your care."

"Witnessed." The four voices spoke in ragged but emphatic unison.

"Bard?"

"Witnessed." As the woman began to shriek profanity, Annice turned and went back into the healer's cottage. The mother wasn't her problem, but it very much sounded as though the child was. Moving slowly, and thankful for the curling driftwood banister, she climbed up the steep and narrow stairs and ducked into the other second-floor room.

It was identical to the one she'd been placed in except that the bed held a small boy and, bending over him, the oldest man she'd ever seen. "Healer Emils?"

The old man turned and squinted in her direction. "I don't know the voice," he said, his own voice a rough whisper, "so it must be the bard."

Annice stepped forward and saw the milky film over both his eyes.

He snickered, as though aware of the direction of her gaze. "Lifted the fog from any number of eyes but can't clear my own. Everything else still works, though. And why are you standing up? After that stunt you pulled, your baby needs you to rest. You know very well where the energy to control the kigh like you did comes from."

"How's Jurgis?"

"Well, he should have frozen solid, but he didn't. My guess is that those water kigh he called somehow protected him."

"How . . ."

"How do I know about that? How do you think? You were questioning the woman right under my window. Sit down on the edge of the bed." Clawlike fingers reached out and grabbed her arm, pulling her to the bed and then pushing her down. "Have a good long look, then get back where I put you. I haven't lost a patient in . . . in . . . well, in a long time, and I'm not going to start with you. Or your baby. How do you feel?"

"Tired." She had no intention of denying it, but she needed to see the child.

The hair fanned out on the pillow was bleached a fine white-blond and against the tanned skin of his face, his brows, the same sun-kissed color, almost glowed. There were smudged circles under his eyes, but whatever else his life had been lacking, at least he seemed to have gotten enough food. Annice smiled as she recognized the line of his jaw and the unmistakable alignment of his features and wondered how six years of bards Walking the north coast had missed it. Wondered how *she'd* missed it when she'd walked through three years before. Her smile slipped a little at the green and purple bruise still discoloring one temple.

"Got a baby on a bard who Sang water," she murmured.

"What?" The ancient healer groped for her shoulder. "What are you talking about?"

"I know who Jurgis' father is."

"Good. Good." The clutching fingers moved on to administer an approving pat on the head. "A man should be told when his seed bears fruit."

She told him three days later, sitting on top of the cliff with the boy cradled on her lap, weaving his father's name in an amazingly complicated descant around her message. It was obvious that Jurgis had inherited the ability to Sing both water and air as the kigh no longer responded with such willingness for her alone.

When they finished, and the pale bodies had disappeared against the clouds, Jurgis pushed his head into the hollow of her throat. "What if he doesn't want me?"

"He will." Annice added just enough Voice that he couldn't doubt her, confident that Petrelis would be overjoyed to discover he had a child. The older bard was one of the finest teachers the Hall had ever had; kind and patient with the fledglings, soothing fears and bringing out the best in each of them. She couldn't think of anyone who'd be a better father.

"Mama doesn't want me."

"Your mother's sick. In her heart. Emils is trying to heal her, but the sickness makes her fight against his help."

"Tell me again about being a bard."

"Well, bards are the eyes and ears and voice of the country. We bring the mountains to the coast and the coast to the river and the river to the forest and the forest to the cities. We're what keeps all the little bits of Shkoder together and ..."

"No." He twisted indignantly until he could stare up into her face. "Tell me the good stuff. About Walking and the kigh."

So she told him while they waited.

Petrelis' answer came just as the cold had begun to seep through layers of clothing and Annice was about to suggest they go back to the village to warm up.

Overjoyed to have a child was putting it mildly.

The kigh who brought the news that he was on his way if he had to bring all three fledglings with him, wove ecstatic circles in the sky.

Watching Jurgis running about, laughing and Singing and trying to catch kigh that whirled just out of reach, Annice shook off a mitten and slid her hand beneath her jacket.

Suddenly, for an instant, it felt as though a butterfly were dancing just under her heart. Her eyes welling with tears, she pressed her fingers against the smooth, soft ball of her belly. The baby, her baby, had moved.

"A man should be told when his seed bears fruit."

"Well, he's mine! *Mine, no one else's."*

"It isn't like that," she whispered.

Jurgis leaped into the air, Singing his father's name.

* * *

"Your Grace!" The teenage boy skidded into the stable, his eyes wide. "There's a fire!"

"Where?" Pjerin was already moving when he asked.

"Lukas a'Tynek's house," the boy panted, scrambling to keep up with his duc's longer stride. "It flared up so fast!"

They could see the smoke rising over the wall as they raced to the gate, Pjerin gathering people as he ran. The greasy black column served as both guide and goad as the inhabitants of the keep threw themselves down the short, steep hill to the village. By the time they reached the house, flames were shooting through the thatch. Men and women threw shovelfuls of snow onto the roof in a desperate but losing race against time.

The melting snow hissed and steamed. The fire leaped past it.

"My little girl!" Bundled into a fur overcoat not her own, an ugly blister across one cheek and her eyebrows all but gone, Lukas' partner, Hanicka, strained against her sister's grip. "Your Grace, my little girl is still in there!"

The door into the front half of the house, into the living quarters, belched flame.

Heart pounding, Pjerin raced around to the back. The double doors were open, the barn empty, not yet on fire but filled with smoke. He stomped through the ice in the outside trough and soaked his scarf in the little bit of water that remained.

"Pjerin!" Olina's voice seemed to come from a great distance. "What do you think you're doing?"

He *wasn't* thinking because thinking would stop him. Eyes squinted nearly shut, he plunged into the barn. The scarf helped but not much. Bent almost double, coughing and choking, he ran for the inside door. His foot came down on the body of a chicken, dead or stunned he had no idea, and without breaking stride he kicked it behind him.

The wooden wall between the barn and family quarters felt hot, even through the palm of his leather mitt. He could hear the fire crackling on the other side as it ate at the logs. Gasping for breath, he stood so that the angle of the door would offer at least a minimum of shelter and then yanked it open. A solid wall of flame burst forth, igniting the straw and driving him back. Twice he tried to get through it, but finally, his clothing smoldering, had to stagger outside and admit defeat.

A heartbeat later, the roof caved in with a roar that almost sounded triumphant.

Dragged to a safe distance by Olina and a villager he couldn't recognize, Pjerin watched with streaming eyes as the beast devoured everything but the thick stone walls. His snarl became lost in the snarl of the fire. Hanicka's keening rose with the smoke.

"Our thanks for the attempt, Your Grace."

He turned, saw it was Lukas a'Tynek, and didn't know what to say. The man had just lost his only child.

Rubbing at the ice-encrusted ends of his beard with a cracked and bleeding hand, Lukas stared into the inferno. "But perhaps it was for the best."

Confused, Pjerin hacked a mouthful of black mucus onto the snow and asked, "What was?"

"That she died. She did this. She was singing to the fire, making it dance. Leaving the Circle even as I watched." His fingers flicked outward in the old Cemandian sign against the *kigh*. "I couldn't have that happen, not in my house."

"What did you do?"

Standing a few feet away, Olina jerked around, drawn by the heat in Pjerin's voice.

Lukas didn't seem to hear it. "I hit her. Not hard. Just to stop her. I'm her father. I couldn't just stand by and let her leave the Circle. She went over backward and the fire . . . the fire . . ." His voice cracked. "Better she die than live outside the Circle."

Pjerin took a step forward, his fingers closing on the other man's shoulder and yanking him around. He caught a bare glimpse of Lukas' terrified expression through the red sheen of rage then he drove his fists, one, two, into stomach and jaw. Hearing nothing over the fury howling inside his skull, he spun on his heel and strode off toward the keep.

Olina looked down at the sprawled body, now surrounded by babbling family, and then at the disappearing back of her nephew. *He makes it so easy,* she thought, careful not to let the satisfaction show. The people's loyalty to their hereditary duc had loomed as a potential problem, yet that could be undermined when, with a subtle twist or two, she blew this incident completely out of proportion.

Finally breaking free of his nurse's grip, Gerek raced down from the gate of the keep to meet Pjerin on the way up. Skidding to a stop, he stared up at his father eyes wide. "Papa! You're all scorched!"

Pjerin shuddered and dropped to his knees, gathering Gerek up into his arms, pushing the boy's hat off so he could lay his cheek against the soft cap of hair.

His face screwed up from the smell of the smoke, Gerek struggled to get free. "Papa!" he protested. "You're holding me too tight!"

Tadeus basked in the warmth of the fire like a contented cat, fingers lightly strumming the lute on his lap. He hadn't played in this particular inn for some time and he wondered why he'd stayed away for so long. He'd had an appreciative audience for his songs, an apparently bottomless ale cup, and enough offers of bedmates to get him through the quarter.

What more could a bard desire?

Head slightly to one side so that thick black curls cascaded forward over his shoulder—a pose practiced and calculated to open both purses and hearts—he listened to the sounds of the inn. Behind him he could hear the distinctive crackles that said a kigh danced in the grate, called and confined by his Song. Before him, he could hear the rise and fall of maybe thirty voices. The news that he'd returned to the River Maiden had filled the small common room—the dull roar would've told him that, even if the innkeeper hadn't.

While he appreciated a full house as much as the next bard—*All right, maybe more than the next bard*—it wasn't going to make his job any easier.

Continuing to strum, he began to separate out the individual voices.

". . . don't worry, I can pay for it. I've got plenty of silver . . ."

There. The accent surrendered origins.

Setting his lute carefully aside, Tadeus rose, throwing

the hair back off his face. Smiling in the direction of an appreciative murmur, he made his way toward the Cemandian trader, threading gracefully around tables and benches and clients with no more than the occasional gentle touch to guide his way.

"Of course he's blind, you unenclosed idiot. Why else do think he's wearing that scarf thing across his eyes?"

Why else, indeed? The scarf was a brilliant red, cut from the same bolt of fabric as his new shirt. The tailor, a cousin of his, told him the effect was rakish. While he couldn't swear to rakish, or even the color, Tadeus had to admit that there was a definite effect. He took a deep breath as delicate fingers traced a pattern on the back of his thigh and regretfully kept moving.

As he approached the Cemandian accent, he sniffed the air appreciatively. Over the winter smells of damp wool and infrequently washed bodies, over the inn smells of smoke, and ale, and grease came a distinct scent of sandalwood mixed with clean hair. *Seems a rough choice of domicile for a trader with a bit of class,* he thought, negotiating the last few feet.

Conversation in the immediate area stopped as Tadeus directed his best smile at the Cemandian, who would, he knew, be staring up at him. **"Mind if I join you?"**

Bereft of eye contact, he couldn't Command, but over the years he'd raised Charm to a high art. He heard the trader swallow, hard, before he managed an answer.

"Please do."

Toning down the smile, Tadeus slid onto the bench, letting his thigh press lightly against his quarry's—intimate conversations could not be carried out across the full width of a trestle table. He waited until surrounding conversations had risen again before saying, "I'm Tadeus. **You are?"**

"Leksik i'Samuil."

His breath was good, too. Tadeus began to hope that Leksik was nothing more than he seemed; a young noble—easy enough to tell from his voice—who wasn't very bright—because only an idiot would mention having plenty of silver in a place like the River Maiden—playing trader for one of the obvious had-to-get-out-of-the-country reasons. He didn't hope very hard, though; a gut feeling told him there wouldn't be much point.

"So, Leksik, what brings you to Shkoder?"

Theron paced the length of the nursery and back, shoved his head into the built-in wardrobe and bellowed down the narrow flight of stone stairs visible under a lifted trapdoor. "Haven't you reached her yet!"

"Almost, Majesty!"

The disembodied voice that came floating up from the darkness seemed to do little to mollify him. Neither did the child's voice that followed.

"I'm okay, Papa! Really!"

"Brigita! I told you not to crawl around down there . . ." he began.

"Theron." Lilyana took his arm and gently pulled him back. "You're not helping by yelling. They're moving as fast as they can."

"I know that!" He shook himself free, then patted her shoulder in apology, muttering, "I should've had all those passageways filled in years ago. Suppose no one had heard her yelling? She could've died, trapped in the walls like a rat!"

"Theron!"

"Father!"

The king ignored both consort and Heir. "The Circle holds no *reason* for this place to be riddled with secret passageways!"

"It's not like they're even very secret," Antavas agreed, investigating an old wooden ship he'd forgotten he'd left in the nursery with all the unconcern of a thirteen-year-old for the fate of his younger sister. "Every time you think you've found a new one, you find a big 'A' and a bunch of arrows scrawled on the wall in chalk."

"Antavas . . ."

He turned, recognizing the tone but unsure of what he'd said to cause it. "Sir?"

Theron broke off what he was about to say as a page slipped past the guard stationed at the nursery door. "I'll speak with you later," he promised his son. "What is it, Karina?"

The girl bowed. "Message from the Bardic Captain, Majesty. The captain asks for an audience."

"Did the captain give a reason for this request?"

"Yes, Majesty. She said to tell you that they've got him."

CHAPTER FIVE

Something had obviously happened while she was away. Annice paused at the edge of the Farmers' Market, her pack propped against the edge of a wagon, and studied the crowd. The buzz of information passing from city dweller to country dweller, as well as the opinions passing back, held too much of an edge to be merely gossip and the clouds of breath billowing out onto the cold morning air gave conversations a heated appearance.

Shrugging her pack off her shoulders, she let it slide to the ground. Although she'd intended to cut through the market and then the nobles' district—the shortest, fastest route through the north side of Elbasan to the Citadel and Bardic Hall—finding out what was going on suddenly seemed more important than getting to the Hall in time for lunch.

Scanning the square, Annice caught the eye of a shabbily dressed young man hanging about on the edges of the crowd and motioned him over. He came eagerly, hands tucked into his armpits against the cold.

"You lookin' fer hire?" he asked, as soon as he was close enough to be heard. "Someone ta carry ..." then he noticed she was a bard, not a cook or innkeeper likely to be buying winter vegetables in quantity and needing help to get them home. His face fell.

Annice flipped him a quarter-gull, enough for a bowl of soup and a hunk of bread at any of the corner stalls in the market.

He snatched the small copper coin out of the air with cracked and bleeding fingers and looked a little more cheerful. "What kin I do fer you, Bard?"

She jerked her head toward the scattered clumps of buying and selling and gossip. "I've just come in from a Walk. What's everyone talking about?"

"Troop of King's Guard rode out this mornin', 'fore dawn."

"Going?"

He shrugged and a hank of greasy, dark blond hair fell forward into his eyes. "Mountains, they say."

"Where in the mountains?"

"Dunno. Just mountains. Unenclosed time of the year ta go ta the mountains, ya ask me."

Annice had to agree. While Fourth Quarter on the coast could be cold and unpleasant, in the mountains it could be deadly—if the mountains could be reached at all. "What could be so important that King Theron would send his guard out in the winter?"

The young man didn't disappoint. "Treason."

"What?"

"His Majesty didn't give me no details." He began to inch away, eyes on a deal just being concluded. "Now, if ya don't mind, Bard, I got other things to take care of."

"How much to carry my pack up to the Citadel Gate?" Her own extra bulk would be more than enough for her to haul around the streets.

He glanced down at the pack, then squinted up at the stone bulk of the Citadel visible over the roofs in the center of the city. "Three gulls," he said at last. "I go that far I won't get no more work today."

A half-gull, Annice knew, would get him a place in a crowded but warm dormitory room in any of the inns down by Dockside. A full gull would get him out of Dockside and into a place where he not only wouldn't have to guard his back but would be fed a heaping bowl of porridge the next morning. Bards stayed in both kinds of places, to keep them honest—a number of songs contemplated whether it was the bards or the inns that were to be kept honest—and Annice knew which she preferred.

"How about two gulls and a Song?"

His eyes narrowed. "What good'll a Song do me?"

"It'll get you past the gate, to the Hall, and into the kitchen where they'll feed you. Cast your lines right and you might even make up that third gull. Cook's always complaining about being shorthanded."

Stomping his feet in a valiant but doomed effort to keep warm, he didn't have to think about it for long. As she watched him make his way around the edge of the market, her pack perched high on his shoulders, and a kigh riding unseen over his head, Annice decided not to mention the incident to Stasya who, coming from a south coast fisher family that argued over every quarter-gull, would not understand.

"I *know*, he'd have done it for half that," she murmured, settling her instrument case across her back. It wasn't that she couldn't barter, it was just that she hated to do it with people who had so little. *Not everyone can be equal in wealth, but no one should have to starve.* Theron had said that, back when he was Heir, and he was doing what he could as king to stand by his word. He was a good king and a popular one, loved and respected by his people.

Annice rubbed at her eyes with the back of a mitten and ground her teeth. She couldn't seem to stop herself from suddenly becoming stupidly sentimental about the most commonplace of things. *Of course, Theron's a good king,* she snarled silently. *And now he's a good king who's sent a troop of guards into the mountains, so let's find out what's going on, spend our last coin on lunch, and go home.*

Information wasn't difficult to come by as every conversation in the market either began or ended or was solely concerned with the guards riding out at dawn. Annice took a slow stroll, filtering out the story as she walked.

"That unenclosed bastard up at Ohrid has agreed to let a Cemandian army through the pass!"

"This Cemandian nobleman, well, he was hardly more than a baby really, he broke down and, well, just told everything to one of the bards, don't you know."

"King Theron's sent a troop of guards to Ohrid to arrest the duc."

"No, no, no! The king's sent a bard to question him, and when the bard finds out the truth, then the guards who are with the bard will arrest the duc."

"We're all going to be murdered in our beds, I tell you."

"They'll take his head. They will. He broke his vows. Only one punishment for treason. Death."

Annice found herself wrapping both arms protectively

around her belly. *All of a sudden, I'm not so hungry. How about you, baby?*

Almost everyone believed the Duc of Ohrid guilty of treason as charged. A few allowed that the Cemandian spy—regardless of what said spy *thought* was going on— might have been planted to sow discord in Shkoder. "To test our defenses!" declared one elderly, ex-soldier-turned-innkeeper, waving his cane with such vigor his granddaughter took it away. Everyone suddenly remembered how many more Cemandians there'd been around over the last year. And they all believed that the bard sent into Ohrid by King Theron would find out the Truth because, after all, that's what bards did.

Training stepped in and Annice held her tongue. Pjerin a'Stasiek, Duc of Ohrid, a traitor? It didn't seem possible. It couldn't be possible. While she *could* call him a number of uncomplimentary names, traitor wasn't one of them. All at once it became very important that she reach Bardic Hall without delay. Someone, somewhere, had made an incredible mistake.

The summons activated as Annice slipped through the Bard's Door, her own Song unlocking then locking it again behind her. Her heart pounding, she listened, glaring at nothing. When it finished and the last note had faded into silence, she hoisted her instrument case and strode purposefully down the narrow corridor, the soles of her boots slapping against the dressed stone. So the Bardic Captain wanted to see her immediately—good, because she wanted to see the Bardic Captain just as badly.

"Pjerin is not a traitor." She'd been muttering it in varying tones of disbelief all the way through the city. The very idea would be laughable if it weren't so serious. "I'll have a few things to say to whatever idiot brought in that information."

She was passing the training rooms, absently noting that one of the fledglings must have started trance work without her, when a sudden realization brought her up short and she stood, frozen to the spot, breath caught in her throat. The sound of approaching footsteps pushed her into an empty room and she sagged against the door as she closed it behind her. She couldn't face anyone, and least of all the captain, until she worked this out.

Still leaning against the door, she Sang fire, lighting the lamp that stood on the table in the center of the room after her fourth attempt. All the training rooms were identical, tiny and windowless, and as soundproof as the Builders' Guild and bardic ingenuity could make them. Distractions were the last things fledglings needed.

Annice dropped her instrument case on the floor and dropped herself into one of the two padded chairs. The captain could read nuance off a brick. She couldn't help but draw the correct conclusions from a hysterical declaration of Pjerin's innocence.

Allowing her jacket to fall open, Annice rubbed at the itchy skin of her swelling abdomen through sweater and shirt. "The Duc of Ohrid has been charged with treason—it's ridiculous, but the charge will stand until he's questioned under Command. The Duc of Ohrid is the father of my baby. By having this baby, I'm committing treason. She sighed deeply. "What a mess. I couldn't have got knocked up by some pretty shepherd. Oh, no— it *had* to be the Duc of Ohrid.

Pjerin was innocent, Annice was as certain of that as she'd ever been of anything—he didn't need her help. All her efforts had to be concentrated on not exposing her baby's paternity to the Bardic Captain because, the moment that happened, the king would be told. Theron was a proud man; no one knew that better than she did. For him to discover she'd committed treason was one thing, for him to discover she'd committed it with a man accused of selling out his oaths was something else again. She had to protect her baby.

In order to do that, she'd have to discuss this whole situation and the Walk she'd made to Ohrid without giving anything away.

Impossible.

So she'd just have to give something else away.

"And your personal opinion of the *duc,* Annice?" Liene's tone made it very clear she'd tolerate no further dancing around the subject. Annice, after skimming a copy of young Leksik's testimony, had given opinions on the political situation, economic prospects for the region, and the feelings of the people on everything from government to the weather, but had mentioned Pjerin a'Stasiek only in passing. The captain had strong suspicions about that omission; if she didn't get a straight answer soon, she'd Command one.

Annice shifted in the chair, searching unsuccessfully for a position that would take the pressure off her lower back. "The duc," she said levelly, "is loved and respected by the majority of his people. Not only because of the hereditary position he holds but also because he's cast in the heroic mold. He, in turn, cares very much for his people and very much considers them to be his responsibility."

"All that was in the recall, Annice." Liene leaned forward, taking in the way the younger bard's fingers had closed over the arms of the chair and tightened while she spoke of the duc. "And you edit your recall of personal material more tightly than any other bard Singing in Shkoder. I want to know what *you* thought of him."

"What *I* thought of him." Annice drew in a deep breath and released it in one short burst, obviously aware she wouldn't be able to put it off any longer. "First and foremost, I thought he was the most gorgeous man I'd ever seen. After a few hours under his roof, I soon came to realize that he's incredibly strong-willed, stubborn, opinionated ..." The words tumbled out as though the dam that had been holding them back had burst. "... arrogant, abrasive, pigheaded, mannerless, self-important, overbearing ..." She sputtered to a stop at Liene's upraised hand, panting slightly.

"Put it to music," the captain suggested, her eyes narrowing. "Did you sleep with him?"

Annice lifted her chin defiantly. "I *wanted* to."

It didn't take a bard to read the implication. "But he didn't want to sleep with you. Why not?"

"*He's* the Duc of Ohrid." The emphasis came without effort. Even stripped to the waist and wrestling a stubborn colt into a halter, Pjerin i'Stasiek had been definitively the Duc of Ohrid.

The captain, as intended, misunderstood.

"And you're only a bard." Liene finished the thought silently. *And you've always gotten what you wanted, haven't you, Princess? If he only knew who you really*

*were; not that pride would allow you to tell him. You
must have been furious.* "The father?"

"Someone willing."

"I see." And she could see it. Exactly. Annice had
probably stormed away from the duc and kicked the feet
out from under the next person she met. Liene spared
the fellow a moment's sympathy and hoped his heart
had been up to it. Then she spared another moment to
Sing a silent and heartfelt gratitude that the fear she'd
nursed had been unfounded.

"So . . ." Leaning back, Liene drummed her fingers
against the edge of her desk in a martial rhythm. "Do
you think the duc has agreed to open the pass to a Cemandian army?"

Annice tossed her head. "Only if they were willing to
put him in charge of it," she snapped.

There could be no mistaking the ring of truth that
statement carried. Satisfied, the Bardic Captain nodded
and relaxed for the first time since the kigh had con-
tacted her with Tadeus' news, the knot of worry that
had settled between her shoulder blades easing away.
"You've had quite an eventful couple of quarters,
haven't you? You bring a baby back from Ohrid, then
you discover young Jurgis while Walking up coast. I
think I'll keep you around the Hall for a while before
you inundate us with children."

"Jurgis is . . ."

"Jurgis is fine. Petrelis is beside himself. They're still
getting to know each other, of course, but the boy has
fit himself into the Hall like a missing puzzle piece and
soaks up music like a little sponge. We have a percussion
lesson, he and I, every other morning."

The thought of Jurgis finding a place where he belonged so perfectly combined with the sudden realization
that she'd done it and her baby was safe jerked Annice's
emotions from one extreme to the other and shoved
them right over the edge. To her horror, she burst into
tears. "I'm sorry," she gasped, both hands waving in the
air as if they were searching for her lost control. "It's
just . . . I mean, I don't . . . He was so . . ."

Liene cleared her throat, at a loss for something to
say. Raw emotion, unconfined by verse or chorus, made
her profoundly uncomfortable. "You're tired," she said

at last, coming around the desk and gathering up Annice's outerwear and instrument case from the floor. "I
think you should go and lie down. We'll discuss this
latest Walk of yours after you've had a chance to rest."

Annice struggled to her feet. "But recall . . ."

"Recall can wait. This interview is *over*." The captain
accompanied her to the door and whistled a piercing
summons down the corridor.

Leonas appeared almost instantly. He gave the captain
a cursory nod and glared at Annice who was scrubbing
at her cheeks with her palms. "What's wrong?" Concern
leaked out around the brusque tone. Not even in the
early days, at her most lost and confused, had he ever
seen the princess cry.

"Nothing," Annice began indignantly but Liene cut
her off.

"She needs to rest."

He snorted. "She's expecting a child. She needs to
rest. She needs to eat properly. She needs to not be out
tramping around the countryside." He pointedly took
the clothing and instrument case from the captain, every
movement a criticism. "Probably walked since dawn,
skipped breakfast, skipped lunch."

"I had breakfast."

"But not lunch," he concluded triumphantly, shoving
the end of her scarf up under one arm and starting down
the corridor. "Come on."

Annice shot an apology at the captain who merely
rolled her eyes and said, "I'll see you when you're
rested. I'm looking forward to hearing Jurgis' story
from you."

All at once, as tired as everyone seemed to think she
should be, Annice fell into step beside Leonas. She essentially played parts of the truth so loud they'd
drowned out the bits she didn't want heard and the performance had exhausted her. *But it wouldn't have
worked if I hadn't been playing a tune the captain wanted
to hear.* When Tadeus got back to the Hall, she'd have
to see what she could do to start clearing the whole mess
up. He *had* to have misunderstood what the Cemandian meant.

"I lit a fire in your rooms when I heard you were in
the building," Leonas told her as they moved in slow

procession up the stairs. "It should be nearly warm in there by now."

"Isn't Stasya back from her Walk yet?"

"Didn't they tell you?"

"Didn't who tell me what?"

"Stasya's the bard they sent into Ohrid."

"They sent Stas?" The disappointment hit her as almost a physical blow; she'd been looking forward to the other woman's company for days. Blinking back yet another unexpected rush of tears, Annice fought to let only the annoyance show in her voice. "She'll be gone for months."

"Needed a bard who Sings a strong air to travel that far in this weather."

"I *know* that, Leonas."

"Stasya was the strongest in the Hall at the time." He snickered. "Got a good blunt Command on her, too. Yours, now, it works because you expect it to. Hers works because she dares it not to. Duc of Ohrid won't know what hit him."

"The Duc of Ohrid," Annice ground out, trying to determine which of them she was so suddenly jealous of and why, "can take care of himself."

"You've been this way before?"

Stasya smiled tightly at the guard riding beside her, leading her horse. "I've Walked this way, Nikulas. It's not the same thing."

Nikulas nodded. "You move a lot faster on horseback."

"You see less and it hurts more," she amended.

"I thought they fixed that at the Healers' Hall in Vidor?"

He looked honestly concerned, so Stasya allowed her smile to relax a fraction. "The memory remains painful," she told him, shifting in the saddle. A bard on foot took eight to ten days, Elbasan to Vidor and, on the way, they talked with the people, observed the minutiae of the kingdom, sang, laughed, made love. The troop she traveled with had done the same distance in four days, pounding down the frozen River Road, pounding past many of her favorite inns, pounding the insides of her thighs raw. Drifting snow between Vidor and Caciz had slowed the pace, even though she used the kigh to push through a path, but the Troop Captain seemed determined to make up the lost time.

Speak of something unenclosed and lo, it appears, she thought as Captain Otik galloped back to fall in at her other side.

"I don't like the look of those clouds," he grunted without preamble. "Could be a storm forming up."

"Could be," Stasya allowed, squinting into the distance where the sky seemed to be resting its weight on the horizon.

"Best Sing it away."

"Excuse me?"

Her tone pulled him around in the saddle and he glared at her from under the fleece-lined edge of his helm. "That *is* one of the reasons you're riding with us, Bard. To control the weather so we can reach this traitor before he's warned and gets away."

"First of all, Captain, I can't control that storm, I can merely redirect the results. Secondly, I won't even do that unless it actively threatens our route. Thirdly, we don't know that the duc is guilty of anything until I arrive and ask him."

"You don't seem to understand the seriousness of this expedition, Bard."

Stasya caught his gaze and held it. "And you don't seem to understand that I take my orders directly from *my* captain and she takes hers directly from His Majesty the King. So go away and stop bothering me before I Command you to stuff your head up your ass where it seems to belong."

The realization that she could do exactly as she threatened spurred the captain back to the head of the double line, temper barely held in check only because lack of reaction made it obvious he'd been the only one to hear her.

"You don't like Captain Otik much, do you?"

Stasya carefully turned. "What gave you that idea?"

Nikulas grinned at her, the ice in his mustache cracking. "Oh, not hearing the last thing you said to him, I suppose. The captain's really not such a bad sort. He's just a bit pompous and he desperately wants to do something heroic. Scooping a traitor out of his mountain stronghold and dragging him back to Elbasan in chains is probably the best chance he'll have."

"We don't *know* he's a traitor until I ask him," Stasya reminded.

"Oh, come on, you don't believe that, do you? I mean, from what I heard, that Cemandian was pretty specific when you guys questioned *him*. The duc's head is on the block."

"Does everyone feel that way?"

The guard shrugged. "Pretty much. They figure you're along as a kind of formality; you know, the icing on the cake."

There wasn't much Stasya could say to that, so she concentrated on clinging to the horse as, up ahead, Captain Otik waved the troop forward into a trot. *Go ahead, take your revenge, you asshole. I should've kept my big mouth shut.*

She'd tried to contact Annice the morning they'd left the city, but the kigh had disappeared with her message and not returned. Obviously, unfortunately, the pregnancy had advanced to the point where earth had completely superseded air. She'd wanted to ask Annice about this man whose head had so suddenly become so perilously attached. She'd wanted to ask what she could expect him to say and how good were the chances of her word being the one that sent him to the block.

She'd wanted to say good-bye.

"As you know, Majesty, the messages the kigh carry are less than explicit without a strong emotional content." The Bardic Captain reluctantly moved away from the fire as a server approached with a load of wood. "I have, however, received reports that the troop is making excellent time and they expect to be in Ohrid in twelve to fifteen days, weather permitting."

Theron nodded and looked up from the map spread out over his desk. Behind him, the frost coating the inside of the windowpanes sparkled in the sun. "They're still following the Hijma River?"

"It's the best route in Fourth Quarter, Majesty. Everything beyond Lake Marienka is frozen solid and, as far as the gorge, it makes a better road than what goes by that name in the area." She spread her hands. "The problem, of course, will be storms."

Stasya woke just before dawn, the sound of the kigh scrabbling at the shutters pulling her up out of sleep. "All right, all right," she muttered, "I heard you the first time."

Crawling out of bed, aching in muscles she hadn't known she had until she'd been ordered up into the torture device sadists on horseback called a saddle, she stumbled across the common room, over and around the sleeping guards. While a chorus of protest rose behind her, she cracked open the door, and looked out.

"Shit."

A short while later, as the sun touched the horizon and the whole troop clattered out of the inn yard, she wrapped both hands tightly around the saddlehorn and began to Sing.

By mid-morning, they'd left the original storm behind them. By noon, they'd ridden into another. By mid-afternoon, when they arrived at a tiny hamlet tucked up tight against the riverbank, their path an eerie eddy of calm defined by Stasya's Song, it became obvious they'd be staying for a while.

Stasya Sang a gratitude and slid off her horse into the waiting arms of a guard. The storm, free of constraint, howled at full strength around them. Astounded villagers, brought to their doors by the final notes of the Song, muttered about stupid lowlanders and hurriedly began to divide mounts and riders into the available shelter.

Still cradled in the guard's arms, Stasya watched as Captain Otik fought the wind to her side.

"Why are we stopping?" he yelled, clapping his hand to his head as a gust threatened to rip off his helm. "We've still got hours of daylight."

Stasya smiled at the three kigh who were trying to knock the captain over. "Look behind you," she told him hoarsely, her voice barely rising over the storm. "What do you see?"

Struggling to keep his balance, he turned and squinted into the blowing snow. "Nothing."

"Well, that's Ohrid. Trust me on this one, Captain, the duc isn't going anywhere."

                        *   *   *

"Expecting someone, Olina?"

Scraping away the ice her breath had laid on the tiny pane, Olina stared out into the courtyard. "I'm watching the storm."

"Yeah?" Pjerin snorted and stretched his feet out nearer to the fire. "What's to see?"

"Passion. Strength." Her voice caressed the words. "Blind and uncontrollable fury wrapped in beauty like a dagger in a diamond sheath."

Gerek scrambled up from his place by the hearth, raced across the room, and pushed under her arm. "I only see snow," he sighed after a moment.

Olina's sigh echoed his as she pushed him gently back into the room and let the heavy tapestry fall into place over the window embrasure. "You are *so* like your father at times."

"Really?"

Unable to resist his smile, she nodded, smiling down at him in turn. "Really."

"I'm going to be just like my papa when I get big."

Not if I can help it, Olina promised silently as he ran back to the fire. *You're going to be civilized. You'll be the first Duc of Ohrid to realize the worth of the title. No drafty, cold stone keeps for you, boy. You'll have glass in all your windows, carpets on all your floors, and a city built at your feet. You'll control crowds of rich and powerful people.* She dropped back into her chair. *And I shall control you.*

If she had a tail, Pjerin thought, watching his father's sister from the corner of one eye, *she'd be lashing it. I wonder what she's up to?* The storm had confined them all day in the keep and the desire for warmth had kept them together in this one small chamber. Only Olina's bedroom and the nursery had been modernized to the same extent and there were reasons for not gathering in either of those places. He personally couldn't believe that in his grandfather's time the entire household had gathered in the Great Hall where the high, narrow windows remained open to the winter and the central hearth had thrown either too much or too little heat and coated everyone in a fine patina of smoke. With most of his people in houses of their own down in the village, smaller rooms and inset fireplaces made a lot more sense and he had to give Olina credit for forcing the changes on his father; no matter how much he disagreed with the changes she tried to force on him.

Attention still apparently on the half-finished carving in his hands, he studied her as she lifted a stone game piece from the small round table beside her. She rolled it between long, pale fingers, its polished surface reflecting firelight, candlelight, and, he'd be willing to swear, the gleam in her eyes.

Without warning, her fist closed around the stone and she flung it into the fire.

Startled by the sudden spray of sparks, Gerek tumbled backward, rolled, and stared at her accusingly, protest cut off by his father's lifted hand.

"Next year," Pjerin said quietly, forcing the words through clenched teeth, "why don't you travel to Elbasan with that tame trader of yours. You could take rooms in town for a couple of quarters. Your rank would ensure you a position at court."

She twisted lithely in her chair, facing sideways to stare at him. "Are you trying to get rid of me?"

"Not in the least," he replied. "But you seem ... bored."

"And with what should I pay for a house in Elbasan, Your Grace; have you considered that?" Her eyes narrowed. "With favors from the king given to honor our historical duty in holding the pass? That should get me nothing and the cup to drink it from. Thank you, no. I'll stay here and make the best of things."

Pjerin straightened and, for the first time, turned to look directly at her. "I will not operate a tollgate between Cemandia and Shkoder."

Her voice was a gentle contrast to the sharpened edge in her smile. "I'm not asking you to."

"No fighting!" Gerek stomped between them, hands on his hips, frowning alternately up at them both. "I'm not allowed to fight. You're not allowed to fight."

The two adults exchanged a startled glance.

"Nobody's going to fight anybody," Pjerin told his son.

The stiff, indignant posture relaxed slightly. Papa had never lied to him, but Gerek wasn't entirely satisfied.

"Well, you sure looked like you were going to," he muttered.

Pjerin's mouth twitched. He caught the disbelieving look on Olina's face, threw back his head, and roared with laughter.

A heartbeat later, Olina joined in.

He is such a beautiful man, she mused as he scooped Gerek up and tossed the boy into the air. She loved to watch the way his muscles moved beneath the heavy, distracting layer of winter clothing. *Such a pity he's in my way.*

Alone in the common room, quitara balanced on her shrinking lap, Annice absently worked through the fingering for a sea chantey. From where she sat, she could see out into the courtyard and watch people scurrying about from building to building, heads bent and shoulders hunched against the driving rain. The days were definitely getting both longer and warmer although it hardly seemed possible that Fourth Quarter was two-thirds over.

Stasya should be at the keep in Ohrid by now. Although Annice knew that the kigh brought daily reports to the captain, she hadn't been able to come up with a reason for those reports to be shared with her. Her ability to Sing air had completely deserted her and not even with Jurgis' cheerful help had she been able to command the kigh.

If it hadn't been for the distraction offered by Jurgis, the middle third of the quarter would've been unbearable. She had no idea how one small boy could so completely fill a building the size of Bardic Hall, but he seemed to manage it with no apparent difficulty. As he was far too young to choose commitment as a bard, his training so far consisted of nothing more than control over his talent and the kind of lessons any six-year-old might have. The former, his father took care of. The latter, he took with the other children of the Citadel.

Annice had never noticed the number of children around before although she supposed they'd always been there. With Ondro and his mother gone for the quarter, there was only the one other bardic child—Or was Bernardas at two still an infant? Annice had no idea.—but a number of the servers had children as well as some of the healers and a few of the guards. Now that she was aware of them, they seemed to be all over the place—running, shouting, laughing, living pretty much incomprehensible lives.

She shook her head as a familiar flutter drummed against the inner curve of her belly. *And it's far too late to change my mind.* The baby only served to remind her of Ohrid and Ohrid reminded her of Stasya and thinking of Stasya reminded her of how lonely she was without the other woman around. This was the first time they'd ever been apart that the kigh couldn't bridge the distance. Helping to train the fledglings kept her fairly busy, and Jazep, who had been going over the Songs of earth with her, filled in some of the gaps, but nothing could relieve the emptiness of the night.

"I had no idea that tune could be played as a dirge."

"Tadeus!"

The blind bard rocked back on his heels as Annice flung herself up out of the chair and into his arms. "Hey, I missed you, too, but ..." then he paused, took hold of her shoulders, and pushed her gently an arm's reach away. One hand dropped to trace the swelling at her waist.

Annice stifled the urge to jerk away. Tadeus was one of only two she'd allow that kind of license. Tadeus, Stasya, and herself had all learned to Sing air together as fledglings. Poor Jazep, with only earth to Sing, had been odd man out that year.

Brows appeared for an instant like the single beat of ebony wings above the edge of the brilliantly yellow silk scarf tied over his eyes and Tadeus lifted his fingertips to her face. After a moment he smiled. "I guess this explains why the kigh kept insisting you didn't exist. I wondered what you'd done to piss them off although I have to admit this *never* occurred to me."

He waited until he felt her smile in turn, then dropped his hand, using the other, still on her shoulder to guide her around to the cushioned bench by the wall. "Let's hope they haven't rearranged the furniture on me."

"They wouldn't dare.

"Good. Sit." He dropped gracefully down beside her, one leg tucked up so that he was half reclining in the high carved corner of the bench. "Explain. Start with why you didn't send me a message through someone else. I assume Stasya knows?"

"She was there when I found out. You know we always try to end our Walks at the same time. And I could hardly send you a message about it when we're trying to keep the whole thing quiet. In case you've forgotten, His Majesty expressly forbade me to have children."

"Children?" He recoiled. "Nees, tell me it isn't twins!"

"Tadeus!" She pushed his name out through clenched teeth.

His whole manner became abjectly, and unbelievably, apologetic. "I'm sorry, really." Then he dropped the pretense. "But it was a stupid, impossible condition for him to put on you and I'm glad you're challenging it." He reached up and tugged on a bit of her hair. "That is, if you're glad. . . ?"

Annice glanced nervously around the common room, suddenly aware that at any moment someone could come in from the library or the hall. Neither door locked; in damp weather one of them barely closed. "Tadeus, can we go somewhere more private and talk?"

"More private? Nees, the best place to tell a secret is out in the open. That way no one suspects you're hiding something." He cocked his head, obviously listening. "There're three people in the library and no one in the hall. I'll let you know if anyone's on their way in."

"But the kigh . . ."

"Are avoiding you as if you were tone deaf. Talk."

"I need to ask you about that charge of treason against the Duc of Ohrid."

"You *need?*" He pounced on the word. "Is this to do with Stasya going into the mountains? Are you worried about her?"

"Of course I am. You know what travel in Fourth Quarter is like. And I *hate* being out of contact." She took a deep breath and fought to relax her jaw. "But that's not it. Is there any chance you could have misinterpreted that Cemandian? I mean, you can't Command . . ."

"No. But the captain can and did and there's no mistake. Leksik believed, heart and soul, that the duc had sold out to Cemandia and would open the pass to an invading army."

"He might have been made to believe that. Lied to."

Tadeus shrugged. "Why bother when we can just ask the duc for the truth?"

"I don't know. But it's just not something Pjerin would do."

"Pjerin?"

"The Duc of Ohrid." Picking at the tasseled corner of a cushion, she watched the expression that flickered across Tadeus' face and disappeared behind the band of primrose silk. His mind worked on circular paths and he knew that she'd done a long Walk into the mountains because he'd gone as far as Riverton with her. With Stasya gone, she needed desperately to share her fears; but she couldn't tell him the one thing that would make him understand. The words just wouldn't come. *He has to ask.*

After a moment of thought, it seemed he'd followed the circle around to its logical conclusion. "Nees." He paused, and pulled her hand off the tassel, folding it in both of his. "Is the Duc of Ohrid the father of your baby."

She nodded, remembered, winced, and said, "Yes."

His grip tightened. "What a mess."

"It's not that I love him, because I don't—I don't even like him very much—but treason is punishable by death and ..."

"You don't want him to die."

Her mouth twisted and she pulled his hands over so that they rested on the swelling below her heart. "It's more than that, actually; I don't want us to die with him."

CHAPTER SIX

"Your Grace, there appear to be people approaching up the valley."

"Appear to be, Bohdan?" Pjerin turned, his breath pluming in the damp of the cellar.

The elderly steward pulled his heavy wool cloak tighter around his shoulders and frowned at his duc. "I sent young Karli up the north gate tower to knock off that icicle, the one that threatens the life of anyone coming or going should we have a thaw—which, all things being enclosed, we'll have to have sooner or later no matter how little it looks like it now—and she came down saying there appeared to be nearly twenty people making their way up from the edge of the woods."

"Were they in trouble?"

"She says not, but who can tell at that distance?"

"Well, if they're not in trouble, why are they traveling in the mountains at this time of the year?"

"Exactly, Your Grace."

"They can't think that the pass is open."

"I personally don't make those kind of assumptions about lowlanders, Your Grace."

Pjerin grinned and lifted his torch out of the ancient metal holder.

Bohdan sniffed. "Barbaric."

"You'd have had more to say if I'd wasted beeswax or oil down here, and a tallow dip would've been useless." Holding the torch over his head, he gestured at one of the huge, square-cut beams. "Does that look like rot to you?"

"No, Your Grace. It looks like frost."

Grin broadening, Pjerin took the hint and led the way up to the relative warmth of the ground floor. "Have

Karli ski down to meet them. The sooner we know who or what they are, the better."

Bohdan clicked his tongue and shook his head disapprovingly. "You could be sending her into danger. Suppose they're robbers, driven out of their winter lair by the cold and storms?"

"Robbers?" Pjerin extinguished the torch in a bucket of half-melted snow he'd left at the top of the stairs for just that purpose. Peering at his steward through the cloud of smoke and steam, he had to wait for the hiss and sputter to die down before he could continue. "Even supposing that Ohrid could support a band of robbers twenty strong, why would they be on their way here?"

"To throw themselves on your mercy, of course. So that you'll keep them fed for the rest of the winter."

"Then they're not likely to slaughter my messenger. Besides, Bohdan, even robbers have better sense than to travel very far at this time of the year."

"A Troop of the King's Guard?" Karli stared at Troop Captain Otik in awe. "And you've traveled all the way from Elbasan?" Elbasan was on the other side of the world as far as she was concerned. "To see the duc?"

"That's right," the captain grunted, plodding forward on a pair of borrowed snowshoes. He spoke the local dialect with an atrocious accent, but bardic tricks had given him a basic command of the language over the tedious days of travel. "A Troop of the King's Guard from Elbasan to see the duc."

"Why?"

"That's between us and the duc."

Stasya watched, jealous, as the young woman poled herself effortlessly over the snow. The town where they'd left the horses could've supplied her with skies, but with the troop confined to the much slower snowshoes there would've been little point. She hadn't wanted to push it as the situation had already left the captain in a decidedly foul mood.

"*There's no forage,*" she'd told him bluntly, "*and past this point, if we find shelter every night—which I can't guarantee—you've no right to have your beasts eat up someone else's winter supplies.*"

"But we're on the king's business."

"And these are the king's people and I don't think he intended them to starve their own livestock for yours. We can carry enough food for ourselves but not for the horses. From here on, we walk."

Fortunately, someone in Elbasan had been thinking ahead and most of the troop turned out to be country-bred even if their captain was not.

"So what am I supposed to tell His Grace?" Karli demanded.

Captain Otik's head jerked up and around. "You'll tell him nothing. You'll travel with us until we reach the keep."

"I don't think so." She glided half a dozen steps ahead. "We may be moving uphill, but there's not much of a slope until I reach the village. I can beat you back by hours."

"You don't understand," the captain told her, all at once sounding as though he were not a person to be argued with. "You haven't any choice in the matter."

Stasya watched the young woman's face, anger rapidly replacing disbelief, and broke in just before the heated protest. "He's an asshole, isn't he?" Half the strength of Charm was to find a common ground. **"What's your name?"**

"Karli i'Celestin." Grinning broadly, she skied to Stasya's side. "What's yours?"

"Stasya."

"Just Stasya?"

"Uh-huh."

"Well, you don't look much like a priest ... "Karli's grin slid into speculation. "... so you must be a bard."

"Right the first time."

"We had a bard here last quarter."

"I know. Annice. She's a friend of mine."

"Really?"

"Really. **Why don't you travel with us to the keep and we can talk about her?**"

"That'd be great. She sang a song called 'Darkling Lover'. Do you know it? It really steamed His Grace."

"I'll bet." Stasya shot Captain Otik a superior look as Karli expanded on just what she meant by *steamed*. The captain had wanted the approaching skier kept with them under threat of crossbow fire.

"If the duc finds out what we are," he'd declared in a tone that suggested no room for argument, *"he'll close the gates and we'll never pry him out. If we keep his messenger, he'll have no idea of what happened; a request for assistance, a broken ski, a sudden love affair. He may suspect trouble, but he won't know for sure."*

Stasya had not taken the suggestion, had argued, and had won.

Weapons remained undrawn.

Karli remained with them.

They'd be at the keep by noon.

"You told her to come right back?"

"I did." Bohdan hunched his shoulders against the cold wind blowing down from the mountains and funneling out through the gate of the keep. "I told her to find out who the travelers were and what they wanted and to return immediately."

Pjerin beat his fist lightly against the stone of the north gate tower as he peered down the length of the valley. Although they were still some distance away, individuals could now be picked out of the moving mass and counted. Twenty-two; twenty-three including Karli. "I wouldn't worry about it, Bohdan. Karli's probably just found someone new to talk to."

His steward grunted and didn't seem reassured.

He wasn't particularly reassured himself.

The Cemandian has spoken to no one since Tadeus found him. The duc cannot have been warned of your coming. Inform me immediately upon questioning.

The messages the kigh carried were high in concept and low in structure and therefore open to interpretation depending on the personal style of the bards involved, but in this particular instance, there hadn't been much room for flexibility.

Stasya lifted her gaze to the imposing bulk of the keep where it perched on a steep-sided spur of rock, brooding over the pass, the village, and the valley below. Even the Citadel seemed open and welcoming in comparison. What kind of a man would such a stronghold produce?

By all accounts, one who knew his own strengths and had every intention of keeping Ohrid safe behind them.

". . . well it's a pretty well known fact that the duc's aunt—that's his father's youngest sister, she lives in the keep, too—wants more trade with Cemandia, but he says that he won't be relegated to just a tollgate between the two countries, that he wants more for Ohrid than that."

"You heard him say that?" Captain Otik barked.

Karli shot the captain a disgusted look. "Of course I have. Well, mostly. *Everyone* knows that's what he says."

As they came closer, it became apparent that distance alone had not created the similarities between the travelers.

"Twenty-one in a Troop of Guard," Pjerin muttered. But who the twenty-second might be he had no idea. Why would a Troop of Guard be sent to Ohrid? He had no need of them. He didn't want them. He didn't care what kind of lowlander lunacy brought them into the mountains in Fourth Quarter. Whatever their reason, they weren't staying and that was final.

He buried the urge to strap on his own skis by joining his forester at the splitting stump, but his unease grew as he returned again and again to watch the slow, inexorable progress up the valley.

"The next trader through here with a distance glass," he growled in frustration, "makes a sale."

When the strangers reached the village but continued on up the steep path to the keep, snowshoes shouldered and Karli mad obvious by the silhouette of her skies, he sent a message to Bohdan and another to Olina. The tabards proclaiming them King's Guard were now visible over bulky winter clothing.

"You didn't mention we were being invaded," Olina pointed out as she arrived at the gate, nodding at the heavy splitting ax Pjerin still carried. "Should I have brought you the Ducal sword and taken the time to arm myself?"

Bohdan, hurrying up in time to hear her question, shot a startled look at his duc. "Your Grace! They're King's Guard. 'Tis treason to deny them."

"And an unenclosed pain to feed them," Pjerin

grunted, laying the ax aside; but not so far aside that he couldn't reach it if he had to. "I wonder what they want?"

Together they stood and watched the twenty-two cover the last bit of ground followed by a chattering crowd of villagers, mundane tasks abandoned in the face of this unusual occurrence. The last time a troop of King's Guard had come to Ohrid, it had been as a part of the army that had secured the mountain principalities for Shkoder.

A similar crowd, consisting of the inhabitants of the keep, had gathered just inside the gate—the majority ranged behind their duc, the more adventuresome risking ice-covered stairs for the better view from the top of either gate tower.

"Is it the king, Papa?" Gerek pushed his way through until he could peer wide-eyed around his father's legs. "Is it the king?"

Before he could answer, Karli called out, "They've come to see you, Your Grace. All the way from Elbasan. This is Stasya. She's a bard."

Pulled forward, Stasya inclined her head; pack and snowshoes precluding a bow. The duc was, as Annice had said, absolutely gorgeous: tall, broad shouldered, narrow hipped, a thick mass of blue-black hair tied at the nape of his neck, dark violet eyes surrounded by a fringe of ebony lashes, high cheekbones, a straight nose, and good teeth. *I suppose for people who like that sort of thing* . . . His bearing stopped just short of challenge. *And Nees has never been able to resist a challenge.*

While he certainly didn't look happy to see them, neither did he look like a man guilty of treason suddenly faced by a Troop of King's Guard and the prospect of being questioned under Bardic Command. *Annice believes he's innocent of the charges.* Tadeus had sent that message right after he'd returned to the hall. Stasya wasn't sure it helped. *Why* did Annice believe the duc innocent? Did she have a rational reason or was it merely the influence of the child she carried?

"Pjerin a'Stasiek, Duc of Ohrid." Troop-Captain Otik dropped his pack and squared off in front of the gate, his eyes narrowed and his beard jutting out aggressively. "You have been charged with high treason; with the breaking of your oaths to Shkoder; with the surrendering of Defiance Pass to the Cemandians, the enemies of Shkoder. These charges have been Witnessed and confirmed."

The crowd, shocked into disbelieving silence by the captain's words, drew in its collective breath. The charges were Witnessed and confirmed. The bards had already determined the truth.

Stasya felt a number of eyes on her back. She kept her own on the duc's face which, so far, showed no emotion at all.

"We are here," the captain continued, "in the name of Theron, King of Shkoder, High Captain of the Broken Islands, Lord over the Mountain Principalities of Sibiu, Ohrid, Ajud, Bicaz, and Somes, in order that you may answer this charge and that the truth may be determined." His tone made it plain that, for as far as he was concerned, the truth had been determined already and every moment the duc spent out of irons was wasted time.

Stasya watched a muscle jump in the duc's jaw, noted how both hands curled into fists, and was impressed by the tight grip he kept on his rage. Although his lips had thinned to bloodless lines, he said only, "Bohdan, open the Great Hall."

"Yes, Your Grace." The old man's voice barely rose above his shock.

Pjerin turned and unfolded one fist long enough to touch his trembling steward gently on the arm. "It'll be all right, Bohdan."

Bohdan nodded and squared his shoulders. "Yes, Your Grace."

There was the strength of belief in this second declaration, belief and trust, and Stasya found herself more impressed than she had been. Guilt or innocence aside, she couldn't let Captain Otik turn this into some kind of power-tripping sideshow.

"Your Grace?" When he faced her, she could feel the force of his emotions, even contained as they were, and had to stop herself from stepping back. "Perhaps," she suggested, "it might be better if this were done more privately."

"No." Pjerin shook his head. "These are my people.

What concerns me, concerns them. I have nothing to hide."

"Pjerin a'Stasiek, Duc of Ohrid, step forward."

Pjerin did as commanded, hating the feeling that he had no choice but to obey. He heard Gerek mutter angrily behind him and wanted to turn and reassure his son, but his gaze had been locked in place by the dark eyes of the bard. His lips parted slightly and he growled, "Go on."

If only because it annoyed Captain Otik, Stasya approved of the way the duc had just declared to those assembled in the Great Hall—his people, the guards, herself—that he was Commanded only because he allowed it to happen. She hoped that Annice was right, that the duc had been set up by Cemandia for whatever reasons, that he wouldn't be witnessed a traitor, that he wouldn't have to die.

"Pjerin a'Stasiek, you will speak only the truth."

The captain advanced half a step ahead of the bard. It would be witnessed he asked the only question necessary. "Pjerin a'Stasiek, have you broken your oaths and agreed to allow a Cemandian army access to Shkoder?"

"Yes."

For a moment, Pjerin had no idea whose voice had spoken, then he realized it was his own. He fought to take the word back, but his throat and mouth defied him. The bard's face was expressionless, the captain's triumphant, and all around him he could see, and hear, shock and horror and disbelief.

Otik smiled. "Who will witness?"

"Wait." Tempted to put Command on the word, Stasya settled for filling the hall with it. "A life is at stake here. That's too important a matter to witness on one question."

"He had no choice but to tell the truth." The captain snapped in Shkoden. "You yourself gave the Command."

"I know." But she could see the inner struggle going on in the man before her and while it might be nothing more than the realization that he had doomed himself, she had to be sure. For Annice's sake if no one else's.

"Very well " In victory, Otik could afford to be generous. "Ask as many questions as you like. You, of all people, should know it won't change things."

". . . next spring, bring an army through." Pjerin remembered saying it, but the memory seemed somehow removed as though it belonged to someone else and as he repeated it, the shape felt wrong in his mouth.

"Are you satisfied?" Otik asked. Many of the duc's people were weeping openly.

"Not quite," Stasya replied, although she personally had no doubt remaining.

"Olina i'Katica, you will speak only the truth."

". . . and I reminded him of his liege oaths and he said that he didn't give a rat's ass about King Theron. That *he* was Duc of Ohrid."

Pjerin remembered the conversation. But it hadn't been like that. It hadn't been treason. Horror growing, he tried to rip the fog aside but found himself flailing at nothing. Found himself agreeing that those were his words.

"Bohdan a'Samuil, you will speak only the truth."

". . . I don't know what they discussed." Tears ran unheeded down the old man's cheeks. "His Grace spoke only Cemandian with the trader. But it was probably nothing. Nothing at all. You see, we're storing some of the trader's packs."

"Satisfied now?" Otik prodded one of the packs with his boot. An opened bundle of crossbow quarrels spilled across the floor, metal ringing accusingly against stone.

Sick at heart, Stasya nodded. *I'm sorry, Nees. But he condemned himself.* Only Pjerin had known what the packs contained. Olina had been furious that the man she'd thought had been lingering at the keep for her company had actually been plotting with her nephew. Bohdan had been sobbing too hard to speak.

"Well, then." The captain moved out to the center of the Great Hall and swept his gaze over the stunned crowd. As the questioning had progressed, they'd pushed back toward the walls in a futile effort to remove themselves from their duc's betrayal. "Who will be the four who witness?"

Lukas a'Tynek was the first to step forward. He had lost weight since the fire and the skin of his face hung slack along his jaw. The bruising of Pjerin's blow, although it had long since faded from his flesh, still showed in the anger in his eyes. He stood alone for a moment, then another man and a woman joined him.

"One more," Otik prodded.

Finally, a second woman shuffled to the center of the hall, her eyes and nose red from weeping.

The captain nodded his approval and pivoted briskly to face the pale and trembling Duc of Ohrid. "Pjerin a'Stasiek, as of this moment, you are found guilty of high treason."

"Witnessed," Lukas' voice sounded over the other three.

"Bard?"

Stasya closed her eyes for a heartbeat. If he'd only look defiant instead of hurt and confused, it would be easier to bear. When she opened them again, nothing had changed. "Witnessed," she said.

"NO!" All at once, the fog was gone. Pjerin charged forward, hands outstretched, unsure of who exactly he was going to grab but knowing that his life depended on making them listen. "I never did those things. I never said those things! It's a lie!"

The first guard hit him low, the second swung locked fists into his gut.

He couldn't feel the pain, he couldn't feel anything but the need to make them understand that he'd been trapped, held prisoner inside his own head while something else answered for him. "I didn't do it! It's a lie!"

It took four guards to hold him down.

"You can't lie under Bardic Command," the captain told him smugly. "Although this isn't the first time some arrogant fool has thought he would get away with it. You've put your own neck on the block. For pity's sake, take it like a man."

"You. . . !" Rage lent him strength. Pjerin dragged one leg free and kicked out.

Captain Otik crashed backward and down, both hands clutching his left thigh.

Misjudged the safety zone, you asshole, Stasya thought, barely preventing herself from saying it aloud. But when the captain stood, drawing his sword, she decided enough was enough. **"Stop it!"** she told him, whirled, stared down at Pjerin, and repeated the command. **"Stop it, right now."** Shaking, she pushed her hair back off her face and swept her gaze over the crowd. "It's over."

In the silence that followed, Gerek twisted out of his nurse's grip and ran to his father's side. He hadn't understood much of what had happened and his nurse's tears had frightened him, but no one was taking his father away. No one.

"Don't you touch him! Not any of you!" Fists flailing, he threw himself at one of the guards kneeling on Pjerin's arms. Taken by surprise, and unwilling to hit a child, the guard rocked back and raised both hands to protect his face.

"Go away! Go away! Go away!" Half screaming, half crying, Gerek stumbled and fell.

"Gerek!" Pjerin scooped the boy up in his free arm. "Hush. Quiet."

Stasya glared the captain into silence. Then she gestured the guards away. They moved slowly and they didn't move far, but they went.

His attention solely on his son, Pjerin got to his feet, Gerek pressed tight against his chest. "Hey. Come on, look at me."

Still sobbing, Gerek raised his head.

Gently drying the boy's cheeks with his palm, Pjerin searched for an explanation. "I have to go away for a while. To see the king."

"They're going to hurt you."

"No. They're just going to take me to the king."

One grubby finger pointed at the captain. "But he said ..."

"He's wrong. There's been a mistake made."

"The king will make everything better?"

"That's right."

"I want to go with you."

"I need you to stay here and look after things."

"Till you come back?"

"That's right. Until I come back. Now, we're not leaving right this moment but ... uh ... but we need to make travel plans. So give me a kiss and go to your Aunt Olina." Olina would keep her head, not frighten Gerek nor lie to him either. Later, when he'd calmed down, the boy could go back to his nurse.

Gerek stretched his mouth up to his father's, then allowed himself to be placed on the floor. "I don't understand," he complained and wiped his nose on his sleeve.

"It's all right, Gerek." Pjerin stroked the soft black curls. "Nothing bad will happen to you."

"Witnessed."

His head jerked up and he stared at the bard, hope warring with fear. She nodded, the motion deliberate and unmistakable, and he felt as though a knife had been pulled from his heart. He could bear whatever happened, whatever the outcome, as long as none of it touched his son. Blinking back tears, he made no protest as two of the guards took his arms and led him from the hall.

Only Lukas a'Tynek met his eyes as he left.

"The block's too good for you," he snarled and spat at Pjerin's feet.

"Majesty."

Theron knew what news the Bardic Captain brought. He could read it in every line of her body, in the forced neutrality of her expression, in the somber undercurrent that darkened her perfectly modulated voice. Combined, they told him she brought death. As well as anger, for he and his people had been betrayed, he felt grief for both the betrayal and the life it would claim. He wished he could send her away, now that her message had been delivered, but the formalities must be played out. "You have a report from Ohrid, Captain?"

"Yes, Majesty." Liene drew in a deep breath and passed the roll of parchment she carried to her king. He took it and laid it on his desk, but his eyes never left her face. "Pjerin a'Stasiek, the Duc of Ohrid, when Commanded to speak only the truth, did admit to dealing with Cemandia, to agreeing to open the pass to a Cemandian army, to the use of his keep as a Cemandian base."

"There is no doubt?"

"My bard was most thorough, Majesty." More than

thorough from the impressions brought by the kigh. It had taken Liene most of the morning to unravel the tangled messages and had the emotions behind them not been so strong she doubted she'd have had much success. "They are returning with the traitor to Elbasan, Majesty. For your judgment."

There was, always had been, only one judgment passed on treason.

"How long?" Theron asked, the parchment roll collapsing beneath the sudden pressure of his fingers.

"They should arrive ten to fifteen days after First Quarter Festival if everything goes well."

It is impossible to lie under Bardic Command. But I heard my mouth twist the truth, twist my words, twist my memories. His mind not on the placement of his feet, Pjerin stumbled and would have fallen had one of the two guards walking close beside him not stretched out her hand. He nodded his thanks. *Careful shepherds, seeing that their sheep makes it to the slaughterhouse.*

I am not guilty of treason. But it's impossible to lie under Bardic Command. Everyone believes that. King Theron believes that. So, by my own words, I'm guilty. Except that they weren't my words. All right, whose words are they? Who can twist a man's mind in such a way? Who can . . .

Up ahead, Stasya began a marching song, her clear soprano drawing in those of the guards who knew the tune. All around him, heads lifted, shoulders straightened, and arms swung out. Pjerin found his feet beginning to move to the rhythm.

Who can twist a man's mind? The answer became suddenly very clear.

But it wasn't this bard. She had no opportunity. It happened earlier.

He remembered a woman who'd matched him passion for passion, who'd sung to his son, who'd brought news of the world into the isolation of the mountains, and taken news of the mountains out into the world. Annice. It had to be Annice. How and why, he had no idea. How and why didn't matter.

It was impossible to lie under Bardic Command.

Everyone believed that.

He was going to die.

No. He wasn't going to die. Not without a fight. They were still in Ohrid and he knew his land. Knew how to live off it, knew where to hide. In time, he could clear his name, but to do it, he had to survive.

It wouldn't be easy. At every stop, that bastard of a troop captain had gleefully recounted the questions and answers that had condemned him. At every stop, he'd seen his people turn against him.

How can they believe me a traitor? For a moment, he felt physically ill. *They believe because the words came out of your mouth.*

The road—no more than cart tracks for the roads Shkoder had promised three generations ago still came no farther than the head of Lake Marienka—followed the north edge of a steep-sided ravine. If he could reach the bottom, he could lose himself in the tangled paths of frozen water courses. Once he was free in the mountains, Shkoder would have to bring an army to dig him out.

Heart pounding, muscles tensed almost to pain, Pjerin waited until the marching song reached its final chorus then, with most of the guards singing, dropped his pack and threw himself off the road. He kept his feet under him for only the first two strides. When he hit snow, he allowed himself to fall.

A winter's worth of snow had been packed and frozen by a day of rain and a subsequent drop in temperature creating not only a solid surface for walking but a slick and dangerous route down the side of the ravine. Ignoring the cries from above, Pjerin concentrated on avoiding the trees and rocks rushing toward him at deadly speeds. He'd been sliding down these mountains all his life. This was a path the guards wouldn't dare to take.

Then the ice ended. He slammed into bare rock, bit back a cry of pain, tumbled, dropped five feet straight down and landed on another strip of frozen snow. Arms and legs flailing, fighting to regain control, he crashed off the trunk of an ancient pine, gouged his jaw on a protruding branch, and spun without slowing through the tearing clutches of a thorn bush. Only a frantic grab for the trunk of a small tree kept him from plummeting over a final drop and onto the jagged bed of stone at its base, the sudden jerk nearly tearing his arm from the socket.

Gasping for breath, Pjerin pulled himself to his knees and froze as a crossbow quarrel thudded into the tree just above his hand.

"The next one nails your hand to the tree. Stand up."

Shaking with disappointment, Pjerin stood.

"Now turn around."

He turned. The ice had taken him diagonally, not straight down. Captain Otik and two guards, bows cocked and aimed, stood braced against a fallen tree about three body lengths from the road. The scrub and rock between them offered nothing to block a shot. He could chance it. Leap off the edge, count on the rock to shield him. Defy the odds that said if they didn't shoot him in the back, he'd break a leg in the landing.

No. It was a long way to Elbasan. There'd be other, better chances.

"Get your traitor's ass back up here," Otik growled, "or I'll have the corporal shoot you through the knee and we'll drag you to Elbasan and the block."

The corporal looked as though she'd be more than willing to pull the trigger.

Hauling himself back up to the road, bruised muscles and joints protesting every movement, Pjerin kept his eyes locked on the captain's face and took a savage pleasure in having the other man finally wheel away. *This isn't the end*, he vowed, blood staining the snow from the wound on his face. *I am no lamb to go meekly to the slaughter.*

Rough hands yanked him over the last distance and threw him down in a circle of boots. He rolled over and squinted up at uniform expressions of animosity.

"Hobble him," Otik commanded. "And after you've got the pack back on him, tie his hands. I should've remembered that traitors have no honor."

Annice stared down at the blank page without seeing it, her attention held by the movement under the loose folds of her smock. Over the last few weeks, the baby had grown increasingly more active and almost impossible to ignore. Her awareness of it ran under everything she did; under her music, under time with the fledglings, right *through* eating and sleeping. *It's like having a house guest you can't get rid of,* she thought, chewing on a handful of raisins. *I can't* believe *some women do this more than once.*

Giving herself a mental shake, she finally laid pen to paper, discovered the ink had dried on the quill, and shoved it back into the well. While she usually enjoyed transcribing recall notes, the thought that the king, Theron, would be seeing them kept distracting her.

What was he like now? The evidence of how he wore the crown was hardly hidden but what kind of a man had he become? What kind of a father had he been? Onele was seventeen, a woman grown. Antavas, at thirteen, tottered on the edge of being a man. And Brigita, the baby she'd never seen other than at a careful distance, was a child of ten. Did he love them? Or were they merely imperial playing pieces as the previous generation of royal children had been—shuffled from lesson to lesson, brought out and put on display when the occasion merited a show of family.

Did he ever think of her?

Would he listen if she went to him and said . . .

And said what? Please excuse the fact that I committed treason with a man you're about to behead for the same crime. Don't hold it against me, don't hold it against my baby. Dream on, Annice. He wouldn't see a coincidence, he'd see a plot. He's a king before he's your brother. She'd learned that at fourteen when he'd rejected everything she was and everything she wanted for herself.

In the early days of her training, when the anger had dimmed until only the hurt remained, she'd dreamed about the day when he'd realize what he'd done and come to her and ask her forgiveness. With every year that passed, the hurt grew and more of the anger returned.

And now, it was too late.

A sudden blaze of light drew her out of a deepening spiral of self-pity as one of the librarians moved around the room tending the lamps. If it was that late, maybe Tadeus had a new message from Stasya.

"Hello, Nees."

"Hello, Imrich. Where are you off to in such a hurry?"

The young man beamed proudly at her, close-set eyes

nearly disappearing in the folds of his smile. "Going to get ribbon for Tadeus." He held up one thick-fingered hand. A scarlet ribbon had been loosely tied around his wrist. "Must match this one 'zacally.'"

"But it's after dark, all the ribbon makers will be closed."

"Not going to shops. Going to Ceci's rooms. Tadeus says she has ribbons to match."

Annice had no idea how Tadeus, being blind, could possibly know what color ribbons the other bard had, or even that she *had* ribbons, but had no wish to confuse poor Imrich by saying so aloud. With one arm curled protectively around her belly, she watched him walk down the hall, stocky body rocking from side to side as he hurried off to complete his errand.

Imrich was what the healers called a Moonchild. They *said* that the name came from the round and flattened features, but Annice suspected that, way back in the beginning, they'd thought the moon somehow responsible—healers were very touchy about outgrown superstitions. The son of one of the cooks at the palace, Imrich had headed for music of any kind the moment he could creep and had finally, to his great joy, been taken on at Bardic Hall as a server. He adored Tadeus, who occasionally had to be reminded not to take advantage of his good nature.

No one knew what caused a baby to be born a Moonchild or why some were more affected than others. Imrich lived a happy, productive, albeit simple life. Others Annice had seen sat grunting in corners, barely aware of self or surroundings. She felt a sudden rush of fear at the thought that her baby could be one of those.

"Are you coming in, Annice? Or did you just come up to lurk about outside my door?"

Jolted out of dark imaginings by Tadeus' appearance in the hall, Annice felt her jaw drop. "What is that on your head?"

"Do you like it?" A gentle shake sent the heavy fringe hanging off the broad brim of his felt hat swinging, the arc just clearing the tip of his nose. "There's only so many ways you can tie a scarf around your eyes before it gets old so, *hokal!*" He threw the Petrokian word in with a flourish and stepped to one side. "My cousin the milliner made it up for me."

Mesmerized by the swaying fringe, Annice slid past him into his room. "I thought your cousin was a tailor."

"I have a lot of cousins," Tadeus declared with satisfaction, following her in and closing the door. "And they're all in the clothing trade."

Blindness forced Tadeus to keep his room compulsively neat and the visitor who moved a chair or set a mug where it didn't belong was never invited back. Carved letters on the edge of his shelves kept clothing sorted by color. There were a great many shelves.

"You're going to have to request a double room soon," Annice observed, "so that you and your wardrobe can continue to live together."

"I'm going to have to go through all this and pass on the no longer fashionable," Tadeus corrected, carefully removing a kettle from his fire and pouring two portions of hot cider. "Shall I arrange it that you get a shirt or two?"

"Thank you, no. I've no desire to look like a slaughtered sheep when that crimson fabric of yours loses its dye in the rain."

"Try to keep up, Nees. That doesn't happen anymore." He passed her a mug and settled into the room's second chair, one slender leg draped nonchalantly over the padded arm. "Sea-trader came back from the south last summer with the secret, and now local cloth, provided, of course, it's bought from my-cousin-the-dyer, will be just as colorfast as the imported. There's this stuff called alum they add to the bath ..." Warming to his subject, Tadeus went into a complicated explanation of the process to which Annice paid little attention.

"Has a message come from Stasya yet?" she asked when he finally paused for breath.

His expression grew instantly contrite. "Oh, center it, Nees, I'm sorry. I meant to tell you right away. You shouldn't have let me babble on like that."

"I've never found a way to shut you up." The smile in her voice took the edge off the words. "So. What's she have to say?"

"The duc tried to escape again."

"Again? How many times is that, three?"

"Four," Tadeus corrected glumly. "Stas is afraid he's trying to goad Otik into killing him out of hand."

"No. He's trying to stay alive. To escape the block. That's all."

"You sure?"

"I'm sure. He was one of the most alive people I ever met."

"Meet a lot of dead people, do you?"

"Tad!"

"Sorry." He didn't look very sorry. "After you leave and I can get a kigh to come around, I'll tell her."

Annice tried very hard not to resent the fact that she'd been cut off from air, that messages had to be passed through an intermediary. She wasn't entirely successful. "Anything else."

"Just the usual mushy stuff." He grinned. "She misses you. I'm to see that you take care of yourself. You're not to worry about her. What do you want me to answer?"

That I'm afraid of dying. That I don't want my baby to pay for its father's crime. That I want her here to help me deal with all this. Leaning forward, she flicked the fringe above Tadeus' nose and forced a calm she didn't feel into her voice. "Oh, just the usual mushy stuff."

"I *can't* keep him under Command all the time! He'll go insane!"

"What difference does that make?" Otik growled. "He's going to die anyway."

"There're twenty-one of you," Stasya snarled. "And only one of him. I should think you could control him without my help."

A few feet away, Pjerin sucked in a shallow breath and grimaced as even such minor movement ground bones together. He'd very nearly made it this last time. Would have made it if those unenclosed kigh hadn't given him away. Arms cruelly bound high on his back, one cheek pushed into the mud, he listened to the argument and almost wished the bard would give in, would give him an excuse not to keep trying and failing and with every failure sliding faster and faster toward despair.

"Get up!"

The boot drove into his thigh hard enough to lift him a few inches from the ground.

"I said; get up, oathbreaker!"

The second kick smashed into his hip. Gagging from the pain, Pjerin struggled to raise himself to his knees, terrified that a third kick would hit ribs already broken. A helping hand buried itself in his hair and yanked.

He fought to stay conscious. He wouldn't give them the satisfaction of throwing his limp body into the back of a wagon like so much carrion. If they were going to get him to Elbasan, they were going to have to fight him every step of the way.

Gerek looked at the family crest etched into the pommel of the Ducal sword and then up at Olina, his eyes red and puffy from crying. He'd been so certain his papa would be back by First Quarter Festival that not even the festival gifts piled by his bed at sunrise had prevented a morning of tears.

Sighing deeply, he wrapped both hands around the wire grip as far as they would go.

"As your papa isn't here, Gerek," Olina had told him as they'd walked hand in hand down to the field, *"you've got to take care of things. It's up to you."*

The gathered villagers murmured approval. Gerek ignored them. They'd said bad things about his papa. He remembered. He wasn't a baby anymore.

Olina released her hold on the sword.

Gerek hung on. The point quivered in the air for an instant then dropped, burying itself in the dirt, marking the first furrow of the new season's ploughing. Legs braced, he stood and watched as the team of slow moving oxen dragged the plough to the far end of the field, peeling back the first trench for the spring planting. Not until they began their turn, did Olina reach down and take the sword out of his hands.

"I'm very proud of you," she whispered as she turned him to face the cheering crowd. "You've woken the earth from its Fourth Quarter sleep and ensured that your people will have bread this year."

He twisted his head to stare up at her. "I have?"

"Yes. *You* have." She smiled at him and was rewarded by a tentative smile returned. In a very short time, this child would be the Duc of Ohrid, hers to teach, to train, to rule.

CHAPTER SEVEN

"... carrying low, so it's likely a girl. Although ..." The heavyset young woman reflectively rolled a ball of damp earth between her fingers. "... as I think on it, my cousin Onele—the one who always said that Her Highness the Heir was named for her—well, she carried so high her tits stuck out like a shelf and still ended up delivered of a fine healthy girl. But, on the other hand, my Aunt Edite when she was carrying my little nephew—such a pretty baby he turned out to be ..."

Annice let the steady stream of chatter flow in one ear and out the other while she sipped at the traditional bard's cup of clear water. *I'm so tired of hearing about babies. Can't anyone think about anything else?* It didn't help that she was Singing fertility and the hope of high yield into the earth. She'd been Singing almost constantly since First Quarter Festival, roaming the city, calling her services out for anyone who might have a bit of garden they wanted Sung—and she rather suspected that a number of people who wouldn't normally bother took one look at her condition and figured it couldn't hurt.

Cup drained and formalities satisfied, she handed the small clay vessel back to her hostess and, so smoothly that the other woman had no idea she'd been interrupted, asked for the use of the privy.

"Oh, certainly, for it's very important that you keep your bladder emptied, not only because of discomfort—and don't I know that babies seem to bounce on it purposefully—but because if you wait, well, infections can grow. I mark how my partner's sister waited too long and ..."

Closing the privy door muffled the stream of information and Annice sighed as she maneuvered her bulk around in the enclosed space. *I think I've seen the inside of every privy in Elbasan. What a recall on city sanitation I'll be able to make. I can only hope that the captain herself gets to read every single word of it.*

It had been the captain who'd pointed out that as she was now Singing earth so strongly and as she was in no condition to begin a First Quarter Walk, she could do some work in the city. Annice had no objection to the Singing, but the symbolic watering-the-bard that followed had floated her through the last twelve days. Out in the country, village bounds were Walked and the area enclosed all Sung at once. One Song, albeit a long one, meant one watering. In the city, outside the rough community gardens of the poorer areas, every individual household wanted an individual Song and poured her an individual cup of water which symbolism required her to drink. Annice had never realized how many people actually lived in Elbasan before.

Nor would it have occurred to me that every single one of them would have an opinion on my belly. As it appeared that the young woman had finally run out of stories concerning childbearing relatives, Annice hastily rearranged her clothing and stepped back out into the small yard.

Although only watering-the-bard was required from the householder, most added a small, easily carried token for luck. In the country, buttons or spoons or combs intricately carved from wood or horn over a long winter trapped inside were usually presented. Annice had a horn spoon so beautifully translucent and skillfully carved that once when eating porridge in an inn, she'd been offered a double-anchor for it. She'd laughed, spun the heavy silver coin on the table, and pocketed her spoon. In the city, coins predominated; gulls for the most part but two half-anchors nestled in the bottom of her pouch and as she moved into the richer neighborhoods she expected to get more. The Hall would take a percentage, the rest would be hers to spend as she wished. Normally, she'd toss the lot at the Hall—fed, housed, and clothed she had little need for money—but with a baby on the way, she supposed it wouldn't hurt to have some set aside.

Back out on the street, she barely had time to finish

her call—*Shall I Sing the earth for you/shall I Sing grow-ing*—before the elderly man from the next house in the row dragged her through a cluttered first floor room to a tiny walled garden identical to the one she'd just left.

"I could hear you over there," he told her as he fussily positioned her in the center of the rectangle of dirt. "See that you Sing mine as well. The rest are out at their jobs, but I'm not so old and deaf that you can pass off any second-rate tune. So you just see that you Sing mine as well as you Sang that babbling featherhead's next door."

"I heard that!"

Annice rolled her eyes as the young woman's voice floated up over the wall and resisted the urge to Sing up a fine crop of thistles.

Eleven gardens, a handful of coins, and a really pretty pair of shell earrings later, Annice decided to call it a day. While the actual Singing was almost effortless and she seemed to pull as much or more energy from the earth as she put into the Songs, she'd had just about as much contact with the middle-class citizenry of Elbasan as she was able to cope with.

The next person who tries to grope my belly is going to find themselves marched down to the harbor and Sung off the end of a pier.

Late afternoon shadows seeped chill into the narrow streets as she hurried back to the River Road and her favorite soup shop. She'd have an early supper before heading back to the Hall. With every mobile bard off on First Quarter Walks to discover how the country came through the winter, the Hall was pretty nearly empty. She found the huge dining room depressing and eating in her own quarters lonely. Even the fledglings had gone off in the company of older, more experienced bards. In an effort to become used to children, she'd been spending time with Terezka, but three days before, Terezka had strapped Bernardas into a padded cart and left to make a round of Riverton, saying, *I know it's not far, but if I don't get back on the road, I'm going to go crazy.*

Annice understood completely.

I think tomorrow I'll head over to the Crescent. At least there I'll be dealing with servants too busy to indulge tactile curiosity.

The sounds and smells of the busy thoroughfare caught her up as Chandler's Alley spilled her out onto River Road and she quite happily jostled along with the crowds, enjoying the anonymity. This having been one of the first rain-free days of the quarter, shopkeepers had done a brisk business and continued to do so even though sunset would bring out shutters in a very short time. Annice watched people, was watched in turn, and found she didn't mind the smiles when they came unaccompanied by a homily and a pat. Humming cheerfully, she stepped around a donkey cart piled high with bundles of dried fish and froze.

In the distance, she could hear shouting and beneath the voices, the clatter of hooves against cobblestones. She glanced around. Could no one else hear it? The sound continued to grow and with it alarm, excitement, anger, until he advance wave finally crashed down on the people surrounding her and dragged them around to point and yell.

"The guard! The guard returns!"

"They have him! They have the traitor!"

Annice shrank back against the rough willow weave of the cart, wishing she was somewhere, anywhere, else.

A thick patina of mud covered horses and guards alike. Only the Troop Captain sat erect, eyes ahead but obviously conscious of the crowds lining the route. *I have saved you all,* his posture declared and the crowds responded. Everyone else sat slumped in the saddle, wearing the exhaustion of a Fourth Quarter march to Ohrid and back. Had Stasya not been Singing a gratitude as she rode, Annice wouldn't have recognized her.

She tried to look away as the prisoner went by and found she couldn't.

He'd been tied to the horse, thick ropes cutting into each leg then secured beneath a mud-caked belly. His hands were bound to the pommel. Blood and dirt encrusted his face and his beautiful hair was a tangled, knotted mass clubbed up in the center of his back. He swayed, hunched over his left side, his left eye swollen completely shut.

It was no worse than she'd expected, given the messages Tadeus had relayed, but it made her feel sick.

An egg smashed into his shoulder. He ignored it but

not with the despair of a broken man. He ignored it because it had nothing to do with him.

You can't lie under Command. Why can't he go to the block with some semblance of dignity?

Annice closed out the babble of the crowd and turned toward the Citadel. Stasya was home. She'd hold onto that.

"You haven't touched the supper I brought up."

"I'm not hungry, Leonas."

"So? Your baby still has to eat." After prodding up the fire, he shoved a thick slice of bread and cheese onto the end of a toasting fork and stood, deaf to her protests, until the cheese melted and the bread beneath turned a deep golden brown.

When he pointedly held it out to her, Annice sighed and pulled it off the fork, unable to order him out because she didn't think she could wait alone any longer. Stasya had accompanied the guard directly to the palace. The Bardic Captain had rushed over to speak with her there. No telling how long before she could come home.

"Good." The server nodded approvingly as Annice bit into the food. "Eat that, promise you'll eat the custard and drink the juice, and I'll leave you be."

"The juice . . ." She couldn't *ask* him to stay, he'd only fuss the more. ". . . it's very, uh, red. What is it?"

"Something my Giz got sent from her sister down coast. They call them bog berries."

She took a cautious sip and her entire face puckered. "It's a little sour."

Leonas snorted. "So's the sister." Then, without prodding, he launched into a long, complicated story of how the berries were being tried out by some of the sea-traders—". . . cheaper than relying only on them imported limes . . ."—and looked as though they might become an important cash crop for the area.

Annice ate while he talked, eyes locked on his face.

At last he paused, head cocked toward the door. "Someone coming," he said shortly, piled empty dishes back on their tray, and turned to go.

"Leonas." She searched for the right words and finally found, "Thank you."

He snorted again. "You're welcome, Princess."

Annice squelched the urge to follow him out into the hall and instead waited by the fire, shifting her weight from foot to foot. She didn't know why she was so nervous, she and Stasya had been walking in and out of each other's lives since they first met as fledglings. *All right, so the circumstances are a little different. I'm playing a duet and she just spent two and a half months helping to bring my baby's father to his execution. That shouldn't affect us.*

When the door finally opened, she found it didn't.

"Center it, Stas, you look like shit."

Stasya sagged against the door frame, one corner of her mouth twisting up in the ghost of a smile. Although she'd managed to find time to wash the dirt from her face and hands, her clothing still bore evidence of the road, bits of dried mud flaking off the cloth with every movement. Her short dark hair lay plastered lifelessly against her head, the shade very nearly matched by the circles under her eyes. "Thanks." She sighed deeply. "I missed you, too."

"So you're still Singing fire?"

"As long as it's already contained." Annice opened the tap from the boiler, tested the temperature of the water, and closed it again. The four notes she Sang to the kigh dancing in the steel pan of charcoal provoked a burst of activity. Satisfied, she used the rim of the tub to pull herself erect, then turned and sat on the broad edge. "I don't think I'd dare Sing fire outside where anything in the Circle might ignite." Reaching under her clothing, she scratched at the stretched curve of skin. "The water'll be hot by the time you get undressed."

She watched for a moment as the other woman fumbled with ties and buttons and finally went over to help. "Are you sure this is a good idea?" she asked. "Maybe you should just have a quick wash in the basin and go to bed. I don't want you to drown."

Stasya emerged from the folds of her shirt emphatically shaking her head. "I have been dreaming about this tub for the last three nights ... ever since we left Vidor. Do you know how long it's been since I've had a nice long soak?"

"Don't tell me." Annice wrinkled her nose and stuffed

the soiled clothing down the laundry chute, trying not to touch the filthy fabric any more than she had to. "I don't think I can stand knowing." Breathing shallowly through her mouth, she checked the water temperature again and this time let it continue to run. "Was it really bad?"

"Tub first, talk later." Stasya repeated the phrase that had brought them down to the bathing room. Her hand on Annice's shoulder, she stepped over the high side of the tub and, sighing deeply, lowered herself into the rapidly rising water. "I'll tell you one thing, though, I don't care what oaths I took or how much my country needs me, I'm never getting on a horse again."

"You've lost weight."

"Weight, teeth, and my sunny disposition."

Annice stopped scooping soft soap onto a huge sponge and whirled around so fast she nearly fell over. "Teeth?"

"Well, not really." Stasya sank lower in the water, rubbing without enthusiasm at the gray of old dirt ground into her skin. "But I'm sure that one of the top ones, on the right, at the back, is loose."

"Stas, you always worry about your teeth." She Sang the kigh a gratitude as the boiler drained and the charcoal went from white hot to barely warm. "And your teeth are always fine. Sit up a bit so I can wash your hair, I'm not as flexible as I used to be."

"How *are* you?"

"I drop nearly everything I pick up, my ankles are two sizes bigger in the evening than they are in the morning, I have to pee all the time, I can't bend, and I'm sick of talking about it. Rinse." When Stasya reemerged and had knuckled her eyes dry, she added, "Elica says I'm healthy, the baby's healthy, and everything's happening right on schedule. Nothing's changed since Tadeus left and we lost touch."

They killed another few minutes discussing Tadeus, and the few after that covering the list of "reminders" Jazep had left when he'd headed out into the country the morning after First Quarter Festival. "I'm telling you, Stas, he's worse than Elica and Leonas combined." Washing Stasya's back, Annice told stories about Singing in the city and silently urged her to bring up the one thing they had to discuss. Finally, she could stand it no longer. "Stas . . ."

"I know." She pulled herself up, reaching for a towel. "I guess I'm ready to go through it again."

"What are you crying about?"

Annice shrugged and swiped at her nose. "I don't know."

"Look, Nees, he's guilty." Stasya drained a mug of water, her voice rough from the recall. "Right out of his own mouth. If he'd just accepted that his stupid plan had failed and resigned himself to fate, none of the rest would have happened." She hated the very concept of defending Troop Captain Otik but found herself doing it anyway. "There was no more force used than was necessary to get him back to Elbasan and he created the need for every last bit of it himself."

"I'm not saying that he isn't guilty, Stas; I mean, no one can lie under Command. I just can't believe I was so wrong about him. I just didn't think Pjerin was the kind of man who'd break a sworn oath."

Stasya's memory ran through a kaleidoscopic review of Pjerin a'Stasiek, Duc of Ohrid, from the moment she'd first seen him scowling down at Captain Otik, through the countless attempts to escape on the trip to the capital, to the final image of him struggling to rise after being cut free of the horse by the palace stables and dumped like so much garbage to the ground. While he managed to remain both arrogant and abrasive even during the increasingly rough handling he'd received, she would've sworn that his pride came from a strong sense of self-worth based solidly in the real world and that he fought for more than just a chance to avoid death.

She looked up and met Annice's gaze. "If I didn't know better," she said heavily, "I wouldn't believe it of him myself."

"Your Grace?"

Pjerin shifted on the bench, enough so he could bring the doorway into the field of his good eye.

"My name is Damek i'Kamila." The middle-aged man stepped into the room and the heavy, reinforced door slammed shut behind him. "I'm a healer."

"You'll forgive me if I don't rise."

"Actually, I'm here to do something about that." He set the small leather bag he carried on the floor and frowned up at the gray light spilling through the one tiny window. "Well, it's not much, but as they wouldn't allow me to bring in a lantern it will have to do. I don't suppose you can slide down to the other end of the bench?"

In answer, Pjerin reached down beside him with his right hand and lifted his left onto his lap. Around the left wrist, he wore an iron manacle, attached by a short length of chain to an iron ring set into the stone wall.

Damek shook his head disapprovingly. "Yes, I see. Then I suppose this will suffice. Can you not move that arm on its own?"

"I can. But I'd rather not."

"Ribs broken?"

"You're the healer," Pjerin grunted, closing his eye. "You tell me."

"Yes. All right, then. Just give me a moment to prepare myself."

Pjerin listened to the other man's breathing fall into a slow, steady rhythm, each lungful very purposefully drawn in, each lungful very purposefully expelled and in spite of himself he began to relax. Although he flinched at the initial touch, he welcomed the warmth spreading out from under gentle fingers and, because he knew it was coming, he managed to bite down on the scream when a sudden burst of heat seared his side. It lasted only an instant and when it faded, most of the pain faded with it.

"Still broken," the healer told him as he opened his eye. "But all the pieces are aligned again and held and it should heal leaving no lasting disability. You know . . ." squatting, Damek opened his case and pulled out a small vial. ". . . there are those who believe that there's a type of kigh within the body and healers manipulate it much as bards manipulate the kigh of the elements. Let me tell you, young man, if that's true, you've got a powerful kigh tucked away in there. It practically grabbed hold of me and drained me dry." He thumbed the wax stopped off the vial and drank the contents in one long swallow. "Much better," he pronounced, standing. "Now then, let's have a look at that eye."

Pjerin allowed his head to be pushed gently around to the right. "How long?" he asked.

"How long what?" Damek muttered, peeling up the swollen lid and peering beneath it.

"How long will it take to heal?"

"What? Your ribs? Oh, a week. Maybe two. Nothing we do is entirely instantaneous no matter what people think. Now then ..." He pulled back enough so that Pjerin could see a reassuring smile. ". . . this may hurt a bit as well, but it should take the swelling down enough for you to use the eye. Fortunately, there doesn't appear to be any internal damage. Try not to jerk your head away."

The warning came a second too late, but the healer's grip was surprisingly strong. Pjerin felt as though his face were held in a warm vise while someone skewered left brow and cheek with a red-hot needle. Then it was gone. Breathing heavily, he blinked and found he was using both eyes.

Damek patted his shoulder apologetically. "Sorry. I guess you can see why most people with minor injuries tend to have us clean them up and then they let them heal on their own."

"And I'm not most people?"

"Not really. No." To cover his embarrassment, Damek ducked his head and closed up his bag.

"They're healing me to send me to the block."

"Yes. Well." The healer shrugged. "No reason to die in pain."

Pjerin sighed. "No," he said bitterly, "I suppose not."

"Do you want a priest sent in? To talk to?"

"No. Thank you."

Damek sighed, picked up his bag, and called for the guard. Then he paused in the open doorway. "If they offer you a chance to bathe before Judgment, I suggest you take it. It's amazing how being clean will help."

"With dying?" Pjerin laughed, a short harsh bark that held no humor. He turned and glowered at both healer and guard. "I broke no oaths. I *am* not a traitor."

The guard spat into the cell. Damek shook his head sadly and walked out of sight. The door swung closed, the iron bolt that held it hissing against iron brackets as it slid home.

*   *   *

"You're going where?"

"To the Judgment."

"Are you out of your mind?" Stasya leaped up from her chair, and ran around Annice to block the door, harp dangling from one outstretched hand. "What if His Majesty sees you?"

Annice frowned. "His Majesty will have enough on his mind without trying to figure out who's up on the bards' balcony."

"But suppose he does look up? What then?"

She shrugged. "He'll see a bard."

"Annice, you're his sister. I don't care how long it's been since he's treated you like one, you're not exactly an unfamiliar face!"

"Every bard in Elbasan will be there, Stas. He won't notice me."

Stasya sat her harp down and crossed her arms. "Great plan. Except that there's bugger all bards in Elbasan right now. They're all out Walking."

"All right." Annice sighed and shoved a fistful of her robe for inspection. "What color is this?"

Stasya's eyes narrowed but, uncertain of where Annice was leading the argument, she answered. "Brown."

"And why is it brown?"

"Because you're Singing earth now."

"And what color is my robe usually?"

"You mean the nonfestival robe you never wear? It's quartered. So what?"

"So if His Majesty does look up, he'll see a bard in a brown robe. I'm sure he knows *I* wear a quartered robe. He'll therefore have no reason to take a closer look. Will he?"

"This is really stupid."

"Stas, I'm going to go. Whether you like it or not."

And she was, too. Stasya recognized her expression and, short of physical restraints, could see no way to stop her. "Fine. Hang on till I get dressed. I'm going with you."

"I hate this sort of thing," Theron muttered, tugging at the high, embroidered collar wrapped about his throat.

Although she knew he referred to the upcoming Judgment and not his clothing, Lilyana reached up and adjusted the clasps. His Majesty's valet could deal with her later.

He caught her hand. She returned the pressure of his fingers, then pulled free.

"Majesty?" The page bowed in the open doorway. "They're ready now."

Theron nodded and squared his shoulders under the folds of heavy black velvet. The king was responsible for every sentence of death passed in Shkoder. There'd been a hundred and twenty since he'd taken the crown ten years before; four other attempts at treason, but most of them men and women who'd committed crimes so terrible that removing them became a necessary surgery for the greater good. Carrying them all, Theron walked slowly out to pick up the weight of the hundred and twenty-first.

Although the gleaming wooden benches in the bards' balcony weren't known for comfort, Annice sagged against the high back with a sigh of relief. She was finding it more and more difficult to negotiate such things as steep, narrow, spiral staircases—around and around and around on tiny wedge-shaped steps, unable to see her feet, the curve of her bulk barely fitting within the curve of the stone.

"What's wrong with stairs in straight lines?" she hissed at Stasya as the other bard sank down beside her.

"Spiral staircases take up less room," Stasya reminded her absently, gaze sweeping the crowds assembling below.

Annice sniffed. "That'd mean a lot more if *I* was taking up less room." She settled back and looked around. The last time she'd been on this balcony, she'd been one of the fledglings touring the parameters of their new lives. She hadn't been back in the ten years since. It seemed smaller than her memory of it.

Cut into the wall on the narrow end of the Great Assembly Hall, high above and behind the right side of throne, the balcony could hold a dozen bards comfortably and twice that if comfort was disallowed. At the moment, it held only Stasya and Annice.

"I guess no one else cared enough to come," Annice

growled, uncertain as to why she was so angry about it. If every bard in Shkoder had crammed onto the balcony, Pjerin would still be condemned to die.

"It's First Quarter," Stasya reminded her. "Every bard who can Sing is out Walking. Stay tucked up against the pillar. It'll block the angle of view from the throne if His Majesty does happen to glance up."

"I can't see as well from behind the pillar."

"And you can't be seen as well either," Stasya pointed out, shoving her so that she slid sideways over the polished wood and into the partially hidden position. "Please stay there."

Because it meant so much to Stasya—but *only* because it meant so much to Stasya—Annice gritted her teeth and decided to be gracious.

Down below, the thirty-two members of the Governing Council were filing in. Dressed in somber black, they moved quietly to stand before the two rows of wood and leather chairs set up at right angles to the throne. Annice recognized a few of them; they'd been on the Council in her father's day and had been passed down from reign to reign, their hard work and experience remaining in the service of Shkoder.

When all thirty-two had taken their places, a pair of guards in full ceremonial armor threw open the huge double doors at the other end of the Great Assembly Hall and the public surged in. This was an innovation of her brother's. Although the common courts had always been open, Royal Judgments had not as their royal father would have rather passed Judgment in a sheepfold than in front of his subjects. Newly a bard, Annice had listened to the criers call King Theron's first proclamation with amazement.

"Neither Death nor Mercy should come in secret. Any who wish to keep silent witness in the Death Judgment of Hermina i'Jelen to present themselves, weaponless, at the Citadel Gate tomorrow at noon."

Yesterday, the criers had called for those who wished to keep silent witness for Pjerin a'Stasiek, Duc of Ohrid.

Well, here I am. She laced her fingers into a protective barrier between her baby and the room below. *Here we are.* Although it was far from hot, damp patches spread out from under both arms.

A solid wall of bodies pressed up against the low wooden barricade that kept the citizens of Elbasan from spilling over into the actual area of the court. Neither as solemn nor as quiet as the Council, they were anxious to see this Duc of Ohrid—who'd intended to have them slaughtered in an unequal war—get the traitor's death he deserved.

Annice could feel the anger rising off of them, could almost see it beating against the molded plaster ceiling like a great black kigh. Heart pounding, she hoped Pjerin would be safe, that the anger wouldn't catch him up and dash him down in pieces. Then she called herself four kinds of fool because he'd be safe only to die.

Suddenly, the Bardic Captain stood before the throne. Instead of her quartered robe, she also wore black, her short hair like a cap of polished steel above it. Slowly, she swept her gaze over the huge room and where it touched, silence fell and spread. At last, she nodded and stepped to one side, her voice falling equally on every ear. "His Majesty, Theron, King of Shkoder, High Captain of the Broken Islands, Lord over the Mountain Principalities of Sibiu, Ohrid, Ajud, Bicaz, and Somes."

Annice started forward, then jerked to a stop even before Stasya's cautioning hand reached her arm. From behind the pillar, she watched the top of her brother's head come through a door in the wall below. *Well, at least he still has his hair.* Biting down hard on the terrifying urge to giggle, she couldn't believe that after ten years and under the present, potentially deadly circumstances she could have such a stupid reaction.

Chewing her lip, she watched Theron move slowly and deliberately around to the front of the throne. Just for an instant, she caught a glimpse of his face. Ten years under the crown had drawn lines around his eyes that hadn't been there before and something, perhaps the Judgment he was about to make, perhaps the Judgments he'd already made, had drawn the mouth she remembered as full, into a narrow, barely visible crease.

He took his seat and disappeared behind the high, carved back of the throne.

The Bardic Captain bowed to her king, then turned and called, "Pjerin a'Stasiek, Duc of Ohrid. Come forward for Judgment."

A small door opened about halfway down the left side of the Great Assembly Hall. Two of the King's Guard marched through, black plumes nodding on the top of ceremonial helmets. The accused followed, dressed in neutral gray, hands tied behind his back. Two more of the King's Guard brought up the rear. The guard's expressions were unreadable. The duc's could only be called defiant. All five marched to the center of the room and then the guards peeled off to stand two on each side of the throne, leaving Pjerin alone between the flanking rows of the Council. The muttering crowd at his back, he faced the Bardic Captain and beyond her, the king.

Annice stared down at him, tried to grab a single emotion out of the multitude she was feeling, and found herself clutching disbelief. No longer filthy and in pain, this man looked more like the Pjerin she remembered. Purple and yellow bruising still colored his face, but he stood straight, shoulders squared, ready to meet the enemy head to head. The Pjerin she remembered could not have done what he admitted doing. Her stomach twisted and a quick kick/punch made her catch her breath. *Right. And my judgment has been flawless lately. . . .* But the disbelief lingered.

Fighting to keep his breathing even, Pjerin glared at a point just over King Theron's shoulder. He supposed that the others who'd stood so exposed had been able to find strength in the inevitability of the Judgment. If they were here, they were guilty—Commanded, Witnessed, condemned. It only remained for the king to pass sentence. It only remained to die. He had no such support. He'd done nothing worthy of death and what was more, he had no idea of what his mouth would say when they put the question to him a second time. Perhaps, this time, he'd be able to speak the truth.

Pjerin dropped his gaze to the bard who faced him and recognized her from his only previous trip to Elbasan. She'd stood in much the same position when the newly crowned King Theron had taken his oaths of allegiance, witnessing his words and no doubt marking him then for the treachery that came to fruition now. The Bardic Captain would see to it that whatever ways Annice had twisted his mind, he would not be able to untwist them here. He allowed his mouth to curl into a sardonic smile and was pleased to see the captain's brows draw in. *How many words of denouncement could I speak before she silences me? And would His Majesty listen to any of them?*

He would draw his strength from the knowledge that he had done nothing worthy of death and they could take the rest of it and shove it right out of the Circle. Swallowing, he lifted his chin and clasped his fingers together hard lest they tremble and the crowd behind him think him afraid.

Annice saw the smile and wondered. Then she saw the swallow and wished she hadn't come. All the rest was bravado. He knew he was going to die.

Her face expressionless once again, the Bardic Captain took a deep breath and began to speak, her voice filling the huge room so exactly that there was no longer room for the muttering of the crowd.

"The oaths of allegiance that bind His Majesty and the lords who swear them are so sacred that the breach of them is the only offense irredeemable by law. From the acceptance of the sanctity of this plighted faith comes the belief of sanctity in all plighted faith. That whomsoever gives their word, be they ever so base, it shall hold.

"Pjerin a'Stasiek, Duc of Ohrid, step forward."

The step was ceremonial. It meant nothing as he already stood apart. He had no choice but to take it anyway.

"Pjerin a'Stasiek, Duc of Ohrid, you will speak only the truth."

Because there was nothing in the Command to stop him, he laughed.

Behind him, he heard the crowd growl; a single sound torn from a hundred throats. He could hear their impatience in it. Knew that if given a chance, they'd pronounce his sentence themselves, and he laughed again.

"Stop it."

Eyes still held by the Bardic Captain, he dipped head and shoulders as far as he was able in a mocking bow.

Cocky bugger. Long years of practice kept the thought from showing on Theron's face. *Just the type to think he could get away with something like this and then refuse to believe it when it turned out he couldn't. What a waste.*

What a stupid, pitiful waste. He shifted on the throne, that small movement silencing the crowds and drawing their attention as he knew it would. In a voice as neutral as he could make it, he asked, "Pjerin a'Stasiek, Duc of Ohrid, are you forsworn?"

NO!

"Yes."

And it began again. But this time, rage not terror fueled Pjerin's battle against the distance that separated the man he was from the man who spoke. Chest heaving, he strained against invisible bonds while words he couldn't control continued spilling from his mouth.

Feeling sick, Annice watched his struggle, hearing neither questions nor answers, barely conscious of Stasya's hand gripping hers. *Why are you so angry? Because you were discovered? Because you're about to die?* Either answer could easily be believed. Neither answer felt right. *Why, Pjerin, why?*

As though echoing her thoughts, Theron leaned slightly forward. "Why did you do it?"

For a heartbeat, the Great Assembly Hall fell perfectly quiet as everyone—Council, crowd, king—waited for the answer. This question was the king's alone and had not been asked before. Even Pjerin stilled, wondering what his reply would be.

"Power, wealth, attention; what have my oaths got me from Shkoder? Empty promises. Cemandia offered me a chance to be a part of something more than sheepshit and a drafty stone keep perched on a mountaintop." Listening to the reasons he gave for the treachery he hadn't committed, Pjerin couldn't help but agree with them, at least in part. The promises made three generations ago when the mountain principalities became a part of Shkoder had *not* been kept. Scowling, he tossed his head back as far as he was able and discovered that with the inner and outer man in agreement, the distance between them had been bridged for that instant. "Shkoder promised roads, Majesty; roads, healers, an end to isolation. Only your tax collectors have come." His voice grew harsher. "And your bards." But when he tried to continue, to accuse the bards of twisting his mind to speak the truth they desired, he found he'd lost control again.

Annice flinched back from the raw hatred. He *hadn't* felt that way. He'd been glad to see her, glad of the news she'd carried. He'd enjoyed her music. He'd left her alone with the son he'd clearly adored. The passion they'd shared had been, if nothing else, real passion. *I shouldn't have come. Why did I come?*

"Nees?"

She shook her head at Stasya's worried whisper. She shouldn't have come, but since she was here, she'd stay until the end.

A muscle jumped in Theron's jaw and his fingers were white on the arms of the throne. Roads took time to build. There weren't so many healers he could order a dozen here, a dozen there. How dare this arrogant young pup suggest his treason was Shkoder's fault. Slowly, he stood.

"Pjerin a'Stasiek, Duc of Ohrid, you stand accused of high treason against the crown and the people of Shkoder, your oaths forsworn. You have been condemned by your own mouth. Have you anything more to say?"

Pjerin knew what was expected. *I wouldn't beg for my life if I was guilty. I'll be unenclosed if I beg when I'm not.* He shook his head.

"Then I, Theron, King of Shkoder, High Captain of the Broken Islands, Lord over the Mountain Principalities of Sibiu, Ohrid, Ajud, Bicaz, and Somes, do on this day declare you guilty of high treason. As of this moment, your titles, lands, and responsibilities pass unencumbered to your son, Gerek a'Pjerin, now Duc of Ohrid. Tomorrow, noon, your life is forfeit. Witness."

The Bardic Captain, who had been standing, eyes locked on the eyes of the accused, the eyes of the condemned, took a step back. "Witnessed," she said.

Pjerin, free of all constraints save the bindings around his wrists, turned his head the fraction necessary to meet the King's eyes for the first time since the questioning began, a wild hope rising unbidden. *Surely, he'll see. Surely, he'll know.* But there would be no sudden realization by the king, no power inherent in his position to see past the surface to the heart. In spite of oaths and loyalties and a golden crown, Pjerin saw the king was just a man.

"Done."

Standing in the shadowed recess of an open window, Annice watched the sun as it rose into position directly overhead. Noon.

The block had been in place before dawn. She knew that because she'd been waiting at this window since sunrise. No one knew she was here. She'd slipped away from Stasya and into the palace using the secret ways she'd discovered on childhood explorations. It hadn't been hard to find an empty room overlooking the small courtyard. It seemed that all the rooms overlooking the small courtyard were empty.

Stasya's probably having fifty fits. She'd apologize later. It was important she be here even if she'd rather be *anywhere* else.

She checked the sun again. It had to happen soon. She didn't think she could bear to wait much longer. She didn't want to think of how Pjerin had spent his morning. His last morning.

A tall, black shape separated itself from the shadows on the far side of the courtyard. Loose tunic, breeches, and the encompassing hood made it impossible to determine if it was man or woman but the broad-bladed ax it held left no question of its purpose. It walked slowly toward the block and a body length away, paused.

A body length away. Someone has a sick sense of humor. She found it suddenly difficult to breathe and had to turn away for a moment and face the empty room instead. When she looked back out the window, the courtyard had filled with guards and Pjerin had nearly reached the block.

He was frightened; she could read it in the bravado that made his walk a swagger.

Desperately, she searched for the king. Theron would be there. The law insisted the king witness the carrying out of his Judgments in order that he never make them lightly.

There! Theron stood almost directly across from her. If she called his name and he looked up, he couldn't help but see her. If she called his name. . . .

Annice wet her lips. One word. That was all it would take. One word.

Pjerin was kneeling now, shirt pulled down across his shoulders. Some time during the night, they'd cut his hair. Cut off all his beautiful hair and exposed his neck for the ax.

He frowned, as though he felt the weight of her gaze, and slowly turned his head.

She almost cried out as his eyes met hers.

"Annice!" His voice echoed against the encircling walls.

All heads but one turned to stare up at her.

The figure in black stepped forward.

"Annice!" She had never heard a curse spoken with the venom Pjerin put into her name. "This is all *your* fault."

Then the ax came down.

"Nees! Annice! Wake up!"

Clutching at Stasya's bare shoulders and gasping for breath, Annice fought her way free of the dream. It had been so terribly, horribly real. She could still feel the stone of the windowsill beneath her fingers, the ache in her legs from standing, waiting for so long. Could still see the spray of blood and hear her name called one last time as Pjerin's head rolled across the courtyard.

"Are you okay, Nees?"

"I, I don't know." She leaned into the light as Stasya lit the lamp with flint and steel.

"Nees, you're crying." Brow furrowed with concern, Stasya drew her fingertips over Annice's cheeks. "You were dreaming about him, weren't you?"

She nodded. "There's something wrong, Stas. Something very, very wrong."

Stasya sighed. "I don't feel exactly great about it either, Nees. But there's nothing we can do." She watched, propped on one elbow, as Annice sat up and swung her legs out from under the blanket. "We've hardly been in bed for any time at all, you can't possibly need to go down the hall again."

"I'm not going down the hall." Her mind suddenly made up, Annice reached for her clothes. "I'm going to go talk to Pjerin."

CHAPTER EIGHT

"Annice, you are *out* of your mind."

Annice, on her knees in the potato bin, probed at the floor with a knife borrowed from the kitchen and ignored Stasya. Fortunately, because of the season, the bin was nearly empty and it had been relatively easy to clear sections of the floor.

"Nees, are you listening to me?" Stasya sighed and rolled her eyes. Stupid question. "Look, you can't just waltz into the palace dungeons and sit down for a heart-to-heart with a man who's going to be executed for treason in a matter of hours."

"So you keep saying." Annice ran the knife along a joining, gouging years of dirt and grunge out of the crack. "Here it is. You'll have to get it up for me." She glanced up at the other woman. "Before he left, Jazep warned me to avoid heavy lifting."

Muttering under her breath, Stasya set the lamp on the edge of the bin and crouched down, allowing Annice to guide her fingers under the hidden lip. "The last thing I should do is help you with this." Slowly, she straightened her legs and a square black hole opened up in the floor. Leaning the trapdoor against the wall, she stared down into the darkness. "What kind of an idiot starts a secret passage in a potato bin?"

"It's a secret, Stas, it's not supposed to be out in the open."

"It's a secret, Stas ..." she mocked, then quickly sobered. "Nees, are you sure you know what you're doing?"

"I'm sure." Annice picked up a small horn lantern and lit it from the lamp. "No one knows these passageways like I do. Sometimes it seemed like I spent half my childhood in them."

"Yeah, okay, so you know the passageways, but are you sure you should be talking to ..."

"Yes."

"You can't *do* anything, Nees. He's going to die."

"Yes. I know." Leaning forward, Annice kissed the other woman lightly. "Don't worry. I'll be careful."

Stasya watched as Annice maneuvered her bulk through the hole and climbed carefully down the ladder. When she reached the bottom, she looked up, almost smiled, then disappeared.

Not until the darkness lapped against the edges of the hole and she could no longer convince herself that she could still see a glimmer of light from the lantern, did Stasya gently close the trapdoor. "Don't worry," she snorted, blowing out the lamp and making herself as comfortable as possible. "Yeah. Right."

Shoulders brushing the walls on either side, Annice moved quickly along the narrow passageway. She hadn't been exactly truthful with Stasya. While she had no doubt she could find her way through the secret routes that honeycombed the walls of the palace, she'd followed the tunnel to the Bardic Hall only once and could no longer remember where the other end began. Hopefully, she'd be able to get her bearings when she arrived.

The lantern flickered and she shielded it with her body as she slid past the opening to another tunnel. From the darkness, she heard the scrabbling of small claws on stone.

Although she knew the rats were unlikely to bother her, she quickened her pace, practically squatting to keep her head from scraping against the low arch of the ceiling. In her memory, the ceiling was higher and the distance between Bardic Hall and the palace not so great.

What else have I forgotten? It's been ten years. Maybe Stasya's right and this is a stupid idea.

She passed two other branches, then the tunnel she followed curved hard to the right.

I don't remember this. Should I have turned?

Something brushed by her foot. She decided not to look down.

Then, just at the edge of the light, she saw a narrow

flight of stairs. Legs aching, more than ready to straighten, she climbed carefully to the top and looked around. A narrow stone passageway, hung with cobwebs and smelling of dust and disuse, stretched off in both directions. Nothing seemed familiar. Not even the darkness.

She probed as far to the left and to the right as she could, arm extended, lantern dangling from her fingertips. Still nothing. There were stories about people who'd gotten lost between the walls, unable to find their way out, wandering hopelessly until hunger and thirst brought a final end to their search. The stories hadn't bothered her as child, she didn't know why she was thinking about them now.

Moistening lips gone dry, she turned right and started walking, her eyes straight ahead, avoiding the shadows. She didn't have the time to indulge her imagination. Pjerin didn't have the time.

Barely ten paces from the tunnel mouth, she came to another t-junction. On the wall, almost hidden under the dust, was chalked a cursive A. Inscribed under it, *kit* and an arrow pointing right.

Murmuring thanks to her younger self, Annice hurried toward the kitchens. From there, she could find any room in the palace.

... life is forfeit ...
... at noon ...

This couldn't be happening. It couldn't be real. It was a long, incredibly involved dream. He'd wake up, just as the ax came down, sweating, panting, and swearing he'd never touch Zofka's mead again.

The short length of chain rattled as Pjerin shifted position, the weight dragging at his wrist. Fist clenched, he jerked his arm forward, the iron links snapping taut between the manacle and the wall. He wouldn't give his word that he'd not try to escape when they'd brought him back to his cell. It had taken three of them to secure him.

This was no dream. The pain in wrist, ribs, heart was too real. The terror was too real. The anger was too real.

He wasn't ready to die.

His arm dropped back to his side, the chain collapsing

in on itself. Dying meant never seeing Gerek again. Right now, more than anything, he wanted to hold his son. Wanted to hear him laugh. It wasn't fair that he should lose all the years they could have had together. He wondered how long it would take Gerek to forget him. Why would he want to remember a father who'd died a traitor's death?

Exhaustion kept him from howling in frustration and rage. Tears prickled against the inside of his lids, spilled over, and burned paths down both cheeks. Perhaps he *should* have begged a private audience with the king, told him what the bards had done, warned him that his kingdom was being eaten away from within. But then, why would he listen?

It was impossible to lie under Command.

And I'll pitch myself right out of the Circle before I beg for anything.

Teeth clenched, Pjerin scrubbed at his face with his free hand. At least when they told Gerek of his death, they'd have to tell him that his father died bravely.

A sound at the door of his cell snapped his head around. It was still the middle of the night, barely hours into the new day; what did they want with him now? He heard the bar drawn back, then the door slowly opened.

To his surprise, the corridor was as dark as the cell.

"Who's there?" His hoarse whisper sounded unnaturally loud and, rather than an answer, it brought movement. Someone slipped inside, pulled the door shut behind them, and remained standing just over the threshold.

"Pjerin. . . ?"

It was a woman, the voice vaguely familiar.

"It's Annice."

Fury flung him to his feet, heart beating with such force he could hardly breathe around it. Stopped short by the chain before he could close his hands about her throat and squeeze the truth out of her, he tossed his hair back off his face and closed his fists on air instead. "Come to gloat, have you?" he asked, amazed at how restrained he sounded.

Annice frowned. She'd expected anger—it was the active side of despair—but she couldn't understand why it was directed at her. "I came because I needed to talk to you."

"Why?" Was this the payoff, then? Had she come to offer him his life in return for ... for what? He still couldn't understand what game the bards were playing, nor was he willing to play along. They'd manipulated him as far as they were going to. *I'll die first.*

"Because ... well, because ..." The baby rolled and kicked. She traced the motion with her fingertips and decided to just say it. "Because I don't believe you betrayed anything."

Pjerin stared into the darkness and then he started to laugh.

It was a wild, almost vicious noise and Annice wanted to Command him to stop but, listening to the pain and fear that ran beneath it, she waited silently instead. The guards were at the far end of the hall on the other side of an iron-banded door and, with the cell door pulled closed as well, they wouldn't hear.

And considering the cells they guarded, they'd probably heard worse.

Staggering back, Pjerin sank down on the bench and buried his head in his hands. "You don't believe I did it?" he managed to choke out at last. "Center it, that's priceless."

This wasn't going at all the way Annice had imagined. "What are you talking about?"

He lifted his head and smiled. They thought he'd be panicking by now, ready to do anything to avoid the block. They didn't know he was onto them. "When did you do it, Annice? When did you put the words into my head? Afterward, when I was sleeping? Or during, when I was concentrating on other things?"

She opened her mouth and closed it again, unable to find the words to answer him.

Leaning back against the wall, Pjerin wished he could see her face. "You can't lie under Command," he said mockingly. "Did you think I'd believe your lies over my own memory? That I wouldn't figure out what you'd done?"

"What I'd done?" Annice repeated. "Pjerin, I don't understand."

Had she not been a bard, he would have believed her.

But a bard could easily layer that kind of confusion onto her voice. "What I would like to know," he continued, "is *why* you're doing all this. Lay your cards on the table so I can tell you to stuff them up your ass."

He'd taken a number of blows to the head on the way in from the mountains—the bruising she'd seen stood testimony to that—perhaps one of them had shaken his brain loose. "You think that *I* put those words into your head? That *I* did something to you so that you'd admit to treason? That *I* want you dead?"

It was Pjerin's turn to frown at an unexpected response. "You. The bards. What difference does it make?"

Annice tried to drag her thoughts around into some kind of order. "You think the bards did this to you?" She didn't wait for an answer. "Why?"

"Who else could wander through a man's mind and change his thoughts?" His lip curled. "It's just a small step from Command, isn't it?"

Forcing herself to consider it objectively, she supposed it was, although she'd never heard of the step being taken. "But *why?*" she repeated.

"How should I know!" Pjerin slammed his free palm down on the bench. "You tell me; you're the story-teller."

"Al right." Annice took a deep breath. "You keep insisting that you're innocent even though you know that it's impossible to lie under Command. This makes you either so stupidly arrogant that you can't believe you've been found out—which, by the way, is what everyone else seems to think—or . . ." Or he didn't actually do it, and it *was* possible to lie under Command and one of the foundations of the kingdom had just been swept to sea. Annice suddenly understood why no one else found it difficult to reconcile Pjerin's personality with what he was accused of doing. The consequences of believing him innocent were just too immense to deal with.

"Or?" Pjerin prodded stiffly. So everyone thought him stupidly arrogant. Well, he didn't give a rat's ass for what everyone thought.

"Or . . ." If she said it, then she made it possible. If she didn't say it, she had no reason to be here and she might as well let him die in peace. "Or, somehow, you were made to lie under Command."

"So you admit it?"

"I'm not admitting anything!" He was beginning to make her angry. "Can we look at this logically? Please?" When he made no answer to her sarcastic plea, she continued. "Someone changed what you think of as the truth. Because we do similar sorts of things, it could have been a bard. But I'm the only bard who's been near you in over a year and I *know* I didn't do it."

He snorted, the sound an eloquent expression of disbelief. "Easy to say."

Annice jerked forward a step; a pointless movement in the complete darkness, but she couldn't stay still. "Look, asshole," she hissed through clenched teeth. "I'm willing to believe you didn't do it. I'm willing to believe something or someone made you lie under Command. But unless you start meeting me halfway, and *considering* the possibility that I had nothing to do with it, I'm out of here and you can . . . well, you can *die*. Do I make myself clear?"

Flung across the cell at him, the words held no bardic artifice. Pjerin shook his head, confused and unable to hold onto his certainty. "But if it wasn't you, then it wasn't a bard. Then who. . . ?"

"Obviously someone who wants you dead." She wiped damp palms on the thighs of her breeches. It seemed that she no longer had any doubts. And that left only one logical action. "I'd ask who you've pissed off lately, but there isn't time for the list if we're going to get you out of the city before dawn."

"What?"

Annice sighed and spoke very slowly. "I don't believe you did it. Therefore, I can't just let you die. So I'm going to get you out of here. Sit quietly for a minute, I'll be right back." She groped behind her for the edge of the door, pushed it open, and reached around the doorframe.

Pjerin heard the door open and was suddenly terrified she'd left. "What are you doing?"

She turned her head toward him just long enough to snap, "Shut up!", then continued her search. *If they've moved it . . .* But they hadn't. She pulled the door closed again. "I was just getting the key to the manacle."

"Oh." This was all happening just a little too fast. A

very short time ago, he'd been standing alone against the world, preparing himself for death. Now, all of a sudden, the person he'd thought responsible had turned up to offer him life. "And I suppose they leave the key hanging on a hook just outside the door?"

"That's right." Holding it tightly in her right hand, she stretched out her left and slid her feet across the floor. The last thing she wanted to do was to bump into Pjerin and have him jump to conclusions about the child she carried. "No reason why they shouldn't. *You* can't get to it."

That made sense. At least it made as much sense as anything else that had happened lately. "Annice, why didn't you believe I did it? Because of the night we spent together?"

She snorted, brushed her reaching fingers against his head, and quickly sidestepped to the back wall of the cell. "Don't flatter yourself, although I suppose that was part of it." From the ring, she found the chain and began tracing it to his wrist. "Don't move. This is going to be hard enough in the dark." Where was Tadeus when she needed him. "I took my memory of the man you were and I held it up against the man you appeared to be under Command and they didn't match."

"But all your training says that the man under Command is the true man."

"Yeah. So?"

Pjerin found himself honestly amused for the first time since he'd seen the distant group of travelers working their way up the valley. "And they're calling *me* stupidly arrogant."

The key turned with a metallic snick and the manacle fell open. Annice managed to snag it before it crashed into the floor, closed it again, and tucked it up into the corner. She rose awkwardly to her feet and moved away. "Come on. We're running out of time."

Pjerin stood, rubbing his wrist. "Come on where? Do we just waltz out past the guards? Are you going to Command them to look the other way?"

"There's a secret passageway between the last two cells in this row."

"How do you know that?"

"I'm a bard. We know everything."

Partway to the door, Pjerin stopped dead. "You'll forgive me if I'm suspicious but, all things considered, I think I have reason. I want a real answer."

"You're getting your life ..."

"I want a real answer."

"What difference does it make?"

"I'm tired of lies!"

"You'd rather die?"

"I'd rather know the truth!"

"You want the truth?" Annice threw her hands in the air and raked the cell with a glare she wished Pjerin could see. "I know where the passage is because I grew up in the palace. Surely you've heard the song of the Princess-Bard? All twenty-seven unenclosed verses of it? Now, can we go?"

He didn't know what he'd been expecting, but that wasn't it. "You're King Theron's youngest sister? Then why didn't you just go to him when ..."

"Look, we don't talk, okay?"

"Not even for this?"

"I have my reasons. Can we discuss them later? Or would you rather discuss it with *him* on your way to the block?"

He felt warm fingers close around his and pull him forward. Still half expecting a trap, he stepped out of the cell. A glimmer of light showed under the door at the far end of the corridor, but other than that, the darkness remained absolute. His skin crawled as he realized that a hundred guards could be standing a sword's length away and he'd never know. An imperious hand pressed him up against the wall and left him there. Straining pointlessly to see, he heard the door close and the bar slide back across it followed by the faint chime of metal against stone as Annice—*Annice, the king's youngest sister. This is getting stranger by the moment.*—replaced the key. Then the fingers found his again and he followed their direction down the hall.

This has all the elements of one terrific song. Pulling Pjerin along behind her, Annice swept the wall with her free hand, searching for the entrance to the secret passage that she'd left slightly ajar. *Let's just hope I survive long enough to sing it.* She bit her lip as the baby kicked an enthusiastic endorsement. *What am I going to tell him about. . . ?* At that moment, she stubbed her fingers on the protruding lip of stone and gratefully dropped the thought for more immediate concerns.

Tucking Pjerin up against the wall once more, she forced the block of stone around on stiff pivots. When she'd opened it originally, she'd been amazed that the tortured rasp hadn't brought the guards running. This time, she was only surprised that they hadn't yet responded to the deafening pounding of her heart, filling the corridor like the beat of a kettle drum. A quick swipe behind her found Pjerin's sleeve. She grabbed at the cloth, dragged him forward and, at the last instant before shoving him through the opening, reached up and yanked his head down—unfortunately, given the soft impact of flesh against stone, not quite far enough.

Biting back a curse, Pjerin shook himself free of her grip and tried the entrance again, this time guiding himself under the low lintel. He was relieved to find he could straighten once he was actually in the passageway and, rubbing at the rising lump on his forehead, he wondered how much longer they were going to spend in the dark. He took four paces, then paused, listening to Annice fight the block of stone back into place.

King Theron's sister. He'd heard the song about the Princess-Bard, years ago, and couldn't remember much of it; something romantic and asinine about her becoming a bard in spite of royal opposition. *She seems to be making a habit of defying the king.*

In spite of the darkness, he knew the moment the passageway was secure. The walls, already barely clearing his shoulders, began to close in. The air grew thicker and his breathing sounded loud in his ears.

"Well?" he whispered.

"Well what?"

"What about a light?"

Annice picked the lantern down off the ledge where she'd set it for safekeeping and thought about denying she had it with her. Unfortunately, they'd never find their way out in the dark. Because there wasn't anything else she *could* do, she fumbled for flint and steel, unwilling to risk fire not answering her Song.

Pjerin closed his eyes as the lantern flared, reasonably certain that she hadn't tried to blind him on purpose. Turning his back to the flame, he opened them a crack, then, with most of the light blocked by his body, opened them the rest of the way. Cobwebs hung like the ghosts of tapestries against the walls, torn and tattered by Annice's earlier passage. He glanced down at his shoulders, saw he already wore the life's work of several spiders and decided not to bother brushing them clean. Better to unwrap them, like a winding sheet, when freedom was finally achieved.

"All right." Pjerin pivoted back around to face her. "Where to n ..." It took a moment for the full implications of what he saw to sink in.

"I came because I needed to talk to you. I'm willing to believe you didn't do it. I'm willing to believe something or someone made you lie under Bardic Command."

"But all your training says that the man under Bardic Command is the true man."

"I can't just let you die."

He hadn't asked her why. Why did she believe in him when everything she *should* believe in said he was guilty? He was suddenly afraid he knew the answer. It was the first detail in a long time that made perfect sense.

"Annice, is ... I mean, you're ... and we ..." This was ridiculous. He wasn't some teenager presented with the evidence of a Second Quarter Festival too enthusiastically enjoyed. "Am I the father?"

Annice watched emotions rise and fade and rise again on Pjerin's face as he realized and reacted to her pregnancy. It wasn't hard to guess what he was thinking—that everything she'd done, everything she believed about him had its root in the paternity of her child. *As though my womb's making decisions for me. All that matters is that he's the father. What an ego.* She didn't have to tell him. She knew she could make him accept a lie.

"Annice. *Am* I the father?"

"Yes." As the word left her mouth she knew for that instant how Pjerin had felt listening to himself speaking without conscious control under Command. *When did I decide to tell him?*

He nodded grimly. "This changes everything."

Annice snapped her fingers, lifting his gaze up off her belly. "How many times *did* they hit you on the head?"

"What are you talking about?"

"This changes nothing."

"You're carrying my child."

"You're due to die at noon." She thrust her chin toward him, daring him to dispute her. "I'd like to *at least* have you out of the palace by then. Turn around and start walking."

Caught up in the discovery of a new life, he'd forgotten that he was due to lose his own. He frowned as the thought snagged on a memory. *"... and if you dare a new life/then you're doomed to lose your own ..."* Why were bits of bad doggerel suddenly chasing themselves around in his head? And then he remembered. "Does His Majesty know about this?"

"I already told you, we don't talk."

"This baby, it's treason."

"You're hardly one to point fingers."

"Annice!" he grabbed her shoulders and hurriedly released her when her expression picked up an unpleasant edge. "How could you do this?"

"As I recall, I didn't do it alone."

"*I* didn't know what *I* was doing."

"Then you're obviously a fast learner because you certainly seemed fully aware of where everything went."

His face darkened. "Don't twist my words. I've had enough of that."

Shadows seemed to crowd around the flickering light from the lamp. Annice stared at the tiny flame dancing lifelessly on the oil-soaked wick then looked up and met Pjerin's eyes. There were deeper shadows there.

"I'm sorry." She took a deep breath. "Look, I decided to keep this baby. I decided to take the risk. I'll face the consequences."

"But you won't face them alone. How many treasons can His Majesty forgive? The treason of the child. Of the child's father. Of tonight."

Annice had been doing her best not to think about that.

"If you'd been any other bard," Pjerin continued, his eyes holding hers, "you'd have gone to your captain with your suspicions and then the two of you would have gone to the king. This is too important for a midnight visit to a condemned man's cell. Why didn't you, Annice? Because you're carrying treason around in your belly and the punishment for treason is death. We *both* know that."

"So you're free and he won't know. The only problem I see now is the time we're wasting. Turn around and start walking."

"Not until I have your word you'll come with me."

"What?"

Pjerin folded his arms over his chest. "I'm not leaving without my child."

"You're crazy."

"He'll find out. Soon or later. Frankly, I'm amazed no one's told him already. He'll want to know who the father is, and when you refuse to tell him he'll put you under Command. When he knows I'm the father, he'll ask you how I escaped. It's treason times three, Annice. What do you think he'll do?"

She turned her head away.

"You know what you believe. If you didn't, you'd have gone to him."

She didn't really believe Theron would execute her and her baby. Did she? Then why was she stumbling about between the walls of the palace in the middle of the night? "I'm *not* going with you." That much she *was* sure of.

"I'm not going without you."

"Oh?" Lip curling, she faced him again. "What're you going to do? Go manacle yourself to the wall and wait for the block?"

"Why not? It lifts one treason off you—maybe with me dead, His Majesty will be merciful."

"Maybe with you dead, His Majesty will decide to complete the set."

"Either you give me your word you'll come with me, or I'm going back to that cell."

"You wouldn't."

"I would."

He would, too; she could hear it in his voice. "This is insane!"

"You're the one holding us up."

"I'm not waddling all over the country with you."

"And I'm not leaving without my child, so I'm not leaving without you."

"You'd rather die?"

"Than risk the life of my innocent child? Yes!"

"Oh, very noble!" What had she ever seen in this man? "All right, all right, I'll go with you!" Anything to get him moving. Once she got him to Bardic Hall, he wouldn't be able to *find* his cell again.

Pjerin smiled. "Swear."

"Why?"

He sighed. "Stupidly arrogant, I might be. Just plain stupid, I'm not. Swear."

"Okay, I swear on my mother's grave."

"Nice try, but I *have* been to court; the late queen was cremated and her ashes scattered, there isn't a grave. Swear on your music."

If she swore on her music, her word would bind her. If she didn't, Pjerin would die and she'd have to face his child knowing she could've saved him.

Eyes narrowed, she snarled, "I swear on my music. Happy?"

"Yes. Now, let's get out of here. Tell me when I have to turn."

Following Pjerin down the passageway, Annice fought the urge to Sing his pants alight. Unfortunately, that sort of reaction had been covered under a previous oath. And the way things were going, the kigh probably wouldn't answer.

"What took you so long?" Stasya growled as she yanked the trapdoor open. "The servers are going to be awake any minute."

Annice passed the lantern up and began to awkwardly mount the ladder. "I ran into a bit of a complication."

"What does that mean?" reaching down, Stasya tucked a hand into the other woman's armpit and lifted. "You couldn't find the cell? You had to subdue a guard? You had to convince His Grace you couldn't take him with you? What?"

Breathing heavily, Annice sagged against the wall of the potato bin. "You were closest on the last one."

"Closest? Oh, Nees . . . you didn't."

Pjerin, twisted diagonally to fit his shoulders through the opening, came up out of the tunnel like an ancient god of the underworld. His eyes were deep pools of shadow, the lantern flame reflecting as a single gleam of

gold. Brilliant white teeth were bared as he fought to
free himself from the confining stone. When he tossed
his head, he tossed a mane of darkness, barely separated
from the night around him.

Stasya broke free of the image with a curse—although
she tucked it and the minor chords accompanying it
away for future reference. Inspiring the greatest song in
bardic history wouldn't be enough to make this reality
any more palatable. "Annice! Are you out of your mind!
I thought you were just going to *talk* to him."

"I did. And talking convinced me that he couldn't
have done what he's accused of. Once I believed that, I
couldn't let him die."

She should've seen this coming. She should've put her
foot down right at the start. "Nees, this belief of yours is
based on air. The fact is, you can't lie under Command."

Annice snorted. "The fact is, I don't believe he did
it!"

"So your emotional response wipes out centuries of
historical precedent?"

"Yes. You said yourself that selling out seemed at
odds with his character."

"So?"

"So if there's even the slightest chance he's innocent,
we can't let him die."

"*We* can't?" Stasya sighed, and turned to Pjerin. Over
the brooding shadow, she laid her memory of the horrified disbelief she'd seen in his eyes when his mouth had
spoken the words that had first condemned him. "Oh,
all right," she snapped, "we can't." She scooped the lantern off the floor and handed it to Annice. "Light this
off the lamp and let's get out of here. I refuse to commit
treason in a potato bin."

"Wait." While Pjerin realized that Stasya had in no
way been responsible for what had happened under her
Command, she brought back memories of the trip down
the mountain—memories he would rather have not had
to confront. He found himself uncomfortable in her presence and he had no intention of following her blindly.
"Where are we going?"

"Our rooms, I think." Annice handed the lantern back
to Stasya and blew out the lamp. Losing the ability to
confidently Sing fire was an irritating inconvenience. "No

one will find it odd to hear voices from there in the middle of the night."

"No."

"Stasya, I gave him my word."

"Tough. You're not going."

"I'm not going without her."

Stasya whirled around and Pjerin stepped back a pace. "Fine. Die, then. But you're not taking her with you."

"I'm not leaving her here."

"In case you haven't noticed, *Your Grace*, she's seven months pregnant."

"With my child."

"Your child?" Stasya glared at him. "Oh, so *you* were the one puking *your* guts out from Ohrid to Elbasan. *You're* the one on the pot every second breath. *You're* the one who spent the last four months being poked and prodded by healers. *You're* the one who gets heartburn so bad you turn blue, screaming pains in your hips and butt, and nosebleeds every other sniffle. And *you're* the one who hasn't gotten a decent night's sleep for the last three months. And here I thought *she's* been going through all that." She swept a gesture over Annice on the appropriate pronoun, then stood, arms crossed over her chest, eyes narrowed, lip curled in a disdainful sneer. "*Your* child, my ass. You may have fathered it, but you don't own it."

"I'm thinking of its safety."

"And what about Annice's safety?"

Pjerin managed to keep a fingernail's grip on his temper. "She'll be in danger if she stays behind."

"She'll be in more danger if she goes with you, you moron! You don't honestly think the king will execute his own sister, do you?"

"Yes. And so do you, or you'd have convinced her to take her suspicions to the king."

Annice swallowed the mouthful of black bread she'd been chewing. As much as she'd been enjoying the argument, the time had come to put an end to it. "We're *not* going to the king—but not for my sake, for Pjerin's. We have no proof he didn't commit the treason he admitted to. His Majesty won't want to believe in the possibility of lying under Command, Stas, no more than you do. The difference is, you love me and you're willing to take a chance on what I believe. He won't be. Pjerin'll end up back in his cell, and I'll ..." She sighed. "How many treasons can Theron forgive, Stas? I don't want to risk it. Besides, I'm the only chance Pjerin has of getting away."

"What? He's going to hide behind you?" Stasya threw both hands into the air. "Maybe we should steal him a horse; you could hide them both."

"Stas, how would you hunt for someone you can describe in detail?"

She shrugged. "I'd ask the kigh."

"You'd ask the *air* kigh," Annice corrected. "Because water is confined and fire is self-absorbed and earth keeps its own council. Only air has enough curiosity to be of any use in something like that."

"Yeah, well, I'd also ask air because that's all I Sing but I get your point." She jerked her chin at Pjerin. "The moment he steps out of a building, or even too close to a window, they'll spot him."

"I can change how I look," Pjerin grunted, pulling at the gray Judgment clothing like he wanted to begin the change immediately. "Cut my hair, grow a beard ..."

"Change the color of your eyes? The way you speak? The way you move?" Stasya snorted. "The captain herself has you on recall from the Judgment. You couldn't change enough to fool the kigh."

"But the air won't go near me. Tadeus said they're so jealous of me Singing earth that they're going out of their way to ignore me and anyone with me." Annice spread her hands. "If I go with him, he has a chance to stay free long enough to find out who did this to him and how. And we have to find that out, Stas, before it happens again and someone dies."

"I'll have to have a bard for that." Pjerin suddenly realized it himself. "I'll have to have someone who can try to get behind the lies."

Stasya ignored him. She slipped to her knees by the side of Annice's chair and gathered both the other woman's hands into hers. "Nees, love, it's too dangerous. You'll be on the run, living the life of a fugitive. You can't expose yourself, or the baby, to that kind of risk."

"So do I just let an innocent man die?" Annice tightened her fingers. "I can't do that, Stas. You can't either."

"Then I should come with you."

"You have to cover our tracks."

"But you're only two months from delivery."

"A lot can happen in two months."

"Maybe if you convinced the captain . . ."

"That it's possible to lie under Command? We'd have more luck convincing the king."

"Fine."

"No."

"He's your brother, Nees."

Annice pulled Stasya's hand forward until it rested under hers and pressed against the movement of the baby. "And he's the one who said that *this* is death."

Stasya laid her head on what remained of Annice's lap. "You're right," she admitted. "I hate it when that happens." She rubbed her cheek gently against the knee of Annice's breeches. When she continued, the clipped and matter-of-fact tones rang out in direct contrast to her position. "Well, after Vidor you can take to the countryside and there won't be enough people in all of Shkoder to find you, but getting to Vidor means the River Road, and that means we'll have to hide you in plain sight. How much money do you have?"

"I've been Singing earth for the city gardens."

"Good. I haven't had a chance to spend anything in months, so if we pool our coin, you should have enough. There's enough junk in the cellars to turn the two of you into a fairly believable pair of traders, but we'll have to hurry—we can't pull this off if you're not out of the Citadel by dawn."

"What are you talking about?" Pjerin growled. "Why are we going to Vidor?"

"We're not," Annice told him, her fingers stroking the velvet nap of Stasya's dark hair. "We're going to Ohrid. You told me that you haven't been farther into Shkoder than Lake Marienka in years, so if we're going to find out who's done this to you, we're going to have to look closer to home."

CHAPTER NINE

"Can't you move any faster?"

Annice shifted the straps of her pack and wished she was back in bed with Stasya curled up warm and protecting around her. "No. I can't. And you'll just attract attention if you try to hustle me along."

Unable to see around the edges of his much larger pack, Pjerin swiveled from side to side, trying desperately to pierce the surrounding shadows—there could be a guard in any one of them. Six times he'd escaped on the way to Elbasan, six times they'd captured him again. He wasn't going back to that cell. "The longer we stay on the streets," he ground out through clenched teeth, ignoring the pain from newly stressed ribs, "the more attention we attract."

"Not if you'll stop acting like a fugitive." Her voice which had been pitched for Pjerin's ears alone, shifted slightly to cover a broader audience. "And I don't care how much you think you can make in Vidor, profits are less important than the health of your unborn child!"

Pjerin started, glared at her, followed her line of sight, and glared at the guard on the bridge.

"And furthermore," Annice continued, beginning to enjoy the performance a little in spite of the circumstances, "you have no business making bets with your cousin that involve me. Leaving Elbasan in the middle of the night, indeed. We'll be in Riverton before the sun's even up. Pay the toll."

"What?"

She sighed. "The toll. Remember? Oh, never mind." As she rummaged in her belt pouch, she looked directly into the guard's eyes and favored him with a smile. "He's the hardest man to get coin out of I've ever met, **believe me**."

The guard, wisely deciding to stay out of what looked to be a nasty domestic battle in the making, stepped silently aside.

"Was that absolutely necessary?" Pjerin growled a few moments later when they had River Road to themselves again. "Why couldn't we slip quietly out of the city by a back way?"

"What did you have in mind, swimming the canal?" A deliberate waddle thrown into her walk emphasized the protruding curve of her belly. "Frankly, I don't think I'm up to it."

"Then why the bullshit? Why not tell the guard to forget he ever saw us?"

"He'd remember me doing it if they put him under Command. This way, he'll only remember two traders leaving the city in the middle of the night—one of them charming, one of them cheap. And since no one but Stasya knows I'm with you, they've no reason to assume that you were one of those traders." If she was going to have to explain the reasoning behind every little thing she did all the way to Ohrid, it was going to be one unenclosed walk.

Pjerin could feel the guard's eyes on his back, even through the bulk of the pack. He fought the urge to turn. "Next time, let me know what part I'm playing *before* you start."

"If *you* can just remember you're a trader on your way to Vidor, *I* can work grunting and glowering into any situation."

"This isn't one of your ballads, Annice. It's real life and all three of us are dead if we're captured."

"All four of us," she reminded him. "If we're captured, Stasya will go to the block with us."

"So, we've got to get away from here!"

The catch in his voice surprised her. "I know." Sighing, she reached out and touched him lightly on the arm. The muscles beneath her fingertips were rigid. "Really, Pjerin, I *do* know. You want to run and hide. Put as much distance as you can between you and that cell. You're feeling frightened and vulnerable, so am I. You have every right to be in a bad mood."

"I'm not in a bad mood. I'm just ..." *Feeling frightened and vulnerable.* He shook the thought off. It wouldn't help. "We need to move faster. It's almost morning."

Annice let her hand fall from his arm. So much for understanding. "I don't go any faster," she snapped.

"What is it, Theron? You've been tossing and turning all night."

Theron glanced over at his consort, her face a pattern of shadow on shadow against the pillow. "Did I wake you? I'm sorry. Perhaps I should get dressed and go for a walk."

"The king roaming about the halls in the middle of the night? You'll give your guards spasms." When he didn't respond, Lilyana sighed and sat up, propping the pillows against the crowned ship carved into the headboard and pulling the heavy linen sheet up over her breasts. "Why don't you tell me what's bothering you?" she prodded gently although she suspected that she already knew.

"It's young Ohrid." Theron heaved himself up beside her. "Something about his testimony felt wrong."

That he was concerned about Ohrid and the upcoming execution was no surprise. But how could the testimony feel wrong? "He was placed under Command by the captain herself."

"I know. *That's* what's bothering me." He rubbed at the stubble on his chin. "The greater part of our justice system is based on the belief that only truth can be spoken under Command, but every instinct says that something wasn't right yesterday in that Assembly Hall."

"You know how you hate to order executions."

"That's part of it," Theron admitted. For weeks after his first Death Judgment, every time he closed his eyes, he saw the ax fall. He'd despised himself for a weakling until his brother, on a rare visit to Elbasan, had pointed out that a king with a conscience was hardly a liability for the kingdom. "But this time, there's more. I just wish I could work out exactly where the problem lies. It might be nothing, but ..."

"It might not," Lilyana finished thoughtfully. "Should we summon the captain and have her do a recall?"

"No, I'm sure it has as much to do with me as anything that actually happened."

"All right, then." She settled back against the pillows and laced her fingers together on top of the sheet. "*You* do a recall. Tell me everything you remember happening and how you felt about it from the moment you entered the hall until you left."

"Are you sure?"

"I wasn't sleeping anyway," she pointed out with a smile. Then she sobered. "That boy goes to the block at noon, Theron. You've *got* to be completely certain that he's guilty."

Perhaps because it had been a Death Judgment, Theron remembered more than he thought possible. He remembered how the rose scent that his chamberlain always wore clung to the area around the throne. He remembered thinking how the crowds had sounded like the sea, building to a storm. He remembered staring past the stocky, black figure of the Bardic Captain at the young Duc of Ohrid and knowing that this one would not beg for his life. He remembered every word that was said.

"It matched the recall of what happened in Ohrid, essentially word for word. Then, when I asked him why he would betray his oaths, he asked me in return what his oaths had gotten him from Shkoder. My great-grandfather promised him an end to isolation and, though it irks me to admit it, that promise hasn't been well kept."

"Justifiable treason?"

"Certainly in his mind. You should've heard the passion as he accused me of sending tax collectors and . . ." Theron frowned, murmuring, "Passion . . ." He twisted on the bed to face his consort. The room had begun to lighten with the approach of day and he could see her staring at him expectantly. "The man who made those accusations was a different man than the one who spoke before and after. Those words had a ring of truth that had nothing to do with being under Bardic Command."

"A sincerely held belief is likely to hold more passion than a mere admission of guilt, regardless of the circumstances they're spoken under."

"But a man of that passion, knowing he was caught, would have been defiant, daring me to do my worst."

Lilyana nodded slowly. "He insists he's innocent. The

general opinion around the palace, and around the city for that matter, is that he's too arrogant to know when he's defeated."

"Where did you hear that?"

She shrugged. "Servers talk. I listen. It makes a nice change."

"Well, he's an arrogant pup, that's for certain, but he's not that stupid. And there's more." Theron wrapped one of his hands around both of hers. "After a Death Judgment, I've been looked at with hatred, fear, numb acceptance, and complete incomprehension, but the expression on young Ohrid's face was, just for an instant, almost identical to the expression he wore when swearing his oaths."

"Which was?"

"*You are my liege.* No emotional loading, just a bald statement of fact."

"You said almost identical. Perhaps yesterday he was thinking, *You are my liege, drop dead.*"

Theron smiled. "No. *You are my liege, do something about this.*" He reached up and yanked on the cord that would summon his valet then he swung his legs off the bed.

"So what are you going to do?"

He paused at the door to his dressing room. "I'm going to have to talk with our passionate young traitor. After that, we'll see."

They reached Riverton just as the sun crested the horizon and gilded the rooftops with light. A few lines of pale smoke drifting into the dawn showed they were no longer the only ones awake. As River Road carried them into the town, a pair of half grown dogs, deep-chested and short-legged, bounded out to greet them, tails slamming from side to side.

"Some guard dogs you are," Pjerin muttered, dropping down to one knee. "No, I don't want my face licked, thank you very much."

Annice rested her pack against the corner of a building, glad of the chance to rest, and watched him dig his fingers deep into fur, reducing both dogs to abject adoration. From the look on his face, this was the most important thing that had happened all night. *There's so much I don't know about him.* She'd arrived in Ohrid only days after both his elderly dogs had been killed by a mountain cat. He'd fought tears when he'd told her what had happened. *A person that animals trust so absolutely can't be capable of the kind of betrayal Pjerin was accused of.* Cliché, perhaps, but it further convinced her that she'd done the right thing.

Pjerin bit the inside of his cheek, struggling to hide his emotions. More than Annice appearing in his cell, more than the midnight trip through secret passageways, more than disguises and leaving Elbasan in the middle of the night, this told him he was free. This was one of the things he believed he'd never do again.

The dogs sensed the desperation in his touch and kept pushing their noses at his face.

"Sandy! Shadow!"

Two pairs of ears perked up and Pjerin knelt abandoned in the middle of the road. He stayed there for a moment, unable to move, hands pressed against the ground so hard his knuckles went white. It had been a child's voice. He forced himself to breathe. If he wasn't going to die, he'd see his son again.

Teeth clenched, he surged to his feet. "Let's go."

Annice snagged the back of his pack as he went by. "Hold on! Try to remember I'm walking for two." He shortened his stride and, smothering a yawn, she fell into step beside him. "First inn we come to that's open for business, we stop for food and a rest."

"No." Pjerin shook his head, eyes squinted almost shut against the sun but locked on the east, locked on Ohrid.

"What do you mean, *no?*" But they had time to scratch dogs?

"What I said, no." There was no room for compromise in his tone. "We eat while we travel."

"Then you can travel without me. The kigh will spot you and you'll be back in that cell faster than I can find a rhyme for door hinge." She knew she sounded equally unreasonable, but she was tired enough and hungry enough not to care.

"Annice . . ."

"You can growl my name all you want to, but it's not going to change anything. You need me to hide you from the kigh, which means we have to stay together, which means you have to travel at my pace." Grabbing his arm, she pulled him around to face her. "Or have you forgotten about *your* child?" The sarcastic tone clearly suggested just how much value she placed on that possessive pronoun. "You remember; the one you wouldn't leave without?"

His mouth worked and she waited for the explosion. It never came.

"They'll have told Gerek I'm dead."

Oh, shit. She swallowed a sudden lump in her throat. *You and your big mouth.* "Pjerin, I'm sorry."

"We *have* to find out who did this to me." Every muscle of his body stood out in rigid delineation.

Annice sighed. Considering everything he'd been through, he was remarkably stable, but considering everything he'd been through, he had every right to go completely to pieces.

"Not now," she told him gently. "While a pair of traders arriving at dawn will attract no attention, that same pair of traders standing in the middle of River Road in a Command trance would give the whole game away." Linking her arm in his, she tugged him firmly down the street. "We'll need privacy and quiet and we'll have plenty of both before we get to Ohrid."

"... so I ask her what she's doing with my shield and she says that they're diggin' a hole in the commons and they don't got a shovel. She's gonna use my shield as a shovel. Well, I give her a cuff up the side of the head and tell her it's not *my* shield, it's the king's, and if she wants a shovel she can just hoof it over to her grandad's place. And she tosses her braid back over her shoulder, and I've got a good idea where she picked up that motion, and says ever so indignantly ..." The guard lifted his chin and pursed his lips, continuing in a piping imitation of a small child's voice. "... but, Papa, you wasn't usin' it."

Aliute grimaced and thanked every god the Circle contained that the night was nearly over. Guarding the door to the dungeons was a dull assignment at best, but spending it forced to listen to story after story about a five-year-old removed it from the Circle entirely. This wasn't what she'd expected when she joined up. She'd wanted excitement, adventure, and never in her wildest dreams did she see herself standing guard so that prisoners, who were both shackled *and* locked in their cells, could have no chance of escape.

Escape; yeah, right. She rubbed an itchy shoulder blade against the rough stone wall and wondered if her partner was awake yet. *What am I thinking, the sun's up. The kids probably got her out of bed ages ago.* Her helm shifted forward slightly as she yawned. *At the risk of sounding dissatisfied with the job, it sure is boring being a guard.*

Footsteps sounded, coming down the spiral stairs that led to the upper levels of the palace. At first, Aliute thought they belonged to the drudge who came every morning to empty the pots, but there were too many of them and they were moving too fast.

The first set of feet that descended into sight wore boots and, over them, greaves enameled with the royal sigil of Shkoder.

The two guards stared at each other in shock.

Inspection? he mouthed, eyes wide and near panick.

At dawn? Aliute returned, shoving her helm straight.

As a second set of identical greaves appeared, they snapped to attention, pikes properly at rest, the effect somewhat ruined by identical expressions of disbelief. Ceremonial armor was worn only by the four members of the guard assigned to accompany the king.

Theron came down the last few steps, a second pair of guards on his heels, and acknowledged the two at the door. "I wish to speak with the Duc of Ohrid," he said quietly.

"Sire!" As senior, Aliute set her pike against the wall and lit a lamp off one of the three tallow candles. Pinching off the smoldering end of the taper, she motioned for her companion to open the door. Shoulders back, head up, heart pounding, she moved into the passageway between the two rows of cells; however peculiar this visit might be, it was her chance to look good in front of the king and she wasn't going to blow it.

At the cell door, she set the lamp in the bracket and heaved up the bar. Motioned aside by one of the other guards, she watched as he picked up the lamp and went

into the cell. He rushed back out a second later, his face
pale, the flickering light illuminating the superstitious
fear in his eyes.

"Majesty, the prisoner is gone."

"What!" Theron snatched the lamp from the guard's
hand and charged forward. Just inside the door, he
stopped. The shackle—closed and locked—was lying on
the braided straw pallet which was lying flat on the
bench. Although he knew it was ridiculous, he squatted
and peered into the shadowed recess between the bench
and the floor.

Off to one side, Aliute strained to see, her mouth dry,
blood throbbing in her temples. If a prisoner was missing, *she* was responsible. She had no idea what the punishment would be. They'd never lost a prisoner before.
Perhaps she'd have to take his place at the block.

"Spirited away," murmured a guard.

"Always knew those mountain folk were unenclosed,"
muttered another.

Yes! Aliute grabbed at hope. *Spirits from outside the
Circle took him! It wasn't my fault.*

"Don't be ridiculous!" Theron snapped, stomping
back out into the corridor, nearly knocking over the two
guards, who'd followed him in. "There's a perfectly logical explanation." His eyes narrowed and his nostrils
flared. "During the night someone let him out and then
locked everything behind him."

Five pairs of eyes turned to glare at Aliute.

She backed up a step, and then another.

"N–no one came in here last night, Majesty," she protested. "I swear it. No one."

Still holding the lamp, Theron half turned and pointed
with his free hand. "You, Janyte, I want the Bardic Captain down here, now."

"Sire!" Janyte took off at a full run, aiming for the
rectangle of light that marked the entry into the corridor.

"Karlis, go back and get the other lamp. Then I want
that cell inspected for loose stones or some indication of
an exit other than by the door."

"Sire!"

The two remaining guards flanked their sovereign and
lowered their halberds, the implication plain. If Aliute

had cooperated with a traitor, she herself was a danger to the king.

Aliute looked down at the weapons and swallowed. Like the ceremonial armor, the halberds were highly ornate, but not even the intricate engraving that extended nearly to the edge of the blades could make them look any less deadly. Without intending to, she scuttled backward another three or four paces.

They let her go. They were, after all, between her and the only way out.

She was at the edge of the lamplight now, the shadows closing in around her. Then, out of the corner of her eye, she caught sight of a pale, translucent streamer against the wall. Her heart leaped into her throat. *The spirits!*

In spite of her terror, she moved toward it. If it *was* a spirit, the king would know she'd had nothing to do with the prisoner's escape.

Not a spirit. Something better.

"Majesty ..." She licked her lips and tried again. "Majesty, I think I've found the answer."

Indicating that the guards should stay where they were, Theron came forward.

Aliute laid the end of the torn and filthy spiderweb carefully across Theron's palm.

Together, they turned and stared at the place it entered the wall.

"We've paid for it, you might as well eat it."

"I'm not hungry." Pjerin pushed his meal aside. All he could think of was the time they were wasting. Time that could be better spent by increasing their distance from Elbasan. "How can you eat eels for breakfast?"

Annice shrugged and swallowed. "I like eels. The Riverfolk eat them all the time."

"You're not Riverfolk."

"So?" She yawned, scraped the bottom of her bowl, and reached for his. "No point in wasting it."

"Something wrong with the food?"

"Not a thing." Annice smiled up at the innkeeper. "*Jorin*'s just in a rush to get to Vidor. He's got a bet on with his cousin."

Dimpled arms folded over a featherbed bosom, the

innkeeper clicked her tongue disapprovingly. "He makes a bet, and you've got to rush. And in your condition, too."

"Oh, I don't mind. After all, half the profits are mine."

"Health first, profits second," she declared. "Why didn't you wait for the river? Current'll be down and they'll be able to hoist sail by the new moon. You could go to the festival—there'll be a bard to Sing up the wind—then ride to Vidor in comfort."

"Riverboat passage costs coin." Pjerin opened his mouth and Annice kicked him under the table. She didn't know what he was about to say and she didn't want to. The story would be easier to keep track of with only her telling it. "Besides, we haven't the time to wait."

"Traders. Rushing here, rushing there. When are you due?"

"Just into Second Quarter."

"So soon? You don't look big enough. When I was that far along, I was much bigger. And you're carrying too low. You don't get enough rest, that's the problem." She turned a dark gaze on Pjerin. "You've got to see that she rests more. Look at those circles under her eyes. Now then, my sister's boy, Bartek the carter, he's heading for Vidor this morning. If you leave now—and I only suggest this since you seem to be in such a hurry—you can still catch him. It'll cost you coin, but you won't have to wait, and you," a sausage finger jabbed at Annice, "won't have to trot along under a double load."

"Thank you." Annice's smile had frayed a little around the edges. "That's a big help, **believe me**." She finished the last mouthful of what was supposed to have been Pjerin's breakfast and stood. "Good business, innkeeper."

"Good business, trader."

A few moments later, they were hurrying toward the carter's yards.

"I wish you'd stop telling people to believe you," Pjerin growled.

"Why?" Annice belched and began to think the second bowl of eels had been a mistake. "It's the easiest way to allay suspicions."

"I don't like you putting ideas into people's heads."
He half turned and glanced behind them. "I know what
it's like from the other side."

"This isn't the same thing."

"Isn't it?" In memory, he heard his mouth speaking
with someone else's voice. How much difference was
there between that and being charmed into a false belief? "Even you agreed that what happened to me *could*
have been done by a bard."

"Yeah?" She was too tired to be diplomatic. "In balance, try to remember that it's a bard saving your butt."

"From the kigh!"

"So?"

"The kigh are controlled by the bards!"

"You *still* think the bards had something to do with
this?"

No. He didn't. "I'm sorry." He brushed his hand over
his eyes. What was his point? He suddenly realized he
didn't have one. "Whenever I remember what was done
to me, I get too tangled up in anger to think clearly."

She had enough energy left for half a smile. "Apology accepted."

Her smile suddenly reminded him of better days in
Ohrid and where her smile had led them. He searched
for a safer subject. "Why did you call me Jorin?"

"I don't know." They turned down a street of small
shops—apprentices opening shutters for the start of the
day's business, artisans calling greetings to neighbors—
and Annice pitched her voice so as not to be overheard.
"I had to call you something and that's close enough to
your name you'll probably answer to it."

"Then what should I call you?" Without her skills, he
felt exposed every time he opened his mouth and could
only mumble, hoping her ears had been trained as well
as her tongue.

"I've always kind of liked Magda. It was my grandmother's name."

"Think you'd answer to it?"

"Probably no . . . oh, boy."

"What's wrong?" Pjerin jerked around. The street behind them was empty except for a yawning teenager in
a wrinkled smock and an equally disinterested black and
white cat.

"Baby just stretched out its little pointy toes and booted me up under the ribs."

Releasing a breath he couldn't remember taking, Pjerin snorted. "It was probably the eels."

"It was *not*. It's just getting crowded in there."

"The innkeeper seemed to think you're too small."

"I am not too small!" Annice practically spit out the protest. "Everyone who's ever had a baby suddenly thinks they're an expert! I'm not too small, I'm not carrying too low, and of course I look tired, I've been up all night dragging your ass out of a dungeon."

"Why not tell the world?" Pjerin snarled. But no one appeared to have noticed, in spite of the vehemence. Sweat trickling down his sides, he turned and checked behind them again.

She shifted her pack. "What do you keep staring at back there?"

"They must know I'm gone. The drudge comes for the slops at sunrise."

Annice grinned at him. "But you vanished out of a locked cell. First they'll have to drag His Majesty out of bed and then they'll have to question the guards. We won't see any sign of pursuit for hou . . ."

The sound of at least three sets of shod hooves spun them both around. Pjerin flung out a hand to keep Annice on her feet as her shifting pack threatened to pull her over. Sight blocked by a curve in the road, the sound echoed between the buildings.

"You were saying!" Heart slamming in his chest, the sound of pursuit almost drowned out by the roar of blood in his ears, he searched for a place to hide.

"No!" Annice dug in her heels, throwing her weight against his. "Stay here! Turn your back to the road, the pack will hide you. You're a trader. Remember that!"

There wasn't time to argue. Pjerin turned just as three horses galloped into view, his hands closing around Annice's, her touch the only thing keeping him from running.

They were on them. They were gone.

"Nothing to do with us," Annice said soothingly, her voice trembling a little in spite of her best efforts. "Nobles."

Pjerin couldn't get his muscles to unlock. "Nobles?"

"Young ones. The kind who think it's funny to gallop through town and make everyone jump out of their way."

"Nobles," Pjerin repeated a second time. He remembered how to breathe.

"Assholes!" bellowed a candlemaker stepping out of his shop and shaking a scarred fist at the clouds of dust. "Unenclosed guards are never around when you need 'em."

"Ain't it the truth." Annice pulled her hands out of Pjerin's loosened grip and flexed the fingers to make sure they still worked. "Come on." She reached up and slapped him gently on both cheeks. "Let's catch that ride to Vidor."

"Well, Captain?"

Years of practice kept Liene's voice and facial expression totally noncommittal although below the surface calm her thoughts churned. "The trail does lead to Bardic Hall, Majesty, but we should consider the possibility that it was made by other than a bard."

Theron stared across the desk at her, his hair and clothing bearing mute testimony to his explorations within the walls. "Do you honestly believe that, Captain?"

She frowned. "Not for a moment, Majesty."

"Then let's leave the realm of fairytales behind, shall we, and cut right to the facts." He raised a grimy finger. "One: the passageways through the palace are not exactly secret and have long been explored by the younger members of the royal family. Although, I might add, that particular passageway is going to be filled before we're all very much older. There's no reason," he growled, "for any of them to have been built in the first place."

The captain decided against mentioning that Kristjan II, the king who'd commissioned the building of the palace, had been referred to by the bards of his time as "out of his royal mind" and there were scrolls and scrolls in the library concerning how best to deal with his "enthusiasms." At the moment, the information would only serve as an unnecessary distraction.

"Two:" Theron continued, "you have such a ... person currently in residence at Bardic Hall. Three: she was the last bard to go to Ohrid before this whole situation came up."

Four: she's not going to want to see the father of her child executed. The sudden realization hit Liene hard enough to set up echoes between her ears. She'd known from the moment the king had so tersely laid his dawn discovery before her that Annice had to be involved. That Pjerin a'Stasiek had fathered her child could be the only logical explanation for her to save him from the block. Not for a moment did the Bardic Captain believe that Annice had sold out to Cemandia.

Quickly recalling the conversation they'd had after the Duc had been accused, she realized that Annice had never denied sleeping with the duc although she'd done her best to misdirect suspicion. *I must be getting old not to have seen through your innuendos. You told me exactly what I wanted to hear without ever telling me an outright lie and when I get my hands on you, I'm going to wring your neck. How could you put me in this position!*

"Captain! I realize this has given you plenty to think about, but *try* to pay attention."

"Your pardon, Majesty." Liene sketched a bow.

Theron snorted. "As I was saying, there is another bard who recently spent time with the duc and who may have, over the years in close proximity, been told the secret ways of the palace."

"Stasya?"

The king nodded. "I'll send for them both and we'll see what kind of an explanation they can give us. I'm sure they'll be a credit to their bardic training."

"But, Majesty, shouldn't the guard be sent after the fugitive immediately?"

"No." The word was both denial and a warning not to argue further.

Liene drummed her fingers against her thighs. At this hour of the morning, she didn't deal well with disaster and she couldn't read the king's mood at all. "If you'll forgive me saying so, Majesty, you're taking this escape—*and the implication of your sister in that escape*—very calmly."

Theron leaned back in his chair and brushed at the cobwebs on his sleeve. "I have my reasons, Captain. Page!"

The door flew open. "Sire!"

"Take a message to Bardic Hall. . . ."

Stasya scrambled into her good tunic and searched amidst the mess on the table for a comb. Things were not going as planned.

"How did he find out so quickly?" she muttered, sifting through a pile of slates, a box of chalk, three scrolls, and a breastband with a broken strap. "There was nothing to connect that escape to Annice. Nothing."

The summons had been for them both.

"Maybe I can say she's in the privy. All things being enclosed, she'd been there often enough lately I can probably make it sound like the truth."

She found the comb at last and dragged it through her hair.

"Maybe this has nothing to do with last night."

One of her boots was under the bed.

"Maybe he's found out she's pregnant and wants to know if it's mine."

The other was propped up in the otherwise empty fireplace.

"Maybe he wants us to sing him a duet over breakfast."

She paused in the doorway and glanced back at the familiar mess. This might be the last time she ever saw it—an execution had already been planned, all it lacked was the guest of honor.

One hand went to her throat as she pulled the door closed with the other. At least Annice was safely away.

"And now off I go to compound treason with lies." She couldn't believe the risks she took for love.

Without appearing to be watching him at all, Liene watched the king carefully as they waited for the two bards to arrive. This would be the first time in ten years he'd seen his youngest sister face-to-face. What was he thinking? Given the circumstances, what *could* he be thinking? Given Annice's condition on top of everything else, this was likely to be an interview of historic proportions and Liene rather wished that someone else were Bardic Captain during it. *I'm getting too old for this.*

In her opinion, he looked too calm. She wondered what he was hiding.

Theron continued to brush at the dust on his sleeve. He could remember only two times he'd been this angry; the first when the sister he'd all but raised had made him look a fool at his father's deathbed, the second when she rejected his offer of forgiveness and demanded *he* apologize for what she had done to him. *And now, she defies me once again. This time, she has gone too far.*

He had no doubt that Annice had helped Ohrid escape and two theories as to why she'd done it. The first, that she'd fallen in love with young Pjerin during her Walk and had acted on that emotion, he found difficult to believe. Love was one thing, but—even for Annice—treason something else again. Besides, her continuing relationship with Stasya seemed to indicate that her emotions were already engaged. No, it wasn't love. He suspected that she, too, had reason to disbelieve the duc's testimony and he looked forward to hearing what those reasons were.

He had no trouble at all believing that she considered her opinion of greater value than the entire justice system of Shkoder.

As soon as he set her straight on that score—and he looked forward to the opportunity—she could retrieve the fugitive and together they could begin the unpleasant task of getting at the truth—the whole truth, not just the words spoken under Command.

And then?

He took a deep breath and found himself considering Annice in conjunction with the terrifying possibility that, if the young duc were innocent, someone had found a way to manipulate a mind under Command. This held the potential for such chaos that royal pain, royal pride, and royal anger could not stand against it.

For the first time in ten years, Theron found himself smiling as he thought of his sister. Somehow, he didn't find it at all surprising she was in the middle of the greatest crisis he'd faced since he'd taken the throne and that this crisis would place the full responsibility of a reconciliation squarely on his shoulders. Annice never did anything by halves.

"Do you think she's a good bard?" he asked suddenly.

Liene started. *Why is he worrying about that when she seems to have just helped a condemned traitor escape execution?* "Yes, Majesty. Annice Sings all four quarters and ..."

"I know what she can *do,* Captain," Theron told her dryly. "I am not without resources. I was asking for your personal opinion."

"In my personal opinion, Majesty ..." The Bardic Captain bowed, thinking, *Resources? What in the Circle does he mean by that? Of course he has resources, he's the king.* "... she's a very good bard. If a little impulsive at times."

"Impulsive?" Theron repeated with a bark of laughter. "I suppose that's one word for it." A gentle knock at the door stopped him before he could voice any others. "Come."

"The bard you sent for is here, Majesty."

"I sent for two."

The young page looked confused and a little frightened by the tone. "Only one came," he offered, tugging nervously on the hem of his tunic.

Which one? Theron wondered, but all he said aloud was, "Send her in."

"Yes, Majesty."

Stasya had never been this far into the palace before. The senior of the guards flanking the door into the royal apartments had questioned the page and checked her for weapons before allowing her entry. *And we haven't been at war for three generations. These guys are paranoid.*

The private areas were a lot less ornate and more comfortable looking than the public ones. She only wished for different circumstances so she could've enjoyed the tour.

The whole place smells like beeswax and whitewash. They must've just finished First Quarter cleaning. Bardic Hall usually smelled like damp wool and ink.

The page who'd accompanied her from the Hall handed her over to another who told her to "wait right-exactly" where she was as he knocked on one of the carved wooden panels that made up the door. He slipped inside and Stasya tried to come up with something coherent to say.

One thing was certain; the truth was about to take a beating.

She wondered if the king would put her under Command.

Still, we now believe it's possible to lie under Command, don't we. Wish I knew how Pjerin managed it. If he managed it. I think I'm going to puke.

The page returned and stepped aside. "His Majesty says you may enter."

Well, this is it. Show time. Drying damp palms on her breeches, she stepped forward and hid a wince as the door swung closed behind her. It was such a depressingly *final* sound.

The king's private office was a surprisingly small room. It had a fireplace in one of the inner walls, a tall window looking out into an interior courtyard, and, instead of exposed stone, richly polished wood paneling. A portrait of the king's grandmother, Milena III, hung over the fireplace—Stasya had seen the artist's sketches and two preliminary portraits in the archives. The furniture—a large desk, three wood and leather chairs, and a set of shelves—sat on a plush burgundy and cream patterned carpet that could only have come out of the Empire.

Having run out of *things* to look at, Stasya surrendered to the inevitable and finally turned her gaze on the people. The king was sitting at the desk. He looked ... actually, he looked amazingly like Annice when she was anticipating something that could easily turn out to be unpleasant. While their features were very little alike, the expression was nearly identical. Stasya hadn't been expecting that. It would be harder to lie into the face of a friend.

The Bardic Captain stood by the window. Stasya really hadn't been expecting *that*.

Oh, shit. I wonder whose side she's on.

As far from the desk as protocol allowed, she bowed, trying to remember if it was right leg forward, left leg back or the reverse and if, under the circumstances, it really mattered anyway. When she lifted her head, the king was staring at her, his expression unreadable.

"So," he said grimly. "She went with him."

He knows. Stasya was as certain of that as she'd been of anything in her life. The question now became, how much did he know? With no point in lying to keep Annice in the clear, Stasya decided she'd better move on to her alternative plan. Just evolved, it involved answering all questions as truthfully as possible and then, the moment the king seemed susceptible, throwing herself— and Annice—on the mercy of the crown. When it came down to it, she wasn't too proud to beg for both of them. "Yes, Majesty."

Out of the corner of her eye, she caught sight of the captain's incredulous reaction and fought to keep from smiling. *It has to be nerves,* she told herself sternly. *This isn't funny.*

Liene jerked forward. "How could you let her ..." she began, then stopped, unwilling to be the one to define Annice's condition before the king.

Theron ignored the interruption. "Do you realize the position you're in?"

Stasya swallowed. "Yes, Majesty."

"Do you realize that you have assisted in the committing of a treasonous act?"

"Yes, Majesty."

"Do you realize that the penalty for what you have done is death?"

She briefly closed her eyes. "Yes, Majesty."

"Then why ..." Theron surged up out of his chair and slammed both palms down on the desk "... by all that's in the Circle, did you do it!"

Because Annice asked me to. She couldn't say it. It felt too much like betrayal.

Theron read the answer off her face, sighed, and sank back into his chair. "Never mind. I understand why you helped her, Stasya; I'm sure she put you in a position where you weren't able to do anything else." He stared into memory for a moment, then lifted his gaze once more to her face. "I would, however, like to know why *she* saw fit to break into my dungeon and release the Duc of Ohrid."

Unexpectedly warming to him, now that his expression seemed more resigned than angry, Stasya saw a glimmer of hope. If the king would listen to the explanation, maybe they'd all survive the experience. Wishing she could use just a little Voice to help her convince—it was more the captain's presence than her oath that stopped her—she wet her lips and tried to sum up Annice's reasoning. "She helped the duc escape because she doesn't think that he did what he was accused of."

"What he confessed to!" Liene snapped, wondering why nothing seemed to be making sense.

Stasya turned to face her captain. "Annice didn't think that confession was valid. She believes him when he says those aren't his words. *Time to stand up and be counted.* "I believe him, too."

"What!"

An imperious hand cut off the captain's protest. The king leaned forward. "Are you certain it's not Annice that you believe?"

Up until that point, Stasya hadn't been sure, but now, all of a sudden, she was. "I began by believing her," she admitted. "I ended up by believing him."

"Why?" Theron asked quietly.

"I watched him, Majesty, all the long way back from Ohrid, and Pjerin a'Stasiek is not the type to commit treason. He'd never allow anyone else to do his fighting for him. If he has an argument with you, he'll face you directly rather than try to stab you in the back."

"Even if he thinks he'll lose?"

"He wouldn't ever think that, Majesty."

"And I suppose your opinion is not likely to be influenced by his physical attributes," Theron mused, raised brows making the statement a question.

Stasya snorted. "You can count on it, Majesty."

"In your unbiased opinion then, leaving aside for a moment whether or not the duc would commit treason in the first place, if he were caught, how would he behave?"

"He'd be defiant, Majesty. No question about it. He'd dare you to do your worst."

Theron nodded. "My thoughts exactly."

Stasya's eyes widened and she took an involuntary step forward. "You don't believe he did it either!"

"Your Majesty, I protest!" Liene charged around the corner of the desk so that she stood between the king and the younger bard. "The Duc of Ohrid admitted his guilt not once but twice when questioned under Command. Belief doesn't come into it!"

"Your protest is noted, Captain," Theron told her calmly. "But belief very much comes into it. If I don't believe the man is guilty, I'm not going to order his death."

"But he was Commanded to speak only the truth!"

"Then, obviously, someone altered the truth."

Liene drew herself up to her full height, her eyes glittering dangerously. "Majesty, are you suggesting that one of my bards . . ."

"No." Theron cut her off abruptly. "I'm not."

Still scowling, the captain was left with nothing to say.

Stasya stepped into the silence. "Majesty, Pjerin said that during the time he was under Command, he felt pushed to the back of his head while someone else used his mouth, and the worst of it was that the words weren't so much outright lies as twisted bits of the truth. He could remember most of them happening but not in the way they came out."

"He said all this to you?"

"To myself and Annice, yes, Majesty."

Theron slammed his fist down on the desk. Both bards jumped at the sudden explosion of sound. "But the arrogant fool would rather go to the block than say any of this to me! The stiff-necked young ass!" Drawing in a deep breath, he exhaled it all in a rush. "And Annice! Would rather commit treason herself . . ." His gold signet flashed as he waved a hand at Stasya. ". . . and convince you to help her with it, than come to me with her suspicions. Did they consider me such a tyrant that I wouldn't listen? Did they think I don't have eyes or ears of my own? By the Center, they *deserve* each other!"

Stasya couldn't help it, her nerves were stretched tight enough to strum and the last she'd seen of Annice and Pjerin they were having a low-voiced but edged argument over the best way to leave the Citadel. She snickered.

To her relief, Theron took no offense. He sat back in his chair and shook his head. "I can well imagine," he said with feeling. "The irresistible opinion meeting the immovable conceit. Well, you'd better bring them back before they kill each other and we can start straightening this mess out."

"Bring them back, Majesty?"

"Yes. Bring them back. Send a kigh with a message." He glanced from bard to bard. Both were looking as though they'd just stepped in something foul and sticky. "Is there a problem?" His tone made it clear that, if there was, they'd best overcome it and quickly.

"The kigh, the air kigh, that is, Majesty, won't have anything to do with Annice at this point in time."

Theron rubbed at his temples. Somehow, he wasn't surprised. Trust Annice to make it difficult. "So," he sighed. "What's she done to alienate *them?*"

"Your pardon, Majesty." Stasya jumped in before the captain could say anything. "But it really isn't our place to say."

"Yes, it is," Theron told her, his temper beginning to fray again. "It's your place to answer my questions. I'm the king. That's the way the system works. Now then, what has my sister done to alienate the kigh?"

The words "my sister" seemed to hang in the air. Even Theron seemed a little startled by them.

A hesitant tapping on the door became a welcome distraction.

At the king's barked command, the page came far enough into the room to be heard, but not so far he couldn't make a quick escape if it became necessary. "I—I didn't want to interrupt, Majesty, but there's a man out here and he has one of these."

The thin copper disk resting on the boy's outstretched palm bore the highly polished, raised image of a crowned ship. It gave the bearer access to the king at any time. In his ten years on the throne, Theron had given out only three.

"Does he have a name?"

"Yes, Majesty. Leonas."

Stasya shot the captain a startled look. The captain frowned.

Leonas walked into the king's private office as though he were walking into a chamber back in Bardic Hall. Stasya half expected to see him set down a tray of food and demand to know why they'd all tried to skip breakfast. He'd taken off his apron but apparently thought that his working clothes were suitable for a visit to his sovereign.

"I heard you sent for *them*," he said before anyone in the room could speak. "So I figured you'd found out and I'd save you the trouble of sending for me, too."

"You helped with this?" Theron demanded incredulously.

"Well, not exactly helped, Majesty, although I tried to see she ate right. But I knew about it."

"Then why didn't you see fit to inform me?"

Leonas shrugged. "Didn't seem like my place to tell you, Majesty. Kept hoping she'd tell you herself." He jerked his head at Stasya. "Where's the princess?"

Stasya opened her mouth but no sound came out. Leonas had been King Theron's spy? Finally she managed a strangled, "You shit! Annice trusted you!"

He stiffened. "And I never betrayed that trust. I served the princess to the best of my abilities." Glaring at the bard, he didn't see Theron's brows rise, but the captain did and she wondered if Leonas was even aware of the shift in his allegiance. He didn't appear to be as he asked, "Where is she?"

Still sputtering, Stasya was unsettled enough to answer. "She helped the Duc of Ohrid escape from the dungeon last night and ended up going with him."

"What!"

"I thought you knew about it?" Theron stood and came out from around the desk.

"Not about this!" The older man looked stunned. "I figured you'd found out about the baby."

"The what!"

"The baby," Leonas repeated. He turned his attention back to Stasya. "What were you thinkin', letting her go off with this duc fellow? I thought that you had more brains than that!"

"Why does everyone seem to think I could've stopped her?" Stasya demanded of the room at large. "You *know* how she is when she gets an idea in her head. And besides, he wouldn't leave without her."

"His baby?"

"Yes." There didn't seem to be any reason to deny it. "But that's not why she went with him. Without her to block the kigh, he'd be picked up again in minutes. It was the only solution; we couldn't just let him die."

"Let me see if I have the gist of this." Theron barely raised his voice, but it filled the room in such a way that the server and both bards gave him their complete attention. "My sister is pregnant . . ." He paused. It was the loudest silence any of them had ever heard. ". . . with the Duc of Ohrid's child . . ." Again the pause. The silence rang. ". . . and they are now hidden from the kigh because of her condition?"

Liene stepped forward. When it came right down to it, Annice was her responsibility, so *this* was her responsibility. "Yes, Majesty."

"How long have you known?"

"About the father . . ." She shot a glance at Stasya heavy with promise. ". . . I found out as you did, Majesty. About the child; since she returned from Ohrid."

Theron's brows drew in so tightly they met over his nose. "I'm only going to ask this once; why wasn't I told?"

At last, an easy answer. Liene met his eyes. "As Leonas said, Majesty, I was hoping she'd tell you herself."

"Then why *didn't* she?"

"I expect it's because she was afraid you'd have her executed for treason."

"Executed? Where did she get such a . . ."

By the will of the late King Mikus, you have permission to enter Bardic Hall. I, Theron, King of Shkoder, High Captain of the Broken Islands, Lord over the Mountain Principalities of Sibiu, Ohrid, Ajud, Bicaz, and Somes, do on this day declare that by doing so you forfeit all rights of royalty, that you shall surrender all titles and incomes, that all save your personal possessions shall revert to the crown. Furthermore, for the stability of the realm, you may neither join nor bear children without the express permission of the crown. To do so will be considered a treasonous act and will be punished as such.

Theron shook his head. "She couldn't have believed I'd go through with it."

"With respect, Majesty . . ." Too skilled to let it show, Liene was enjoying herself for the first time since she'd been jolted out of her bed by an urgent summons from the king. ". . . the proclamation laid it out rather clearly.

While Annice might not have believed it at first, when it became obvious that you no longer considered her a member of the family, it became easier for her to believe the rest."

"You could've told her she was wrong!"

"If you'll recall, Majesty, when I attempted, just after you took the throne, to suggest that you had been, perhaps, a little harsh, and that you might reword the proclamation to lessen its impact, you told me that it was necessary for the smooth running of the kingdom that the king's word be perceived as law."

He stared at her for a moment, fully aware of the sarcasm behind each word and equally aware that the captain had far too much control for him to call her on it. "It is *also* necessary for the smooth running of the kingdom that the king be perceived as able to change his mind," he ground out through clenched teeth. "And, if *you'll* recall, I attempted to forgive her, but *she* decided she didn't want to be forgiven."

"She didn't want the forgiveness of her king." There could be no fault found with the captain's respectful tone. "She wanted the understanding of her brother."

"They are the *same* person!"

"Majesty?" Stasya decided to explain before the king lost his temper and the bards lost their captain. "I think Annice was too proud to go to you when she thought you wanted nothing to do with her. I think she finally found something you'd have to notice, a guaranteed way for *you* to send for *her*."

"By throwing my own words in my face?"

"I don't think she thought that . . ."

"I doubt she thought at all," Theron snapped. "Go on."

"Well, before you found out . . ." Stasya hid a wince as he glared at the captain who stood listening impassively. ". . . this whole thing with the duc happened. She couldn't tell you then. Her baby was under the weight of a double treason—hers and its father's. There has to be a limit to how much a king can forgive." She stressed his title.

"I take it you agreed with her assessment?"

"Yes, sire."

"So she couldn't come to me with her suspicions because of the child?"

"We didn't know you suspected that the duc had been set up, Majesty. We didn't think you'd believe her and we couldn't take the risk only to have His Grace still go to the block."

Theron pulled at the collar of his tunic. Annice had thrown her unwillingness to compromise in his face right from the beginning. He couldn't back down from that kind of a challenge.

Now she was pregnant and on the run with a man accused of treason. He didn't doubt for a moment she was challenging him again. But this time, more than just the two of them were involved.

The collar button twisted off in his fingers and with an annoyed growl he tossed it onto the desk. "What were you planning on telling people," he demanded of Stasya, "when they noticed she wasn't around?"

"That the execution had upset her, Majesty, and she'd gone to stay with my family down coast."

"Good. Then that's where she is."

"But, Majesty, there won't *be* an execution."

Theron smiled grimly. "Oh, yes, there will."

Stasya's hand went to her throat.

"Executions are witnessed by five people," he continued, "Myself, the Bardic Captain, two guards, and the executioner. They take place in an interior courtyard without an audience. The executioner is . . ." His lips pursed as he searched for the right epithet. ". . . discreet, the captain will *speak* with the guards, and you, Leonas, will get some fresh blood from the kitchens. The servers will expect to have to scrub the cobblestones."

"Begging Your Majesty's pardon, but this is beginning to sound like a fledgling's ballad." Liene's nostrils were pinched with the effort of keeping her opinion even that restrained.

"Someone has worked very hard to make us believe that the duc is guilty of treason, Captain. If they think they've succeeded, we'll be one step closer to catching them." Theron perched on the corner of his desk. "The quickest way to discover who rearranged young Ohrid's memories would be to put him back under Command and ask him but, as I understand it, as long as he remains with Annice, you," he nodded at the captain, "can't find him."

"Essentially correct, sire."

"And if I send the guard out after them," he continued thoughtfully, "I've no doubt I'll alert that someone and throw away our one advantage."

"You can't just leave the princess out there, about to have a child!" Leonas protested.

The set of Stasya's shoulders said much the same thing.

"I can't send the guard after the duc," Theron mused, then all at once he smiled. "But there's nothing that says I can't send the guard after Annice."

Stasya felt her jaw drop. "She'll be furious, Majesty."

The king's smile never faltered. "Good. I found out about the baby, she ran, and I want her back. There's nothing anyone can use in that."

"How're they going to bring her back without hurting her?" Leonas asked, arms folded across his chest. "She won't just come 'cause you order it, Majesty; not the princess, no, she won't."

"I could go after her, Majesty," Stasya offered, eagerly. "I know which way they've gone."

Theron thought about it for a moment then shook his head. "No. Only the four of us know what's actually going on, I can't afford to have you out of whatever plan we create to capture the real traitor." He picked up the collar button and rubbed it between his fingers. "Still, it's essential we get the duc back and find out exactly what's been done to him. It'll have to be the guards."

"The duc'll fight if the guards try an' take her," Leonas insisted stubbornly. "Then the guards'll know who he is."

While Theron appreciated the affection the old man had for Annice, his attitude was becoming annoying. "He's not likely to identify himself," he snapped. "I've plenty of guards who've never seen the duc and all they'll know is Annice has run off with the man who fathered her child and I want them *both* brought back to Elbasan. I think a troop of guard can handle one pregnant bard and the Duc of Ohrid. They won't hurt her and if they have to knock him on his ass to get him here, maybe next time he'll consider confiding in his king."

When Leonas opened his mouth again, Theron abruptly raised a hand. "Enough. Annice is going to have to live with the consequences of her actions. If she'd come to me with her suspicions, none of this would be necessary."

"Your pardon, Majesty?" Liene recognized the tone in the king's voice and decided she'd better speak before he felt the urge for another proclamation he'd come to regret. It was time to remind him that Annice was by far the least of his concerns. "Who would want you to believe Pjerin a'Stasiek is a traitor?"

"A good question." Theron agreed to be distracted. "And there's only one logical answer. Queen Jirina of Cemandia."

Liene frowned. "Why would Cemandia want you to discover a plot involving Cemandia?"

"This is how I see their reasoning; Queen Jirina has made no secret of wanting a seaport and has to know we've heard about the mercenaries she's been importing. I know Defiance Pass at Ohrid is the only way she can bring an army into Shkoder, so I strengthen it. *Unless* I think I've discovered their plan and neutralized it, thereby removing the threat.

"*But* the plot involving the duc was a blind, a setup I was intended to discover. They not only want me to believe I've taken care of the threat, but they want me to remove young Pjerin from their way." His voice hardened. "I don't like being used."

"It seems logical," Liene admitted after a moment of turning it over and examining it from all sides. "But why not let them know they've failed?"

"Two reasons. First, if the duc isn't the traitor, someone else is—or Jirina wouldn't think she could get an army through the pass. I want that someone." His expression darkened. "I'm going to lay out a path to the block and dance them down it."

The sudden crack of the carved wooden button snapping between his fingers jerked everyone's gaze to his hands. Theron took a deep breath and let the two pieces fall to the carpet. "Secondly," he continued as though nothing had happened, "if the someone in Cemandia is able to work around Command, I want to know how and who and I want to know it now, not later when they've made an attempt we didn't discover."

"*If* the Cemandians are able to work around Command, Majesty." Liene's tone suggested that the king could believe what he wished. While she'd give him the rest, she wouldn't give him this. Not without a fight.

"*If* they can do it, I'm sure you can as well." It was less an observation than an order. "We'll need a way to undo it and a way to guard against it ever happening again. I'm sure His Grace will be eager to help when he's returned to the capital."

Her lips had thinned to a pale line and she barely opened them as she spoke. "Yes, Majesty. And if it can't be done?"

His smile held a warning. "Assume it can. You'll find the two dungeon guards with my four. I want all six of them Commanded not to speak of the escape but explain why before you do it—they may not have a choice, but they'll at least have the reason."

"That won't stop them from speaking the truth if they're Commanded, Majesty."

"I know that, Captain, but who's going to Command them? I'm not. You're not." His smile suggested she drop the subject. "Leonas, get the blood, then return here. You're roughly the same height as the duc and no one looks too closely at the person in the Judgment robe. I'll take you into the Duc's cell by way of the so-called secret passageway, then you, Captain, will show up with the dungeon guards to escort him out."

Liene bowed and turned on her heel, muttering, "I am *not* singing a dirge for a bucket of chicken blood," as she left.

Leonas bowed as well, with the air of a man who knew his duty even if he didn't like it.

Theron allowed them both to leave and sat staring down at the two half circles of wood at his feet.

Stasya stared at a point just over his head and wondered why he hadn't dismissed her with the others.

Finally, he glanced up. "I know you're worried about her. I wish I could send you after her."

"Thank you, Majesty." This wasn't what she'd expected. And he looked as worried as she felt. "She really wants this baby, Majesty. She won't do anything to endanger it."

"Perhaps you'd better reassure Leonas."

"Yes, Majesty."

"Stasya . . ." He paused, uncertain of how to go on. "Did Annice deliberately challenge my authority with this?"

"She didn't get pregnant on purpose if that's what you're asking, sire."

"An accident?" Sighing, he bent and picked up the broken button, his tunic gaping at the collar. "Trust Annice to have an accident this complicated. Is she happy about it?"

"Stasya, when I think about this baby, I feel the way I feel when the Song works; that sense of everything snapping into place and being, if only for a little while, absolutely right."

Stasya smiled. "Yes, Majesty."

"Is she healthy?"

"Yes, Majesty."

"Do you really believe she did this just so I would send for her?"

"Not consciously, Majesty, but, yes; I really believe it. She misses you, misses her family, misses her past."

"I wish I'd known this sooner."

Stasya sighed. "So do I, Majesty." *Because then she wouldn't be on her way to Ohrid, almost eight months pregnant, a hunted fugitive, protecting a man she wouldn't eat breakfast with.* No point in saying it; there was nothing the king could do, no way he could find her. *No way I can find her. Shit.*

Theron remembered a little sister who followed him like a shadow. When he met Stasya's eyes again, his own were bright. "I sent for her, about eight years ago, but she wouldn't come."

"It still hurt too much, Majesty."

"I know."

Stasya bit her lip as she realized why he understood about Annice's pain, but before she could think of something to say, he continued.

"And then, when I heard that song, all I could think of was how she'd taken something that should have been private between the two of us and deliberately used it to undermine my authority throughout Shkoder."

" 'The Princess-Bard'?" Stasya was so astonished, she took a step toward the king. "Annice had nothing to do with that, Majesty, and I doubt you hate it more than she does. If you'll forgive me, the two of you are a lot alike. I think that's your biggest problem. You were both too proud to bend first."

"A king cannot appear weak before his subjects. A weakness in the king is perceived as a weakness in the country." Theron sighed and his shoulders slumped. "I did what I could."

"Leonas?"

"He watched over her for me. Kept me informed." He drummed his fingers on the desk. "Apparently not as well informed as I thought." *A baby.* He couldn't deal with the concept. The Annice of his memory was fourteen. Or five. But he didn't know this Annice at all. "I missed her."

Stasya snorted, sounding remarkably like Liene. "Tell her, Majesty, not me."

Theron nodded. "When this is over."

Recognizing a dismissal, Stasya bowed. Her hand was on the door when the king's voice stopped her.

"I'm going to want you to go to Ohrid, but we'll speak again before you leave. This deception must be closely planned if it's to work."

Annice woke, aware something was wrong but unable for the moment to determine what. *Where am I?* The rocking motion suggested riverboat, then the cart hit a bump and she remembered.

"Heard they had terrible trouble with mice over Fourth Quarter," Bartek the carter confided, slipping the two gulls they'd settled on for the fare into his pocket. *"I got oats, barley, spring wheat, and some corn. Just so much extra here, but if I get it to market in Vidor by the new moon, I figure I can make a killing. Climb on board, make yourself comfortable. You both look like you could use some shut-eye."*

With the sacks of seed grain molded to her aching back, Annice fell asleep before the cart was out of Riverton.

Now she was awake and she wanted to know why. The baby was quiet. Nothing hurt. The sun poured heat over her like molten gold.

The sun.

Directly overhead.

Noon.

She opened her eyes and looked for Pjerin.

He was sitting rigidly upright against the side of the cart, one leg raised, his forearm resting across his knee. The shirt that Stasya had found for him was a bit small and with the fabric pulled tight across his chest, Annice could see each shallow breath. There were hollows in his cheeks that hadn't been there in Third Quarter and the bruising around his eye made him seem achingly fragile. She had the strangest desire to go over to him and let him rest his head on her shoulder while she stroked the long fall of dark hair.

Out of the Circle with that! I refuse to get maternal about him.

His other hand worked against the bag of corn beside him, grinding the kernels together.

The grinding was the sound that had woken her.

Reaching out one arm, she poked him in the calf of his outstretched leg—all she could touch without moving. "Hey. You're alive."

Violet eyes found hers, dark with anger, not pain.

"And I'm going to stay alive." It was more a threat than a promise. "And when we find out who did this to me, I'm going to make them wish they'd never been born."

CHAPTER TEN

"Traders in the pass!"

The voice drifted down from the high watchtower, echoing off the stone of the mountain and sounding remote but clear in the lower bailey.

Olina shook her head at Gerek's questioning glance. "That's only first warning. You've time to finish your practice." When he was old enough to learn the sword, she'd hire an armsmaster—as her father had done for her and Pjerin's for him—but the Ducs of Ohrid trained with the mountain bow from the time they could walk, the bow growing taller as they did.

The boy sighed and set another arrow to the string.

"Traders at the wall!"

If Gerek squinted, he could just make out the tiny figure waving from the top of the wall-tower. Responding to the cry, the men and women of the keep began to make their way toward the gate. Gerek turned and looked hopefully up at his aunt.

"If you hit the target with this last arrow, you can come with me to meet them," she promised.

Brow furrowed with concentration, Gerek pulled and released. Although the target wasn't far, it was at the edge of his range and the arrow wobbled a little in flight. Perhaps pushed on by the intensity of the violet stare locked onto it, it managed to just reach the lower edge of the bundle of straw.

"It hit! It hit! And it *stayed*," he added, just in case his aunt hadn't noticed.

"That's very well done, Gerek." Olina smiled down at the boy. "I'm very proud of you."

Gerek preened. "I'm gonna shoot like my papa. My papa can hit anything."

"Your papa is dead, Gerek." She'd tried being gentle, she'd tried discussing it with him—she'd finally given up and merely repeated the bald statement as often as she was given cause.

His lower lip jutted out and Gerek prepared to do battle.

"No." Her hand chopped off his protest before it began. "I am not going to argue with you. Your father is dead. You are now the duc. Gather up your arrows, and put your equipment away. You should be finished long before the traders reach the gate." He hesitated, obviously still considering a defense of his absent father. "Or would you rather not see the traders at all?"

The threat worked where reason stood no chance. Olina watched the boy run to the target and wondered how much longer she was going to have to put up with his nonsense. *The boy isn't quite five, surely he'll soon forget.*

With the First Quarter rains over and the roads passable—*Or what stands for roads in this unenclosed part of the world . . .*—Olina expected a courier from the king with the official notification of the Judgment. Not that she needed to be told what had happened; the part of the plan that removed the stewardship of the pass from her nephew's hands was foolproof. The penalty for treason was death and she knew that Pjerin would rather die than throw himself on anyone's mercy. Therefore, Pjerin was dead.

But if the child won't believe me, maybe he'll believe the king.

She smiled and stretched in the sun like a cat. Gerek had been repeating to everyone his version of Pjerin's last words. *"They made a mistake. The king will make everything better and then my papa will come back."* He had half the village and most of the keep partially convinced as not even those who personally found their duc somewhat arrogant and overbearing had wanted to believe the evidence they'd heard. When that piping cry changed to a howl of *"The king killed my papa!"*, neither His Majesty nor the thought of Shkoder rule would be very popular in Ohrid.

Gerek bounced out of the armory and raced toward

the gate of the keep, short legs pumping. "Come on, Aunty Olina! Come on!"

Still smiling, she followed the boy to the gate.

"You want to set up a *what* outside the village?"

"A fair, gracious lady." The portly trader swept off his hat and managed to actually bow more-or-less from the waist. He spoke the local dialect with a Cemandia accent. "Why, we asked ourselves, should we travel to distant foreign cities to sell our wares when there is a market eager to buy just over the border."

Eager? Olina snorted silently. *Try slavering.* The villagers seldom reaped any benefit of the scanty trade that traveled through the pass; sheep and timber being in abundance on both sides. The pass itself was their only worthwhile commodity, and Pjerin, the fool, had refused to take advantage of it. Nor would he have allowed so many Cemandians to remain so near the keep but would have insisted they move on and provided an escort to see that they did.

"We have strong markets in Cemandia for both fleece and timber," the trader continued as though reading her mind. "And I have a client who has interest in strong mountain rams for cross-breeding purposes."

"My nephew was recently executed for conspiring with a Cemandia trader. He planned to allow a Cemandian army through the pass."

The trader blanched and his hand rose to trace the sign of the Circle over his heart as the small crowd of villagers began to mutter. "War, gracious lady, is so bad for business. I assure you, we have no ulterior motive but profit."

It was impossible not to believe he was sincere. "If you wish only to trade in peace," Olina raised her voice so that those watching would hear and pass it on, "I will bring the matter up with my duc." Her fingers closed around Gerek's narrow shoulder. "Shall we let them have their fair?" she asked him.

He looked up at her, brightly colored caravans reflecting in wide eyes. "What's a fair?"

"Like a market day, only better."

Gerek bounced. "Fairs are good," he declared.

The trader bowed again and produced from the

pocket of a voluminous trouser leg a small crimson top which he presented with a flourish. "So we have your permission, Your Grace?"

"Yes." Gerek took the top quickly, before any of the adults standing around could decide he wasn't to have it. " 'Cause I am taking care of things till my papa comes back."

A slender man with short blond curls, who leaned negligently against one of the smaller wagons, smiled.

". . . your duc was accused by bards, was he, lady? We don't have much use for bards in Cemandia. Now you won't find finer pins than this anywhere . . ."

". . . fine-looking young ram and I can give you a good price for him, too. Folk in Cemandia appreciate the work that's gone into breeding for him, let me tell you . . ."

". . . save you an incredible amount of work, they will. I can't imagine no traders from Shkoder have brought them in. Well, never mind, I can beat their prices right out of the Circle . . ."

Olina walked slowly around the small fair, admiring the subtle—and occasionally less than subtle—working of Cemandian influence. She stopped for a moment to watch a fair young man keep half a dozen clubs in the air in a spinning cascade. His golden-blond curls gleamed in the afternoon sun and a breeze chased itself through the gilt. Below the pushed-up sleeves of his cotton shirt, the muscles of his forearms danced under the pale sheath of skin. As the small crowd gathered around him gazed open-mouthed at his skill, Olina dropped her eyes to the fit of his breeches.

"He's no more than a mountebank really." The portly trader stood suddenly by her side, wiping his jowls with a huge square of linen. "But we've found that a little free amusement makes people less willing to argue a price."

"He looks very . . ." Her brows dipped speculatively. ". . . coordinated."

"Yes. I suppose."

"When he's finished, could you tell him I'd like a private performance. Tonight. In the keep."

"He warned me that you'd eat me alive."

Olina laughed. "Maybe later." She stretched out her legs and crossed her feet at the ankles. "I like you with those short blond curls. It makes you look younger, more vulnerable."

Albek helped himself to a cup of beer. "Thank you." He wore a rough homespun vest over his wide-sleeved shirt and his manner echoed his clothing; his voice less polished, his speech less subtle. "Rumor says the king accused Pjerin of treason, sent a bard to condemn him, and a hundred guards to drag him away."

"There were twenty guards, but rumor got the essentials right. It was too much for poor old Bohdan. He's tottered off to his daughter's and taken to his bed."

"So the new duc will need a new steward. Unless you intend to do the job yourself."

"Don't be ridiculous. I have someone suitably sympathetic to Cemandia in mind."

"You're certain Pjerin is dead?" Albek asked, leaning against the mantel.

"It probably happened some time ago, but you know what the roads are like at this time of the year. I'm expecting the official messengers to ride up any day now, covered in mud and glad to be done with it."

"I told you it would work."

"Yes, you did. Now, tell me why you've brought so many little friends with you across the border?"

"Two reasons." He turned a chair and sat straddling it, arms resting along the top of the back. "Albek always traveled alone so *Simion* does not. Albek was an aristocrat of traders, polished and urbane. These people are as far from that as I could stand traveling with. And . . ." He took a long pull on the cup and wiped his mouth on the back of his hand. ". . . as I had to check out the situation anyway, I thought I could use the opportunity to stir up a little sedition. Nothing overt, just a bit of *Cemandia good, Shkoder bad*."

Olina looked thoughtful. "So these traders work for you?"

"Not directly. But the Cemandian crown will be buying more fleece and timber than it really wants this year."

"The crown seems to be spending a lot of money on this considering the pass is open to them now."

Albek/Simion shrugged. "Wars are much more expensive and the longer they take to win, the more they cost. We have a saying in Cemandia that the word is not only mightier than the sword, but it's cheaper, too. By the time Her Majesty's army comes through that pass, I want the only resistance to come from parents who don't want their children to join up."

"That might not be so difficult to accomplish." She told him how Gerek had unwittingly been adding to the *Shkoder bad* opinion. "By the time the child's finished, Pjerin will be a martyr to half of Ohrid."

"But Pjerin was anti-Cemandia."

"*Cemandia good,* remember? We're looking for an emotional response." Olina slowly stood. "They were left so emotionally flayed by his betrayal that they're very open to suggestion and will only remember that Shkoder killed him."

"It sounds as though you've been busy."

"I may have dropped a word or two in the right ears."

He could feel her strength, the heat of her focus, from across the room. "And the other half?"

"Pjerin was going to sell them out. They hate him. If he was anti-Cemandia, they're for it."

"But he was going to sell them out *to* Cemandia."

"You're forgetting that in an emotional response rational thought has no place. If you can manage to invoke two or three conflicting emotional responses, rational thought has no chance. Those who aren't convinced to help the invasion will either be so confused that they won't hinder it or easy enough to remove." She reached up and pulled out the pins holding the weight of her hair. It cascaded down over her shoulders like a fall of night. "Come here."

He stood and wet lips gone suddenly dry. It was a long walk to her side and his past walked with him, murmuring in his ear, anxious for the release she could offer.

Strong fingers reached out and snaked through golden curls, pulling him forward over the last couple of feet. "It's time Cemandia showed me some return on my investment."

Later, much later, Olina took the edge of his ear in

her teeth and murmured, "Many of them fear the bards, fear the Singing of the kigh."

He twisted under her grip, unable to remain still. "No one Sings the kigh in Cemandia."

"Yet another convincing reason to for them to switch allegiance." The nails of one hand scored the inside of his thigh. "Half of them already believe there are things that should not be allowed in the Circle. After all ..." She smiled as he cried out. "... who knows what fell powers these bards can exert if they so desire."

"Annice, what are we doing here?"

"We're traders, remember?" She stepped over a small, foul-smelling pile she had no wish to investigate too closely and turned down a narrow street that led toward the center of town. "We're going to trade."

Pjerin grabbed her arm and pulled her to a stop. "We are not traders," he snarled after glancing around to make certain he wouldn't be overheard. "And we're going to Ohrid."

She glared at him until he removed his hand, then she asked, "If we aren't traders, what are we?"

"We're just *telling* people we're traders." His nostrils above the dark bristle of incipient mustache were pinched almost shut. The six days' travel up River Road, afraid to open his mouth for fear he'd be recognized and dragged back to Elbasan, had rubbed his nerves raw and he'd had as much as he was going to take. "I'm tired of pretending to be something I'm not."

"And you think I'm not tired of it?" she demanded incredulously. "The bards have a corner in every inn along River Road. I could've slept warm and dry and well fed inside. Instead, because we're *traders*, I slept under a cart and worked at not being seen by people who might know me. I had to constantly keep reinforcing our story. I couldn't relax. I couldn't sing. I couldn't play."

Pjerin had no intention of dispensing sympathy. From the moment he'd faced Command in his own ancestral hall to the moment just past when they'd left the carter's yard, he'd been swept along by events beyond his control. It seemed he was as helpless to affect his destiny now as he had been when beaten and bound by the

King's Guard and there was nothing he hated more than feeling helpless. "At least," he spat, "you had a choice!"

"A choice?" Annice stared up at him in astonishment. "Oh, sure I had a choice; I could've chosen to let you die!" She spun away from him and started walking again, not caring at that moment whether he followed or not.

He watched her go, remembered the kigh, swore, and hurried to catch up. The worst of it was, he'd heard the genuine sorrow in her voice when she'd said she couldn't sing or play. "Annice? I'm sorry."

Oh, no, you're not. You're angry because you've got to depend on me, can't be His high-and-mighty Grace the Duc of Ohrid standing alone on his mountaintop. Well, tough shit. Half-turning, she glared up at him. "If we don't *act* like traders, no one will believe we *are* traders. They'll start asking questions. Questions we don't want. Ohrid is on the other side of Vidor so, since we have to go through town anyway, we're going to get rid of some of the expensive luxury items we've been packing from Elbasan and pick up things that'll be of more value where we're going. If we make enough of a profit, we can pick up a pack mule."

Pjerin's glower shifted into astonishment. "A what?"

"Well, I personally would prefer a good-sized cara-van," she said sarcastically, shifting her weight from foot to foot as the baby started to kick, "but as the whole idea is to disappear into the wilderness after Vidor, I'm willing to compromise."

"What's wrong with horses?"

Annice sighed dramatically and took a certain satisfac-tion from Pjerin's reaction to it. "I have walked from one end of this country to the other in all kinds of weather, carrying everything I needed on my back and in my voice. I'm willing to walk beside you to Ohrid carrying this baby, but I'll be unenclosed if I carry a pack as well. I realize," she held up a hand as he tried to interrupt, "that you'd rather gallop off in a cloud of dust, but you're stuck with me and I'm not putting this body, in this condition, on a horse. Even if we could afford one—let alone two—which we can't. While you're thinking about it, and realizing I'm right, I'm going to go find a privy."

He caught up to her again in four paces. She thought she could hear his teeth grinding.

"If you weren't carrying my child," he growled. "I'd take my chances with the kigh."

"Your child?" Annice turned to face him again. Their conversations traveling River Road had been nearly nonexistent; they'd never really been alone. The carter hadn't exactly been intrusive, but he'd always been a presence they'd had to account for. "Let me tell you something, Your Grace ..." Almost biting her tongue with the effort, she broke off as a chattering cluster of teenagers pushed past them. Overhead, a pair of neighbors leaned out third-floor windows and discussed the weather. "Never mind. This isn't the place. But when we get on the road again and it's just you and I, we're going to have a little *chat.*"

"I'll be looking forward to it."

"I wouldn't," she advised tightly.

How do you know about all this trading stuff?"

They were the first words he'd spoken to her in hours and, although he still sounded more annoyed than interested, Annice found she was actually glad he'd finally broken the silence. They might as well make an effort, if only a superficial one, to get along.

"Bards and traders often travel together for short distances," she told him as they circled around the perimeter of Vidor's smaller permanent market, trusting the babble of voices buying and selling to cover hers. They had almost everything they needed—their packs lighter by a considerable amount of trade goods and their purse heavier by a reasonable amount of coin—and as soon as she found some halfway decent jerky, they could get the mule and get out of town. "I can recall most of what I've been told over the ... Oh, shit!"

Pjerin froze, his hand dropping to the hilt of the long, heavy dagger now hanging at his side. It wasn't a sword, but *traders* didn't carry swords and *he* wouldn't carry any of the twisted timber they called bows in the lowlands. "What is it?"

"Crier. There's a Bardic Hall in Vidor and there's always someone there who can Sing air. They've probably got your description from the captain and given it

to him. Don't run." Her voice teetered on the edge of
Command as he tensed for flight. "The *last* thing you
want to do is attract attention."

"Fine." A muscle jumped in his jaw but he stood
where he was. "What's the *first* thing I want to do?"

"Keep your head down and try not to look like yourself." Fingers wrapped around his, Annice guided him
slowly between the two outside rows of stalls and toward
the nearest exit from the square. It only took a moment
for her to realize they weren't going to be away in time.
Passing a meat pie vendor, she paused long enough to
hand over a half-gull and shove one of two pies at Pjerin.
"Eat this."

"I'm not hungry."

"You don't have to be, it'll distort your face."

Even with six days' growth of beard, clothes that
didn't quite fit, and dirty hair clubbed back at the nape
of his neck, Pjerin's looks attracted attention. It didn't
help that a disproportionately high number of the crowd
seemed to be Riverfolk and he towered over them.

*Maybe we should've gone around Vidor. Hiding him
out in plain sight is one thing, but maybe this was an
unnecessary risk.* Annice fought for calm as the baby
reacted to the turmoil, twisting and pushing against the
flesh that confined it. *And it's a fine time to think of
unnecessary risk now.*

"Oy-yay! Oy-YAY!" The ambient noise of the market
dropped slightly as the crier began. Trained at the
Bardic Hall in memory technique and voice projection,
the criers kept the largely illiterate public informed and
Annice had completely forgotten about their existence
in Vidor.

How could I be so stupid? She couldn't hope to Command a crowd this large.

But the crier never mentioned the escaped Duc of
Ohrid.

"I don't understand," Annice muttered, tossing the
remains of the pie at an emaciated orange cat.

"He must've already done it."

"No." She shook her head. "It should be called every
day until you're caught."

Pjerin stepped aside as a burly server, his basket
loaded with fernheads and frostpeas, pushed past them.

The mix of meat and pastry had congealed into a fist-sized lump just under his ribs. "A trap, then." It was the only answer. "To lull us into a false sense of security."

"Too complicated. Why would they bother when . . ." She frowned as she caught a floating scrap of conversation.

"Annice?"

Still frowning, she lifted a hand to silence him and cocked her head toward the babble of voices rising out of the center of the market.

Pjerin was getting more than a little tired of her imperious attitude. He opened his mouth to tell her so. He never got the chance.

"Wait here." Sliding out of her pack, she shoved it into his hands with enough force that he took a step backward between two tottering piles of willow baskets and could only watch, fuming, as she pushed her way into the crowd.

Although he never actually lost sight of her, by the time she returned a few moments later he'd worked an edge up on his temper. "You walk off on me again like that," he snarled, "and I won't be there when you get back."

Annice shot a glance at the basket seller. Deep in a spirited defense of his bottom-weave with a less than satisfied customer, he wasn't likely to overhear anything she said. Shoving her hair back off her face, she glared up at Pjerin. "Maybe you won't be. The fishmonger said a troop of King's Guard rode into Vidor about mid-morning."

Pjerin's fingers closed around the upper edge of Annice's pack with enough force to buckle the frame. "They must've been right behind us. We should've kept going!"

"No!" She took a step forward and winced as the baby objected to her vehemence by drumming its heels on her bladder. "They're looking for the escaped Duc of Ohrid and we've spent the day convincing the city we're traders. I'm telling you, we're safe."

"Fine." His smile was tight. "Tell that to the six guards who've just come into the market."

"What?" She whirled around, careening off the surrounding stacks of baskets. Ignoring the muffled yell of protest from the basket seller, out of sight behind his dangerously swaying stock, she could see no farther than a cluster of people grouped around the egg seller's stall.

From his advantage of height, Pjerin had no difficulty following their progress. "Someone just sent the corporal to the fishmonger's."

Annice heaved her bulk up onto her toes. She thought she might be able to see the sun glinting off the upper edge of a helm, but she wasn't certain.

"Let's get out of here." Enough was enough, Pjerin reached forward and grabbed her shoulder. "Now!"

She shook him off. "The fishmonger never saw you."

"Then why is he pointing this way?"

Eyes wide, she turned to stare up into his face. "Are you sure?"

"No! I'm kidding! Center it, Annice! How could I be unsure about something like that!" This time when he grabbed her shoulder, he actually managed to get her moving. "I'll carry your pack, just go!"

Too late.

"There they are!"

The crowd, in the way of crowds, parted and Pjerin found himself staring down a wide and unobstructed aisle at the corporal. She was young, with a wide mouth and legs too long for her body. He could take her down, get her sword, sell his freedom dearly. They weren't taking him back to Elbasan. They'd have to kill him first.

A cascade of baskets broke the tableau.

And the crowd, in the way of crowds, closed in to see what was going on.

"This way!" Annice grabbed his arm and dragged him to the right. "There's an alley!"

Over the shrill shrieks of the basket seller and the swarm of rising speculation, they could hear the corporal demanding that they stop in the king's name. Although Annice was running as fast as she could, even laden with both packs, Pjerin reached the mouth of the alley first.

Not quite as wide as even Annice was tall, the cobbles of the market square cut off abruptly at its mouth. From wall to crumbling wall and as far as he could see down its length, the footing was a treacherous mix of churned mud and garbage. One of the clay pipes intended to carry rain from the roof to a cistern dribbled water into

the mess and from the stench, it appeared that chamberpots were emptied out of upper windows more often
than into the honey wagons. Pjerin doubted a rat could
keep its footing.

"We can't go down there," he barked as Annice
caught up, stopping her before she could step off the
cobblestones. "We'll have to go around."

"Not us," Annice panted. "Them. Take them ages.
Follow right behind me and stay close."

Holding her belly with both hands, she took a deep
breath and Sang. Then she jogged forward, still Singing.

Pjerin stared in horror at the ground. It looked, just
for a moment, as though she were moving over the bent
backs of squat, earth-colored . . . things. And then it was
just a path, displaced flies buzzing agitatedly above it.
Not very wide and not very dry but infinitely preferable
to the surrounding alley.

It formed beneath her as she advanced and stretched
back behind her—as he watched, the solid ground far-
thest from her feet dissolved back into mud. Her reason
for telling him to stay close all at once became obvious.
Teeth clenched, he leaped forward and landed on the
disintegrating edge of the path. He felt himself begin to
sink, the stench of rot becoming infinitely worse as his
boot heels broke through the thin greenish-gray crust.
Leg muscles trembling with the effort, he somehow con-
trived to propel himself and both packs up onto solid
footing, then, trying not to inhale, he hurried after
Annice.

He reached the end of the alley one step behind her,
and, well aware that he shouldn't, he turned and looked
back the way they'd come just as the half dozen guards
were arriving at the other end. It was the first really
funny thing he could remember happening in over a
quarter and he felt he deserved a moment to appreciate
the variety of profanity that rose as three of them
charged forward and sank almost to their knees.

Annice finished Singing the gratitude and clutched at
a fold of Pjerin's jacket, suddenly dizzy. She wouldn't
have made it down the alley if she hadn't been pulling
strength from the earth, but now the kigh were gone,
she wanted nothing so much as a chance to collapse.
Unfortunately, she wasn't going to get that chance for a

while. "Pjerin, come on." She tugged on the jacket. "We haven't gained that much time."

"I'm not so worried about them." Pjerin turned away as one of the three managed to struggle back to firm footing. "But your fishmonger said a troop of King's Guard rode into town. There're twenty-one guards in a troop." He was intimately familiar with the number. "Where are the rest of them?"

"Not here." At the moment, that was all Annice had the energy to worry about. Breathing heavily, she led the way through a maze of back streets and alleys, all of them damp and stinking of rot but none as bad as the first. Twice they narrowly missed being drenched with the contents of chamberpots and once skirted a shower coming straight from the source. The middle-aged man blew a kiss to Annice as she looked up and then another at Pjerin. At one point, a group of ragged children dogged their heels, screaming insults until a shrill voice from a shadowed doorway brought their game to a sullen stop.

Finally they reached a narrow opening between two buildings in better shape than most they'd been passing and Annice wedged herself into it. Pjerin had to slide out of his pack to follow.

"Watch for the dead cat," Annice hissed as, arms trembling, he set the packs down.

"Dead cats," he growled back, leaning sideways to see over her head, "are the least of our worries. Where are we?"

"One street away from the Center," she told him, moving enough for him to get a look at the slice of the city defined by the buildings tight on either side of them. In the near distance loomed the round bulk of the Center of Vidor, a nearly new and smaller copy of one in Elbasan. "I don't see any of the guards. Let's go."

"Wait a minute. Go where?"

"I can't run if they catch up to us again, Pjerin. We'll have to hide and slip out of town after dark."

He stared out at the wide, tree-lined boulevard that led to the Center. "I think we've gone past the possibility of hiding in plain sight," he said dryly.

"Don't worry." She reached behind her and gripped his forearm for an instant. "I know a place."

Because he had no better option, he picked up both packs, stepped over the dead cat, and followed her out onto the street. "Why," he asked, "am I not surprised?"

"Just stroll," she told him quietly as he fell into step beside her. "Act like we have every right in the world to be here."

"Are we still traders?"

"For the moment."

The Center loomed closer.

"There they are!"

There was no mistaking the source of the cry. As they started to run, Annice found herself wondering if guards were trained to achieve that particular doom-laden timbre or if it came with the uniform.

"They won't give us sanctuary!" Pjerin yelled as they pounded toward the Center.

Annice didn't have breath enough to answer.

They reached the curved wall of the building not very much ahead of the guards. As Annice began circling right, Pjerin shouted, "Where are you going?"

"Around!" she answered.

"No!" He headed for the double doors under the fire sigil. "Go through."

Annice turned and ran after him. They burst through the doors and into the round chamber, their pounding footsteps echoing under the high arch of the vaulted ceiling. A quartet of priests turned from the altar as they passed but weren't in time to stop them. By the time the following guards came through, they were at the water door and the priests had moved out and were ready to intercept. They were outside again with a little more time bought.

Annice spun to her left and Sang. A narrow door swung open where a moment before there'd been only stone.

"Wha . . ." Pjerin came to a dead stop.

"Bard's Door!" she gasped, grabbing his arm and dragging him forward. "Go on!"

He dove through the opening and she threw herself in behind, Singing it closed as she moved.

Tumbled together on the stairs, they heard shouted questions, pounding footsteps, and then, mercifully, silence.

Pjerin felt her weight fall against him and dropped her
pack to grab for her. Together, they sank down to the
stairs. "Annice! Are you all right?"

What a stupid question. She wanted to smack him.
"I'm not . . . exactly in shape . . . for much running."

Half-cradling her against his body, he twisted around,
wincing as his pack straps dug into still tender ribs.
While they sat in semidarkness, the top of the stairs were
lit by diffused sunlight. "What's up there?"

"Balconies, for Singing from. A gallery around. Not
much else." Fingers trembling with the effort, she clawed
at the buttons of her smock. The air in the narrow stair-
way was cooler than that outside but she could feel rivu-
lets of sweat running down between her breasts. Elica
had told her she could walk all she wanted, but she
wasn't to overheat. *Oh, baby, I'm sorry. I couldn't . . .
there wasn't . . . don't . . .*

A sudden cramp threw her head back and it slammed
into Pjerin's chest. The noise she made was more from
fear than pain.

"Annice?"

She could feel his breath warm against the top of her
head as he bent over her and she swatted ineffectually
at his hands until he caught her wrists.

"Annice, calm down and tell me what's wrong."

There was a note of command in his voice she'd never
heard before and a strength that had nothing to do with
ego. She caught her breath on another cramp and then,
to her horror, burst into tears. "The b . . . baby . . ."

"Open the door." He started to rise. "We're getting
you to a healer."

"No!" She pulled him back down and fought for control. "Just let me rest."

"Are you sure?" He didn't sound like he believed her.

She didn't believe herself, but if they went to a healer
now everything would be lost. *Baby, I'm sorry.* She
wiped her nose on her sleeve. "Yes, I'm sure."

Pjerin settled back down on the step, sliding his arms
out of his pack straps but leaving it behind him. He *had*
to trust that Annice knew her body. Gently, he pulled
her back into the circle of his arms. "All right. Rest."

She sniffed again but didn't pull away. After a moment, she let her head fall into the curve of his shoulder

and sucked in a long shuddering breath as a third cramp
twisted the muscles of her lower back.

It seemed the most natural thing in the world for his
free hand to come up and stroke her hair. "I'm sorry I
got you into this," he murmured.

"Me, too." Her heart had slowed a little so that it
wasn't slamming so frighteningly hard against her ribs.
"When we catch up with whoever's responsible, you owe
me a piece of them."

He smiled and brushed a sweat-damp strand of hair
up off her forehead. "Agreed."

"A pregnant woman cannot just disappear, Corporal."

The corporal kept her eyes locked on a point just over
the captain's shoulder. "The man with Her Highness was
a trader, he must have contacts in the city."

"The man with who?"

"Uh, I mean the bard, Captain." The corporal could
feel the blood burning in her ears, and knew they were
an embarrassingly brilliant red.

The captain snorted. "Remember that. She made her
choice a long time ago."

"Yes, Captain."

"Well, don't just stand there. You know what section
of the city you're supposed to be searching."

"Yes, Captain." The corporal spun on her heel and
hurried from the room, the warning verses from the
"Princess-Bard" echoing in her head. She didn't really
believe His Majesty would execute his sister for treason.
Not really. But she'd taken her squad the long way
around the market just in case.

The captain, fully aware of where the sympathies of
most of her troop lay, watched her go and sighed deeply.
Not for the first time, she wished she could share the
private orders His Majesty had given her.

*Don't listen to anything they say and tell them, when
you catch them, that* all *is forgiven.*

"You look like you've had pleasanter duties."

She started and snapped her attention back to the
here and now. "Otik. What are you doing here?"

"I'm on leave," Otik explained coming into the room.
"I've family in Vidor." He sauntered over to the table
she was using as a desk and peered down at the maps

of the city spread across it. "Nicely done. Must be bard work."

"They are." She folded her arms as he bent over and began tracing the streets with one finger. He wore civilian clothes like he was still in uniform. *And moves like he's got a poker up his butt.* "I meant, what are you doing *here*?"

"A troop of King's Guard rides into Vidor and I'm not supposed to be curious why?" Otik snorted. "Please, Luci, you'd have checked it out, too."

"Yeah, I guess." But she admitted it grudgingly. Self-interest had motivated too many of Captain Otik's previous actions and he was now clawing his way toward commander with what she considered a disgusting amount of ass kissing. If there was a way to get in good with the brass, he headed straight for it. On the other hand, as he'd likely make commander some day, she couldn't afford to alienate him too badly. *More's the pity.*

"So." He pushed the maps aside and perched on the corner of the table. "What are *you* doing here?"

Unfortunately, there wasn't any reason not to tell him. "We're looking for His Majesty's sister, the bard. It seems she's committed bodily treason."

Otik blinked. "What?"

"She got knocked up. His Majesty found out and we've been sent to bring her and the proud daddy back to the bosom of her family. As long as you're around, you might as well make yourself useful." Luci reached over and picked up a piece of paper closely covered with cramped writing. "They were spotted this afternoon."

"Your penmanship stinks," Otik muttered, scanning the description around the blots of black ink. Then he read it again. He'd started it a third time when Luci plucked it out of his hand.

"Now, if you'll excuse me, Captain," she said pointedly, "I have work to do."

"Yes, yes, of course. Good hunting, Captain."

He's onto something, she thought as he strode out the door. *Fortunately, I don't give a shit what it is.*

It's impossible. He's dead. Unaware of anything around him, Otik kept turning the description around in his mind, fitting pieces of it into memory, trying to understand what could possibly be going on.

The Duc of Ohrid was executed. it was witnessed. It happened.

So why did the trader with His Majesty's sister appear to be the same man?

Coincidence? He brushed past a friend of his mother's without seeing her or hearing her speak. *No. He's too unenclosed distinctive looking for it to be coincidence. It's him. I know it's him. I gave him that black eye he's still wearing the shadow of.*

As impossible as it seemed, the Duc of Ohrid had escaped, with the king's sister, the Princess-Bard, and was, it appeared, the father of her child.

All at once, it wasn't so impossible that the duc had escaped.

"Bards!" Otik spat out the word. They were nothing but trouble. He understood completely why King Theron had kept the truth from Captain Luci. *His own sister, caught up in treason, selling her country to Cemandia for a tumble.* It made him sick to think of it. Obviously, His Majesty was hoping to recapture the pair of them with no one the wiser.

King Theron would be very pleased with whoever cleaned up this little mess for him. Very pleased.

Otik smiled. He had two advantages that Luci and her troop didn't. He knew where the fugitives were heading—Ohrid and the border—and he knew that as the duc was already technically dead, there was no need to go to the trouble of bringing him back alive.

CHAPTER ELEVEN

Annice woke with a start, jerking out of a dream where she'd fallen in the middle of River Road, her legs unable to hold her weight. With the thunder of hooves against the hard-packed earth filling the world around her, she'd only been able to desperately try to roll clear. Trained to recall her dreams and use them for inspiration, she shoved this one aside. *There's a limit to art imitating life.*

As she lifted her head, Pjerin shifted behind her, flexing the arm she'd been resting against.

"Welcome back," he said quietly.

Yawning, Annice heaved herself awkwardly to her feet, rubbing the imprint of the stone step out of her butt. "How long was I asleep?"

"Long enough for my legs to go numb." He shook them out and pushed himself upright against the wall, wincing as a thousand points of pain danced from ankles to hips.

"You could've moved me."

He gestured around the narrow stairwell and asked, "Where? Look, don't worry about it," he went on, trying to pound some feeling back into his calves. "It was more important that you sleep. How are you feeling?"

"Better," she admitted. The baby stirred as though it, too, were just waking. She smiled and traced the motion with her fingertips. "I think everything's all right."

"Good." Leaning against the wall, Pjerin realized he sounded abrupt and wondered if he should tell her how frightened he'd been that she was going to lose the baby. *No,* he decided. *That's over. Time to move on.* "So," he asked instead, "what now?"

Annice sighed. "I have to use the privy."

Pjerin managed to stop himself before the *of course you do* left his mouth. "So do I."

Together they turned and stared at the dark curve of wall at the foot of the stairs.

Annice, being closer, reached out and laid her hand flat on the cool stone.

"Do you think it's safe to leave?"

She shrugged, then realized he probably couldn't see her, and said, "I don't know. Even if the guards aren't around, people are going to notice a pair of traders going out the Bard's Door."

"Perhaps it's time we stopped being traders." He spoke lightly, not intending to start another argument. To his astonishment, she agreed, turned, and started up the stairs. "Where are you going?" he demanded as she squeezed past.

"If we're not going to be traders," Annice explained, pausing just above him, "we have to be something else. Sometimes—like now, in First Quarter, when most of the bards are out Walking—a bard will have to Sing more than one Quarter during a service. When that happens, they leave extra robes in the gallery behind the balconies." She started climbing again.

He caught her arm. "We're going to be bards?"

She threw a smile back over her shoulder. "Why not? They're looking for traders."

Mouth pressed to a thin line, Pjerin let her go and returned to working on his legs. He'd been able to see her face clearly as she passed, her cheeks were flushed, her eyes were gleaming, and she'd obviously forgotten the lesson the guards had taught them. They weren't on an adventure destined to last for only six verses and five choruses, they were fighting to stay alive. The sooner she remembered that, the better chance all three of them would have.

Annice stepped off the stairs, sliding her boots along the floor to muffle her footsteps. The angle of the light slanting through the carved stone screen that separated the gallery from the chamber told her it was nearly sunset. She'd have to hurry. Bards by no means Sang every service but they couldn't risk the chance of discovery.

Water came up empty, so she circled around to her right toward air.

If only Pjerin would realize that there's more to staying

safe than putting his head down and charging for Ohrid.
She'd hoped the chase scene they'd played out with the
guards had taught him that, but, obviously, from his
comments, it hadn't.

There were no robes in air. Silently pleading with the
baby to stop bouncing on her bladder, Annice hurried
around to earth and practically threw herself at the
hanging brown fabric. The robe could've been made for
her and her condition although, from the lingering scent
of sandalwood, she suspected it belonged to Tymon, the
head of the Hall in Vidor. He was short and fat and
unwilling to carry an ounce more than his own weight.

She was certain of it when she reached fire and found
a second robe, identical but for the color. Although he
Sang all four quarters, a necessity if he was going to run
the Hall, Tymon had apparently not Sung one of either
air or water at the last service he'd done. The third quarter he *had* Sung, would've been the robe he wore home.

Fighting the urge to step out onto the balcony and try
to Sing the altar candles alight, Annice walked as quickly
as she could for the stairs, feeling suddenly hollow.

*I need to be a bard again, if only for a little while. I
miss it all so much. I miss Singing. I miss recall.* She
rubbed a bit of robe against her cheek. *I hate wearing
robes and I even miss them.* At the top of the stairs she
looked around the curve, past water, toward air. *And I
really miss Stasya.* Before, when they'd been apart,
there'd always been the kigh to link them together. *I
hope she's okay.*

Which was when she realized.

Pjerin heard the noise from the top of the stairs and
whirled around, his hand dropping to the hilt of his dagger. He squinted up into the fading light and could just
barely make out a familiar silhouette. "Annice?"

She started toward him, but her movements were so
stiff that he raced up to meet her. "What is it? What's
wrong?"

"They've got Stasya. I have to go back."

He caught hold of her shoulders and turned her, unre-
sisting, to face him. The stricken look on her face closed
a fist around his heart. "Who's got Stasya?" he demanded. "What are you talking about?"

Tears spilling unheeded down her cheeks, Annice had to swallow hard to find her voice. "The guards," she said at last, "called out, *There they are!* There *they* are, Pjerin. Stasya was the only one who knew we were together. Getting you out of that dungeon was treason and she helped and now she's going to die. I have to stop it."

"How?" When she shook her head blindly and tried to pull away, he tightened his grip and repeated the question. "How, Annice? By surrendering yourself and the baby to that same death? Listen to me, the only chance she has is if we prove my innocence and I need you to do that. Stasya *needs* you to do that."

"What if she's already dead?"

"Then going back won't do her any good."

Her head snapped up and she glared at him. "You shit!"

"That's better," he nodded approvingly. "Be angry. Be angry at me. Be angry at them. But don't give into despair."

She rubbed at her cheeks with the palm of her free hand and remembered the Duc of Ohrid had made six attempts to get free during the long trip from Ohrid to Elbasan. Six attempts surrounded by a troop of guards and a bard who could find him wherever he ran. "If she's dead, I'm going to Sing His Majesty a song that will bring the palace down around his ears."

Pjerin released her. "Witnessed," he said softly.

Pavel i'Gituska woke with the memory of music in his ears. Pleasant music, pretty music, music a man could sleep to. He stretched, scratched, and went out into the evening to check his rented corral. Business hadn't exactly been brisk and he still had five of the eight-mule string he'd come to Vidor with.

He frowned and counted again.

There were only four mules in the corral.

A shriek of outrage had begun to form when he caught sight of the purse hanging off an upright. It wasn't very full, but that didn't end up mattering as the coins it held were silver.

Pavel looked down at the two half-anchors and the double-hawser gleaming on his palm and quite sincerely hoped that his unknown customers would be happy with the mare they'd so drastically overpaid him for.

                              *   *   *

Annice came out from behind the bush designated as
the privy and stared in astonishment. A couple of hours
out of Vidor, they'd camped at a spot she remembered
vaguely from a fledgling Walk; near where a small
stream dropped off a series of stone shelves and rested
for a moment in a deep hollow in the rock. Last night,
the water had been cold enough to bite at the throat
and it wasn't hard to believe that the reflected moonlight
was a tracery of frost.

"Are you out of your mind?" she gasped.

Pjerin sucked air through his teeth as he turned and
the water lapped higher on his body. "I hate being
dirty."

"But you're fond of frostbite?"

His grimace didn't even pretend to be a smile. "You
lowlanders don't know what cold water is," he growled
and ducked under.

Annice almost screamed in sympathy then reluctantly
raised a hand to her own limp tangle of hair. "All things
being enclosed," she muttered the hand dropping to her
belly, "it's a good thing I've got an excuse not to be in
there with him."

She watched appreciatively as he surfaced, muscles
rigid, the tendons in his neck standing out in sharp relief,
hair flung up in an ebony/crystal arc spraying water
across the pond. "Very nice," she said as he waded with
dignified haste toward the shore, "but wasn't that bigger
the last time I saw it?"

Pjerin glanced down. "Shut up," he snarled.

Lips curved but obediently closed, Annice pulled a
cloak up off the pack and handed it to him with exaggerated solicitude.

"I thought I'd let the sun dry me off."

"It's barely up," she pointed out. "And so's . . ."

"Annice!"

"Sorry. I'll get some food ready and we can move
on." With plenty of dry deadfall around, she had a small,
very hot fire going in minutes, and water nearly boiling
in their squat iron trailpot shortly after.

Pjerin was dressed and had the packs ready to load by
the time the oatmeal was done. "You put raisins in it."

She nodded and carefully unwrapped her horn spoon.

"Stasya says that oatmeal without raisins is called a hot grain mash and you feed it to hor ..." Her mouth worked, but the last syllable wouldn't come out. All at once, she wasn't hungry. She set the bowl aside.

Pjerin put it back into her hands, wrapping her fingers around the wooden curve and holding them there until they gripped on their own. "You have to eat."

"I don't want to."

"Tough. The baby hasn't made that choice."

"You don't understand. I forgot. I hadn't thought of it all morning."

"As you said, the sun's barely up."

"What about last night? We were alone. We could've tried to find out what was going on. All we did was sleep."

"Annice, you were barely in command of yourself last night, you couldn't have Commanded me, and you certainly didn't have the energy to begin to untangle the mess in my head."

"But ..."

"No buts." He pushed wet hair off his face. "You can't think about injustice all the time."

Annice lifted her head, nearly choking on the lump in her throat, and met his eyes. "Can't you?" she asked pointedly.

They sat like that for a long moment.

"Eat your oatmeal," the Duc of Ohrid told her at last.

"Ya said ya wouldn't want her fer days yet." The owner of the livery stable squinted up at Otik as he mounted. "Ya shouldn't oughta just take her out like that. Not without warnin' me."

Otik sighed, settled in the saddle, and threw the man a purse. "Look, she's my horse, I can take her when I want her. The full sum we agreed on is in there."

A quick weighing on the palm brought a gap-tooth smile. "But ya said ya wouldn't want her fer days and ..."

"Never mind what I said!" Otik snapped. "I'm taking her now!" He yanked the mare around, put his legs to her, and trotted her out of the livery yard.

The stable owner shrugged and pocketed the purse. "Can't say as I didn't try to tell 'im."

*   *   *

Otik had grown up in Vidor. In order to head due east—and Ohrid was due east—there was only one way out of town. A few questions in the right places and a gull or two changing hands had elicited the information that a man and a woman and a mule had passed that way early the previous evening. The woman had been quite pregnant. The man, taller than average, broad shouldered, and dark haired.

"Good lookin' mule, too, yer honor."

A muscle jumped in Otik's cheek. "I don't care about the unenclosed mule!"

Given the woman's condition, they wouldn't be traveling very fast—or very far in the dark. He knew the road and had a good idea of where they must've spent the night. It was mid-morning when he turned his horse off the track, dismounted, and saw he'd guessed correctly.

"Probably pulled out just after sunrise," he muttered. "And likely heading for Turnu. The bard'll know of it, even if the duc doesn't." A day's travel from Vidor in good weather, Turnu was the last village of any size heading east. If they needed any supplies, or even one last chance to sleep in a bed, they'd stop at Turnu.

Back on the track, Otik pushed his horse into a canter. Fields and trees rolled by on either side with gratifying speed; he'd be on them long before they could reach the village. His free hand slipped down to pat the crossbow hanging from his saddle.

The mare stumbled.

Otik catapulted headfirst over her shoulder, landed, and rolled dangerously close to still moving hooves. Impact jolted the reins from his hands and, through bones driven into dirt, he felt her jog away. He lay there for a moment, taking inventory, then slowly got to his feet blinking away multicolored flashes of light. All things being enclosed, he was lucky nothing had broken, although the arm he'd landed on would be black and blue and too stiff to use very shortly.

Swearing under his breath, a habit he'd gotten into when he'd made captain, he limped down the track to where his horse had stopped to pull at the new grass, weight resting off her left foreleg. The moment he saw her stance, he knew what he would find when he lifted the hoof.

The shoe had been loose when he'd left her at the stable upon arriving at Vidor and he had given explicit instructions that it was to be immediately taken care of. Running his fingers over the cracked horn, for the shoe had not cast cleanly, Otik added a snarled opinion of the stable owner's lineage to his stream of profanity.

He had no choice. He'd have to walk the horse back to Vidor and have a farrier repair the damage.

"A reprieve," he muttered, catching up the reins, "nothing more. Tomorrow, they are *mine*."

"I want you to Walk directly to Ohrid by way of Marienka. Act in no way that would draw suspicion on yourself but don't delay. I need you as my eyes at that pass as soon as possible."

Stasya stepped off the stern deck of the riverboat and onto the dock at Vidor, exhausted but pleased with herself. Although "as soon as possible" was not a speed often traveled by bards, she'd used the season to her advantage; moving quickly upriver as King Theron had commanded without alerting possible enemies. That she'd done it with everyone from Elbasan to Vidor watching, made it a particularly bardic solution.

She'd have enjoyed her accomplishment more, however, if every note hadn't been tinted with worry for Annice.

"You've a right powerful Song there," the pilot told her as his family swarmed over the boat. "Be a good omen fer the season, first boat travelin' so fast." He spat into the water. "River willin'."

"River willing," Stasya echoed, spitting carefully just beyond the reach of a lingering kigh. The last thing she needed was to have the ritual thrown back into her face. Her voice rasped against the sides of her throat and her head throbbed with the echoes of her Singing. She'd spent almost every waking moment of the last four days ensuring that the huge, square sail remained full and would no doubt spend the next four regretting such prolonged contact with the kigh.

The Riverfolk traveled downstream with the currents from the mountains and upstream with the winds that blew inland off the sea. Although the kigh might not fill another sail all season, after the breakup of the ice the symbolic first boat was always Sung upriver. Only the kigh could hope to move even the nearly flat-bottomed riverboats against the First Quarter currents. Stasya had seen no reason why she couldn't be that bard and the captain had agreed.

She rescued her instrument case from an overeager teenager and let the congratulations of the gathering crowd wash over her. First boat attracted a lot of attention. Although she wouldn't be able to leave until after the blessing and the celebration that followed, it had still been a much faster trip than walking River Road.

Passed from one set of admiring hands to another, Stasya soaked up the goodwill of the crowd, but even while she wished she would surrender to the moment, she found herself scanning the surrounding faces for the familiar curve of Annice's smile. Which was ridiculous. If Annice was in Vidor—a possibility not entirely removed from the Circle for all she'd left some days before—she'd have—they'd have, for the duc would be close by her side—no reason to be hanging about the docks. Connected by the kigh for as long as they'd known each other, Stasya hated this sudden separation. It was one thing when she knew Annice was safe and secure back at Bardic Hall and another thing entirely with her pregnant and wandering Shkoder. *With,* she added silently, struggling to control her expression, *His Grace, the unenclosed Duc of Ohrid.* The urge to write a scathing song about the man that would last for centuries was intense.

She had no idea how she was going to manage the next month and a half of ignorance and couldn't understand how His Majesty had turned his back for ten years.

That was, however, not the only question the king had avoided answering before he dismissed her.

"The captain will contact you through the kigh the moment we've constructed a plan, so there's no need for you to waste the limited time we have waiting around here. Given that the actual traitors believe their plot has succeeded, you should be in no danger until the Cemandian army arrives. Before you arrive, we'll have come up with a reason for you to be there and then a reason for me to follow with an escort of guards." His Majesty's expression had been grim. *"If you've managed to discover the iden-*

tity of the traitor, I'll hold a Judgment and ensure the keep is in loyal hands. If not, we'll face the army together."

His Majesty obviously had more faith than she did in what a king, a troop of guards, and a bard could hope to accomplish facing an army.

With a noncommittal smile and ears tuned to catch any comments directed specifically at her, Stasya let the celebration sweep her into her appointed role, all the while wondering just how the king intended to get to Ohrid *with* his guard without attracting the kind of attention he'd commanded her to avoid.

"Suppose," the Bardic Captain said thoughtfully, turning from the window where she'd been watching a team of gardeners pack up their tools for the day, "you went to Ohrid to accept the allegiance oath of the new duc."

Theron looked up from the maps spread out over his desk. On the topmost map, the border that split the ancient mountains between Shkoder and Cemandia had been thickly traced in red. The pass at Ohrid appeared to have been circled in blood. "Why would I do that?"

"Because you acknowledge that Pjerin a'Stasiek made a valid point when he accused the crown of failing in its obligations to the principalities, Majesty." Liene stepped forward, the soles of her boots crushing the plush nap of the carpet. They'd discarded a score of ideas since Stasya had left for Vidor, but she was certain this one would work. "If you go to Ohrid rather than have the duc come to you, you'll be showing a willingness to break the isolation."

"And strengthening the ties between Ohrid and the crown," the king mused, tapping a fingernail against the smooth curve of the ivory button closing his vest. "A logical and politically astute move, seeing as the last duc committed treason and we'd like to prevent that from happening again."

Liene nodded. "It would also be seen by your people as a way of showing the Cemandians you intend to hold the border."

Theron almost smiled. "Makes so much sense, even the Cemandians should have no trouble believing it.

And I'd be a tempting enough bait that we'll be able to schedule the arrival of the invading army."

"Bait, Majesty?"

"If they hold their attack until I'm in the keep on my alleged diplomatic mission, they have the chance to not only enter Shkoder through an undefended pass—thanks to the traitor they think we don't know about—but also to remove Shkoder's king. Queen Jirina's no fool, she'll see the opportunity and she'll take it."

Liene frowned as she considered the implications. "Your Majesty, we can't put you in that kind of danger."

"Captain," Theron spread his hands, "we don't have any choice."

"But, Majesty, suppose the traitor is still unidentified when you arrive? It would only make sense for this person to kill you before the invasion actually occurs. You'll have no idea of the direction of the threat, so you'll be unable to defend yourself. The army will pour through the pass unopposed and down over Shkoder with your head on a pike before them."

"Could happen," Theron admitted. "All things being enclosed."

Liene took a deep breath and let it out slowly. Although she was only twelve years older than the king, there were days—and this was one of them—when she felt those years stretch to at least a century. Squaring her shoulders, she twitched the edge of her tunic straight. "Your pardon, Majesty, but you can't go to Ohrid."

"Captain, I'm going." He sat back in his chair, the tooled leather creaking under his shifting weight, his jaw set in an obstinate line the captain had seen on both his father and his youngest sister. "I'm going for a number of reasons. When the traitor is found, only I can pass Judgment. It's the law. I alone can carry the weight of that death." Something in his tone said that this particular weight wouldn't add much to the burden he already carried. "Now, if the traitor *hasn't* been found before I arrive, you're probably right and he or she will be unable to resist trying to kill me. My presence there will force the culprit into betraying himself, and that is, after all, what we want."

"He can betray himself right out of the Circle, Majesty, but it won't do us any good if you're dead."

"Then I'll just have to stay alive." His face and voice grew grim. "But, essentially, I'm going to Ohrid because Cemandia made this a personal battle when they set *me* up to remove Pjerin a'Stasiek from their way."

Liene knew it wouldn't do any good to remind him that kings seldom had the luxury of indulging in personal vengeance. Finding the traitor before the Cemandian army arrived was the only way to avoid a war they couldn't hope to win. Tempting the Cemandians with the King of Shkoder ensured they'd attack on Shkoder's schedule. Theron's presence in the keep was the best way to prod the traitor into betrayal.

The king traveling to Ohrid to take the oath of Gerek a'Pjerin was a perfectly believable way to set the whole plan in motion. She wished she'd never thought of it.

She could just see herself explaining to the new queen, as she hurriedly armed the country, how it was her father had died confronting a Cemandian invasion he knew was going to occur backed up by nothing more than a diplomatic entourage. *I'm getting too old for this shit.*

Then she realized they'd missed considering one vital component of the whole convoluted mess.

"What of the duc, Majesty? The guard hasn't found him yet. Suppose they don't? Suppose Pjerin a'Stasiek arrives in Ohrid before you do? He could destroy the entire plan."

"As I understand it, he has to remain close to Annice to stay undetected by the kigh and she won't be moving very quickly in her condition. Even if Captain Luci and her troop prove themselves completely inept, I doubt that they'll arrive before Stasya. If Stasya makes herself visible, Annice will contact her, and Stasya will explain what's going on. Simple."

"Simple, Majesty? The duc has an even greater personal stake in this than you do. If I read him correctly, he's as likely to single-handedly storm the keep as listen to anything either Annice or Stasya have to say."

Theron shook his head. "He won't jeopardize his chance to get his hands around the throat of the person who did this to him."

"And what of that person?" Well aware she was getting nowhere with her arguments, the captain felt she had to keep trying; for duty's sake if nothing else. "I need the duc to find out who that is?"

"He may know by the time he arrives," Theron pointed out thoughtfully. "He is traveling with a bard, remember. Once Stasya explains, I think he's politically astute enough to work with me on this. And if he isn't, Annice is."

"Are you willing to risk your life on the possibility that Annice can control him?"

Was he? Theron thought about it. Thought about a fourteen-year-old who'd thrown away everything—family, privilege, responsibility—to follow her own desire. "I think," he said slowly, "he's met his match in Annice." *And but for Annice,* his hands curled into fists, *this whole problem could have been solved ten years ago.*

". . . join with Prince Rajmund, Heir of Cemandia."

Annice's eyes opened wide in astonishment. "I will not."

It took Theron a moment to find his voice in the face of such bald denial and he fought to sound reasonable. "It won't happen immediately. You'll be betrothed first, the actually joining won't happen until you're both eighteen. This arrangement is for the good of Shkoder . . ."

"But what about me?" Annice broke in, reaching forward and grabbing his sleeve. "You know I want to be a bard. You *know* I do, Theron. I've just got to get permission from His Majesty."

"He won't give it and you're living in a dream world if you think he will, Annice. It's time to grow up." He pulled his arm free and squared his shoulders. "You have a responsibility to the royal family, a responsibility to the country."

She stared up at him in confusion. "I always thought you understood how much being a bard means to me and that if His Majesty wouldn't give permission, then, when he died, you would."

If she believed that, Theron knew it was because he'd given her reason. But that was before the Cemandian ambassador had come to him—to him because the king had no interest in anything but his own mortality and the lingering death that had been moving slowly closer to him for almost a full quarter. Theron, tired of waiting for power, had grasped the opportunity.

Annice paced the length of her solar and back, her shoes slapping a staccato beat against the tiles. "You have to speak to His Majesty for me, Theron. You're the Heir, he'll listen to you."

She read the answer off his face and took a slow step away from him, eyes locked on his. "Father didn't arrnage this, did he? You did." Her expression changed from confusion to betrayal. "This isn't for the country! This is for you! I'm not stupid, Theron, and I had the same tutors you did! You don't even see *me* in this!"

Too close to the truth. The healers said the king was dying, but he'd been dying for too long, and if Theron wanted to strengthen his position, his youngest sister was the only card he had to play. "Nees, you've got to understand . . ."

"Oh, I understand." Her chin lifted defiantly. "Let me tell you something, Your Royal Highness, my life isn't a prize you can trade for the chance to be taken seriously!"

He forgot his reasoned arguments of how this joining, this family link, would give them a chance to bridge the gap growing between their two cultures, to build a permanent peace with Cemandia now that the much larger country had begun to press against their border. Forgot the arguments that might have made her see there was more to it than his own personal agenda. "Don't fight me on this, Annice, because you can't win." The words were forced out through teeth clenched so tightly his jaw ached. "Remember, in a very short time I will be your king."

Her face flushed as she stomped to the door and threw it open, waiting pointedly beside it for him to leave. "Well, you're not king yet!

"Majesty?"

Theron shook off the memories. It had been a long time since he'd played that scene through.

"Majesty? Are you all right?"

"I'm fine." He tugged on a vest button, pulling at the indigo brocade, and exhaled noisily. "I was just thinking of how different things would be if I'd handled Annice better. If I'd actually taken the time to explain why I wanted her to join with Prince Rajmund."

In all the years since he'd taken the throne, in all the years the captain had stood as one of the throne's primary advisers, this was the first time the king had ever been willing to discuss that bit of family history. She smothered a sigh. The time was long past to set the recall straight. "Your pardon, Majesty, but Annice and Prince Rajmund would never have been joined, regardless of the reasons, or the benefits, or any political maneuvering."

Both the royal brows rose. "Because you wanted her for Bardic Hall?"

"Because she was qualified for Bardic Hall, Majesty. Queen Jirina would never have allowed her son to be joined to someone who Sings the kigh. You know how the Cemandians feel about that. Their version of the Circle holds neither kigh nor bards.

"But Annice wasn't a bard . . ."

"She was born with the ability, Majesty. We only trained it."

Theron swore as his vest button twisted off in his fingers. "But the Cemandian ambassador came to me!" he protested.

"And was horrified when he discovered what he'd very nearly done. And was called home. And was, if I recall correctly, executed for daring to suggest the Heir to the royal house of Cemandia join with someone who Sings the kigh."

"The Cemandian ambassador is still after a similar joining."

"Neither of your daughters Sing the kigh, Majesty. You can be certain he's checked."

"It's been ten years," Theron growled. "Why didn't you tell me any of this before?"

Liene closed her eyes for an instant, weighed the potential for disaster, and decided. "Because you wouldn't listen, Majesty. Just the same way *she* wouldn't listen. It's taken the threat of war to force you to look beyond your personal—*and,* she added silently, *highly inflated*— sense of injustice."

His expression unreadable, although the tips of his ears were red, the king made no answer for a long moment. The captain began to fear she'd misjudged the timing. *Bloody fool thing for a percussionist to do.*

Finally, without looking up, he said, "Do you believe in destiny, Captain."

She bowed. "I'm a bard, Majesty. Destiny is my stock in trade. Why?"

"It seems as though there's been an incredible series of events to bring us to this moment." He turned the button over and over in his fingers. "Including the difficulty between my sister and myself."

"Could as easily be coincidence, Majesty." She bowed again. "Also a bard's stock in trade."

Theron looked dubious. "I've always considered myself above both."

"I can't say as I'm surprised, Majesty." It had been a long day and Liene felt she was entitled. "So does Annice."

"Annice." Pjerin had reached the end of his limited supply of patience. "Recall, if you would, that we're trying to be forgettable."

"You're the one who said I needed a bath. That," she jerked her thumb back toward the village, "was our last chance at hot water."

"And a good chance at being remembered if the guards are behind us."

"The guards still think we're in Vidor."

"You don't know that."

Annice smiled across the mule at him. "They've got horses, Pjerin. If they were after us, don't you think they'd have caught us by now?"

He jerked the mule to a stop. "Do you want to go back?" he asked, spitting the words out through clenched teeth.

"Too late." A nudge in the ribs got the mule moving again. "If we suddenly reappear now that we've wandered past, they'll definitely remember us.

Pjerin brushed his hair back off his face with a barely under control sweep of his hand. "Then maybe we could look for a campsite before it gets dark?"

"A sheltered campsite." Annice glanced up at the horizon to horizon blanket of gray-green cloud. "It looks like it's going to storm." She squinted into the gathering shadows. "We'd better hurry."

Pjerin only ground his teeth and continued to scan

both sides of the road. He was well aware it was going to storm and that sleeping rough would be harder on Annice than on him. He felt obliged to lessen her discomfort as much as possible. Which irritated him right out of the Circle. She wasn't an easy person to be considerate of.

A rectangle of darkness loomed up suddenly out of the dusk.

He frowned. Although there were walls on the narrow ends, the sides were open to the night. It didn't look like any kind of building he knew. "What is it?"

Annice leaned awkwardly forward and peered around the barrier of the mule. "Flax shed. This is a big linen-producing area. It's mostly just a roof to keep the rain off while they're hackling. There won't be anything in it right now, but there should be water nearby and possibly a fire pit so they don't have to depend on the weather for drying the stalks after retting."

"Are you sure?"

Her eyes narrowed at his tone. "Yes. I'm sure."

"Good." Pjerin began turning off the track.

"I don't think so." It was a young man's voice, rough edged but not unfriendly.

Pjerin glared at Annice.

She shrugged.

Together they turned and looked back the way they'd come.

There were three of them. Although none of them were very big, they moved with an aggressive cockiness that suggested no one had better mention it. They wore breeches with ridiculously wide legs, a style gone out of fashion with the young toughs of the cities but apparently still popular in the country, and all three heads of hair had been clubbed up into greased topknots. One of them had the beginnings of a scruffy beard; the other two might not have been old enough to manage even that.

"Where did they come from?" Pjerin growled.

"They followed us from the village. I saw them hanging around outside the alehouse." Her chin rose as he swiveled around to stare incredulously at her. "I guess I forgot to mention it."

Pjerin opened his mouth and closed it again. He

couldn't think of anything to say. Well, that wasn't quite true; he could think of several things to say but they'd all take time and would have to wait.

"Throw us the lead rope." The suggestion came from the bearded young man and was the same voice that had hailed them initially. He stood a little in front of his companions, obviously in charge. "We'll have a look-see through your packs, pick out a few trinkets, and no one will get hurt."

Annice smiled sweetly at the trio. "Go away, we'll forget we ever saw you, and no one will get hurt."

All three of them looked confused for a moment, then their spokesman shook his head and flicked a dagger down from a wrist sheath.

Increasing darkness made it difficult to focus on a single pair of eyes, so Annice opened her mouth to Sing. Perhaps she could get the kigh to open a large, deep hole in the road under their feet.

"Annice." Pjerin's fingers closed around her wrist like a vise. "I'll handle it."

"But ..."

He shoved the lead rope into her hand. "I said," he snarled, "I'll handle it."

He moved back up the track, hands carefully out from the long dagger hanging sheathed at his side. An opportunity to actually *do* something, to hit back at the unenclosed chaos his life had become, was an opportunity not to be missed.

The three looked smaller in comparison, Annice realized; smaller, younger, less dangerous. But there were three of them. And one of them had a blade ready.

"Should've kept her quiet," the leader said genially, flashing broken teeth. "Now, we'll have to cut you."

Pjerin returned his smile. "You've got to the count of three to run."

They looked at each other and laughed.

They were still laughing at three.

They weren't laughing at four; had anyone still been counting.

Breathing heavily and pressing the edges of a shallow slice across his forearm together, Pjerin returned to where Annice waited.

Watching as two of their attackers limped into the

night, dragging their moaning leader back toward the village, Annice had to admit she was impressed. To herself. She had no intention of admitting it aloud.

"Feel better?" she asked as Pjerin took hold of the rope and began to lead the mule off the road.

He flashed a grin back over his shoulder. "Much better. Thank you."

"I'll have a look at that arm when we get settled."

"It's nothing."

"Your nose is bleeding."

"It'll stop."

Shaking her head she stepped over a muddy ditch as they left the track, heading for the flax shed. *Please,* she begged the life nestled under her heart, *be a girl.*

CHAPTER TWELVE

"Ow!" Pjerin yanked his arm out of Annice's grip. "That hurt!"

"Oh, don't be such a baby." She dipped the kerchief back into the trailpot of hot water propped precariously between a pair of rocks at the edge of the fire pit. "You know that cut's got to be cleaned. I don't even want to think about what could've been on that blade."

"Then don't think about it."

"Pjerin!" He started to move away, but she grabbed his wrist and yanked him back down beside her, ignoring his hiss of pain. "This'll only take a minute if you'll just let me do it." Dragging his arm across her lap, she dabbed at the dark line of red. The flesh beneath her fingers felt both hard and yielding and very, very warm. *Forget that,* she told herself sternly. *Those sorts of observations are what got you into this mess.*

As though in response to the thought, the baby stretched, pushing hard with an elbow or a knee and bringing an entirely nonmaternal comment to Annice's lips.

"The baby?"

"Uh-huh."

The contours of his face softened and an almost hungry expression rose in his dark violet eyes as he stared at the folds of her smock.

Watching him, Annice came to a decision. *Which I'll probably regret later.* She lifted the hand she still held, turned it, and pressed the palm against her belly.

Pjerin stared at her, then at his hand.

Nothing happened.

For some time.

"This is deliberate." Annice blew a strand of hair back off her face. "I'm sure of it. Maybe if I pretend I'm about to go to sleep and would like a little peace and quiet, the rhythm section will star ... There! Did you feel that?"

He nodded, eyes wide.

Annice had seen priests look less reverent at prayer and she felt kinder toward Pjerin than she had at any time since her Walk to Ohrid. Or more specifically, since waking up freezing beside him and discovering he'd stolen all the covers.

After sitting quietly for a moment, barely breathing, he gently lifted his hand away. "Thank you," he said, softly. "I hadn't realized it would mean so much to touch my child before it's born."

His child. Annice sighed and tugged at the edge of her smock. *I knew things were going too well between us.* "Pjerin, we have to talk." That said, what next? She leaned against her pack, taking the strain off her lower back, and scratched at a bug bite. "You have to understand that this isn't *your* child." She fought against sounding defensive and thought she'd succeeded.

He paused, halfway to his feet, his legs bent at awkward angles. "Are you saying I'm *not* the father?"

"No. That's not what I'm saying."

"Then what?" When he sat again, their small fire burned between them and the embers painted his face with shadow.

Nice symbolism. Why do I get the feeling he's not going to be reasonable about this? "Look, I know that Gerek was a contract birth." She let her voice fall into the rhythmic cadence that should, at least, keep him listening. "I know that he stayed with his mother until he was weaned and then moved in with you. I've seen the two of you together and I know you're a good father—he's happy and healthy and curious about everything—but this is *my* baby." Hearing an echo of the mad woman from the fishing village, she hastily added, "Not mine in the sense of ownership but mine because ..." Because she so desperately wanted it to be? ". . because, I'm the one who's going to raise it." Remembering the expression on his face when he'd felt the baby move and unwilling to lose that completely, she added, "I'm willing to witness a contract acknowledging you as the father, though."

"And as the father, I have every intention of raising *my* child." There were flames reflected in Pjerin's smile.

"You've already got Gerek," she offered, feeling her way around an anger she could sense rising in him but couldn't understand.

"Does that mean I should ignore this child, then?"

"Not ignore." Although Annice had to admit that a complete lack of involvement on his part was the solution she'd prefer. "Just trust me to raise it. I mean, I am its mother."

"Its mother?" He laughed and she jerked back at the sound, wondering what he had to be so bitter about. "And what kind of mother are you going to be?"

"What?"

"You spend your life running around the countryside, never staying in one place for more than a couple of days." The accusations poured out as though they'd been rehearsed. "You don't have a home to give a child. You're like some kind of human butterfly; living here and there, thinking only of yourself."

Mouth open, Annice stared across the fire, her initial flash of disbelief quickly overwhelmed by rage. "Myself?" She slapped the word at him.

He looked almost as though he regretted what he'd said, but she didn't give him a chance to speak.

"You seem to keep forgetting that if I thought only of myself you'd be dead! Do you think I want to be out here with you? Is your ego so huge that you think I'm enjoying this? Do you think I'm happy that someone I love might have died for you?" She could feel the muscles knotting across her back, knew that she should calm down for the baby's sake but couldn't. "And as for the rest, you don't know ratshit about how I spend my life. I'm a bard, and better to be raised by a bard than by some obnoxious, narrow-minded, arrogant bigot who thinks he's the center of the Circle even though he's spent his whole life hiding in a mountain keep with his head up his ass."

"Hiding?" His features hardened, regret gone. "I am responsible for every life in Ohrid and *I* take my responsibilities seriously."

"And I don't? You have no idea what my responsibilities are!"

"I know you agreed not to have children!" He dropped his gaze pointedly. "This doesn't say much for your ability to keep your word."

"Is that so? Well, if I'm an unfit mother, what kind of a father are you when it comes right down to it? You've been judged guilty of treason ..."

"Falsely!"

"But still judged guilty! Right now you haven't got anything but what *I've* given you, including your life! You've got no business making plans for my child when you've lost the one you've already got!"

When the anger left his face, Annice knew she'd gone too far. The realization that she'd intended to cut that deeply, that she knew his fears for and of Gerek and she'd chosen her words in order to do as much damage as she could, only made it worse. She closed her eyes because the utter lack of expression hurt more than pain would have; opened them again when she heard him stand.

"Pjerin, I'm sorry. And I'm wrong."

"No." He could barely force the denial past the constriction in his throat although he wasn't sure if it was anger, grief, or pride that choked him. "You're right. About the first part at least. I owe you my life and my continued liberty and therefore any chance I have of clearing my name. But I will clear my name and I will get my son back and then I'll fight for the child you're carrying."

She didn't have the energy to start screaming at him again. "It's a fight you won't win."

"Annice, I can reverse the King's Judgment because I didn't actually commit the treason I was accused of. You're carrying yours with you. You created an innocent life just so you could throw it in your brother's face."

He moved out of the circle of firelight and Annice, breathing heavily, wrapped both arms protectively around her body. She had to believe that his parting shot had oozed out of the wound she'd inflicted. Had to believe it because if she didn't, she'd have to pick up her pack and start the long walk back to the safety of Bardic Hall leaving Pjerin to the kigh; to recapture; to the block. And she couldn't do that.

Thunder rumbled over the still distant mountains. A

few moments later, a flash of lightning showed Pjerin standing at the edge of the open shed, staring out at the night. He looked as if a movement would shatter him into a thousand pieces.

This time, they'd gone too far for apologies.

Blinking away the afterimage and ignoring the single track of moisture that spilled down each cheek, Annice dug her flute out of her pack. For the pretense of being traders, she'd had to leave her quitara behind. It could neither be hidden nor explained away as a simple hobby; the moment she played she couldn't help but show what she was. Although she'd recognized the danger, she'd refused to travel without any instrument at all. The polished rectangular flute case could be thought to hold any number of other treasured items.

Her hands steadied as she fitted the pieces together. Something had to be said, but she didn't know the words, so she closed her eyes and let the music speak.

When the last note slipped away into the darkness, she opened her eyes to see Pjerin sitting back on the other side of the fire, carefully laying wood on the embers as the storm broke and a cold, damp breeze crept in under the eaves of the shed.

"I remember," he said, prodding the fire to life, "when you played like that in Ohrid. You were up on the top of the high watchtower and you either didn't know or didn't care that the whole valley could hear you. I stood there listening and wondering at the kind of courage that allowed you to throw so much of yourself into the music." He swallowed and locked his eyes on her face. "Can we go back?"

She shrugged, flute cradled against the curve of her body. "How far?"

"To the beginning? We had the time you were in Ohrid and one terrific night together and we've been assuming we know each other ever since. We don't. But we need to." When she hesitated, he added, "Our lives are irrevocably entwined, Annice. We can't change that. We've already proven we know enough to hurt each other. We have to learn enough to stop."

"I wouldn't know how to start."

He gestured at her flute. "You've already started."

"All right. Then I wouldn't know how to go on."

"How do people usually get to know each other?" He half smiled. "They ask questions."

"What kind of questions? Things like, uh ..." She searched for something frivolous. It wasn't easy. There didn't seem to be a lot frivolous between them. Everything came weighted with the life she carried. "... like, what's your favorite color?"

His open hands sketched compromise in the air. "I don't think we have time to be quite so thorough."

Annice nodded. "You're right." There was really only one question she wanted to ask, but she suspected it was the one question he couldn't answer. Not directly. Not in so many words. She knew how complicated her own reasons for wanting the baby were and—*in spite of what His Grace might believe*—wasn't egotistical enough to suppose his were any less complex.

Start thinking about this man, Annice. Stop merely reacting to him. You're a bard. Finding truth in information is part of what you do.

"Pjerin?" She used his name to lift his gaze to hers. "What was your father like?"

The rain fell straight down, securing the open shed behind translucent walls.

Pjerin shifted uneasily. "My father?" It wasn't the question he'd expected. Perhaps he didn't have the courage of her music, but he'd be unenclosed if he didn't at least try to meet her halfway. "He was, well, he was very strong."

"Did he love you?"

"Yes." The fire had burned down enough so that he couldn't see her face, only a constant shadow amid the flickering ones. It made it easier to respond. It almost seemed as though he were talking to himself. "I was lucky, I never doubted it."

"How did he do it? How did you know?"

Pjerin thought he heard an undercurrent of yearning in her voice, almost dismissed it, and then remembered who she was. Who her father had been. As a monarch, the late king had the reputation of being a shrewd politician and, as a father, of being a monarch. Although it should have been her turn to hand over a piece of *her* soul, he answered anyway. "It's hard to explain. I always knew that I was the center of his life. My earliest memory of him is of the day he fought and got me back from my mother."

"From your mother?" Annice repeated. She had a strong suspicion she knew what accusations the old duc had shouted as he retrieved his son and heir. *Oh, baby, it isn't going to be easy to get your daddy to let go.* "Were you a contract birth?"

"No. They were joined." Pjerin could hear the bitterness in his voice and didn't bother trying to soften it. "My father was an attractive man *and* a duc. She saw him in Marienka; she wanted him; she got him. She didn't think much of Ohrid, though; there was no one there to appreciate her prize. You've been in the keep. It wasn't the kind of place to keep a woman like her happy. She wanted bright lights, attention; love wasn't enough."

"How old were you when she left?"

A flash of lightning lit the distance and the thunder grumbled overhead.

"She didn't know I existed when she left. Father finally heard she'd had a child, found her, and got me back three years later."

And told you these stories all your life. Well, that answers my question. Annice shifted position and traced comforting circles against the taut drum of her skin. She braced herself for the inevitable question about her father, about her family, about leaving them, about being alone. "Your turn."

"What does it mean to be a bard?"

All at once, she wished she could still see his face. "Why?"

"Because I have a good idea of what it is to be a princess and I want to know why you gave it up."

He's more than just a pretty face, baby. But, to be fair, she already knew that. If he'd answered her questions less than honestly, she could've spun him a story with enough truth in it to satisfy. As it was . . .

"Bards are the eyes and ears and voice of the country." It was what she'd told Jurgis when he'd asked. *A thousand years ago.* "We bring the mountains to the coast and the coast to the river and the river to the forest and the forest to the cities. We're what keeps all the little bits of Shkoder together—the people, the land,

the kigh. We keep the pattern whole. We harmonize
the physical and the spiritual, the intellectual and the
emotional, joining body and soul." But that was only
what bards were, what they did, not what it meant to
be one.

Lifting the flute, she traced circles in the air. "Most
people are aware of only their own little Song. Bards
find the connections between Songs, find them and gift
them to others. To keep someone with the ability and
the desire from the training to use it, is to condemn
them to glimpses of the world through prison bars.

She paused for breath, then raised a hand too late to
stop the shaky laugh that followed. "It just occurred to
me that I should've probably told all that to Theron."

"Probably," Pjerin agreed, not the least surprised that
she hadn't. "What did you tell him?"

Her second laugh held little more humor. "Essentially,
that he'd be sorry if he tried to push me around."

Pjerin knew he was treading close to dangerous
ground but he had to ask. "And now you're calling his
bluff?"

*"You created an innocent life just to throw it in your
brother's face."* Annice recognized the gentler version.
"No. I want with this child what you have with Gerek.
Is that so hard to understand?"

"No." He stood. "But so do I."

"Then we're back where we started."

"We're a long way from where we started." He smiled
down at her. Annice remembered that smile. The last
time she'd seen it, they'd made a baby. "We've managed
to stop the bleeding from the damage we inflicted earlier. Not a bad evening's work. Let's get some sleep."
Without waiting for an answer, he moved into the darkness at the far end of the shed to check on the mule—
dubbed Milena after Annice's older sister and tethered
inside with a small pile of hastily gathered forage lest
she destroy the surrounding shoots of flax.

*And he dares to call me imperious. He's pushy, isn't
he, baby? But I think I might be starting to like him.*

A little while later, the packed dirt floor of the shed
having shifted about to cradle her bulges almost comfortably, she peered across the fire pit and sleepily asked,
"Pjerin, what *is* your favorite color?"

"Blue," he murmured, then, to her surprise, went on. "The sapphire blue of the sky over the keep just after sunset. When the day's gone but the night hasn't quite arrived over the mountains."

If they hadn't been treading around each other so carefully, she'd have accused him of being bardic.

Stasya Sang the kigh a gratitude and watched as it swooped down to run its fingers through the pinfeathers of an annoyed pigeon, spun up to swirl once around the pennants flying from the top of Bardic Hall, then finally raced off to Elbasan to tell the captain that her message had been received.

Shivering a little in the cool dawn air, Stasya looked out over the sleeping city and wondered if behind one of the half-timbered walls, Annice was stirring, complaining about being roused, racing for the privy. Or were they already on the road?

Are you seeing that she eats? she asked the duc silently, grinding the question between her teeth. *Are you making sure she rests? If you're giving her a hard time, I can guarantee I'll find out about it, and you'll pay.*

Stasya had arrived at Bardic Hall very late, directly from the riverside celebrations marking the safe arrival of the first boat. She knew that the guard troop Theron had sent after Annice and "the father of her child" still hadn't caught them, but she didn't know much else.

"And I *hate* not knowing."

Although she knew she'd get the same response she'd gotten on other mornings, she whistled up a kigh. It appeared almost instantly, frisking around her like an ethereal puppy, eager to please until she Sang the notes that made up Annice's name, then its elongated features twisted with distaste and it tried very hard to drag her off the balcony as it left.

Fingers wrapped white-knuckled around the rail, Stasya tried to calm the pounding of her heart. "I don't think I'll try that again," she muttered, forcing herself to release her grip. "At least not unless I'm on solid ground." Brow furrowed, she backed in off the small balcony and pulled the shutters closed behind her—a First Quarter sun, just up, shed nowhere near enough heat to leave them open.

The king was going to Ohrid to take the liege oath of the new duc.

Tymon would receive a similar message later in the morning and by noon the criers would be telling all of Vidor.

"And I'm to prepare Ohrid for His Majesty's arrival." She sighed. "As quickly as I can."

Vidor to Ohrid at the less than frenetic bardic pace would take her about twenty-eight days. Unfortunately, the message had stated, as explicitly as was possible with the kigh, that she had about half that much time.

"Good thing the ice has moved out of the rivers." She pulled her tunic off the pile of clothes she'd dropped on the floor when she'd finally headed for bed the night before. "Sounds like I'm going to be Singing another unenclosed riverboat all the way to Marienka."

"But why must you leave so soon, Theron?" The paneled door closed behind the server and Lilyana picked up a piece of cheese. "By law, the new duc has four full quarters to swear the oath."

"Two reasons." Theron reached for his soup, head bent so that he wouldn't have to meet his consort's eyes. It had been her suggestion that they lunch alone—no servants, no courtiers, just the two of them—and he strongly suspected it was because she knew he hadn't told her everything and wanted to give him one last chance. He'd managed not to actually lie to her, but he'd done it by not telling her the full truth. He didn't count the Duc of Ohrid's faked execution because she'd believed the lie he'd told the country. "I want Queen Jirina to see Shkoder's immediate presence in Ohrid now that her plot has been discovered. We must make her realize that we control the pass. And secondly," He paused, took a mouthful of the chowder, and took his time swallowing. "Secondly, things are quiet in all other areas—there's nothing Onele won't be able to handle if I leave now. Who knows what the Circle'll contain if I wait—or if I take my time on the way."

"Who, indeed," Lilyana murmured at a delicate crescent of clam.

They ate in silence for a few moments.

"You'll have to take four nobles, to witness the oath," she pointed out at last.

"I know." Theron ripped a roll in two, spraying poppy seeds over his desk. "The chamberlain's informing the four I want." Three of them carefully chosen from a list of those both politically expendable and likely to consider it an honor to die in a hopeless cause at the side of their king should the worst occur; the fourth, although equally expendable, not likely to consider it an honor to die in any cause and so might just ensure that they didn't. "I'll be talking to them this afternoon."

"Will the chamberlain be telling them they'll be expected to spend thirty days in the saddle?"

"Only parts of thirty days," he protested. "If a bard can walk from Elbasan to Ohrid, from one edge of the country to the other, in thirty-six, thirty with horses isn't setting a killing pace." Theron hadn't actually been pleased at the time the journey would take. The messenger he'd sent to inform Gerek a'Pjerin, the seventh Duc of Ohrid, of his father's execution would cover the distance in sixteen. Travel arrangements for kings, however, were more complicated.

Lilyana thoughtfully sectioned an orange, imported into Shkoder from the southernmost reaches of the Empire. Theron watched, fascinated, as she pulled the pieces apart with strong, sure twists of her fingers and hoped she wouldn't do the same to the story he'd had to tell her. But all she said, as she wiped her fingers on the linen napkin, was, "Are you sure one troop of guards will be enough?"

No. "Any more and we'll have to take supply wagons. There's a limit to the number of people I can expect to have fed on route in First Quarter."

"I'm rather curious about you leaving Mathieu behind."

Theron studied her expression but saw nothing that gave him any clue as to what she actually meant. "Mathieu is Constable of Shkoder. Why would he accompany me on a state visit?"

"Because you need four nobles, he's one of your oldest friends, he'd enjoy the chance to get out of the capital, and you'd enjoy his company."

"Unfortunately, I need him here."

"Oh?" Her head tilted to one side, Lilyana placed the empty lunch dishes back on the silver tray. "Why?"

"To calm the Council. Onele will need his help." He tried not to think about how much Onele would need the constable's help if he didn't succeed at stopping the Cemandian army at the border. It was a little like not thinking about a blue goose—his mind kept circling back toward it. But if the possibility of disaster showed on his face, Lilyana gave no sign.

"Then why not take Antavas?"

"Antavas?"

"Our son. He'd old enough to be no trouble and young enough to think the whole trip a grand adventure."

"No." He saw her brows go up and merely shook his head. "I can't."

Lilyana sighed and stood. She took a moment to smooth the folds of her skirt, then she lifted her head, caught the king's gaze, and held it. "Theron, I trust you and I trust that whatever it is you're up to is for the good of Shkoder, but if you get yourself killed up in the mountains, there is nowhere in the Circle your spirit can hide from me. Do you understand?"

Theron smiled and stood as well. He stepped around the desk and took her shoulders in his hands. "I understand," he said softly. "I love you, too."

She lifted her mouth to his but broke the embrace when a knock sounded at the door. "You won't be leaving for a few days," she said pointedly as he tried to pull her back against his chest. "We'll have time."

With not entirely exaggerated reluctance, Theron stepped away. "Come."

"Bardic Captain's here with another bard, Majesty. Uh, Majesties," the page corrected hurriedly.

"Tell the captain I'll be with her in a moment."

"Yes, sire."

"You'd better have that bard doing recall every step of the way," Lilyana warned him. "When you get home, I'm going to want a full and complete accounting." She reached out and straightened his tunic, then turned and swept from the room.

A moment later, Theron stared across his desk at the beautiful young man standing beside the Bardic Captain.

"Uh, yes, well, I'm sure you're an excellent bard, but this will be a long trip with much of each day spent in the saddle and, well, you're ..."

"Blind?" Tadeus flashed a brilliant smile in the king's direction. "As long as the horse can see, Majesty, I'll be fine."

"More importantly, Majesty, Tadeus Sings a strong air and will be able to keep you in contact with both Stasya and myself."

"Then he'll have to know what's actually going on."

"I took the liberty of informing him already, Majesty."

"Liberty, indeed," Theron growled.

"Majesty?" Tadeus took half a step forward, an expression of intense sincerity visible around the fringed scarf. "Please don't be angry. I made such a nuisance of myself that the captain had to tell me why she wanted me to see you in order to shut me up." The smile blossomed again. "Let me go with you, Majesty. I know I can do what you need and it would mean so much to me."

"Well ..." Apparently enthralled by the graceful movements of Tadeus' hands as they danced in the air, Theron sat listening to the young bard explain why he was the *best* bard for the situation. "It could be dangerous," he managed to interject at last.

"More dangerous for you, sire. Could I send my monarch into a danger I'd avoid myself? Besides, if Stasya hasn't found the traitor when we arrive, I can be very useful." His voice deepened. "No one ever suspects me of anything."

Don't lay it on too thickly, Liene thought acerbically as Tadeus sketched possibilities. And although it seemed to be working at present, and had certainly gotten her out of a sticky situation, she would have to tell him later to stop flirting with the king.

There were no footprints, no mule prints, no trail of any kind in the mud. With the rain in the night and the ground not yet dry from First Quarter thaw, there should have been a trail a child could read.

Otik scratched at the stubble on his jaw and stared through the dusk toward the mountains.

With Captain Luci and her troop still quartering

Vidor, he'd followed the fugitives to Turnu and through the village. He'd found the flax shed where they'd spent the night. Then he'd lost them.

They hadn't gone back to the track.

They hadn't gone over or around the new shoots of flax surrounding the shed.

It was as though they'd sprouted wings and flown away.

But if they had, they were still flying to Ohrid.

And so was he.

"Annice. They're still doing it." Pjerin stepped forward and the ground rippled behind him, absorbing the imprint of his foot.

"Oh, center it, I forgot to tell them to stop." She lifted her head, wet hair dripping down her face, and softly Sang a gratitude. The earth rippled one last time, then settled into stillness. "I guess they thought it was a good idea."

"Thought?" Pjerin bent and picked the trailpot off the fire. "I didn't know the kigh could think."

Annice shrugged. "I'll tell you what the captain tells the fledglings; all living creatures think." She bit her lip as she remembered Stasya's incredulous, *"Even men?"*

Don't be dead, Stas. I couldn't bear it.

It wasn't difficult to read her emotions from her expression. Pjerin knew he should say something but didn't know what. As there wasn't any comfort he could give, he gently pushed her head forward and poured the warm water in the pot over her hair. "That got the last of the soap. Come over by the fire so you don't get chilled."

"Bards don't get chilled." She rubbed the water off her shoulders and accepted his offered hand. At his snort of disbelief, she pulled herself to her feet and said, "No, it's true. We're incredibly healthy, especially when you consider that we're always so exposed."

His brows went up and she shook her head, pulling on her smock and buttoning it. "That's not what I meant!" But he'd made her laugh and in a much lighter frame of mind she walked over to sit in the small lean-to Pjerin had built upwind of the fire. The reflected heat off the cedar boughs made it almost warm inside.

Although they'd stopped in early evening—rather

than a stop to eat and a final stop hours later when they'd nearly lost the light—Annice was tired and she contentedly watched Pjerin refilled the pot from the spring and begin to prepare a meal. Her hands twitched. She wished she'd thought to bring some knitting. "Maybe it's something to do with the kigh."

"Maybe it's the fresh air and exercise."

"Maybe." She yawned. "What are you making?"

Before he could answer, something screamed off in the bracken.

Annice jerked erect, but Pjerin raised a hand and smiled triumphantly. "Rabbit stew," he said. "I set the snares earlier."

"Are you sure you're ready?" They were face-to-face, cross-legged under the lean-to, knees touching, the fire just high enough for Annice to see his eyes.

No. He wasn't ready. The last thing he wanted was to once again find himself trapped in his own mind. The loss of control terrified him as much as it enraged him. Wiping his palms on his thighs, he snarled, "Go ahead."

She knew that not all the shadows on his face were caused by the night but knew as well that he'd shake off any offer of reassurance. "I'm going to use the exact wording of the Judgment, even though you obviously won't be able to step forward."

"Just *do* it."

Annice nodded and locked his gaze with hers. **"Pjerin a'Stasiek, step forward."**

Pjerin jerked as the compulsion hit.

"Pjerin a'Stasiek, you will speak only the truth."

He swallowed, waiting.

Annice took a deep breath. "Did you betray your oaths to Cemandia, agreeing to allow a Cemandian army passage into Shkoder through Defiance Pass?"

It was happening. "Y . . . yes."

"Is that the truth?"

The pounding of his blood between his ears nearly drowned out the question. "Y . . . yes."

Annice frowned. "Let's try that another way. When you say yes, are you telling me the truth?"

"No." Pjerin's eyes widened and he stared at her in astonishment. "No. No, I'm not telling the truth! I d . . .

di ..." But the momentary control was gone. "I betrayed my oaths."

Hurriedly grabbing his hands, Annice leaned toward him. "Calm down," she said as his chest began to rise and fall with frightening speed and the air barely whistled through his teeth before it whistled out again. Sweat plastered the hair to his temples, reflecting flame as it ran down the sides of his face, and tension radiated off him in a palpable force. "Pjerin! **Calm down!**"

Pjerin closed his cold fingers around her warm ones. Slowly his breathing steadied, making time with hers, and his heartbeat quieted. "Why," he asked, ready to close his teeth on the words if they began to slide out of his control, "could I answer that?"

"I think because it's not a question that you'd ever be asked during Judgment because everyone knows you can't lie under Command. There was no need to guard your answer. Do you want to keep going?"

"Yes!"

As he was still under Command, she couldn't doubt his desire, but she watched him closely. She had no wish to provoke the kind of internal conflict that might kill him. "Are your memories of this betrayal true memories?"

"Y ... yes."

"Pjerin, please stop fighting this. The answers aren't as important as the questions."

He couldn't look away, but there was nothing to stop him from scowling. "Then ask the right questions."

"I'm working on it." Annice thought for a moment. She had to stay far away from anything that might be asked during Judgment. Considering what they were trying to find out, that shouldn't be hard. "Who told you these are true memories?"

"Albek!" Pjerin's lips drew back off his teeth in a wolfish grin. "Albek," he repeated.

"Interesting when you consider that he essentially made himself useless for any further intrigue by setting himself up as your Cemandian contact."

"You consider it," Pjerin growled. "I'm going to consider wrapping my hands around his neck and squeezing until the bones crush."

"Ow!" Annice managed to maintain eye contact but

only just. "The only bones you're crushing are in my hands!" She shook feeling back into her fingers as he released his grip. "All right, now we know who, let's find out how. How did Albek twist your memories so that you'd believe a different truth?"

"I don't know."

"Do you remember him doing it?"

"Yes."

"But you don't know what he did?"

"No."

"Did it happen at the keep?"

"Yes."

"Were the two of you alone?"

"Yes."

"When did it happen?"

"The night before Fourth Quarter Festival."

She shook her head in exasperation. "At this rate, it could be Fourth Quarter Festival again before we get anywhere. Pjerin, I'm going to Command you again."

"Again?" He tried to drag his gaze free, but he continued to be held in the depths of a pair of hazel eyes. "I'm still *under* Command."

"I know. But it might not be enough. You're not a bard, you're not trained to do recall." She saw he understood. "I won't do it if you don't want me to." She could feel his hands trembling where they touched her knees, so she gathered them up in hers again. He would have to actually break bones to do much more damage than he already had. "Pjerin?"

It seemed that the surrounding night waited for his answer, even the constant piping chorus of frogs pausing to hear.

"Do it."

"Pjerin a'Stasiek, remember the night Albek twisted your memories. Remember and tell me everything that happened . . ."

". . . mulled wine. Your cook has a very fine touch with it."

"I know. How old are you?"

The question seemed to take the other man by surprise. "Twenty-six."

Pjerin glanced down at his accounts and then jerked his head at the other chair. "Sit. If you can. I suppose we can find something to talk about that won't have us at each other's throats."

They started with the weather. Pjerin, used to the extreme conditions of the mountains, considered lowlanders to have no weather at all. Albek didn't change his mind with a vivid description of the wind screaming down over the Cemandian plains, destroying everything in its path but he did grudgingly admit that it might have, as Albek said, "a terrible beauty."

As Albek refilled both cups with the last of the wine, they discovered a mutual love of hawking and that started a conversation that carried them through to the dregs.

"No." Pjerin set down his empty cup and slapped his palm against the desk. He blinked and stared at it for a moment, surprised by the amount of noise it made.

"No, what?" the trader prodded, gently.

"No . . ." Frowning, Pjerin tried to recapture the thought. "No seeling. Cruel to sew a bird's eye shut when a well-made hood works as . . . works as . . ." He slumped back in his chair. "Heavy . . ."

"Tired," Albek suggested.

The duc tried to nod. "Yes. Tired."

"Isn't that the door to your bedchamber?"

Pjerin swiveled his head around. "Yes. Door."

"I think I'd better put you to bed. Will your man be waiting for you?"

"My man?" He snorted. "Mountain ducs can dress and . . . undress themselves."

Albek smiled. "Not tonight, I think."

It was cold in the bedroom and the Cemandian swiftly stripped the larger man and slid him under the heavy eiderdown.

"Not . . . coming in with me," Pjerin warned.

"More's the pity," Albek replied, sitting on the edge of the bed. "Actually, we have some things to discuss, you and I." He stretched out a long-fingered hand and turned the other man's head to face him. "Can you see what I'm holding, Your Grace?"

"Hunk . . . of clear rock."

"Technically correct. It's called quartz crystal. It's pretty, isn't it. See how it catches the light from the candle and scatters it about."

Pjerin wet his lips and stared dreamily up at the spinning

crystal. It was pretty. Spinning around and around and around. Orange and yellow and white. And around and around and around. It seemed to be catching the liquid cadences of Albek's voice and throwing it about as well. And around and around.

"Your eyelids look very heavy, Your Grace. Why don't you close them."

They were heavy. He couldn't remember them ever being so heavy. He didn't so much close them as just stop keeping them open—they fell closed on their own.

Albek's voice filled the darkness. "What I'm going to tell you, Your Grace, you will remember as the absolute truth every time you hear the phrases 'Pjerin a'Stasiek, step forward,' and 'Pjerin a'Stasiek, you will speak only the truth.' You have betrayed your oaths to Shkoder . . ."

". . . and then he told me that I would remember nothing of what he'd done. I'd remember only that we'd talked until the wine was gone and then he'd left." He was panting as though he'd just run a race and sweat ran down his face and neck.

"Pjerin, how would you describe Albek's voice?"

"Beautiful. Like music."

Annice broke eye contact. "Witnessed," she said softly. They'd heard all they had to.

Pjerin's head fell forward.

Although she wanted to give him a moment's privacy, Annice knew that after so long in one position she wouldn't be able to stand without his help. Because there wasn't anything else she could do, she twisted sideways as much as the unyielding bulk of her belly allowed and began to rebuild the fire from the stack of dead branches they'd gathered and left ready.

When the flames licked again at the darkness, she reached out and gently touched his shoulder. His hand whipped up and snared hers, the action strangely impersonal, as though the memories continued to hold him. She could still only see the top of his head. There was a danger in being too long under Command and Annice began to fear that in Commanding him the second time she'd passed the barrier. "Pjerin?"

"He must have drugged Olina, too. She certainly gave him enough opportunity." Slowly, he lifted his head.

Knowing that he had been helpless and under Albek's control made him feel violated, his will raped. "I'm going to be there when he comes back through that pass and I don't care if he has the whole unenclosed Cemandian army behind him, I'm going to tear him limb from limb."

The power of that promise lifted the hair on the back of her neck and ran a line of ice down her spine. Annice pulled her fingers free. She understood Pjerin's anger and to an extent she shared it, but hers was directed in another way. "I feel sorry for him."

"Who? Albek?" He glared at her in disbelief. "Annice, he's a spy and saboteur and . . . and . . ."

"And in Shkoder, he would've been a bard."

Pjerin surged to his feet, stumbled, and caught himself on the edge of the lean-to. "What are you talking about?"

"You must know what Cemandians do to those who show signs of being able to Sing the kigh. If they can't be *reeducated,* they're executed. Albek's got the ability or he could never have twisted you around and made it hold up under Command. He's had to repress it all his life, but he's managed to find the one acceptable thing he can do with it that won't get him killed."

"Wrong. *I* am going to kill him."

She rubbed the back of her hand over her cheeks and nodded. "I know. He might even thank you."

CHAPTER THIRTEEN

"I was instructed to deliver my message to the seventh Duc of Ohrid, Lady."

Olina steepled her fingers together and looked over the triangular peak of buffed nails at the messenger.

He squirmed.

After a long moment, she spoke. "Were you not informed that the seventh Duc is a five-year-old child?"

"Yes, Lady, but . . ."

"And did it not occur to you that your news would cause this child great distress?"

Having been distinctly uncomfortable at the thought of recalling his message for a little boy, he fidgeted with the edge of his tabard, the crowned ship over his heart warping first one way then the other. "Yes, Lady, it did."

"Then give the message to me." Her smile held the promise of deliverance.

He clutched at her offer. "Yes, Lady."

Under her scrutiny, it took him three tries to slip into the memory trance that the bards had taught him and he thought, for the first time since he was found to have the ability, that maybe the quiet, stay-at-home life of a crier might have been the better idea. "Theron, King of Shkoder, High Captain of the Broken Islands, Lord over the Mountain Principalities of Sibiu, Ohrid, Ajud, Bicaz, and Somes, did sit in Death Judgment on Pjerin a'Stasiek, sixth Duc of Ohrid, and did find him guilty of treason, condemned by his own mouth. Pjerin a'Stasiek, sixth Duc of Ohrid was executed according to law on the twenty-first day of the third moon of First Quarter. Gerek a'Pjerin is as of that day the seventh Duc of Ohrid. His Majesty expresses the desire that, treason routed out and destroyed, Ohrid and Shkoder will continue to observe their historical loyalties."

When his eyes focused again, his heart leaped into his throat and he suddenly knew how a mouse felt under the unblinking stare of a stooping hawk.

"So. It's official. My nephew is dead."

"Yes, Lady."

"He was ..." The deep magenta curves of her mouth twisted and one brow rose. "He was an idiot."

Mesmerized by the ebony arch of brow, the messenger nodded. "Yes, Lady. I mean; no, Lady. I mean ..." Under the heat of her gaze, he didn't know what he meant, so he sputtered into silence.

Olina studied him. He wasn't frightened of her, merely tongue-tied. *More's the pity.* There was evidence of a wiry strength it might have been interesting to explore. "Do you return to Elbasan immediately...?"

"Damek i'Kofryna, Lady. And no, I go on to Cemandia with further messages."

"Cemandia? You go on, then, if I grant you the use of the pass."

"I am a King's Messenger, Lady."

"Of course you are. I was merely making an observation. You'll stay the night?"

He glanced toward the small, thick panes of the window. The day had fulfilled its promise of rain. "If I could, Lady."

"You can."

Only an idiot would miss the dismissal in both voice and manner. Damek bowed and hurried from the room, vaguely aware he should be grateful, not wanting to probe too deeply into what he should be grateful about.

Alone, Olina looked down into her laced fingers. Pjerin was dead. She remembered the day Stasiek had brought him home; she'd been fourteen and just becoming aware of her power, he'd been three and willing to follow her like a puppy. She'd gone away, to Marienka, to Vidor, to Elbasan, and when she'd returned he'd become a beautiful young man, realizing the family potential. She remembered taking him to her bed when his father died, that year the only time his guard was ever lowered far enough for her to get past it.

Pjerin was officially dead.

It made little difference; she'd essentially buried him when the guard had taken him away.

Actually, at the moment, she had more interest in the messages Damek i'Kofryna was carrying into Ohrid. Fortunately, she had a way to find out what they were.

"I bet you're glad you're inside."

Damek turned, wiping drops of rain off his face. A server had led him to an upper room in the original part of the keep and he was sitting with his elbows on the wide stone sill, staring out at the storm pounding the valley. "I do prefer being dry," he said neutrally, studying the young man in his doorway.

Albek stepped forward, fist held out. "Simion i'Magda." His accent was pure Shkoder, educated but not noble. "Traveler, trader."

Standing, Damek touched the other man's fist lightly with his. "Damek i'Kofryna. King's Messenger."

"I know." Albek smiled broadly. "I saw you come out of your audience with the new duc's great-aunt. She's one terrifying lady, isn't she?"

"Not exactly terrifying," Damek protested. But something in his visitor's voice made him add, "Although she's a bit like a serrated blade, isn't she?"

"Well put!" Laughing, Albek sat on one end of the windowseat, making it the most natural thing in the world for Damek to sit beside him. "I hear you're heading for Cemandia tomorrow."

The messenger nodded.

". . . has a message for Shkoder's ambassador to take to Her Majesty, Queen Jirina. His Majesty, King Theron, and so on and so on, regrets to inform her that not only have his people apprehended a spy—the unfortunate Leksik—but that her ambassador is, for the time being, under house arrest. He's requesting an immediate response."

"Well, he's likely to get one, isn't he?" Olina turned from the window. She'd been contemplating the city that would rise to cover the valley when Shkoder and Cemandia were one. The city she would control. "Will the army be ready to move when His Majesty's messenger arrives?"

The Cemandian frowned as he worked out times and distances. "It'll already be moving."

"Will they kill him?"

"Do you care?"

"No." Ice-blue eyes glittered. "I wondered."

"Probably not. The ambassador from Shkoder has been under house arrest since the pass opened. Damek i'Kofryna will be company for her."

"And after?"

Albek smiled. "We'll all be one big happy country."

"So we will." Olina crossed the room and dropped gracefully into a chair, long legs stretched out and booted feet crossed at the ankle. "How nice."

Recognizing her expression, Albek felt his pulse begin to race. *A serrated blade. If the initial thrust doesn't kill you, removing it will. His Majesty's messenger has a way with description.* He took a step forward.

"Don't presume, *Simion*. If I want you, I'll tell you. Interest isn't always invitation." She smiled up at him, well aware of his reaction. "As it happens, I'm expecting someone. I'm taking your *advice* and appointing a new steward."

Lukas a'Tynek had been marking time since the fire that had destroyed his house and killed his only child. When Hanicka, his partner, left him and returned to live with her mother, Lukas flicked his fingers out in the sign against the kigh and bid her good riddance. It was her blood that had forced their child out of the Circle, not his. No one had ever been able to Sing the kigh in the entire history of his family and no one ever would be. His family knew what belonged in the Circle and what didn't.

Unlike Pjerin a'Stasiek, the sixth Duc of Ohrid. The dead Duc of Ohrid.

"The coward gave me no chance to defend myself. Couldn't be a hero, so he took it out on me." Lukas repeated the whispered insinuations that drifted through the village and made them his own.

Then the coward was found to be a traitor as well and his hatred of the duc made Lukas more than happy to witness. While he personally had no objection to a Cemandian presence in Ohrid—was, in fact, pro-Cemandia if only because Cemandia was anti-kigh—he had even less objection to the arrogant Pjerin a'Stasiek going to the block.

"You told them what kind of a person he was, but they wouldn't listen."

He didn't know who said it to him first. It didn't matter. *"I told you what kind of a person he was,"* he pronounced grimly. *"But you wouldn't listen."*

Some of them began to listen.

Now, he'd been called to the keep.

After hanging his dripping cloak on the hook indicated by a less than approving server, he combed his fingers through his beard and tried to make himself presentable. He looked forward to the meeting with equal parts anticipation and dread. The Lady Olina preferred younger men. He was five years her junior. While he fit no other observed preference, why else would she have sent for him?

Olina knew what he was thinking the moment he walked into the room. She could read it in his strut, in the set of his shoulders, in the self-conscious color that burned on each cheek above the damp mat of beard and she hid a smile. She would've laughed aloud except that since the fire, she'd put a considerable effort into shaping him as her tool.

Over half the villagers now looked to this man—this selfish, superstitious, sublimely self-motivated man—as a leader because he had been the only one who'd seen disaster coming. She would use that. That the remaining villagers despised him for the very qualities she found useful, well, she would use that, too.

It amused her that he was beginning to sweat.

"The seventh duc needs a steward," she said abruptly, leaning back in the huge, ornately carved chair and crossing her legs. "I've decided to give you the position."

"Steward, Lady?"

"Yes."

"B—but . . ."

Olina tapped one finger slowly against the broad wooden armrest and watched, eyes narrowed, as he struggled to change his expectations.

"I, uh, I would be honored, Lady."

"Good. You will take your orders from me."

"But the duc . . ."

"Is a child." She was pleased to see him flinch at her tone. "In return for absolute power under me, you will give me absolute power over you. Is that clear?"

Absolute power. He weighed the price, although she had no doubt of how he would respond. "Yes, Lady." She wouldn't have made the offer had she thought he'd answer otherwise. He'd take anything she could hand out for the chance to lord it over everyone else.

"Bohdan is well enough to acquaint you with your day to day responsibilities. Listen to him. You will move into his old suite in the keep. You will be accorded the same rights and privileges he was. That's all."

"Yes, Lady. Thank you, Lady."

He'd have no opportunity to really abuse the position; she planned on keeping him too busy for that.

Under normal circumstances, a man so easily manipulated placed in a position of authority would find no one to follow him. Fortunately, Olina had seen to it that these were not normal circumstances. They might not follow him for long, but then, they wouldn't have to.

If all went according to plan, and Olina saw no reason why it shouldn't, the moment the situation stabilized her new steward would be easy enough to dispose of. Enough people hated him that she wouldn't even have to do it herself.

It had taken him eight days, but Otik knew he'd finally found the trail again. Branches scattered but with ends cut not broken—obviously a lean-to. He fanned his search from that point and found charred rocks that had lined a fire pit at the next night's camp. The trail was days' old, but it narrowed his search to a specific direction, and in the foothills there were a limited number of routes that could be safely taken with a very pregnant woman.

All three of them emerged in the same small valley.

"You just went."

"Well, I have to go again."

Pjerin muttered expletives under his breath but pulled Milena to a stop. "All right, go on. We'll wait for you here."

Wondering when Pjerin and the mule had become a

"we," Annice hurried into the trees. Considering how often she had to squat, breeches had become more trouble than they were worth and she'd changed to the preferred clothing of expectant countrywomen—a full, calf-length, linen shift beneath a tabardlike wool over-dress. Her body temperature seemed to have risen enough to make clogs comfortable in spite of the season, although she did slip on a pair of heavy wool socks at night. The outfit was so unlike anything Annice had ever worn, she figured that any guard still searching for them would walk right by her without a second glance.

With one hand pressed against a tree for support and the other against her belly in the hope that the pressure would still the sudden flurry of activity, Annice started ... then stopped. "If you don't mind!" she snapped at the kigh who had risen out of the ground practically under her raised skirts. **"Go away!"** It looked as disappointed as its features allowed but obediently sank back into the earth.

"What took you so long?" Pjerin demanded a few moments later as she made her way out of the bushes, viciously shoving the new growth aside.

"Kigh," Annice snarled, kicking off her clogs and jamming them under the straps that secured her pack. "Every single time, I have to tell one or more of them to get lost. Why do they keep hanging around?"

"Your cheerful disposition?"

"Drop dead. What are we standing around for?"

"Second Quarter Festival," Pjerin grunted. He flicked the lead rope at Milena who lifted her head from the new growth on the track and ambled forward.

Annice sighed and settled into a long, rocking stride that would hopefully lull the baby to sleep. She knew she was being a bitch, but she couldn't seem to help herself. *At least, I've stopped crying.*

There had been a couple of days when everything had reminded her of Stasya—birdsong, bluebells, the stripped and scattered bones of a deer taken down by some large predator. A breeze would touch her cheek and she'd start to cry. Rain would dribble off her hair and run under her collar and she'd start to cry. Pjerin would ask if she was all right, and she'd start to cry.

As much as it annoyed her to admit it, Pjerin had been

wonderful throughout. Terse and not exactly sensitive perhaps, but tolerant of her mood swings and quietly strong when she needed him to be.

Unfortunately, now she was feeling better, the old Pjerin had reappeared.

Watching movement of his muscles across the top of his back, flesh rippling under the rough homespun shirt he wore, she touched a ripple moving across her belly and wondered how much like its father her baby would be. *You can have his looks, baby, but I'd really prefer my temperament.* Then she smiled. *All right. I'd really prefer Stasya's temperament. Or even Jazep's. Something a little less extreme.* Prolonged exposure and training in observing the obvious had forced Annice to realize that she shared a distressing number of character traits with His Grace, the Duc of Ohrid.

It wasn't an observation she planned on recalling to him.

"Hey!"

Jerked out of her thoughts, she stumbled and had to grab a pack strap for support. "What?"

"Are you sure we're going the right way?"

"Of course I'm sure."

Pjerin looked dubious. "We should've followed that creek."

"It wasn't going anywhere. This way's faster."

"Not if we get lost."

"Bards don't."

"Oh. I see. So the sun's lost?"

Annice squinted at the sky. So the sun was a little more to the left than it should be. Big deal. The track they were following was taking them in roughly the right direction and they were moving a lot faster than they would forcing their way along an overgrown creek. She said as much to Pjerin. He glowered.

Suddenly the trees ended and they found themselves standing on a ridge, looking down into a broad valley. At the far end, they could see a cluster of tiny buildings, some cultivated land, and a half a dozen animals grazing in a meadow.

Annice began to pick her way carefully down to the valley floor.

"Where do you think you're going?" Pjerin demanded.

"The ridge gets steeper farther along." The bottom of a run-off gully firmed into a path under her feet. "This looks like the best place to descend."

"If we were going to *descend*."

Annice, no longer flexible enough to twist, turned right around to face him. "Pjerin, there's no way these people, whoever they are, are looking for either of us. Right?"

Against his better judgment, he growled agreement.

"And we could use some supplies. Right?"

"What about the guard?"

"What *about* the guard? They're not already down there. We left nothing they could follow. And if I don't get to talk to someone besides you, I'm going to push you off the next cliff we come to."

They locked gazes and after a moment Pjerin smiled. "Good point," he acknowledged. "Unfortunately, considering your condition, I can't make the same plans." Tugging Milena into movement, he gestured toward the valley with his free hand. "After you."

Off the ridge, it quickly became obvious that the homestead was farther away than it appeared and it was late afternoon when they finally reached it. While one of two dogs remained guarding the small herd of long-haired goats, the other charged toward them, barking and snarling.

"Steady," Pjerin said softly as the mule backed to the end of her lead rope, ears flat against her skull and whites showing all around both eyes. "Annice, don't move."

Annice shot him an incredulous glance. "Well, I'd actually *planned* on screaming and running for the hills."

Pjerin ignored her, all his attention focused on the dog. A scar parting the thick tricolored fur along one heavy shoulder as well as the tattered remains of an ear, showed the animal willing to follow through on the snarled threats. His free hand dropped to the handle of his dagger. "Annice, move very slowly and take the lead rope."

Impressed by the calming cadences of his voice, she stretched out her arm, inch by inch, until she could close her fingers around the taut line of twisted hemp. "Got it."

A body length away, the dog stopped and danced stiff-legged on the spot, lips pulled up off its teeth, hackles raised, still barking.

Pjerin released his hold and swung his arm around in front of his body in a graceful arc, hand open, the movement as nonthreatening as he could make it. "It's all right. We're not here to harm anything of yours. Quiet . . ."

Eyes narrowed, ears flat, it crept forward.

". . . that's it. We don't smell like trouble, do we? No." He kept his weight on the balls of his feet, ready just in case. His hand held out at waist level, the dog barely had to lift its head to sniff his fingers. It backed up a step and began to bark again, the snarl not so prevalent.

"Safety! Come here!"

Caught in mid-bark, the dog's ears went up, it spun around, plumed tail beating the air, and galloped toward the young woman advancing from the buildings.

Without turning, Pjerin reached behind dim. Annice gave him the rope. "Very impressive," she said.

He shrugged. "What do bards do when this happens?"

"Well, I once spent three hours in a tree until the family came home from picking berries. The mutt pissed on my pack and I made up a song about the trials of the road."

" 'The Trials of the Road'? That's yours? I *like* that song."

Annice rolled her eyes at his tone. "You needn't sound so surprised."

"Hello." With one hand resting lightly on Safety's broad head, the young woman stopped a careful distance away. Her eyes widened slightly as she noted Annice's condition, but her expression remained basically neutral. "You're a long way off the beaten path."

Aware that Pjerin awaited her lead, Annice weighed her options. They still had small items to trade, but they were no longer posing as traders. She knew there *had* to be other travelers with reason to be crossing this isolated valley, but she couldn't remember either travelers or reasons. Her memory had grown worse as the baby had grown bigger and she wasn't thrilled about it. *Oh, out of the Circle with it!* Taking a deep breath, she Sang the notes that made up her name.

When she finished, Pjerin appeared to be grinding his teeth and the young woman was smiling broadly.

"You're bards! By the Circle, you're bards!" She hurried forward, both hands outstretched.

Safety, taking its cue from its mistress, raced on ahead and leaped around them, barking wildly. Pjerin told it sternly to be still and, panting happily, the big dog sat on his foot.

"Oh, be welcome! Be welcome! Bards! Wait till Gregor hears! We haven't seen anyone but each other for almost four full quarters!" She thrust her fist at Annice. "Adrie i'Marija."

"Annice." And added as she lightly touched the other woman's fist with hers, "This is Jorin a'Gerek. He isn't a bard, but he is responsible for the extra weight I'm carrying and decided not to let me Walk alone."

"I should certainly hope not." Adrie stepped back for a more thorough examination. "When are you due?"

"Around Second Quarter Festival."

"So soon? You should ..." An angry wail from the largest of the three buildings cut off the advice. "Oh, no, Mari's awake. You can turn your mule out with the goats for the rest of the afternoon. The dogs will watch her. We bring everything in at night because of the wolves." The wail became an insistent shriek. Adrie ran for the house. "Hush, baby, Mama's coming."

"Wolves?" Annice repeated.

Pjerin shook his head. "Oh, no, you're not changing the subject that easily. Why didn't you just tell her who we *really* are? Make it easier for them. You've forced them to take a moment and figure it out on their own."

"Try to pay attention," Annice told him, as he began to undo the straps holding the two packs on Milena's broad back. "They haven't spoken to anyone for nearly four full quarters. They don't know about the Duc of Ohrid's treason and they've no reason to think you're him."

"And what about the troop of guards we know is looking for us? They're going to be able to get a pretty good description when they show up here."

"If. There's a lot of country in between here and

Vidor for them to get lost in and we didn't leave tracks, remember. If they even managed to find out we left Vidor, they could easily think we doubled back, or were swallowed by the earth, or a great winged serpent came and carried us away."

"Annice, they're trained guards. They can't all be totally incompetent." He ground the protest out through clenched teeth. "If they think I'm a traitor, they'll also think I'm heading for Ohrid to try to get through the pass to Cemandia. This place is between Vidor and Ohrid."

"If they thought that, they'd be guarding the pass, not chasing after us. They know that as long as you're with me, you *can't* go to Cemandia because although you may be safe—depending, of course, on how Queen Jirina feels about failed traitors—I'll be under immediate sentence of death for being able to Sing the kigh."

His brows met over the bridge of his nose. "You must get tired of being right all the time."

Annice smiled sweetly at him. "Haven't yet."

". . . was here to Sing earth for us and take a recall of what we've done to the place back to His Majesty. Late First Quarter it was. His name was uh, Jaks?" Gregor twisted one end of his mustache. "No, that's not it."

"Jazep," Annice offered. "Now that you've spoken of it, I remember his recall. Four years ago, you petitioned His Majesty for the rights to this valley, promising that in five years you could be paying taxes directly to him. In return, King Theron was to grant you his protection should anyone try to move in on you. As neither Vidor nor Ohrid claimed the valley, and His Majesty was impressed by your . . ." She paused, searching for the word.

"Balls?" Adrie suggested, glancing up from Mari's suckling. Gregor reddened.

Annice nodded, her hands gratefully busy with newly acquired knitting needles and wool. "Balls are good. I was thinking of initiative, but balls are definitely better. Anyway, His Majesty was impressed and agreed to the bargain. Jazep's been by every First Quarter since."

"You beat him this year. We thought when we first heard the dogs it might be him." Gregor leaned back against the wall of the house and stared down the broad length of the valley; grass, trees, and goats painted gold by the setting sun. "Do you remember what Jazep said? I mean, about how we're doing?" He wasn't very successful at sounding like it didn't matter.

Actually, she did. Last year, with only two left to go, Jazep had said it would take a miracle for the valley to begin producing surplus in the time remaining. "Well, he said you've gotten a remarkable amount accomplished." Which he had.

Gregor nodded, satisfied, then he stood. "It's getting dark. Time to bring in the animals. Easier for the dogs if they're all in one place at night."

Pjerin stood as well. "Adrie said there were wolves?"

"Didn't you hear them coming through the hills?"

"Once or twice off in the distance, but never very close."

"You're in the distance, Jorin," Gregor told him dryly. "If this part of the Circle didn't enclose so many deer, we wouldn't have a goat left."

As the two men walked off, Adrie added, "If not for the dogs, the deer would strip the gardens." She glanced down beside Annice's stool. "You haven't finished your goat's milk."

Annice made a face. It tasted like cooked lamb smelled. "I, uh, I don't really like it very much."

"It is a little strong at this season," Adrie admitted. "But it's good for the baby."

"Maybe, but *I* have to drink it."

Adrie shrugged and returned her attention to the infant fussing at her breast.

Annice sighed. There was no point in being prepared to argue when the other person refused to cooperate. She hated the assumption that she was mature enough to realize what was best for all concerned—it made it impossible to create elaborate justifications for not doing the right thing.

Picking up the heavy clay cup, she frowned down at the contents, then swallowed the milk as quickly as she could. *You better appreciate this, baby,* she thought as her entire body shuddered at the aftertaste. *'Cause I wouldn't do this for anyone else.*

Later, after an evening of singing and storytelling and edited news of the world beyond the valley, Annice and

Pjerin bedded down in the loft Gregor had spent part of Fourth Quarter constructing across one end of the small house. Adrie had offered the only bed, but they'd both argued that the loft was fine. The bed, while large enough for two, insisted on a level of companionship they wouldn't be able to maintain.

Next morning, Annice woke to a familiar bounce on her bladder. She sighed and dragged her shift over her head. While she had no real objection to the baby being up before dawn, she didn't appreciate having to be awake as well.

Crawling around Pjerin—*They look so innocent when they're asleep.*—she very carefully swung out onto the ladder, waited a moment for various bits to catch up to the movement, and climbed slowly down to the floor.

The arc of sky was pearly gray, touched with a blush of rose-pink over the mountains to the east. Annice came out of the privy, allowed an investigation by Safety and her mother, Honor, and walked a short distance from the house. Although she was still tired, she had no real anticipation of being able to sleep again—not with the baby awake and kicking.

Climbing to the top of a small knoll, she turned to the east and dug her toes into damp ground. Almost without meaning to, she started to Sing.

It began as a simple welcome to the day, a fledgling Song, pure tones chasing each other joyously up and down the scale. When the first light crested the mountains, it became the Song she'd Sung to the earth in the gardens of Elbasan. As the day lifted out of shadow, it gradually changed again, becoming more complicated. Swaying, Annice spread her arms and opened her heart, pouring hopes and fears and dreams and self into the Song. Eyes half closed, she filled the valley with her voice, feeling it respond, Singing to that response. The more she Sang, the more energy she seemed to be pulling up through the soles of her feet and the more she poured into the Song.

When the last note lapped against the valley walls, she laid both hands lightly against the curve of her body and smiled. "Feels good, doesn't it, baby?" she murmured, replete. "It's been a while since we really Sang."

Stepping forward, she frowned, confused, at the

ground. The grass on the knoll, cropped nearly to bare dirt by the grazing goats, had grown up thick and green and ankle high. As she watched, the whole valley seemed to ripple as her Song settled into the earth. Bees droned to the heavy heads of early wild flowers and birds answered her Song with a chorus of their own.

Annice turned, slowly, trying to take it all in.

Off to one side of the house, the tiny apple trees that Adrie had carefully dug out of her father's orchard were in full bloom, a thousand white blossoms touched with pink lifted to the morning sun. The day before, what few blossoms there were, had been ragged and unlikely to fruit.

Standing just outside the house, Pjerin, Adrie, and Gregor stared at her in amazement. Leaking milk soaked Adrie's shift over her breasts and both men had erections. Only Mari, balanced on her mother's hip, seemed unaffected. She giggled and pointed as a bluebird dropped for a bug right at Gregor's feet, then took flight again with an iridescent flurry of sapphire wings.

Annice smiled at them a little self-consciously. Her Singing had never evoked quite that expression of stunned reverence from an audience before; not to mention the physical response. Something told her there'd be seconds of goat's milk this morning—a less than appetizing proposition—and more than enough eggs to go around.

Squatting, both hands spread flat on the earth, Jazep hummed thoughtfully to himself. The kigh had lifted his bedroll, dumped him naked into the dawn, and insisted he listen to the Song resonating through the earth.

There could be no mistaking the emotional signature. Annice.

It seemed that a minor ability to Sing earth had absorbed the other three quarters and become a talent to equal his own—with obvious variations he could never achieve.

"Which brings us to the question," he said, straightening, "of just what Annice is doing Walking so far from a healer so near to her time." He ripped away the vine that had grown over his pack during the night, Sang an admonishment to the kigh, and began to pull on his clothes. Not for the first time, Jazep wished he could Sing air. Or that earth would occasionally concern itself with less indigenous matters.

Fortunately, he could track her easily as her condition, combined with the season, set up sympathetic resonances within the kigh. He wondered, briefly, if she had any idea of what was likely to happen when she gave birth and decided that it probably hadn't even occurred to her to ask as she'd been away on a Walk when Terezka had Bernardas. Terezka Sang only air and water with no earth ability at all, and it had still been interesting.

After a quick breakfast, he shouldered his pack and Sang a request, the bass notes thrumming in the air. A path opened up through the underbrush. Humming softly, he hurried down it.

Although the sun was setting when Jazep reached the valley, not even dusk could hide the effects of Annice's Song. Shaking his head in amazement, he stared out over an area of such fecundity he had to loosen his breeches and think very hard about bathing in pools of winter run-off. He'd never been aware of so many kigh so active in such an enclosed area and he thanked every god the Circle contained that the valley hadn't been any smaller.

"Guess Adrie and Gregor are going to make their surplus this year . . ."

He Sang as he walked toward the homestead, calming the kigh and doing what he could to curb their more extreme reactions. Once or twice, the mating song of spring frogs nearly drowned him out.

Darkness had settled by the time he got close enough to be heard and he Sang the notes of his name at the flickering light in the open window. Both dogs bounded around the corner of the house, barking wildly. Jazep froze on the spot, not willing to chance that they remembered him from almost a full year before.

"Safety! Honor! Be quiet!" Gregor appeared in the doorway, a silhouette against the light within. "Is that you, Jazep?"

"It is." He walked forward and frowned as he drew close enough to see the other man's expression. "What's wrong? Has something happened to Adrie, or the baby?"

"No, they're fine." A smile flashed for an instant between the drooping ends of the mustache as Gregor touched his fist to the bard's. "Mari's almost walking. It's just that ..." He paused, threw up his hands, and stepped back out of the doorway. "It's just that it's complicated. I'd best save it till you're in and sitting down."

Confused, Jazep followed him into the house.

"... so then this Captain Otik rides up, oh, mid-afternoon and says that Annice is really His Majesty's sister and she's wanted in the capital for treason and Jorin a'Gerek is really Pjerin a'Stasiek, the Duc of Ohrid and he's escaped from his execution."

Dusting his fingertips lightly over the stretched skin of his tambour, Jazep frowned. "He's right about Annice, although I doubt His Majesty intends to pass Judgment, but I was in the Bardic Hall in Vidor the day the duc died. Unless the king himself is involved, he certainly didn't escape his execution."

"Then the captain was lying?" Adrie hugged herself and shivered although the night was warm.

Because he Sang only earth, Jazep spent most of Third and Fourth Quarter at the Citadel and often sat gate duty, giving him more contact with the King's Guard than most bards. Even the most determinedly neutral opinion of Otik had included a variation on "insanely ambitious." "Did the captain say why he was after Annice and this man?"

Gregor nodded, one end of his mustache twisted so tightly around his finger that it pulled his upper lip out at a painful-looking angle. "He said that His Majesty wanted Annice brought back to Elbasan but that Judgment had already been passed on the duc."

"And he said that because we were here on the king's sufferance," Adrie continued miserably, "if we didn't cooperate, we'd lose the valley."

Jazep suddenly knew what had happened. "You told the captain which way they went. Showed him their trail." The lap drum whispered under his fingers.

"We've put our lives into this valley." Gregor pleaded for understanding. "We thought he was a traitor ..."

"It's all right." Jazep used enough Voice to be believed. *No wonder these two are wound so tightly with*

guilt. They must realize that Annice saved their valley this
morning. And then they had to sacrifice her to save it this
afternoon. "Otik's a Captain in the King's Guard. You
did what you had to." He couldn't go after them until
sunrise. "I don't know who this Jorin a'Gerek is, but
Annice isn't entirely helpless."

Adrie looked even more wretched. "I thought bards
took an oath not to Sing against other people even to
save themselves."

"That's true." Jazep drummed out a faint heartbeat.
"But she can Sing to save her baby." He just hoped
Annice remembered that.

Otik watched their camp from downwind, his position
carefully screened by trees. He could take them now,
while they slept—one arrow for him and a second to
keep her silent. The crescent moon and stars combined
shed enough light to hit a motionless and unsuspecting
target. Slowly, he raised the crossbow.

Slowly, he lowered it again.

He'd wait until he got a good look at the traitor in
the morning. He didn't want to make any mistakes.

Annice cracked open her eyes and stared sleepily up
at Pjerin. From the length of the shadows it couldn't
have been much past dawn. "What are you doing?"
she muttered.

"Checking for bruises," Pjerin grunted, twisting
around and trying unsuccessfully to get a look at his own
right shoulder blade. "There was a great big unenclosed
pointed rock the size of my fist jabbing into me all
night."

"Then why didn't you mo . . . What is your problem?"
she snapped as the kigh pushed her up into a half reclining position. "I can get up on my . . ." She fell silent as
she realized that something had the kigh very upset.
"Pjerin! Get down!"

The crossbow quarrel caught him just under the left
shoulder, spun him around, and dropped him face first
into the pile of bracken he'd used for bedding.

"Pjerin!" Annice heaved herself to her feet and
started toward him.

"Not another step, Bard, and not a sound, or there's one for you, too."

Annice froze. There was an inch of bloody steel poking out through Pjerin's back and a line of crimson dribbling down from the wound. She couldn't tell if he was breathing, but the quarrel hadn't gone through anything vital, so he couldn't be dead. He *couldn't* be.

Light crossbow, at the edge of its accurate range, she found herself thinking as she listened to the footsteps cautiously approaching from the brush behind her. *A heavy crossbow, or a closer shot would've gone right through him.*

"Go back to where you were sleeping and sit down. And remember, even so much as a cough out of you and I'll shoot."

The voice was educated. *An Elbasan accent over Vidor origins; and what difference does it make?* She couldn't risk the chance that he was bluffing. Not with another life dependent so completely on her. *Pjerin, don't be dead,* she pleaded silently as she sat. *There are times I can't stand you, but I don't want you to be dead.*

When Otik walked out of the bush, weapon ready, it confirmed her worst fears; the guard had caught up to them. How they managed it wasn't really relevant. Then she frowned. Here was the captain, but she couldn't hear the rest of the troop.

"Very good, Highness," Otik piled sarcasm on the honorific. "Stay there and stay quiet and you'll be able to throw yourself on His Majesty's mercy at your Death Judgment. Move and you'll pay the price for treason now." He hoped she believed him because he didn't think he could actually shoot her. It was one thing to realize she was with child and another thing entirely to be confronted with it.

His attention locked on the bard, Otik circled the fire pit and squatted by the duc's wounded shoulder. It wasn't a heart shot; he'd known that the moment he pulled the trigger, but it *had* hit close and it was entirely possible that the position of the body hid a spreading pool of blood.

Still watching the bard, crossbow cradled in his right arm, the captain reached out and dug his thumb, hard, into the duc's side. Any reaction, and he'd shoot the unenclosed traitor again before he turned him over.

In a single motion, teeth clenched against the pain, Pjerin twisted, wrapped his right hand around Otik's wrist and slammed the fist-sized rock on his left, into the other man's head.

The wet crunch of bone shattering at Otik's temple, drowned out the single grunt of surprise he managed. As he fell, his finger spasmed.

Annice screamed as the ground dropped from under her and the quarrel punched through the place where her head had been. Heart pounding, she scrambled to her feet and raced through the kigh to Pjerin. "You're not dead!"

"Not quite," he gasped, rising to his knees.

Before she could stop him, he grabbed the fletched end of the quarrel and yanked it back out of his flesh.

"You idiot!" Annice caught him as he swayed. "How did you know that wasn't barbed?"

"Guards use smooth diamond tips." His face had taken on a slightly greenish cast. "Same going out as going in."

Calling him every insulting name she could think of, she snatched up his shirt and stuffed it against the hole, her fingers stained red.

"You could've waited . . ." she began.

Pjerin shook his head and wished he hadn't as the world tried to slide sideways. "No time. His troop has to be close. We've got to move."

"Not until I've bound this up!" She hurriedly tore, and wrapped, and tightened. "And what about Otik? Who knows how long he's going to be out. What do we do with him?" Hands still working, she half turned.

Otik lay crumpled on one side, the pink and gray ruin of his head facing the sky. His eyes stared sightlessly into the bracken, and a fly minced daintily along the moist lower curve of his lip.

"What do we do with Otik?" Pjerin repeated grimly. He hadn't intended to kill him, but remembering every detail of the long journey from Ohrid to Elbasan under the captain's control, he couldn't find it in himself to care that he was dead. "We leave him for the worms."

CHAPTER FOURTEEN

Jazep Sang the kigh a gratitude and stared thoughtfully down at the earth that now covered the body of Captain Otik. The captain had been killed with a blow to the side of the head. That much was obvious. That *alone* was obvious.

Red-brown bloodstains on the bracken were still sticky. Someone besides Otik had been injured.

The kigh were little or no help. Whether that was because they considered whatever happened none of their business or because they were protecting Annice, Jazep had no idea. He sighed and Sang for the trail. With one of them injured and Annice pregnant, or Annice injured and pregnant, they couldn't be very far ahead of him even with the addition of Otik's horse. With the help of the kigh, he'd be with them by noon.

And then Annice had some explaining to do.

Sometime later, he found himself back in the clearing by Otik's grave. The kigh had led him in a circle.

He Sang a question and frowned. Annice had asked them not to let anyone follow and they were including him in their compliance. There wasn't anything he could do about it either—the kigh had decided to protect Annice and her baby and nothing he could Sing would breach what they considered that protection to include.

Sliding out of his pack, Jazep sat and mulled over the possibilities. Why had Otik been killed? Because he'd wounded either Annice or her companion. Simple so far. But Otik must have known he'd have a fight on his hands if he tried to take them back to Elbasan, and risking that with a man Gregor and Adrie described as both large and fit didn't sound like the captain at all.

"Then let's suppose he didn't risk it," Jazep mused aloud. "Let's suppose he tried to remove the threat, maybe attacking the man in his sleep, botched the job, and was killed." Unfortunately, King Theron disapproved of his guard conducting summary executions and Otik was far too ambitious to risk the king's displeasure. "Unless . . ." The bard's eyes widened. "Unless Otik was right and Jorin a'Gerek really was the Duc of Ohrid, with a Judgment of Death already passed." Why was Annice with him? Jazep counted back. Because during Annice's Walk to Ohrid, the duc had fathered her child. Where were they headed now?

He stood and brushed off his breeches. Given the distance and direction they'd already traveled, they had to be headed for Ohrid.

Why?

"I guess I'll have to ask them that when I get there."

"You sent for me, Lady?"

"Yes. I did." Olina leaned back against the crenellations edging the tower roof and studied the new steward. In the seven days since she'd appointed him, he'd wrapped himself in the privileges of the position and gloried in the power, all the while keeping half an eye on her lest she change her mind. She turned and waved a hand down into the pass. "This is my great-nephew's heritage. If you want to cross the mountains into Cemandia or from Cemandia, you do it here."

Lukas moved forward until he stood by her side.

She allowed it for the moment. "I believe that the Duc of Ohrid has the right to exploit his heritage in such a way that all his people prosper. Don't you agree?"

"Yes, Lady."

"Do you know what that is?"

Lukas squinted along the line of her pointing finger. "The palisade, Lady."

"There, at the base of the palisade!"

He cringed slightly under the whip of her voice. "A crack in the lowest supporting log, Lady. But it's always been there."

"Don't you think it's time it was fixed?"

"But . . ."

She was rapidly losing her patience. "Don't make me repeat the question, Lukas. And don't make me regret I appointed you steward." The coiled ebony mass of her hair reflected the sunlight with an iridescent shimmer. "Fix the palisade so that my great-nephew can make Ohrid prosper."

"Yes, Lady." Stroking his beard he stared down into the pass, then suddenly turned to face her. "Yes, Lady," he repeated enthusiastically. Eyes gleaming with a mixture of fear and greed, Lukas bowed and hurried off.

He wasn't entirely stupid.

Olina smiled and flicked a bit of loose mortar off the top of the tower. Although she was certain he hadn't intended to, Albek had taught her the simplest way to get around Bardic Command. The truth was much more subjective than most people dreamed. "*I* told him to fix the palisade," she told the sky. "The palisade is an important part of Ohrid's defense."

Historically, the truth often depended on who won and, therefore, on who asked the questions. Olina intended to have as many of the right answers as possible, regardless of how much it presently looked like Cemandia would be the clear winner in the upcoming conflict.

Stasya stared up the length of the valley at the keep of Ohrid. When she'd been here in Fourth Quarter, it had brooded bleakly over a landscape of ice and snow, its high thick walls of black rock appearing to be more a grim growth on the side of the mountain than the result of a stonemason's art. She'd thought at the time that the dark impression was most likely a result of her errand.

"And I was wrong," she muttered, swinging her pack back onto her shoulders.

New growth had tinted the landscape a delicate green but nothing else had changed.

"Come to think of it, I'm on the same unenclosed errand." She shook her head and started up the track, a little surprised that the area got even enough traffic to cut the imprint of wheels into the grass.

The trip from Vidor upriver to the head of Lake Marienka had been one worth a song and the recall, when she finally got a chance to do it, would inspire fledgling compositions for generations. Among the Riverfolk, the young woman who'd risked her small boat on the chance that Stasya could out-Sing First Quarter currents had been considered a fool at the beginning of the journey and an unenclosed lucky fool at the end.

Whistling up a kigh, Stasya Sang it a short message to take back to Elbasan and the Bardic Captain. *"I'll be at the keep by sunset. I'm sure they'll be thrilled."* She hesitated briefly before adding, *"Any news of Annice?"* The guard had tracked them out of Vidor and then, as she'd predicted, lost them in the wilderness between the plains and Ohrid. Stasya wasn't sure that she wanted to be told, yet again, that there was no news, but she couldn't stop herself from asking.

By the time she reached the gates, she had a small parade of children accompanying her, dancing and leaping about to the music of her pipes. When she stopped playing, a howl of protest arose.

"Oh, so hard done by," she told them, laughing, gesturing with her empty hand at the two people waiting just outside the keep. "I'm not going to ignore the duc's regent for you lot. Run along and I'll play for you tomorrow."

"Are you going to thtay?" lisped a tow-headed boy through the gap where his front teeth had been.

"I'll be staying for a while," Stasya promised, watching the edge of her vision for a reaction from either of the listening adults. "His Majesty, King Theron is coming here for a visit and I'm to wait for him."

"Is that the majesty that killed Gerek's papa?" asked a child of indeterminate sex, small brows drawn into a frown.

"Yes. But he didn't want to." Four younger brothers had taught her that, moral position aside, children might just as well be told the truth because no adult could predict how they'd react to it. "Sometimes kings have to do things they don't want to, just like other people."

"Like going to bed when you're not thleepy?"

She nodded. "Just like."

"Gerek's not gonna like him," another child warned. "And he's sposed to be His Grace now. Maybe you could play for him 'cause he likes singin' and stuff."

"Well, I very definitely will." She knew it wasn't going to be anywhere near that easy and wondered if anyone had taken the reaction of a five-year-old duc to the king who killed his father into consideration during the planning stages. If they hadn't why not; and if they had, why hadn't they told her. "You guys had better get home before your parents think you've been carried off by ducks."

"Duckth don't do that!"

Stasya screwed her face up into a ferocious scowl. "Scat anyway." She watched them race at full speed down the track that led from the keep to the village nestled against its flank, then turned to face the gate and Sang the notes of her name.

"You're Stasya," Olina said, stepping forward. "The bard who put Pjerin under Command."

Bowing as deeply as the weight of her pack allowed, Stasya decided that the whole unenclosed family was just too good looking. While she appreciated Pjerin's dark and brooding beauty aesthetically, her reaction to his aunt's was a little more visceral. *Guess I was too distracted the last time to really notice her.*

Olina sensed Stasya's response with a predator's instinct and hid a smile. *Wouldn't it be interesting to discover if bards can be as easily controlled by desire as lesser folk.* It appeared she'd have time to find out. "Did I hear you correctly when you told those children that His Majesty, King Theron, is coming here?"

"You heard correctly, Lady." Getting her mind back on the situation at hand, Stasya slipped into a light recall trance. "His Majesty wishes to assure Gerek a'Pjerin, the seventh Duc of Ohrid, that the crime of his father will not in any way mar the historical relationship between Ohrid and Shkoder. His greatest desire now is to strengthen the ties between himself and the new duc. To such end he travels to Ohrid to accept the duc's oaths of fealty, rather than insisting on the duc coming to him in Elbasan."

"How generous of His Majesty." Olina's tone was dry. "But why didn't he send this news with the messenger that came to tell of my unfortunate nephew's execution? He was here just ..." She paused and counted. "... nine days ago."

"By the time His Majesty had come to the decision, the messenger had already left." Stasya spread her hands and smiled modestly. "Only a bard could be apprised of changing plans while on the trail."

"And when does His Majesty intend to arrive?"

"At the rate he's traveling now, he'll likely be here just after the Third Moon of the Quarter."

Olina glanced up at the rapidly darkening night sky. A crescent of moon rose on an arc of sapphire blue. Half moon in four nights and the Third Moon arrived seven nights later. Any time after that, King Theron. She needed to speak with Albek. "We have a room set aside for those few bards who manage to walk this far. My great-nephew's steward will escort you to it."

Lukas started, made as if to speak, and thought better of it.

Well, he's *up to something,* Stasya decided. *I've a dozen days to find a traitor before the king arrives; let's hope it's this obvious.*

Lukas motioned her through the gate. His hand continued to rise as she passed and once he was safely out of her line of sight, his fingers flashed out in the Cemandian sign against the kigh.

"King Theron coming here?" Albek froze, half out of his leather vest. "Are you certain?"

"The bard was."

"But why?"

Olina smiled although the ice remained in her eyes. "His Majesty wishes to strengthen the ties between Shkoder and Ohrid so unfortunately loosened by my late nephew. He's coming here to accept Gerek's oath of fealty."

"Here . . ." Slowly, Albek let the vest slide off his arms. "What an opportunity. At first light, I'll have to head back over the border. If it's at all possible, the army must arrive while Theron is in the keep."

"Of course it must," Olina agreed. She beckoned him forward and extended a booted foot.

Almost absently, he bent to grasp the leather. "What about the bard?"

"No doubt sent on ahead to sniff out any remaining treason. It's what I'd do in the king's position."

"What if she discovers what you've done in the pass? That could be dangerous, all things considered."

"Not to me." Olina offered him the second boot. "I've already been cleared under Command. By this very bard as it happens. The only thing she found me guilty of was being used by a certain Cemandian trader as an excuse to visit and remain at the keep." Her voice became a warning as she finished.

Albek knelt gracefully by her chair and softly kissed the fingers of a captured hand. *She has to believe she has her hooks in you. If she ever suspects for a moment you've used her, she'll close the pass with you in it.* And if Queen Jirina's army arrived at a pass he'd guaranteed open to find it closed, he didn't want to think of how Her Majesty's anger might manifest. His heart began to pound as Olina twisted out of his hold and gripped his chin painfully tight. He swallowed as she pulled his head toward hers. *She has to believe it,* he reminded himself. *You don't.*

But the voices had grown louder as he'd watched the bard approach and, now that she was in the keep, they surrounded him with constant pleading. Pain had always been used to silence the voices.

"You sent for me, Majesty?" With one hand raised to discover his headroom, Tadeus paused at the entrance to the king's tent.

Theron turned, gestured, then flushed and said, "Come in, Tadeus."

The blind bard ducked gracefully through the triangular opening, took three strides forward, and stopped. A breeze followed him in. It danced once around the tent, billowing the canvas walls, then lifted his curls on invisible fingers and left to a softly Sung gratitude.

"Kigh?" Theron asked curiously.

"Yes, Majesty." Tadeus smiled in the direction of the king's voice. "They're usually hesitant to enter even so flimsy an enclosure, but as I asked them very nicely and as they know how much of a loss I'm at when I'm in a place I've never been before, they agreed to help.

"Somehow," Theron told him dryly, "I can't imagine you ever being at a loss." Over the seventeen days they'd been traveling, certain impressive stories had filtered up as far as the royal ear.

Tadeus heard an undertone of those stories in the king's comment. Knowing full well that many of them were blatant exaggeration—because he'd been the one doing the exaggerating—his smile broadened and he graciously inclined his head.

Lowering himself carefully into the folding camp chair, Theron nodded a dismissal to his valet who disapprovingly uncorked a small clay bottle of wine, set it sharply on a tiny table beside two silver goblets, and left, nose in the air.

As the tent flap slid shut, Tadeus sighed theatrically. "He doesn't approve of the company you're keeping, Majesty."

"He doesn't approve of this entire trip," Theron corrected. "But it would've broken his heart if I'd left him behind."

"The Lady Heduicka said much the same of her servant, Majesty."

"The one always giving the Troop Captain advice?"

"Yes, that's Irenka. I believe, Majesty, that she was Lady Heduicka's nurse and moved out of the nursery with her charge.

"She must be older than she appears."

"By quite a bit, Majesty, but she's as tough as boot leather and not only passionately devoted to Hedi, uh, Lady Heduicka, but convinced the lady in question would be unable to so much as dress without her. I personally believe Irenka could take on the entire Cemandian army on her own. Just take them by the ear and march them back to their own side of the border."

"Good." Theron scrubbed at his face with both hands and hoped they wouldn't need her. "Please sit down, Tadeus." He gestured to the second chair and flushed again but before he could speak, Tadeus had crossed the tent—deftly avoiding the hanging lamp—swung his lute around to rest in his lap, and sat.

Wondering how long it would take him to remember both the bard's blindness and how little it hindered him, Theron bent forward and poured the two goblets full of dark wine.

Under the black silk scarf he wore over his eyes, Tadeus' nose twitched. "Is that one of the bottles you were given in Caciz, Majesty?"

"Kind of distinctive, isn't it?" Theron smiled as he watched the younger man carefully lift the offered goblet to his lips. "I had a feeling it wouldn't travel well."

"You're probably right," Tadeus agreed after a moment's serious consideration. "But, that aside, it's actually quite good."

Theron lifted his own cup and settled back in his chair. They drank in silence for a moment, then Tadeus asked quietly, "Was there a reason you wanted to see me, Majesty?"

"Not especially," the king sighed. "It's just that you're the only person in the company I don't have to lie to. You know why we're going to Ohrid and you know what's likely to happen when we get there."

"Stasya will point out the traitor, you'll pass Judgment, the sixth duc will pop out of the forest with Annice, who'll present you with a healthy niece or nephew, the Cemandian army will realize they can't win by treachery, sue for a treaty, and go home."

"Do you always look for the best to happen?"

Tadeus shrugged elegantly. "It's just as easy as looking for the worst, Majesty. And it lets you sleep at night."

"And if Stasya hasn't found the traitor?"

"Then we will."

"And if Annice ..." He couldn't finish the thought. The heavy embossing on the goblet cut into his fingers as he tightened his grip.

"Healer Elica says she was perfectly healthy when she left, Majesty, and that there should be no reason she isn't perfectly healthy still." Tadeus chose not to mention the obvious reasoning behind Elica being chosen as the king's healer for the journey over the elderly man who'd been Theron's personal healer all the king's life. "Bards spend most of the cycle walking and Annice was never one to overdo it, regardless of her condition."

Theron took a long swallow. "I can't believe the guards missed them in Vidor."

Tadeus could, but he chose not to mention that either. "Bards can take care of themselves, Majesty. You've no need to worry about either Stasya or Annice."

"And should I not worry about a Cemandian army marching through an open pass with only a troop of guard and an ex-nurse to greet them?"

Dark brows rose from behind their palisade of silk. "And what am I, Majesty? Fish guts on the pier?"

Theron couldn't prevent a smile at the injured tone. "Bards are forbidden by oath to use the kigh against other people."

"And what about the water kigh at the battle for the Broken Islands?"

"That was a bluff they chose not to call."

"And what about using kigh against enemies of the state?"

"Too easy to split hairs over the definition of enemies, as you very well know."

Tadeus drained his cup and flashed the king a brilliant smile. "Then I shall charm their army, capture their hearts, and send them all home prisoners of love."

There was such an absolute lack of doubt in his voice that Theron started to laugh and continued to laugh until tears ran down his cheeks and his ribs ached. Finally, he drew in a deep breath, let it out slowly, and said, "Thank you. I feel much better."

Rising, Tadeus bowed. "I live to serve," he murmured. "Now, Majesty, if you'll get into bed, I'll ensure that for tonight the cares of the future will have no power to keep you awake."

Theron rose as well, one arm pressed to the stitch in his side. "What did you have in mind?"

Silently commending himself for his restraint, Tadeus resisted temptation. "I thought perhaps I could sing for you."

Still smiling, Theron crossed to the narrow cot and shrugged out of his robe, wondering if he should be insulted at not being given a chance to turn the young man down. "Singing would be fine."

Holding the base of the lamp steady with one hand, Tadeus blew out the flame, and checked to be certain it was out with a string-callused finger. Returning to his chair, he settled his lute, briefly tightening one of the pegs which had a tendency to slip.

Before he could begin, however, Theron quietly muttered, "When I get my hands on my sister, I'm going to wring her neck."

"Begging Your Majesty's pardon ..." Tadeus stroked his thumb over the strings. "... but you haven't had any contact with your sister for ten years."

"Are you saying I haven't the right to throttle her?"

"No, Majesty, I'm just saying that there are others with stronger claims and you may have to wait in line."

"If I thought I could find that bird," Pjerin muttered at the dawn, "I'd wring its neck and make stew."

"It hasn't done anything for a few minutes," Annice pointed out, yawning. "Maybe it's done for the morn . . ."

The three note sequence was not only loud but had the same piercing quality as an infant's scream. It couldn't be ignored; it certainly couldn't be slept through. Annice surrendered and let the kigh roll her up onto her feet. *Oh, well, I had to pee anyway.*

When she got back from the designated privy, Pjerin was kneeling on his bedroll, shirt off, lifting the make-shift bandage wrapped over and around his shoulder.

"What are you doing?"

"Checking for infection." He didn't look up.

"Let me." Annice lowered herself carefully to her knees in front of him. His cheeks above the edge of his beard were pale and there were deep purple half circles under his eyes. "I'm really looking forward to cauterizing this if it gets infected," she muttered, peering under the dressing and sniffing. "Hot irons, searing flesh. What fun. I can't smell anything but sweaty Duc of Ohrid, so I guess it's all right."

Pjerin captured one of her hands. "Has anyone ever told you that personality-wise you're a lousy healer?"

"Has anyone ever told you that a person who gets shot through the shoulder by a crossbow quarrel—oh, and then rips it out of his body with one mighty tug—can't go on acting like nothing happened?"

"You've told me, Annice." He released her. "With every other breath. All day yesterday."

"And I'm likely to keep telling you today because I don't think you're listening. After all the effort I've put into getting you this far, I don't want you to die." She sat back and gently pulled his remaining shirt up over the bandage then settled his injured arm into its sling. "Do you think we lost them?"

Pjerin began a shrug, regretted it almost immediately, and arrested the motion. "You can't move a troop of guard through the bush, especially not up the slopes we've been climbing without making some noise. You haven't heard anything; I haven't heard anything. I think we've lost them for now." He stood and reached down with his good arm. Annice took it and he helped her haul herself back to her feet. "But I think we're going to have to keep losing them every day until this is over."

"Oh, great," Annice grumbled, glancing up at the sky. On top of everything else, it looked like rain.

After a hurried breakfast—fortunately goat cheese had a flavor distinctly different from the milk it was made of—Pjerin loaded Milena and Otik's horse while Annice had the kigh erase all traces of their camp. She couldn't be sure of it, but it seemed that the squat brown bodies were increasing in girth even as she did. Their new shape disturbed her and she hated thinking she appeared as unappealing to others as they did to her.

As unappealing to Pjerin? she wondered, as they started walking east, slowly climbing higher into the mountains. *No. That's ridiculous.*

"It occurs to me," she said after a while, "that talking might make this go a bit faster."

"Talking about what?"

"I don't know." She scratched through the shift at the tight curve of skin just over her hip. "But we managed to find common ground at least *once* before."

Pjerin glanced down at her, caught her meaning, and half smiled. "I don't remember that we talked much."

"Well, I remember you making a number of pretty strange sounds."

"Me? I wasn't the one howling."

"You *could* consider that a compliment."

Pjerin's smile blossomed suddenly and Annice couldn't help but appreciate the view. *Let's hope he passes those great teeth on, baby.*

"You know," he said, "I had no idea that you were who you are. Or were. That is, while you were at the keep, I had no idea that you were the ex-princess."

"It isn't an idea I want people to have."

"Yeah, but even after I knew, well, sometimes I still find it hard to believe."

"Why?" Annice demanded. "I don't act like you imagine an ex-princess should act?"

He laughed. "Actually, it's more that you don't look like a princess. You've got that little bump on your nose and your hair's kind of—well, no easily identifiable color, and your eyes crinkle up at the corners when you laugh, and . . ."

"And if you stick me in expensive clothes and drape me in jewels and surround me with courtiers, I can look pretty unenclosed princesslike, thank you very much." She snorted and pushed a strand of blowing hair back out of her eyes. Stasya said it was like poured honey. What did he know?

Pjerin sighed. He should've known better. "I was trying to pay you a compliment, Annice. You were one of the most *real* people I'd ever met, that's all I was trying to say. And . . ." His tone picked up an edge. "I'd have to say you act exactly like a princess; high-handed, always wanting your own way, always assuming you're right and everyone else is wrong."

"I don't *always* assume I'm right," Annice protested, deciding at the last minute not to let the branch she'd pushed out of her path spring back and smack him in the face. "It just usually turns out that I am and, oh, center it, I knew it was going to rain." She draped the lead rope over a bush and turned to rummage the oil-skins out of the pack.

Thunder cracked directly overhead, the clouds opened, and within seconds they were both drenched to the skin. So early in the season, so high in the mountains, it wasn't a pleasant sensation. To her horror, Annice found herself bursting into tears as she wrapped her long cloak around her soaked shift.

"Annice?" Clumsily tying off the mare's reins with one hand, Pjerin came around the mule. "Are you crying?"

"No. Shut up. Who asked you anyway?"

"What's wrong?" He tried not to sound annoyed, but she wasn't making it easy.

"I'm wet. And I'm tired." Annice had no idea where this was coming from, but she couldn't seem to stop it. "And I'm fat."

Pjerin rolled his eyes. "You're not fat. It's a baby, remember?"

"It's a baby, but I'm still fat." A kigh rose out of the ground at her feet and lightly touched her knee. "Go away!" she sobbed. It left, but slowly. "I can't Sing anything but dirt anymore." Rain ran down her hair and dripped off the end of her nose. "And Stasya's probably dead because of me."

Shaking his head, Pjerin gathered her up against the uninjured side of his body. The fact that she allowed the embrace gave him a pretty good idea of how upset she was. He didn't understand it, but at the moment that wasn't really important as he dropped his head, murmured words of comfort into her hair, and gave her a shoulder to cry on.

Gradually, Annice found her lost control and, cheeks flaming, pushed away. Unable to meet his eyes, she muttered her thanks into his chest.

"Hey, I'd do the same for any friend."

His voice was so gentle that she had to look up.

He smiled. "Ready to move on?"

Still uncertain of her voice, she nodded and reached for Milena's lead rope. *He's really a very nice person, baby. Sometimes. And I know he's a good father. I suppose that if Stasya is dead and I need some help raising you, I could do worse.*

"We'll stop as soon as we find shelter. Make sure the kigh warn us if we enter any run-off gullies. Keep the mule on a tight lead."

On the other hand, he can be a bit of an authoritarian asshole and I'd probably kill him before you were walking.

From the top of the inner tower, Gerek glared down at the lone rider disappearing between the high cliffs of the pass. It wasn't his fault if nobody listened to him. He rubbed his nose on his sleeve, the upper half of his small body wedged into one of the crenellations. He'd told everybody that the new man Aunty Olina liked was the same as the old man and they hadn't listened.

"Think I meant he was a Cemandian," he sniffed. "Think I'm a baby, don't know anything." People should listen to him now he was the duc.

His lower lip trembled. He didn't want to be the duc. His mama had come and asked him if he wanted to go live with her, but he didn't want that either. He wanted his papa back.

Gerek hunched his shoulders as Nurse Jany called for

him down in the courtyard. Even if she figured out where he was, he knew she was too fat to climb the tower stairs.

"I'm going to stay up here for the rest of my life."

The rider was long out of sight when he heard the footsteps behind him and sullenly turned. He never got to do anything he wanted.

"You can really see a long way from up here." Stasya smiled at him and held out her fist. "You must be Gerek." She'd decided to use only his name as his title might remind him of where he'd seen her before.

Unfortunately, he didn't need a reminder. "You're the bard who took my papa!" With a shriek of fury, he launched himself at her legs.

Unwilling to hurt him, Stasya found herself at a distinct disadvantage as Gerek had every intention of hurting her. Although she managed to grab hold of his flailing arms and twist the lower part of her body back out of his way, he got in a couple of painful kicks to each shin.

"Gerek!"

The voice cut through his hysteria and left him hanging stiffly from the bard's grip. Stasya turned them both so she could see who'd spoken although she really had very little doubt.

Olina stood at the top of the stairs, head set at an imperious angle above the slender column of throat, pale blue eyes narrowed and full lips set in a thin disapproving line. "That is not the way that a Duc of Ohrid behaves to a guest in his keep."

"She made my papa say bad things!"

"She made your father admit to the truth."

Cautiously, ready for a rematch, Stasya released him. When his lower lip started to tremble and his violet eyes filled with tears, she almost told him what the truth actually was.

"My papa promised he'd come back!"

Stasya felt her mouth open of its own volition and snapped it shut.

"Your father is dead, Gerek." Olina's voice had gentled. "And now the king is coming to Ohrid to fix the damage your father did."

"He's not coming here!" One booted foot stamped

hard on the dressed rock. "He's not. I hate him!" Sobbing wildly, Gerek pushed past his aunt and pounded down the stairs, screaming "Hate him! Hate him! Hate him!" until his voice was muffled by distance and the comforting bulk of his nurse.

Olina turned from staring down the stairwell and met Stasya's gaze evenly. "The sooner he knows that King Theron is coming," she explained, "the sooner he can get used to the idea. I apologize, though, for the way he treated you."

"Please, don't worry about it, Lady Olina." Stasya bent and rubbed her shin, as much to break the heat of the other woman's gaze as to acknowledge the bruising. "He obviously loves his father very much, and anyway, bards develop thick skins about rejection."

Over the next few days, that thick skin came in very useful. Half the inhabitants of both keep and village viewed her much the way Gerek did; as at least partially responsible for the execution of Pjerin a'Stasiek. The other half flashed the sign against the kigh whenever she approached and went out of their way to obviously avoid her. When she went to visit Bohdan, Pjerin's old steward, his daughter's partner stiffly refused to let her see him and finally slammed the heavy door in her face.

Many people wore Cemandian styles and she saw Cemandian influence in nearly every facet of the villagers' lives. Only one woman was openly welcoming, but as she insisted on reciting long and boring verse that she knew would sound wonderful set to music, Stasya considered that a mixed blessing at best.

She was never able to sing or play for the children again, although she put herself in places where they might have approached her if they'd dared. Gerek, she saw only from a distance as he glared at her from a window or around a corner. Finally, Stasya gave up trying to speak with him, just as happy not to have to see the accusations in his eyes.

Against such strongly held prejudices, Charm would have no effect. Although Tadeus might have been able to use it, Stasya knew it was beyond her abilities. More than once she was tempted to Command the information she needed, but Command was less than subtle and at the first hint of an inquiry, the traitor would be away out of His Majesty's reach.

She Sang the attitudes she faced onto the kigh. The king needed to be prepared.

Eavesdropping became her greatest source of information; fortunately, it was a skill bards were trained in and her presence at the keep brought up old discussions of the treason. It wasn't long before she learned that the young duc's regent was considered to have ideas for the advancement of Ohrid, was strengthening the defenses in the pass, and was someone it was safer never to cross. Surprisingly enough, for a duc who had supposedly made a deal with Cemandia, Pjerin's greatest fault was remembered as his being too restrictive with the border.

"Holding out for the best deal," muttered one villager within Stasya's hearing.

While Pjerin had been respected for his strength, he hadn't been feared. Olina's strength, on the other hand, generated as much fear as respect.

With a bard's right to wander where she willed, Stasya walked one day out into the pass and stared up at the huge timber palisade that held back enough rock to fill the narrowest section two body-lengths deep. Ingeniously crafted by the third Duc of Ohrid, it could be triggered by releasing a single wheel which, in turn, released the tension on the entire system. It had been tested twice, Stasya recalled—amidst much grumbling when it came time to clear and refill, one rock at a time—but had never needed to be used. She squinted up at the people climbing along the top edge and wondered if the kigh could tell her what they were doing.

"You shouldn't be here," Lukas grunted from behind her. "It's dangerous."

Stasya turned quickly enough to catch the end of his sign against the kigh. She was tempted to go ahead and Sing but instead asked, "What are they doing up there?"

"Maintenance." His tone said it was none of her business. "You should go. It's dangerous."

"Isn't it more dangerous for th . . ." The last word got lost in a mad scramble backward as a rock the size of her head fell a body length from where she'd been standing, shooting shards of stone in all directions.

"No," Lukas snapped, white-faced and glaring up at

the top of the palisade as he clutched at a gash in his forearm.

Stasya, thanking every god in the Circle that she hadn't been hit, reached without thinking for his arm. "Here, let me look at that."

The duc's steward recoiled and pointed out of the pass with a bloody finger. "Go!" he spat. "I wouldn't have even been down here but for you."

Stasya went.

"He hates you because his only daughter was killed by the kigh."

"What?" Stasya stared at the cook, who'd been forced to speak with her in order to prepare for the coming of the king. It hadn't been hard to twist the subject to the new steward as the old staff despised him. "How?"

"She was Singing fire and it burned up the house with her in it. Happened early Fourth Quarter."

"But Annice was here in Third Quarter. She must've tested the girl for ability."

The cook snorted. "Lukas a'Tynek would no more let his child be tested by a bard than he'd, he'd . . ." She glanced around the kitchen for inspiration. "Than he'd bake a cherry pie. He follows the old Cemandian ways that came over the mountain, back when. Believes the kigh are outside the Circle."

"Why do you think the Lady Olina made him steward?"

" 'Cause she can't be regent and steward both, much as she'd think things would go better with her running it all, and Lukas is someone she can push around. Lots of folk up here follow the old beliefs."

"But his daughter died because of them." Stasya sighed and shook her head. "What do you believe?"

Suddenly aware who she was speaking to, the cook busied herself with rolling pastry. "I believe," she said, her gaze fixed firmly on the job, "in keeping my own counsel."

Olina i'Katica seemed to be the only person in all of Ohrid who had no opinion on Stasya's involvement with the sixth duc's treason. Stasya suspected that was because she was still so furious at Albek's betrayal, at being used by the Cemandian to gain access to her nephew.

Albek had to have tampered with her memories as well, for under Command, Olina's testimony had matched Pjerin's. If Stasya could Command the older woman again, she might be able to find out how he'd done it and who the actual traitor was he'd left behind. Was it Lukas? Had Olina appointed him because of something Albek had left in her mind?

Or was it Olina herself? Had she agreed to his tampering in order to control a child duc? Stasya watched her and wondered. While she was both self-centered and ambitious, could she actually be cold-blooded enough to frame her own nephew and send him to the block?

The problem was, Olina had no more to gain than anyone in Ohrid, for Stasya doubted that Queen Jirina much cared who she set up after conquest as her puppet in the keep.

Stasya was certain of two things only; that when King Theron arrived, Lady Olina was going back under Command; and that she wasn't going to be the one who told her so.

Four days later, she heard about Simion.

"I sent him away the morning after you arrived." Olina wiped her hands and smiled across the table at the bard. "He was a very pretty Cemandian mountebank who came through the pass with the first lot of traders. I think I was using him to get back at Albek."

"Why did you send him away?" Feeling a surge of sympathy for the unknown young man, Stasya toyed with the fork beside her plate. Although common enough in the capital, she was surprised to find the utensil in use in Ohrid. The silversmith's mark was not one she knew, so the set had to have come from Cemandia.

"I just told you." Smiling, Olina pushed her chair back from the table. "You arrived."

The room was suddenly very warm.

"Before the Riverfolk discovered that the Circle encloses all beliefs, they had a Goddess." Training kept Stasya's voice steady. "She was dark and beautiful and lived in the deep still places of the river. Whenever any of the Riverfolk drowned, it was said they'd gone to the bed of the Goddess."

"My bed is drier."

"Perhaps, Lady." Stasya stood and bowed. "But I'd be just as unlikely to survive. If you'll excuse me?"

Complimented by the comparison, Olina regally inclined her head.

Needing air, Stasya headed for the high watchtower. At the far end of the keep, its base as high on the mountain as the inner watchtower's roof, it gave an unobstructed bird's-eye view down into the pass and along it into Cemandian territory. She knew the observation post stood empty as Olina had commented on it, saying, *"There'll be no invasion now the traitor has been discovered."*

"Everything in this place has two meanings," she muttered, her thoughts in such turmoil that she had no idea she was being followed.

By the time she reached the top of the tower, her pulse beat hard in her ears and she sagged gratefully against the stone. There were no kigh around, and she thanked whatever parts of the Circle were responsible. She had neither the energy nor the inclination to deal with the kigh right now.

Her weight on her elbows, she leaned out over the pass, staring toward Cemandia. No armies approaching. That, at least, was mildly encouraging. Then she sighed and looked back along the outer wall of the keep.

Frowning, she straightened and moved around the arc of the tower for a better look.

"Center it!"

She pursed her lips to call the kigh, but the only sound that emerged was a soft grunt as Lukas smashed the rock in his hand down on the back of her head.

CHAPTER FIFTEEN

"Are you out of your mind?"

Her tone was ice and iron, and Lukas shrank back, knowing as he did that distance would be no protection from the implied threat. "She was at the high tower, Lady. Looking down *into* the pass! I had to stop her!" His hand flicked out in the sign against the kigh.

"Looking down into the pass?"

"Yes, Lady."

And things had been going so well.... Frowning, she prodded Stasya's limp body with the toe of her boot. The dark hair was matted and sticky with blood and the back of the bard's tunic showed a crimson stain. "You're certain she's still alive?"

Lukas dropped to his knees beside the crumpled body. "Yes, Lady. She breathes and her heart beats."

So much easier, Olina reflected, *if he'd just killed her outright.* Had Lukas killed the bard, she'd merely have him confined, convinced that she'd arrange his escape before the king arrived to sit in Judgment. During that escape, she'd have him killed. The kigh could go ahead and tell the bard traveling with His Majesty everything they saw because none of it would arouse suspicion.

To ensure an easy and early victory, Theron must be in the keep when the Cemandian army arrived. It was vital he not receive any information that would make him cautious enough to postpone the end of his journey.

While the kigh *might* have seen Lukas strike the blow, Stasya would very definitely Sing everything she knew the moment she regained consciousness. Therefore, she mustn't be allowed to Sing. Olina remembered being told that a bard's death attracted the kigh. She had no memory of who had told her or how true the observation might be, but now that she could be implicated in was a risk she had no intention of taking. Stasya would just have to be put where the kigh couldn't reach her.

"Carry her to the old section of the keep," Olina commanded at last. "If you let anyone see you, I will be *very* angry. Do you understand?"

Very angry. Thankful that he remained on his knees, for they would have surely given out, Lukas nodded. "Yes, Lady."

"I'll meet you in the small chamber at the north end of the Great hall." She fixed her gaze on him and was pleased to see him tremble. "Remember, no one is to see you."

Gerek had spent a wonderful morning pulling weeds from the fields autumn-sown with corn. It was a task that all the village children participated in from the time they were strong enough to beat the weeds until they were strong enough to move to larger tasks. Each child had a row—some of the smallest children were paired—and there were races and singing and trophies passed from grubby hand to grubby hand as a particularly long rooted foe was vanquished.

Although Gerek had been able to stay for the midday picnic and a lovely mud fight that had been too quickly broken up, he wasn't allowed to remain for the afternoon's fun.

"You're the duc now," his Aunty Olina had told him. *"And you have responsibilities the other children do not."*

He'd settled back on his heels and stared up at her. *"It's the 'sponsibility of the duc to share in the work and know what's going on."* Experience had taught him not to preface such announcements with, my papa said.

Aunty Olina had smiled. *"Very well. But only for the morning."*

"And the picnic."

Her brows had risen, but after a moment she'd nodded. *"Of course."*

Urmi, the stablemaster, had come to get him and the pleasure of riding home on Kaspar, his pony, had almost made up for having to leave. From the stable, aware that he was going to be late and knowing how his aunt felt about that sort of thing, he'd take a shortcut through the old section of the keep.

Still a spiral staircase and a narrow corridor away from the nursery, the sound of boots ringing against the floor froze him in place. Only his Aunty Olina walked like that, like she was slapping the stone with her feet. Was she looking for him? Was she maybe angry with him? Gerek looked around for a place to hide.

Dropping to his stomach, he squirmed under a carved stone bench and tucked himself as tightly as he could against the wall. The footsteps grew louder, then he saw a pair of black boots stride past his hiding place. Grinning broadly, he hugged his knees as they passed. *You don't know I'm here,* he thought. *You don't . . .* Then he frowned as a tooled leather strap dragged by. Why was his Aunty Olina carrying the bard's stuff?

"Did anyone see you?"

"No, Lady."

"Good. And the bard?"

Wrapped tightly in the folds of an old horse blanket, Stasya moaned.

Lukas stared down at her, then up at Olina. "She lives, Lady."

"So I can hear." She shifted the weight of Stasya's pack, hastily stuffed behind closed shutters with everything the bard had brought to Ohrid. "Follow me."

Heaving his burden back over his shoulders, Lukas followed.

Leading the way through the ground floor of the keep, Olina took a moment to light a torch with flint and steel and then descended into the cellars, the steward with his burden treading closely on her flickering shadow.

"Are we going to leave her down here, Lady?'

She didn't bother to answer.

They crossed two rooms, long unused even for storage. In the third, she stopped, and let pack and instrument case slide to the floor. "Put her down and open that," she said, gesturing at an iron grate set flush with the rough-cut stone.

In the end, it took both their strength thrown against the grate to lift it.

Lukas stared through the narrow opening into a darkness so complete it seemed solid. "What is it?" he panted, mouth working against the dank smell of ancient decay rising into the cellar.

"It's an oubliette," Olina told him, scrubbing her palms together. At his blank expression, she added dryly, " A hole in the ground. An old Cemandian custom."

"I never knew this was here."

"Why should you?" She jerked her head toward the pack. "Get that down there and then her."

"Down there?" Lukas backed a step away from the hole.

Olina's eyes narrowed as signs of incipient panic began to appear in the steward's manner. She didn't have time for this. "Try to remember that killing or attempting to kill a bard means a Death Judgment and that *you* struck the blow. *I* am only trying to help you stay alive." Icy blue eyes fixed unblinkingly on his face.

After a moment, Lukas picked up the pack with visibly trembling hands and shoved it through the hole. He threw down the instrument case, listened to it land and bounce, and turned to stare at the feebly moving body of the bard.

"Lady . . ."

"Do it!" Olina snapped, seeing the rest of her well worked plans come unraveled in his hesitation. "Or shall we just drag her back outside and give the kigh a good look at what you've done?"

He had to swallow before he could speak. "No, Lady."

Stasya moaned. Voices slammed about within her skull with such force that she couldn't make out the actual words. She tried to push against the scratchy fabric confining her, but her arms refused to respond.

She moaned again as something dragged her over a surface both hard and cold and poured her into emptiness.

Her thoughts cleared just long enough for her to realize that she was falling, then a brilliant flash of white light exploded against the inside of her head and darkness claimed her again.

His small body pressed into the recessed doorway, hid-

den in shadows barely touched by the pale sunlight slanting through high, narrow windows, Gerek watched as his
Aunty Olina and Lukas came up from the cellars. *What
did they do with the bard?* he wondered. Were they mad
at her, too, because of what she did to his papa? He
watched the torch ground out against the threshold and
left lying on the stone, then he watched them walk away.

Brow furrowed, he padded over to the doorway and
squatted to look at the torch. Remembering something
he'd seen Rezka do once at the kitchen hearth, he
leaned forward and blew on the blackened end. Nothing
happened. Eyes narrowed, he leaned closer and blew
again.

A thin wisp of smoke climbed up to be lost in shadows
of the ceiling.

Pleased with himself, he picked up the torch carefully
in both hands and kept blowing until, suddenly, it was
alight.

His papa didn't like him playing with fire.

But if he wasn't even allowed to yell at the bard, how
come Aunty Olina was allowed to leave her in the cellar? He was the duc. He should at least get to yell.

"I'm blind."

The words bounced back and forth through the darkness, making it clear, even through the pounding pain,
that she was in a very enclosed space. There was no
panic behind the words; not yet, she figured she'd save
that for when she had the energy to make it worthwhile.

Moving slowly, Stasya forced herself up into a sitting
position and fought the urge to vomit. With both hands
pressed hard against her mouth and her throat working
convulsively against the bile, she sat motionless until the
need became less than all she was.

Sucking damp, musty air through her teeth, she
reached behind her and gingerly searched the back of
her head where the pain seemed the most intense. Her
fingers came away sticky and she swallowed her most
recent meal for a second time as, involuntarily, she
jerked away from her own touch.

Obviously, she hadn't been alone looking down at the
palisade and someone had done a thorough job of stopping her from passing on what she'd seen.

Feeling as though her head were an egg, cracked and ready to fry, she groped around her, trying to identify the objects she'd half landed on. Her pack was easy, the bent cedar frame had dug a painful bruise into her shoulder—a bruise she accepted with gratitude as its padded bulk had kept her head from connecting with the stone of the floor. Untangling her legs from a blanket that smelled strongly of the stable, she bent too far forward, the world tilted, and she cracked her nose against her knee.

Her eyes welled with tears and she let them fall, fighting for control only when she felt hysteria rising.

A flailing arm brushed a familiar curve of padded leather.

"My harp!" Anger became a useful distraction, blocking everything else until she held her harp on her lap and could run her fingers over its strings; the harp case had exceeded its maker's guarantee and the soft whisper of sound calmed her enough to wonder, *what next*.

She'd get no response if she Sang the kigh. Not even for Tadeus would they come so far into a building.

Tadeus.

Blind.

Eyes opened or closed, the darkness pressed against her with identical intensity. All at once, she couldn't breathe. Her heartbeat grew louder, louder, louder. Blood roared in her ears. Her fingers tightened convulsively. The dying note of a snapped harp string brought her back to herself.

"Careful." Her voice shook, but for the most part she had it under control. "You won't find any replacement strings down here."

Down here.

At the moment, being blind was the least of her problems.

Stretching out an arm, she found a wall and had to stop herself from trying to drive her fingers into the damp rock. With the mountain supporting her, for her prison had clearly been dug not built, she managed to stand.

"Bard? Hey, Bard? Are you down there?"

"Gerek?" Shoulder braced against the wall, Stasya

looked up. Relief hit her so hard, she almost fell. Through the outline of a narrow grate she could see a flicker of flame. She wasn't blind. Blinking away tears, she reached for the light, but as near as she could tell the opening was an arm's length again above her fingers. "Gerek! Go tell your Aunt Olina where I am!"

"She knows." Gerek leaned forward, resting the end of the torch in one of the holes in the metal, squinting until he thought he could see the bard's face in the darkness. "Her and Lukas put you there. That'll teach you for taking away my papa."

Oh, shit. Shit. Shit. Shit. Stasya sagged but the wall caught her. *Found your traitor, Majesty. Now what?*

"Hey, Bard? Can you get out?"

Let's not waste this one chance. She pulled herself erect, as close to the grate as she could get. "No, Gerek, I can't."

"So what'll happen?"

"I'll die." Die. Die. Die. The word lingered. Stasya tried to ignore it.

Gerek chewed his lip while he thought about it. "Good," he declared after a moment. "I want you to be dead. Just like my papa."

Stasya's heart contracted at the pain in his voice and she came to a sudden decision. "Gerek, I need to tell you a secret." She couldn't Command because she couldn't see his eyes and, under the circumstances, she doubted Charm would be very effective. All she could do was work her voice so that he had to believe her. "It's a very important secret and you mustn't tell anyone."

He liked secrets and the anticipation of hearing one made him forget his plans to yell at the bard. "What?"

"Promise you won't tell."

"I promise."

"Your papa isn't dead. It was a mistake, like he said, and the king is coming to make it better."

"My papa isn't dead?"

She put everything she had into the repetition. "Your papa isn't dead."

Kneeling by the grate, both hands holding tightly to the smoking torch, Gerek turned over the words in his mind, examining each one. The world, pressing so tightly around him, suddenly loosened. His papa wasn't dead. He knew it. He'd known it all along. His papa had said it was a mistake. Just wait till he told his Aunty Olina.

Halfway to his feet, he frowned and knelt again. The bard had made him promise not to tell.

"Why can't I tell?" he demanded.

"Because we don't want the bad people who *really* did what they said your papa did to find out he's alive."

"Oh. Is he going to catch them?"

"Yes. And he's coming here. Really, really soon." Down in the pit, Stasya hoped it'd be soon enough. "He's coming with Annice, the bard who was here in Third Quarter. Do you remember her?"

Gerek sat back on his heels. "Of course I remember."

He sounded so indignant, Stasya couldn't help but smile. "I was supposed to watch for them, because they'll be sneaking up to the keep, but I can't do that now . . ."

" 'Cause you're in a hole."

"That's right, so I need you to do something for me. I need you to go visit Bohdan."

"Papa's steward. I like him better than Lukas even if he told me to do things more."

"That's good, because when you're alone with him, I need you to tell him what I told you about your papa." Bohdan, for all he was a sick old man, was the only person remaining in Ohrid who might possibly have enough authority to stand up against Lukas and Olina. Based on what she'd seen back in Fourth Quarter, he was also the only person in Ohrid she'd trust with the truth.

"But I promised not to tell anyone."

Grinding her teeth sent knives of pain through her head. "Anyone but Bohdan," Stasya amended. "Do you remember what to tell him?"

"That Papa isn't dead and it was a mistake and he's coming with Nees."

"What a good memory you've got."

Gerek snorted. "I'm five."

"Of course you are. And I need you to tell him where I am and who put me here."

"Okay."

"But don't tell your Aunt Olina!"

" 'Course not, I promised. Papa says you never break a promise." He stood. "Besides, Aunty Olina knows where you are. I gotta go 'cause my fire is going out."

"Gerek?" No, she couldn't ask him to leave the torch. She had no idea how far he'd have to travel in the dark without it. "Never mind."

"Okay." He was almost to the next room when he remembered something and returned to the grate. "Bard? I don't want you to be dead no more."

Her back against the wall, Stasya lifted her head one last time toward the light. "I'm glad, Gerek."

"In case you're curious, we're in Ohrid."

Pjerin pushed the mare to one side of the path and turned to stare in confusion at Annice. "How do you know?"

"By the way the kigh react to your presence."

Her tone hinted that any idiot should know that, but, remembering the morning's tears, Pjerin gave her the benefit of the doubt and kept his own voice neutral. "Excuse me?"

"The kigh recognize you as the person responsible for this area of land." Annice pushed an overhanging branch out of her way, waiting until the shower of water droplets ceased before she continued walking. There was no point in taking shelter from the storm and then being drenched by its aftermath. "Surely you've heard the idea that the lord and the land are one?"

"Well, yes, but . . ."

"When you took the title, didn't you make a cut with the family sword and bleed on the earth? At First Quarter Festival, don't you make the first cut for the plow? And at Second Quarter Festival, don't you spend the night in the fields, spilling your seed?"

"Annice!"

She grinned at him. "Well, don't you? It's your right; you're not too old, or too young, I imagine you have plenty of choices, and I *know* all the parts work."

"Annice!" When she looked as if she was going to continue, he raised his free hand and cut her off. "All right. I do. Now drop it."

"I was only about to point out that all these things—and others—tie you to the land." She nodded toward the earth at his feet. "The kigh know that you've come home."

The door to the armory, which was heavy and had a tendency to stick, would have defeated him had one of the stablehands not chanced by to open it for him. Gerek thanked her, explained he could close it by himself, and waited until she'd rounded the corner before he went inside.

While Nurse Jany had fussed and scrubbed him and helped him dress, Gerek had made up his mind. Bohdan was old and sick and couldn't help the bard anyway.

Taking bow and quiver from their pegs, he checked them as he'd been taught, slung the quiver over his shoulder, and wrapped the bowstring tightly for traveling. He had a cooked sausage in his belt-pouch and he had a plan.

Gerek stared up at his papa's sword. It was the duc's special sword his Aunty Olina had said when she'd handed it to him at First Quarter Festival. His papa was the duc. He was going to take his papa his sword.

Hung high above his reach, he had to stand on a bench and use the end of his bow to knock it off the wall. The blade bounced partway out of the scabbard when it landed, hilt ringing loudly against the stone floor of the armory, but Gerek shoved the pieces back together and wrapped it awkwardly in his best cloak. He wasn't allowed to play with the sword, so he figured he should hide it until he was out of the keep.

No one saw him as he made his way to the gate, struggling a little with his heavy load. Relishing his role as a secret messenger, he stayed in the shadows close to the walls. Once outside the walls, he slipped off onto a narrow path too steep for anything but goats or children, screened from above by the lip of the track. He had to let the sword slide down alone, but it didn't seem to have hurt it when he retrieved it at the bottom.

With one wistful glance toward the shrieks of laughter coming from the fields on the other side of the village, he darted into the tangle of growth bordering the creek that ran from the base of the keep to the forest. He wasn't a baby. He knew that if he kept to the track, they'd find him and bring him back.

He also knew, although he couldn't put the idea into words, that there could be no going back. His Aunty Olina wasn't the type to forgive such treachery.

"Stop crying, Jany!" Olina snapped. "I can't understand a word you're saying. Gerek spent the afternoon in the fields when I expressly forbade it and he's going to be punished." Although the boy's disobedience had actually been convenient as she'd had enough to take care of without supervising his lessons, that didn't negate the fact he'd disobeyed.

Gerek's nurse choked back a sob and lifted her face from a damp, crumpled square of linen. "He didn't spend the afternoon in the fields, Lady. I washed him and I dressed him and I sent him down to you."

"Just because he was washed and dressed doesn't mean he didn't return to the pleasures of mud," Olina pointed out, drumming her fingers on the arms of her chair. Gerek had obviously become too much for the old woman to handle. He needed a tutor, and the moment the Cemandian invasion was complete, she'd get him one.

"No, Lady, I spoke with Gitka. He wasn't there. No one has seen him all afternoon."

"No one?"

"No one, Lady. What if he's . . ." The thought became too much for her and she burst into fresh sobs.

"What if he's what? Hurt? You're not helping him, Jany." Olina stood, lips set in a thin line. Although fond of the child, she had no doubt that he'd be found tucked into a corner somewhere, happily oblivious to the panic he'd caused his nurse. Meanwhile, she could use this incident for other ends. "Find Lukas; he can organize a search of the keep."

Eventually, the search spread out from the keep to the village and the surrounding valley. Torches were lit as night fell and the voices calling his name grew strained and frightened. Parents held their own children closer and remembered all the dangers of the darkness.

Olina stood by the entrance to the old cellars, staring at the stub of the torch and the print of a small foot outlined in crumbling flakes of earth. Gerek had gone into the cellar carrying the torch she had used when they got rid of the bard and then come out again. What had he seen? And what, if anything, had he been told? Things had just become much more complicated.

"Has anyone checked the palisade? He may have gone to watch the work and . . ."

"Lady!" Urmi pushed her way through the crowd gathered in the outer courtyard. "I've just searched the armory! The duc's sword is missing!"

The little fool has probably taken it and trotted off to challenge the king! Olina slapped control around her relief. *At least he's not hiding in the keep with what he knows. Now, I can deal with this.* "Has anyone seen the bard?"

No one had.

The server sent to check Stasya's room raced back crying that the bard was gone.

An ugly murmur ran through the crowd. Olina listened and did nothing although she could have stopped it with a word—reaction would serve her better than reason. She was pleased to see Lukas flash the sign against the kigh and more pleased still to see it mirrored around the courtyard.

"The bard can't have gone far!" Urmi cried. "She's on foot. We have to get Gerek back. We have to go after her!"

"And face the kigh at night?"

Urmi turned on the man who'd spoken, her lip curled. "*I'm* not afraid of the kigh!"

"You should be." Lukas stepped forward, but stayed in Olina's shadow. "You saw what the kigh did to my house and my daughter."

The muttering grew more apprehensive and less militant. Even those who personally despised Lukas couldn't deny that his house had burned and his daughter was dead.

"Remember that this is the bard who took Pjerin to his execution." Olina's voice cut through the babble, leaving a sharply defined line of silence behind it as assumptions were hastily shuffled.

"Shkoder is destroying the Ducs of Ohrid!"

The babble became a roar.

"But why?" someone called.

"Because Shkoder is afraid!" came the answer from the back of the crowd. "We're all that stands between them and Cemandia, and suppose we don't want to be a living barrier anymore?"

"His Grace—that is, His Grace's father—saw it coming. He tried to make a deal with Cemandia and they killed him."

Olina hid a smile. It was such a small step from oathbreaker to martyr.

"What has Shkoder ever done for us?"

"Cemandia sends us trade!" bellowed one of the villagers who'd made a handsome profit at that first fair. "Once a year, Shkoder sends us a bard to let us know what we don't have."

"Sends a spy!"

"King Theron's probably coming with an army!"

"Do the bards work for Theron or does Theron work for the bards?"

"He's ruled by the kigh!"

"Kigh are not enclosed in the Circle!"

Again the sign against the kigh flicked out, but this time, hands that had never made it before traced the gesture, caught up in the mass hysteria of the mob.

"Send a message to Cemandia! Let them know what's going on! Cemandia has no dealings with the kigh!"

Well pleased with the result of her suggestion, Olina raised both hands to silence the cries of agreement. "There's nothing more that can be done tonight. Go home. See to your children. And think on how we will greet King Theron when he arrives." With any luck, they'd jump him when he entered the valley and deliver his whole party to her in pieces.

"But what of Gerek?" Urmi protested as people began to turn away.

"What good will you do him if the kigh strike you down?" Olina asked her.

"Well, none, but ..."

"No. We can only pray that he remains unharmed and plan our vengeance if he is hurt."

"I could ride ..."

"Can you track the wind?"

The stablemaster's face fell. "No, Lady."

Olina watched her walk away, watched them all walk

away, until there was only Lukas standing beside her on the steps to the Great Hall, the torch he held isolating them in a circle of flickering light.

"What about the boy?" he asked, eyes shifting nervously from side to side. "He *isn't* with the bard." His tongue darted out to swipe at his lips. "Is he?"

"Don't be ridiculous," Olina snapped.

"Then why?"

Olina turned to stare full at him. "Are you questioning my judgment?"

"No, lady. Only ... That is ..." Lukas took a deep breath and found enough courage in it to carry on. "Do you know where the duc is?"

"As he wasn't found in the valley, I can only assume he reached the forest. He probably took his father's sword and went off to challenge King Theron with it."

"But why?"

"I imagine he saw you deal with the bard."

Lukas paled, his face between beard and hair bone white even by torchlight. "Lady!"

"You've nothing to worry about. Haven't I arranged it so that no one will go after him? So no one will wonder about the absence of the bard?"

"Yes, Lady. Thank you, Lady." When she started to walk away, he scuttled after her. "But suppose he reaches the king and ..."

"And nothing. The king is still approximately ten days away. Gerek is barely five years old. I'll be very surprised if he even survives the night." She pushed at the weight of her hair and muttered, "The stupid little fool. Had to be a hero. He's dead—" She turned on Lukas so suddenly he stumbled and almost dropped the torch. "—because you couldn't think past the moment."

"I'm sorry, Lady." He scrubbed his free hand against his tunic, leaving damp smudges of sweat on the fabric. "I couldn't be more sorry."

She stared down at him for a long moment. "Yes, you could," she said at last. She'd been going to mold Gerek, turn him into the kind of duc neither Pjerin nor her brother had had the courage to be. And this sweating, stumbling idiot had lost her that immortality.

He was alive because, at the moment, she didn't need

any more unanswered questions. When the moment ended, so did he.

Her back against the wall, every piece of clothing from her pack either on her or under her to fight the damp and cold, Stasya considered her companion. The chill air had helped preserve enough integrity that it had been a body, not just dry and dusty bones that she'd found folded in on itself against the far wall. The remains of a tangled beard had given him gender and the intricate carving she could trace on a buckle and a pair of wrist bands suggested he'd been a man of some means.

How long ago, she wondered, knees tucked up against her chest and arms wrapped tight around them. *How long has he been down here? Does anyone remember him? How long did he live before he died?*

She rested her head on her knees, eyes closed to give an illusion of choice in the darkness. *Were the ends of his fingers broken and split from trying to claw his way out through the heart of the mountain? Had he screamed and fought? What had he done when he'd realized that no one would come?*

Ten days. The king would arrive in ten days.

With luck, Annice and the duc would contact Bohdan sooner.

But she had to count on surviving for ten days.

There'd been trail food for a couple of days still in her pack that could be stretched to provide meager rations, but her water skin had been empty. She'd have to lick the moisture off the walls and hope the bit of water she'd crawled through earlier would continue to collect at the lowest point of the floor.

Ten days.

Her head throbbed and standing left her so dizzy that the mountain had to act as her support as well as her prison.

Ten days.

I could made a song out of this that would pull night terrors from the most flint-hearted listener. Let's hope I last long enough to sing it.

Long past rot, the faint smell of continuing decay was an omnipresent reminder of the alternative.

*   *   *

Tired and hungry, Gerek plodded between the tower-
ing trunks of ancient pines, dragging his father's sword
behind him. Above him, each needle stood out in sharp
relief against an ominous gray-green sky.

The sword caught on a half-buried stick and the sudden jerk threw the small body to the ground. "That
didn't hurt," he gasped, getting slowly to his feet and
trying desperately hard not to cry.

Exhaustion had brought him a few hours of fitful sleep
tucked in the hollow between two giant roots. A dense
layer of fallen needles had made a comfortable enough
bed, but with the moon hidden behind cloud and the
forest noises so loud and so close, he'd spent most of
the night staring wide-eyed and terror-stricken out of his
refuge. The scream of an owl heard from the safety of
his nursery was not the same sound heard alone in the
dark; Gerek had screamed in turn and thrown the protection of his cloak over his head. Fortunately, the larger
predators had been hunting elsewhere.

Yanking the sword free, he wiped his nose on his
sleeve and started walking again, too young to notice it
had grown ominously quiet.

He'd eaten the sausage in triumph when he'd gained
the safety of the trees without being seen from the keep
and he'd licked the grease from his fingers exactly the
way that Nurse Jany always told him not to. At dusk
there'd been only water sucked up from the stream to
quiet the first rumbling of hunger. At sunrise, he'd left
the stream for the easier walking under the pines. At
mid-morning, with a sharp ache behind his belt, he'd
tried to eat a handful of red berries he'd found in a
clearing, hanging plump and thick next to pretty purple
flowers, but they'd tasted so bitter he'd spit them out
without swallowing and continued to spit for some time.

Now his stomach hurt, and he wondered why his papa
was so far away.

Thunder boomed directly overhead and Gerek froze.

A few moments later, he was drenched to the skin as
the huge trees bent and swayed like saplings. Nearly
solid sheets of water poured through the holes in the
canopy. Whimpering, his back pressed hard against a
sticky trunk, Gerek lost himself in the fury of the storm.
The wind howled like the demons Nurse Jany said still

lived in the mountains, and even stuffing his fingers in his ears couldn't keep out their shrieking. When a branch as big around as he was crashed to the ground in a deafening cascade of smaller twigs, he panicked and ran.

Pushed in front of a wind strong enough at times to lift both child and sword from the ground, Gerek scrambled blindly forward, screaming for his father. Oblivious to welts and scratches, he plunged out from under the pines into an area of younger trees and thicker underbrush. The sword caught again.

Sobbing in near hysteria, Gerek yanked on the belt, his only remaining coherent thought that he had to get the sword to his papa. Jammed in a tangle of poplar suckers, the sword refused to move. He threw his weight against the leather. A sudden, violent gust of wind added its strength to his. The sword flew free. Gerek tumbled backward and lost his grip.

Coughing and sputtering, he fought his way back to his feet and looked frantically around him. The rain made it nearly impossible to see. He took two jerky steps forward and clutched frantically at a sapling for support as the sodden earth slid out from under his feet and down into a deep, steep-sided ravine.

Another gust of wind blew the curtain of rain aside just long enough for him to see that the sword lay, half covered in mud, on a ledge a little way down from where he stood.

He had to get the sword to his papa.

Rubbing the water from his eyes, he crouched, still holding the sapling, and stretched out his other arm. The rain pounded against it and his fingers dug into the ground a handbreadth short.

Gerek set his jaw, panic pushed aside by determination. Releasing his anchor, he inched forward. His fingers touched the scabbard, then his hand wrapped around it.

Unfortunately, the sword weighed much more than the child could lift one-handed. It began to slide. Blinking away rain and scowling furiously, Gerek refused to let go. His free hand flailed for the sapling, couldn't reach it, and dug into the earth instead.

The handful he held fell with him.

Wind and rain and the roar of water below drowned out his cries.

"Pjerin, I have to sit." With one hand pressed tight against the curve of her belly, Annice lowered herself to a rock still damp from the recent rain.

"But we just sat out the storm."

"I know." She let the lead rope slide through slack fingers and the mule dropped her head to graze.

Something in her voice pulled Pjerin to her side. He dropped the mare's reins, knowing she wouldn't wander, and peered anxious down at Annice. "Are you all right?"

"I don't know." An attempted smile didn't quite reached her face. "It hurts."

"What hurts? The baby?"

"I think so."

He stared at her in disbelief. "You *think* so?"

"Well, I've never . . ." The stiff set to her shoulders suddenly relaxed. "It stopped."

"What stopped!"

"Every now and then, it . . . that is, this," she tapped the curve gently, "gets all hard, kind of tightens from the top down."

"So it's happened before?"

Annice nodded. "But it never hurt before."

Pjerin felt a sudden line of sweat bead down the center of his back. "You're not . . . I mean . . . you couldn't be . . ."

"I'm not due until Second Quarter Festival and that's . . ." She stopped and looked up at him, eyes wide. "That's soon, Pjerin. I didn't realize it was so soon. What are we going to do?"

He dropped to one knee beside her, ignoring the wet that began to immediately soak through his breeches. "The moon was almost full last night; remember how it looked before the clouds came down?" When she nodded, he continued, his voice low and soothing although under the calm facade his heart slammed against his ribs. "That means we're got a little better than fourteen days to Second Quarter Festival. All we've got to do is get to the keep. There's a midwife in the village. A good one. She'll see that everything goes all right."

Annice reached out and brushed a strand of damp hair back off his face. "But they think you're a traitor at the keep. You condemned yourself in front of them under Command."

"So if you've got time, you'll put me back under Command and we'll tell them what really happened. And if you don't," he captured her hand with both of his, slipping his wounded arm out of the sling, "they'll lock me in a room for a few days until you're well enough to straighten things out. But, Annice, whatever they think of me, won't affect how they treat either you or my child."

"My child," she corrected automatically. Then, realizing that was the response he'd expected, smiled. Leaning forward, she kissed him softly on the forehead. "Thank you."

"Just don't have that baby while I'm the only one around to deal with it." Although he spoke lightly, he'd never meant anything more.

"I'll do my best." The last word came out like a small explosion and they both stared at the billowing folds of shift and overdress.

"Was that a foot?" Pjerin asked, awed.

Less awed by what had become a frequent occurrence whenever she stopped walking, Annice nodded. "Both feet." The tiny body rolled and kicked and, teeth clenched, she pushed herself up on Pjerin's good shoulder. "On second thought, I'm ready to have it now."

Pjerin stood as well, tucking his arm back into the triangle of cloth that theoretically held it immobile. "It can't be far to the keep."

Annice snorted and pulled Milena forward. "It had better not be."

Late that afternoon when they were watering the animals, Pjerin peered upstream. "I know where we are," he announced triumphantly. "That ravine widens out the farther you go into it and there're caves cut into the sides. When I was thirteen, my father led a hunting party down it to kill a bear."

Leaning on the mule's warm flank, Annice looked disgusted. "Why didn't he just leave it alone?"

"It had already been wounded," Pjerin explained, "probably in a fight with another male, and it was hang-

ing around the valley attacking the livestock. People
started to worry about losing children, so Father went
after it." Bending, he slurped water up off his cupped
palm. "If I can find the cave, we'll sleep warm and dry
tonight."

"If it isn't already occupied."

He grinned at her, spirits lifted by familiarity. "Bards
think too highly of themselves to share?"

"Bards think too highly of themselves to be eaten,"
she told him.

They'd just reached the edge of the ravine where raw
dirt walls, too steep for any but the most tenacious
plants, marked the depth the water had risen in the past
when, all at once, Annice stopped.

"Pjerin!"

He turned so quickly he stumbled and nearly fell. "Is
it happening again?"

"What? No, it's the kigh!" She stared at the ground.
"I've never seen them so ... Here!" She thrust the lead
rope into his hands, carefully lowered herself into a
squat, and Sang a question.

Pjerin backed up one incredulous step. As Annice
Sang, the earth in front of her heaved and rolled. He
stared, amazed, and could almost make out the individual shapes of the agitated kigh. Amazement grew as the
earth continued to move even after Annice stopped
Singing. Then he caught sight of her expression and
amazement turned to fear.

"You've got to follow them, Pjerin. Hurry!"

He opened his mouth to ask her why, but her next
words snapped it closed.

"Gerek's been hurt. They think he's dying."

The disturbance in the earth moved up the ravine as
though a giant mole were digging just below the surface
at full speed. Through the roaring in his ears Pjerin
heard Annice say she'd catch up as fast as she could,
then he was running in pursuit of the kigh.

They remained exactly the same distance in front of
him as they had when he began. Pjerin's lungs began to
burn as he raced toward his son. His wounded shoulder
ached as loose dirt and stone forced him to flail about
with both arms lest he lose his balance. He'd been run-

ning forever, he was certain of it, when he saw the tiny
body lying half covered in muddy water.

"Gerek!"

Diving to his knees, Pjerin caught up the still, pale
body of his child. A part of him knew that the boy could
have internal damage and that moving him was the worst
thing he could do, but all the other parts only wanted
to hold him.

Scratches and welts covered every inch of exposed
skin and slack lips had already taken on a hint of blue.
His son draped across his lap, Pjerin lowered his head
until his left ear rested on what seemed a minimal curve
of chest. He couldn't remember Gerek being so small.
The tears began when, faint but unmistakable, he heard
a heartbeat.

Hands trembling, Pjerin pulled off sodden clothes and
searched for broken bones; arms and legs were bruised
but solid. A blue and purple lump covered half his forehead from his hairline to just over his right eye.

"So cold . . ." Stripping off his shirt, ignoring the tearing pain as he stretched tissue that had barely begun to
heal, Pjerin pressed the child's limp body against his
torso, skin to skin. Body heat was all he had to give.
"Papa's here," he murmured, "everything's going to be
all right." Holding Gerek in place with one arm, he
began frantically massaging chilled flesh with the other.

Annice arrived a few moments later, gasping for
breath, her knuckles white around the pack strap she'd
been clutching so that the trotting mule could support
some of her weight. She stared down at Pjerin still rubbing Gerek's unresponsive body and got a sick feeling
in the pit of her stomach. She'd seen dead children before and although the kigh said Gerek still lived, she
knew that he'd be taking his place in the Circle soon. If
they could get him to a healer . . . but the nearest was
in Marienka, and he wouldn't live five hours let alone
five days.

She watched Pjerin's back as he tried to rub warmth
and life back into his son and couldn't think of a thing
to say. Finally, she knelt across from him, reached out,
and gently touched him on the shoulder.

Pjerin jerked his head up and stared at her for a moment with no idea of who she was. His whole world had

become the child in his arms. Then he remembered. His
hand wrapped around her wrist and he dragged her
closer. "Sing!" he commanded. "Sing and make him
better."

He was hurting her, but she made no move to pull
away. "I'm not a healer, Pjerin. I can't."

"You can!" he insisted, eyes burning into hers. "The
healer who came to me in Elbasan told me that some
believe the body has a kigh and that's what they heal.
You Sing all four quarters, Annice. Sing five!"

"That's not how it works," she began, but he cut her
off, his voice breaking, tears streaming down his cheeks.

"It has to work! I'm begging you, Annice." He
searched for a way to make her realize how important
this was. "Gerek's dying. I'll give up all rights to the
child you carry if you can just save him. Please. You
have to try."

"But . . ."

"Annice, please."

Her own cheeks wet, Annice swallowed and opened
her mouth to Sing him comfort, something that would
help to take the edges off his pain, when she felt a gentle
touch on her knee.

The kigh nodded when she glanced down at it. And
when she glanced past it, a whole circle of kigh nodded.

Annice drew in a long shuddering breath and pulled
her hand from Pjerin's grip. It wouldn't hurt anything
to try. She touched Gerek lightly with her fingertips,
and Sang.

She had to Sing earth, it was all she really could Sing
now, but she tried to put into it all that she'd felt that
morning in the valley when everything had been new
and anything was possible. Because love crossed all four
quarters, she Sang Pjerin's love for his son and her love
for the baby beneath her heart.

The kigh moved closer.

Gerek's heartbeat became slower, fainter.

So she Sang Gerek. Everything she knew about him.
Everything she'd seen, everything she'd guessed, everything Pjerin had told her.

It wasn't going to be enough.

She knew it.

She heard Pjerin moan. He knew it, too.

The kigh began to Sing with her; a familiar rumble of sound, felt rather than heard.

Familiar . . .

Eyes closed, Annice began the first anthem Sung to earth at Final Quarter Festival. The kigh took it up. When she finished, she began water. Behind her, the music of the stream slowed. Impossibly, she heard a liquid ripple of Song. Fire. Orange tongues of flame danced over the grass on the bank. Air. It was more a plea than an anthem. Her voice took the music and begged with it. Just as she thought it doomed to fail, her hair lifted off the back of her neck and cold fingers traced patterns on her skin.

Tears streaming down her face, Annice ran up the last notes of air and right into the joyous welcome of the sun throwing herself into the Song. Light returns. Life continues.

And another voice Sang with her. A silent voice. A gentle voice. A strong voice.

It Sang healing.

Gerek's heart beat faster. Stronger. His skin began to warm.

One by one, the kigh fell silent.

The silent voice and Annice continued on a moment longer together.

Then only Annice Sang.

Cradled in his father's arms, Gerek coughed and started to cry.

Annice felt the kigh catch her as she fell.

CHAPTER SIXTEEN

"Papa? I think she's awake."

Annice winced as Gerek's piping voice drove slivers of sound deep into both ears. She whimpered and that hurt, too. If she could have turned off the pounding of the pulse that boomed like a kettledrum within the confines of her skull, she would have.

"Annice?"

Pjerin's voice was low, very nearly a whisper, and much less painful. He sounded worried. She struggled to open her eyes but couldn't seem to remember how her eyelids worked.

"Annice? Can you hear me?"

Of course I can hear you! she wanted to snarl as he spoke a little louder. *You're echoing!* But all that emerged was a strangled croak. Her throat felt as if she'd tried to swallow a dozen knives and they'd all gotten jammed point first between jaw and collarbone.

A sudden sharp blow against her spine diverted her attention with a sudden sharp pain and her concentration focused on the movements in her womb. She realized with incredulous joy that she could hear the soft, steady rhythm of her baby's heartbeat.

"Help me move her onto her back, Gerek."

"Are you gonna give her a drink?"

"As soon as we move her so she won't spill it."

The voices, the noises of movement, were making it harder and harder to hold onto the fragile sound of the unborn life. Annice fought to keep the contact, but gradually it slipped away, lost in the surrounding sounds.

"Papa, she's crying."

"Annice?" A warm finger brushed moisture from her cheek. "Are you all right?"

She didn't know.

"Annice?"

She could feel each thread of the clothing pressed against her, feel Pjerin's breath warm on her face, feel the weight of his concern. Slowly, she opened her eyes.

There wasn't a lot of light, but Pjerin was so close that she didn't need much light to see him. He'd shaved off his beard and the white skin of his lower face looked ridiculous against the upper tan. She tried to tell him so but, again, all that emerged was a dry croak.

He slipped his arm behind her and lifted her head. "Here, drink this. Not so fast," he cautioned as her mouth gaped and she desperately gulped at the liquid.

The water felt like silk on the inside of her throat, stroking and soothing abraded flesh. Her hands came up and grabbed the cup. The metal was cool and beaded with moisture, but when she tried to tip it higher, she couldn't budge it against Pjerin's strength.

When it was empty, she managed a single word. "More."

Pjerin handed the cup to Gerek who scrambled to his feet and raced from her limited line of sight.

Because he was all she could see, Annice watched Pjerin watching her. The intensity of emotion on his face puzzled her and she wondered why he held her hands as though afraid to let them go.

Then Gerek came back with the second cup of water and she realized what that meant.

Gerek lived.

She'd somehow done the impossible.

As she drank, she tried to sort through what had happened, but her memories were cloudy and uncertain. The kigh had Sung with her and so had ... so had ... The harder she tried, the less clear it became, so she sighed and let it go. Later, she'd have someone put her into a recall trance, but for now it would have to be enough that Gerek lived.

The cup empty, she flinched as the baby squirmed, trying to find a comfortable position in what was becoming too little space.

"Pjerin?"

He leaned even closer to hear her.

"I've got to ... pee."

His smile seemed to spread from ear to ear, but there

was a new gentleness in it that she found she rather liked the look of. "Of course you do."

He had to lift her to her feet and then he had to half carry her out of the cave. To her surprise, her helplessness made her neither resentful nor embarrassed. Pjerin's strength was there for her to lean on, but it wasn't a threat and it wasn't a challenge.

This mood can't last, she mused, as he shooed Gerek away and left her tucked behind a bush, braced against the flat side of a boulder. When she finished, she managed to stand by herself and, using the rock as a support, came back around it into the sun.

The sun.

"Pjerin, how long . . ."

Squinting, he followed her line of sight, then gave her his arm so she could lower herself onto a shelf cut out of the side of the ravine. "Almost a full day."

That explained how stiff she was but not much else. "How's Gerek?"

"Gerek's fine." Pjerin dropped to one knee beside her. "How are you?"

"I feel as though I've been . . . peeled. Like an apple. My core is exposed and bits of me are turning . . . brown and mushy." Her voice dragged itself through the ruin of her throat. "And I seem to have become a . . . bass-baritone."

Pjerin shook his head, his nose wrinkled with exaggerated distaste. "What a wonderful analogy," he said, then he grew serious. "Annice, there's no way I can thank you for what you did and I meant what I said. You've given me back my son, so I'll step aside. This baby is yours."

Annice drew in a long breath, tasting the scent of running water, of the pines that towered over the edge of the ravine, of the sun-warmed rocks, of the man by her side. Just on the edge of awareness, she could hear the Song that held everything together. She wasn't even really worried about her voice. Considering the extremes she'd forced it through, she'd have been more surprised had it not sounded like a dull saw ripping soft wood. And now, Pjerin had offered her the only thing she wanted from him; her child. Hers. With no danger of him ever winning its heart and taking it away.

"Don't be ridiculous," she told him. "This isn't my baby anymore than it's yours."

He looked confused as she took his hand and placed it on the arc of her belly.

"Ours," she said softly. Her baby deserved the kind of father Pjerin had proven himself to be and he had as much right to its love as she did.

Pjerin swallowed and she laid her fingers around the curve of his jaw. He turned his head and pressed his lips against her palm.

"Papa?" Gerek's head poked out of the cave. "Can I come now?"

Not trusting his voice, Pjerin nodded and Gerek launched himself across the distance between them, careening into the circle of his father's arm—Pjerin winced at the impact against his wounded shoulder but only pulled the boy closer. Gerek peered up at Annice with brilliant eyes and, as far as she could see, he seemed none the worse for his ordeal. "Are you okay, Nees?"

"Mostly."

"Papa was real worried." Suddenly becoming aware of the position of Pjerin's other hand, Gerek frowned. "Hey, I wasn't allowed to touch."

Annice smiled. "You can touch now."

"Really?" His small hand pressed against her. "Is it a baby?"

Briefly, she wondered what else he thought it might be. "Yes. It's your sister."

"Brother," Pjerin corrected absently.

Annice contemplated smacking him. "Don't start."

Stasya was alive! Stasya was alive! Annice's heart Sang the words, Sang the notes that made up Stasya's name, Sang the words again. *Stasya's alive!* However Theron and hence the guard had discovered that she and Pjerin were traveling together, it hadn't been through Stasya. And whatever questions Theron and the Bardic Captain had asked, Stasya hadn't been put under Command, hadn't been charged with treason, hadn't been executed.

"Annice, are you listening?"

She started. "Of course I'm listening. The king is coming to Ohrid. Stasya brought the news." Stasya was alive!

Pjerin rolled his eyes. "I suppose it hasn't occurred to you that the king coming to Ohrid is going to destroy our plans."

Annice let go of her joy long enough to snort. "Pjerin, we didn't have a plan. You were going to go to Ohrid and clear your name. That was the full extent of it."

He opened his mouth and closed it again.

"You were going to make a plan when we got closer," she reminded him. Although still hoarse, she'd regained sufficient control of her voice to layer on a fine shading of sarcasm. "I don't want to rush you, but this seems like a good time."

"A little difficult to make plans without information," Pjerin growled staring at the dusty, cracked leather of his boot tops.

"Well, you might have made a plan to get information."

"I thought I'd leave that up to you." He glowered at her. "Isn't that what *bards* do?"

"Yeah? Well, bards also . . ."

"I'm not done," Gerek interrupted indignantly.

They were sitting just outside the cave, soaking up the late afternoon sun, listening to Gerek's story. Annice had been pleased that Pjerin had waited until she could hear it as well and understand when it became obvious he hadn't made a conscious decision.

"He was alive," Pjerin had explained as Gerek squirmed out of his arms. *"And I was alive. And the beard scared him . . . Between that and your condition, we didn't have time for anything else."*

"Anyway," Gerek continued as both adults returned their attention to him, "I was mad at Stasya the bard 'cause she took my papa away back when it was cold. But Aunty Olina said I couldn't yell at her 'cause I was the duc and that's not what ducs do." He paused to consider that. "Papa, you yell at people."

"Not at guests."

"Oh." He looked for a moment like he wanted to argue but decided against it and went on. "The bard told me that you weren't dead. That it was a mistake like you said and the king was coming to make it better so I came to find you and Nees and bring you your sword so you could fight the bad guys."

"Gerek, why didn't you tell Olina that I was alive?"

"Bard made me promise not to." He looked down at his toes digging holes in the dirt. "I was s'posed to tell Bohdan, but he's sick."

"Why did Stasya make you promise not to tell Olina?" Annice asked, sure she knew the answer. Pjerin wasn't the traitor. Someone else had to be.

Gerek sighed. " 'Cause Aunty Olina put her in the hole."

"What?!"

"The hole. In the cellar. It's dark and I don't like it there."

Pjerin's hand snaked out and grabbed Annice's wrist. "You can't help her if you fall over three paces from where you're standing."

Numbly she nodded and sat back down. She wasn't going anywhere before tomorrow at the earliest. And Stasya was in a hole.

Pjerin waited until he was certain Annice was going to stay put, then he asked, "Gerek, why did Olina put the bard down the hole?"

He shrugged. "I dunno. Lukas helped."

"Lukas? Lukas a'Tynek?"

"Uh-huh. Bohdan got sick and he's the steward."

"Lukas a'Tynek is the steward! Has Olina lost her mind?"

Gerek shrugged again. "I dunno."

Annice slid forward until she was sitting cross-legged on the ground, the kigh cradling her, her eyes at a level with the child's. For Stasya's sake she had to find out exactly what was going on. "Gerek, we need you to tell us everything that happened at the keep since your papa went away."

"Everything? I don't 'member everything."

"Yes, you do. Gerek, look at me."

"Annice!" Suddenly realizing what she was about to do, Pjerin gripped her shoulder and half turned her around. "No. I won't allow it."

"We can't go in there blind." She kept her voice calm. The last thing they needed was Gerek choosing sides in an argument. "We have to *know* who your enemy is."

His face grew bleak at her emphasis. "Olina," he muttered.

"We have to know," Annice repeated. "It won't hurt him. I promise."

Olina. Eyes closed, Pjerin nodded.

Annice came out of the cave after singing Gerek to sleep and made her way carefully to where Pjerin stood holding the Ducal sword in both hands and staring at nothing. Her knees still had a disturbing tendency to buckle and she wouldn't want to Sing anything for a few days, but tavern crawling with Tadeus had left her in worse condition. "Any sign of the guard?"

He shook his head. "Never around when you need them. I went back as far as the mouth of the ravine. We could be the only three people in the world."

The name of a fourth person hung in the air between them.

After a moment, Pjerin sighed and let the sword point drop to the ground. "She always said I wasted the power I had. She never understood the power that came from belonging. Of *being* the Duc of Ohrid."

"How could she?" Annice asked softly. "She never *was* the Duc of Ohrid. But Ohrid was important to her, or she'd have left it long ago."

"And gone where?"

"Court. Either in Shkoder or Cemandia. She'd have made a fine politician."

"You don't think much of politicians, do you?"

Annice shrugged. "They're a necessary evil."

"She was my family, my father's sister. We were tied by blood. I could almost understand her killing me cleanly because I was in her way, but she set me up, made me appear to be a traitor, an oathbreaker. Dishonored me. Dishonored Ohrid." He swung the sword in a sudden vicious arc and a young alder fell behind the stroke. When he spoke again, he ground out the indictment from between clenched teeth. "She would have raised my son to think I was a traitor when *she* plans to give Ohrid over to Cemandia without a blow being struck."

Turning, he held out the sword for Annice's inspection. "This sword has been the sword of the Ducs of Ohrid for seven generations. The first duc brought it with him out of Cemandia and he was probably the only one who ever used it as a weapon. The balance stinks, the grip is too small for my hand, and the last time it was sharpened was when I took the title and had to be blooded." His brows drew in and the violet of his eyes darkened. "I'm going to pin Olina to the doors of the keep with it."

Stasya forced herself to stop sucking at the floor. Still thirsty, all she could do was wait for more moisture to seep up through the stone.

Shaking with the cold, she crawled back to her pad of clothing and wrapped her cloak around her shoulders. It had only been one day—perhaps a little longer but she doubted it. For a while at least, eliminating wastes would give a fairly good idea of the passage of time.

And for a while at least, the oilskin of her pack would keep those wastes contained.

One day.

How was she going to survive another nine?

"Still no message?"

"No, sire." Tadeus turned to face the king, his expression frankly worried. "I haven't heard from Stasya since sunrise yesterday." He waved a hand toward the west, toward a setting sun he couldn't see. "This is too long. Something has to have happened."

Theron frowned. "Is she dead?"

Tadeus blanched. "Dead? No, sire. The kigh would know that. They just can't find her."

"Can't or won't?" Theron asked thoughtfully. "Perhaps Annice and the duc have arrived in Ohrid, and whatever it is that's keeping the kigh from Annice is now covering Stasya as well."

The blind bard's smile was enough to make Theron believe the number of conquered hearts supposedly laid at the young man's feet.

"I'd forgotten all about that, Majesty." Tadeus brushed a curl of dark hair back over a scarlet shoulder and visibly relaxed. "That's very likely the case and given how long they've been apart they'll probably . . ." He paused. "No, probably not considering Annice's condition."

Theron cleared his throat. He didn't need to hear

speculation on his sister's ... physical relationships. "Suppose Annice hasn't reached Ohrid. Could there be any other reason that the kigh would have trouble reaching Stasya?"

"It has been storming a lot lately, and sometimes that makes them less willing to cooperate." His tone belonged to someone who preferred silk but who'd spent most of three consecutive days wrapped in oilskin. Then he sobered as he weighed the alternatives. "Or she could be unconscious. Or locked far enough inside that the kigh can't get to her. But I can't see how that could happen without her Singing at least a quick call for help."

"If they knocked her unconscious first?"

Tadeus looked miserable again. "Yes, sire, that could work."

Thumbs hooked behind his belt, Theron paced to the edge of the rocky outcrop and stared down at the camp. Three days out of Marienka they had only one remaining official visit to slow their arrival at the Duc of Ohrid's keep. Thanks to Tadeus, he was as fluent as he was likely to get in the local dialect. And he was very tired of subterfuge. "I'm sending a rider out to Lady Dorota's. We won't be stopping after all. I'll meet with her briefly as we pass and explain."

"You think that Stasya's in danger, Majesty?"

"I think that there's someone in that keep who's already arranged to have one person die and thousands of others killed in a war of conquest. All things being enclosed, I think it's time we hurried."

"Pjerin, wait." Annice sagged against the side of the mule. "I've got to rest."

"Is it happening again?"

Teeth clenched, she nodded.

"Gerek, take the animals into that clearing and let them graze."

"Is Nees going to have the baby now?"

"No!"

As a wide-eyed Gerek led the mule and Otik's mare away, Annice transferred her weight to Pjerin's arm. "No?" she said as the kigh created a hillock for him to lower her to. "How can you be so sure?" If she herself hadn't been worried about exactly the same thing, his look of near panic would've been hysterical.

"Annice, by tomorrow night you'll be safe with Bohdan's daughter. Can't you wait?"

"I don't exactly have a choice." She decided that hysterical definitely described how she felt and she fought to remain calm as the pain in her abdomen briefly intensified. "Trust me, you're not my first pick for a midwife."

His hand gesturing impotently, his expression struggling toward supportive, Pjerin swallowed hard and asked, "What should I do?"

"How should I know!" Annice stared up at him incredulously. "I've never done this before!" Then she burst into tears, hating herself for what was rapidly becoming her habitual response but too tired to fight it.

Relieved, Pjerin slipped his injured arm from the sling, sat beside her, and gathered her up against his chest. This, he could deal with. "Don't worry," he murmured into her hair. "We'll manage. You're a bard, remember? You must be able to recall something about having a baby."

She rubbed her nose on his shirt. "Yeah. I guess."

"And I'm not a city duc. Remember, I've helped mares foal and cows calve and goats ..." He paused, trying to think of what it was goats did, then realized that Annice had pulled away.

"Oh *that*," she declared with scornful emphasis, wiping her eyes on her sleeve, "makes me feel much better! Should I go down on all fours and moo? Will that help?"

"Annice, I didn't mean ..."

"What? That I look like a cow? Well, thanks for nothing! Oh!"

"What!"

"It's stopped."

Pjerin closed his eyes and counted to ten. "Don't do that," he said quietly when he opened them again. "Or by the time we get to the keep, I'll be too gray for anyone to recognize me."

"Nees?' They turned as Gerek held out a cupped hand, the fingers stained a brilliant red. "I picked some strawberries to make you feel better."

Annice felt her eyes grow dangerously wet. *"You are*

not going to cry again," she told herself sternly. "Thank you, Gerek."

He dumped the squashed fruit onto her palm and smiled at his father. "It's okay, Papa. I tied up the lead ropes to a bush."

"Why don't you show me," Pjerin said, standing and taking his son's sticky fingers in his. "And then maybe we'll both pick some more berries for Annice." He reached back with his free hand and gently stroked her cheek. "Are you going to be all right?"

She nodded. "I just need to sit for a minute or two."

She watched them walk away and began to slowly eat the warm fruit, trying to calm the frightened pounding of her heart and wondering why she hadn't told Pjerin about the blood.

Three days or four, Stasya wasn't certain. Night and day had no meaning in such utter blackness and time became too unstructured to hold.

The water continued to seep up through the stone. She was thirsty but not desperately so, not yet. More than anything, she was cold. The chill ate through clothes and flesh and settled in bone. She tried to keep moving, but it didn't seem to help. Her muscles were knotted and her feet and hands had begun to ache. Sleep came fitfully if at all.

She'd had one screaming panic already, throwing herself against the stone, stopping only when the injury to her head exploded orange and yellow lights behind her eyes and brought her to her knees. She didn't know how much longer she could prevent another one.

She sang. She told herself stories. She recalled her last few Walks. She thought about Annice. She began to pick the embroidery off the sleeves of her shirt.

And it had only been three days.

Or maybe four.

Lukas opened and shut his mouth a few times, but no sound emerged. Finally, he managed a strangled, "But, Lady, if a Cemandian army comes through the pass . . ."

"It will be followed by wealth and power." Olina traced the carved sunburst in the arm of her chair, her eyes half closed as she thought of how close success lay to hand. The end of isolation. The end of near barbarism. Although the woodworker had likely not intended it as such, the sunburst was a symbol of the Havakeen Empire. *The first Emperor started with less.* "I will control the only route between West and East Cemandia. Any merchants desiring to use their newly acquired access to the sea trade must travel through Ohrid and will have to pay dearly for the privilege."

"Every merchant," Lukas repeated, his tongue appearing between beard and mustache to wet his lips.

She could see him adding up the possibilities. He'd had a taste of power over this last quarter and wouldn't be willing to give it up. Nor would he be likely to realize that her plans were a great deal more complicated than she'd allowed him to see and that they included the removal of Lukas a'Tynek the moment the dirty work was done. But if he wanted to believe she'd be content operating a tollgate, or more precisely having him operate a tollgate for her, she had no intention of correcting him.

"But His Grace," he began hesitantly, a wary eye on her reaction, "the duc—that is the last duc—was executed for agreeing to open the pass to Cemandia."

"And what does that have to do with the current situation?" Olina asked him, steepling her fingers and staring at him over their tips. "Pjerin a'Stasiek broke his oaths. I swore no oaths to Shkoder and neither did you." No point in mentioning that the duc's oaths were expected to hold the people as well. "I would have thought you'd prefer a Cemandian overlord."

Dark spots of color burned on Lukas' cheeks. "They admit the kigh are not part of the Circle."

As far as Olina was concerned, Cemandian religious beliefs were of no importance next to their potential for economic exploitation, but she recognized the strength of their influence on the people. Especially after she'd worked so hard behind the scene to promote the usefully bigoted opinions of her new steward.

Lukas leaned forward, his eyes darting from side to side. Olina wondered if he were searching the room for hidden listeners or if it were the habitual action of a thoroughly unpleasant man that she'd just never noticed before. "There are still those," he said softly, "who will not want Cemandian rule."

"Really?" She sat back in her chair. "Do you know their names?"

"Yes, Lady." Lukas took an eager step towards her. "I heard Nincenc i'Celestin say the Cemandians were an intolerant bunch of superstitious louts and he'd personally remove them from the Circle if they set foot on his land and Dasa i'Ales said she wished there were more bards and . . ."

The list was surprisingly short. Without a leader to continuously remind them that Cemandia was the enemy and with Cemandia pouring money and goods into Ohrid, most of the people really didn't care. After all, what had Shkoder done for them lately except execute one duc and run off with another? The moment she had Theron safely in the keep and it no longer mattered what the kigh reported to him, she'd have Lukas arrange accidents for those too shortsighted to see where their best interests lay. If it could look like the kigh were involved, so much the better.

"I want you to speak to . . ." She paused and considered the numbers that Stasya had said were accompanying the king. Forty people on horseback, crammed into the outer court could easily be taken care of by half that number. ". . . twenty of those who have no wish to see Ohrid remain a backwater province of a tiny country. Archers may bring their bows, but I will arm the rest." Albek's crossbows and quarrels were still in the armory. "The moment that King Theron's party is sighted at the end of the valley, they're to come to the keep. Once His Majesty has been disarmed, he will be held until the Cemandian army arrives.

"I don't want the kigh reporting a plot to His Majesty, so you will speak to these people in ones and twos and have them come to the keep individually—keeping weapons covered. Once they're here, it will matter less what the kigh tell him as he'll be expecting a crowd to gather.

"When Theron is safely in my control, I will speak to the people of Ohrid, tell them we have the chance to prevent a long and bloody war and profit immediately from the proper use of the pass."

Lukas left off nodding his continual agreement to look

suddenly frightened. "But Lady, King Theron's bard will tell the bards in the capital."

"Where they have been left leaderless and in complete disarray. Helpless before the army that will roll down on them out of the mountains." Olina smiled and stood. "I have planned this too well for it to fail."

Pjerin stared out at the village, the Ducal sword an unaccustomed weight at his hip, betrayal a greater weight on his heart. How many did Olina have? How many were willing to bow their necks under the Cemandian yoke? Shkoder may have been less than willing to spend coin in principalities with so little chance of return, but at least it had left them free; something Cemandia would not do.

His hand closed around an obscuring branch and he savagely shoved it down out of his way.

The keep, built to ensure the independence of the first duc and his people, tested by steel and blood in the time of both the second duc and the third, would become no more than a way station for fat merchants traveling to the sea. A city would grow at the mercy of trade; dependent, parasitic, vulnerable. His people would labor for Cemandian overlords, ape Cemandian ways, subscribe to Cemandian beliefs. Priests would come and build a Center and children who showed any ability to Sing the kigh would be ripped from their mothers' embrace and put to the sword.

Ohrid would exist only at Cemandian suffrage. Better it be destroyed before that. The end would be cleaner if the mountains themselves rose up and crushed it, earth and stone wiping it from the map.

The sudden crack of the branch breaking shattered the dusk, cutting off the evening song of birds and frogs. A crow broke out of the canopy high overhead, hoarsely screaming a protest, ebony wings beating against a sapphire sky. Pjerin could feel Annice's glare in the prickling of the skin between his shoulder blades. He ignored it.

After a moment, he made his way to where she sat, Gerek sprawled half asleep over what was left of her lap, horse and mule stripping the underbrush of green and tender plants. They'd pass a sheepfold on their way to the village where they'd leave the animals. With lambing over, the fold would be empty, but there'd be food and water and a stout door to bar against predators.

"We'll wait until full dark," he said softly, dropping to the ground by Annice's side. "Most of the villagers will be asleep by then; morning comes soon enough at this time of the year."

"Your people work hard," Annice murmured as Gerek resettled himself on his father's lap.

"We aren't like lowlanders. We depend on no one." Pjerin traced the curve of Gerek's cheek with the back of one finger, the gentle motion a direct contrast to the edge in his voice.

"Maybe they work a little harder than they need to."

"What are you talking about?"

Annice pushed a kigh away from her belly. "Granted," she said thoughtfully, "that neither my most royal father nor His Majesty, Theron, King of Shkoder, High Captain of the Broken Islands, and so on, and so on, have exactly beat a path into the mountains, but neither have you done anything to remind them of their obligations. You don't take the seat you're entitled to on the council, nor do you send someone to represent you. You sit up here with your head in the clouds and you say, *if they don't want us, then we don't want them*."

"*You* weren't exactly unwelcomed," he growled.

"Because you didn't have to do anything to get me here. There's a whole wide world out there, Pjerin. Why not make an effort to be a part of it?"

"I take care of my people."

She nodded. "I know. And now you're being replaced by the entire Cemandian nation."

The weight of his son across his legs kept him from leaping to his feet. Red waves of rage washed over him, leaving him trembling, muscles knotted with the effort to remain still. "Are you saying," his voice was dangerously soft and his eyes so dark they absorbed the shadows, "that Olina was justified in what she did? In what she's doing?"

"No." The denial was almost Sung, impossible to disbelieve. "But I think that when you've dealt with *what* she's done, you might consider *why* she did it."

His lip curled up off his teeth. "I don't need a lecture

from you, Annice, not about the choices I've made. You haven't always chosen wisely yourself, have you?"

Annice regarded him levelly, wincing slightly as the baby stretched. "I don't regret a single decision I've made," she told him.

His brows rose. "Not even spending ten years isolated from your family?"

"That wasn't my choice," she snapped, slapping at an insect, all at once not so eager to meet his gaze.

"Wasn't it?" Pjerin asked bluntly. "I don't recall you meeting anyone halfway. If they didn't want you," he added, "you didn't want them."

Annice started as he threw her own words back at her. "It's not the same thing."

"Isn't it?" Tucking Gerek more securely into the curve of his arm, he stood. "Maybe we both have something to think about."

Ignoring the kigh leaning against her hip, she watched as he settled the boy onto the mare's saddle. Still only half awake, Gerek clung to the saddlehorn and blinked owlishly into the night. When he turned back to her and held out his hand, she hesitated for a moment, then laid her fingers across his palm. He pulled her to her feet. She held on a moment longer.

"Maybe," she said, "you're right."

Pjerin's smile was a flash of ivory in the darkness, his lips a warm pressure against the top of her head. "Don't strain anything," he advised.

Candlelight flickered through an open window on the far side of the village, the only evidence that anyone remained awake in all of Ohrid.

"Dasa i'Ales," Pjerin murmured. "She'd like to be a poet. While she's creating, you could walk right past her singing at the top of your lungs and she wouldn't notice."

"I remember her," Annice murmured back. *She's terrible.* But she kept that opinion to herself as she had no desire to challenge the protective note in Pjerin's voice. This was his land. These were his people.

Bohdan's daughter's house was very nearly in the middle of the village. The three of them picked their way carefully toward it—the moon, a day off full, lighting their path, the wind pushing at their backs.

"The dogs need to catch our scent," Pjerin explained quietly as they passed the first of the gabled stone buildings. "They need to recognize who we are, then they'll know there's no reason to give the alarm."

"Every dog in the village knows you?" Annice whispered incredulously.

"Dogs like Papa," Gerek piped up, much refreshed by his nap. "And me." He frowned. "Hope Dasa's geese aren't out."

In many ways, geese were better sentries than dogs. They couldn't be bribed and they didn't like anyone.

"If they are . . ." Pjerin reached down and laid a cautionary finger across his son's lips. "Annice will sing them a lullaby."

Annice rolled her eyes. "I don't do lullabies for geese," she muttered.

Pjerin's voice buzzed against her ear. "You do now."

A few steps farther and a half a dozen of the village dogs raced out to meet them; ears up, tongue lolling, and great plumed tails beating at the night air. Gerek, being closer to the ground, had his face thoroughly licked. One of the dogs went into such ecstasy at Pjerin's touch that it made a nuisance of itself and finally had to be told sternly—but quietly—to go home.

Fortunately, the geese were conspicuous only by their absence.

When they reached Bohdan's daughter's house, Pjerin lifted the latch and silently swung open the heavy door. The odor of roast pork permeated the building; obviously they'd just culled one of the suckling pigs before weaning the litter and sending them out to the forest with the village swineherd for Second Quarter foraging. Annice couldn't decide whether the smell—a familiar one at this time in the year—made her feel hungry or sick.

Holding a clog in each hand for it was impossible to move quietly wearing them, she followed Pjerin and Greek down the main room of the house to a pair of doors set off center in the far wall. The polished planks of the floor felt strange after earth under her feet for so long.

It appeared that Pjerin was having trouble deciding which room Bohdan slept in. Annice sighed and pointed to the left-hand door. The door on the right, set farther from the outside wall, defined a larger room. Logically, because Bohdan's daughter and her partner would need a larger bed, they'd have to have the greater amount of space. When he continued to look doubtful, she pushed forward and opened the door herself. They didn't have time for this.

A high, narrow bed stretched the entire length of the left wall. At its foot, the thick stone wall of the cottage held a small hearth—which shared a chimney with the other bedchamber—and a narrow window. The single shutter had been left open and the moonlight painted silver-white highlights across the bed.

The man in the bed was old, his body barely lifting the blankets draped over him. His cheeks had sunk on both sides of a jutting nose where the flesh had wasted off the arc of bone. Yellowed parchment stretched over the dome of his head. His eyes were deep in shadow, untouched by the moonlight. The one hand resting outside the quilt looked translucent, veins and knuckles swollen through the thin skin.

Pjerin couldn't believe that Bohdan had aged so much in such a short time. When he'd been falsely accused, when the guards had taken him away, his steward had been elderly, yes, but vigorous. A man, if not in his prime, equally not in his dotage. This ruin appeared one breath from death.

His throat tight, Pjerin touched the old man lightly on the hand.

Gray-lidded eyes flipped open, widened, and then Bohdan's lips twisted into a smile. His voice echoed the dry rasp of fallen leaves stirred by the wind. "Have you come to take me into the Circle, Your Grace?"

"I'm not dead, Bohdan," Pjerin told him softly, taking up the skeletal hand in his. "I'm as alive as you are, and I need your help."

"Alive?" The parchment brow furrowed. "Alive?" Gnarled fingers pulled free and crept up the younger man's arm. Breathing heavily, he dragged his hand across the broad chest so that it rested over Pjerin's heart. Rheumy eyes filled with tears. "Alive."

CHAPTER SEVENTEEN

Bohdan's daughter, Rozyte, set down the wooden platter of bread, cold pork, and cheese on the table, then slid onto the bench beside her partner. Her eyes locked on Pjerin, Duc of Ohrid, she pushed the platter toward Annice and in a low voice instructed her to eat.

Annice picked at the food, too tense with worry about Stasya to be hungry.

"I'm sorry to be of so little help, Your Grace," Bohdan sighed. Discovering the duc he loved had not betrayed him had erased years from the ruin they'd found in the bed, but he still looked old and tired. Scrawny shoulders rose and fell in a disappointed shrug. "I've been sick. I don't get out." He sighed again. "I would like to think that the whole village would stand behind you, our rightful lord, but . . ."

"But?" Pjerin prodded when the old steward paused.

"But most people would rather be ruled by Cemandia than Shkoder," Rozyte answered.

Pjerin's face grew dark. "Ruled?"

Rozyte raised a cautioning hand. "Your Grace, please, don't wake the children. I can only tell you what I've overheard."

"But Shkoder doesn't rule in Ohrid," Annice pointed out, her tone only slightly less sharp than Pjerin's had been. "The treaty is a partnership. Ohrid guards the pass and has access to Shkoder's greater resources. Shkoder gains security and provides Ohrid with those things it hasn't the size or population to acquire on its own. All five principalities retained their independence."

"We have not overly benefited from that partnership," Rozyte replied shortly. "But since His Grace has been presumed dead, Cemandian traders have done very well by us."

"Cemandian traders have bought you!" Pjerin spat. Annice closed her fingers around his arm, and he settled back onto the bench, seething.

"We were without your leadership, Your Grace," Rozyte's partner, Sarline, spoke for the first time.

Pjerin nodded a tight acknowledgment of her words, but Annice heard the shadow of another meaning and took a long look across the scarred planks of the table. Sarline pushed a graying braid back over her shoulder and pointedly refused to meet the bard's gaze.

"Olina will close the keep if she finds out I'm alive." He pronounced his aunt's name like he hated the taste of it in his mouth. "A siege will place us and His Majesty—when he arrives—right in the path of the Cemandian army."

"But, Your Grace," Bohdan protested, "we don't know for certain there will *be* an army."

Pjerin laid both hands flat on the table. "Olina knows what capturing King Theron will mean to a Cemandian invasion."

"Granted," the old steward allowed, "but how would Cemandia find out that His Majesty was arriving in Ohrid?"

"Rozyte said that Olina's new toy left for home just after Stasya arrived. No doubt she sent a message with him."

"But, Your Grace, to change the course of an army he would have to gain access to the throne and he was only a mountebank."

"He was Albek."

All five adults at the table swiveled to stare at Gerek standing in the door to Bohdan's room.

Rozyte shook her head. "Simion was nothing like Albek," she said sternly. "Father asked me to check when he arrived, Gerek. The two were very different."

"They had different hair and different clothes," Gerek snorted. "But the person was the same."

"Gerek . . ."

Pjerin's raised hand cut off Rozyte's protest. "How did he react to your Aunt Olina," he asked.

Gerek beamed. He knew his papa would understand. "Just exactly the same."

"Come here."

The boy ran to his father's side and clambered up onto the bench looking pleased with himself.

"Since you don't seem to be sleeping anyway," Pjerin told him, "and since you apparently kept a pretty close eye on things while I was gone, you might as well join the council."

"Your Grace! He's only a child!" Rozyte's lips drew into a tight, disapproving line. She had insisted from the moment she'd been awakened with the news that her and Sarline's two children—both twice Gerek's age—be left strictly out of the night's deliberations.

"For a time, he was the seventh Duc of Ohrid. This concerns him more than any of us save myself. And I am getting into that keep tonight." Pjerin's tone settled the matter. "The only question is how."

"What about the path through the thornbushes Gerek used when he ran away?" Bohdan wondered.

Gerek shook his head. "Papa's too big. *I'm* almost too big."

"What about secret passageways?" Annice demanded, ripping a crust of bread into crumbs. "The palace is full of them."

Bohdan almost smiled. "Unfortunately, my dear, we are sadly deficient in secret passageways. A regrettable lack of foresight on the part of the first duc."

"What about the drain?" Gerek asked. "That's sort of like a secret passageway. 'Cept it's not secret."

Pjerin turned and stared at his son. "Have you been playing near the drain?"

The question merited consideration. "Not 'zactly."

"What does not exactly mean?"

"I wasn't playing." He picked at a loose thread on the edge of his tunic. "I was looking."

"What did I tell you about that area?"

Gerek sighed deeply. "Not to go near it 'cause it's dangerous and yucky and maybe I could get drowned. But, Papa ..." His small face grew serious as he fearlessly met his father's scowl. "I was the duc. And you said a duc's gotta know every bit of his land and stuff."

Pjerin gripped his son's chin between thumb and forefinger. "You are no longer the duc. Do you understand?"

The small chest heaved with the force of a second sigh. "Yes, Papa."

"So, what *about* the drain?" Annice prompted. "We have to get to Stasya, Pjerin. We have to get to her as soon as we can."

"Not that way. The drain exits under the road in full view of the gatetower. If Olina has someone on watch, we couldn't get to it without being seen."

"Even at night?"

"It wouldn't matter, Annice. They'd hear you trying to get in. There's a heavy iron grille and it's bolted right into the mountain."

"The third duc's stonemason and smith installed it together," Bohdan explained. "It would take a stonemason at least to free it."

"Or a kigh," Annice said pointedly.

"Earth and stone are not the same thing."

"They are eventually. If that grille has been in place since the third Duc, it's begun to wear. I can Sing it loose." She twisted around and glanced at the shuttered window, trying to judge how much of the night remained. Stasya had been six days in that pit. She wouldn't leave her there one day longer.

"Your Grace, while I recognize the necessity of your retaking the keep and rescuing the young bard, may I remind you that the drains are barely four feet around. You'll have to crawl up a steady slope through debris that will be unpleasant at best. And don't forget, you're wounded, without full use of both arms. Why not just show yourself to the people? Surely when they see you're alive . . ."

"Some of them may try to remedy the situation." Pjerin stood, lifting the makeshift sling over his head and tossing it down onto the table. "We don't know who, besides Lukas, Olina has corrupted. Gerek, I want you to stay here." Gerek began to protest but cut it off at his father's expression. "Annice, once you've freed the grille, can you make it back here without being seen?"

She stood as well. "I'm going in with you, Pjerin. *After* Stasya's out of the hole, you can be a hero on your own."

"No. You're not taking the baby into the drains. Do you realize what you'd be climbing through?"

"Nothing will touch the baby. I'll breathe through a damp cloth if it makes you happy, but I'm going with you."

"I won't allow it."

"You don't get in without me."

He glowered at her. "We haven't time to argue . . ."

"Then let's not."

They left the packs. Pjerin slung the Ducal sword across his back and Annice slid her flute case into the deep pocket of her overdress. As they slipped out into the night—Gerek glowering with Bohdan's hands clamped firmly on his shoulders—Sarline's hand flicked out in the sign against the kigh.

"Well?" Pjerin demanded, the force of his whisper lifting the hair around Annice's ear. "Can the kigh get it off."

Perched carefully on a shelf of kigh above the gully's highwater mark, Annice gave the grille another shake. While brute force might be able to bash the heavy iron free, it would be, as Pjerin had said, impossible to work quietly. As to whether the kigh could manage . . .

Fortunately, although the keep could hold the whole village in need, not many people actually lived within its walls and the area around the drain stank less than she'd feared. On the other hand, it still stank. Annice sucked a shallow breath through her teeth and very softly Sang a question to one of her attendant kigh.

"It's attracting their attention that takes the volume," she'd murmured to Pjerin as they'd hurried through the village. *"And right at the moment, attracting their attention is hardly something I have to worry about."*

The squat brown body with its pendulous breasts and bulge of belly disappeared and tiny gray figures—identical in every respect to the first kigh save in color and size—flickered beside each of the bolts.

Frowning, Annice pitched her voice for Pjerin's ears alone. "They can do it, but it's going to take a while."

"How long?"

"As long as it takes." She rubbed her fingertips over the exposed bones of the mountain. *Stasya? Do you know I'm here?* "Apparently, no one's ever tried to influence nascent earth kigh before. I'll have to keep Singing in order to keep pulling them from the stone."

"Can you Sing so they don't hear you in the keep?"

Annice looked up, past the drain, over the lip of the gully to where the crenellation on the gate tower appeared like dark teeth against the stars. "I don't have a choice, do I?"

The Song was so quietly insistent that Pjerin felt almost compelled to drive his fingers into the rock and yank the bolts free himself. He locked his hands together and tried to listen for any sign they were discovered—tried *not* to listen to the Song.

Stone became earth, very, very slowly.

Pjerin waited as patiently as he could, glancing only occasionally toward the east where the bulk of the mountains hid the approaching dawn. It wasn't until the Song grew both softer and deeper that he realized that the coming of the sun was not the only thing that could defeat them.

Only three days before, Annice had Sung her voice to a rasping croak. It couldn't have fully healed. He thought about stopping her, then he thought about what would happen if Olina closed off the keep with him still outside, and he let her Sing on.

Annice could feel her voice sliding from her control as the pain became harder to ignore. She struggled to hold the Song, allowing it to drift into a lower key, whispering the same request over and over. Stasya had been in that pit for six days. There *would not* be a seventh. Finally, the whisper faded and the kigh, taller and darker than when she began but still very small, disappeared.

The sky behind the mountains had lightened to a hazy blue-gray.

Wrapping her hands around one of the heavy iron bars, Annice yanked at it with all her strength. Was that movement or had her imagination supplied what she so desperately desired? Adjusting her grip, she yanked again. It was movement, definitely movement. The bolts were loose but still a long way from free.

Turning to explain, she saw the expression on Pjerin's face and silently moved out of his way.

Bracing his feet on opposite sides of the pungent mud

in the center of the gully, Pjerin threw his weight against the grille. Flakes of rust dug into his palms. The bolts rocked in their anchorage, but held.

Breath hissing through his teeth, he continued to pull. The veins stood out on his forearms, muscles knotted across his back. The new tissue closing the hole the crossbow bolt had left in his shoulder tore and it felt as though hot knives were twisting in the wound. He bit off the cry of pain, couldn't stop the sudden blurring of his vision.

Then over the roar of blood in his ears he heard a single low note throb in the stone.

The grille began to shake.

Slowly, the bolts began to pull free.

One inch. Two. A handbreadth.

Panting, Pjerin collapsed against the bars, drenched in sweat, muscles trembling. Forehead resting on his arm, he managed to turn in time to see Annice break down her flute and slip it back into its case. "I thought," he gasped, "that you had ... to Sing the ... kigh."

"You do." He had to strain to hear her. "But the right notes will call them." She swallowed, wincing as the motion wrenched abraded flesh. "I thought calling them back might make room around the bolts."

"Seems you were right." Grunting with pain, he straightened, shifted his stance, and made ready to pull again. A handbreadth's worth of space between the grille and the mountain would do them no good at all.

"Pjerin?" She poked at one sweat damp arm. "Wouldn't it make more sense to use a lever now?"

He looked at the grille—at the space between the grille and the mountain—and allowed his hands to fall to his sides. "Yes," he sighed, "it would."

Although the valley still lay in the mountain's shadow, a cock had crowed in the village when the grille finally slid down to rest in the mud.

Pjerin squared his shoulders and turned to face the greater challenge.

"It's all right," Annice told him, the stiff line of her back clearly stating how little she liked what she was forced to admit. "I'm not going with you. Not," she added hoarsely, "because of a few bad smells." She chopped a gesture at the dark hole. "I can't bend. And what's more, there's too much of me sticking out—I couldn't climb up into the keep at the end. Happy?"

He was.

Her hand came up to hold her throat, as though to lend strength to her voice. "Swear to me you'll get Stasya out first."

"Annice, if Olina . . ."

"Swear!"

He could see whites showing all around her eyes and her palms pressed against his arm were far too hot. "Annice, the baby . . ."

"Swear!"

"All right! I swear." She took a deep breath and Pjerin watched, relieved as she calmed. "If I go up the laundry drain, I can get to the cellars without being seen. I'll free Stasya and then take care of Olina."

"And Lukas?"

"Without Olina, Lukas is nothing." He pulled himself up into the drain. "Will you be able to get back to Bohdan?"

She nodded. "Be careful."

"Don't worry."

As he disappeared into the darkness, she closed her eyes and murmured, "Soon, Stas. Soon."

Although masking shadows grew fewer with every step, Annice made little effort to hide while returning to Rozyte's house. Without Pjerin, she was completely unrecognizable as the bard who'd visited the keep back in Third Quarter. Just another pregnant woman waddling about on business of her own.

The ache in her temples finally forced her to unclench her jaw. Pjerin had given his word. Stasya would soon be free. But what did Pjerin know about bards? Stasya needed her and here she stood, helpless on the sidelines. It made no difference that her own somewhat latent good judgment had placed her there or that honesty and near exhaustion combined forced her to recognize that she needed to lie down.

Then she saw the small basket of potatoes tucked up against a low stone wall.

Pjerin couldn't just walk in the front gate of the keep. But nothing said *she* couldn't.

Just another pregnant woman waddling about on busi-

ness of her own ... We'll look like a villager, delivering something to the kitchens, baby. I can't be the only person in Ohrid shaped like a gourd.

With the village coming awake, she had no time for deliberation. Any hesitation and this chance would be lost.

Stasya's going to need me. I can't not be there.

Already sprouting, the potatoes had obviously been saved from last year's harvest and, now that the ground had warmed, would probably be planted any day. Annice squatted and awkwardly stood again. A chicken, scratching in the garden, paused long enough to give her a stupidly superior stare, but no one else appeared to have seen. *When this is over, I'll see that these are returned,* she promised silently.

With the basket balanced on one shoulder, screening her face from watchers on the walls of the keep, Annice picked her way onto the track and began the long curving climb up to the gates.

Sarline quietly pulled the heavy wooden door closed behind her and shoved her feet into her clogs. It had taken her until dawn to come to a decision. Lying in the darkness beside a sleeping Rozyte, she'd weighed the alternatives.

Pjerin a'Stasiek was neither oathbreaker nor traitor, and he was their rightful duc.

But Pjerin a'Stasiek supported the dangerous belief that the kigh were enclosed in the Circle and he had fathered a child on a bard.

While Sarline by no means approved of everything that had allegedly been happening over the last two quarters, she could not allow the kigh to return to Ohrid in such strength.

Lukas a'Tynek was her cousin. As he was still steward of Ohrid, she'd give him the information she had and wash her hands of it.

Bare feet making no sound against packed dirt, Gerek ran to the shelter of a building and peered out at his quarry. Sarline had thought he was asleep, but he'd seen her staring at him with her face all twisted. He'd been frightened, for she'd looked a bit like Lukas did and he knew now that Lukas was a bad man.

When she'd snuck out of the house, he'd got his bow and arrows from his papa's pack and followed her.

Pushing his quiver back behind his hip, he dashed forward and ducked behind a garden wall as an early riser called out a greeting. Sarline answered without stopping.

Eyes narrowed in an unconscious imitation of his father's glare, he watched her pass the last house and head up the track toward the keep. When the curve took her out of sight, he raced for the narrow twisting path under the thornbushes.

Calves burning, Annice sagged against the cool stone of the gatetower. Buildings swam across her vision, then steadied into the solid black rock of the keep. She'd never wanted so desperately to sit down.

"You don't look so good."

Somehow, she managed to turn to face the owner of the voice.

Sandy brows drawn into a deep vee, he took the basket from her slack fingers and set it at her feet. "You shouldn't be carrying stuff like this. Here, let ... Hey! You're not ..."

As the realization she wasn't who he thought replaced the concern in his eyes, Annice caught his gaze and snapped, **"Go on with what you were doing."**

The young man shook his head. "Not until I get you where you're going. You really don't look like you should be walking around on your own. Are you Anezka's sister? I heard she was visiting from Adjud."

Annice knew she was staring at him and tried to stop. Her voice hadn't been strong enough to carry the Command. Hand on her throat, she sank back against the wall, hoping she didn't look as frightened as she felt. What if her voice was never strong enough again?

"You're, uh, not ... that is ..."

She dropped her gaze to follow his line of sight and forced herself to think. The baby. He thought she was having the baby. "Uh, no. Not now. Soon."

"Soon?" The word slid up an octave and shattered. "Look, you stay right here. I'm going to go get the midwife." Before she could protest, he was gone, bounding down toward the village.

The baby twisted and Annice clutched at the curve of her belly. *Not now,* she pleaded silently. *Not now.*

Abandoning the potatoes, she moved as quickly as she could toward the laundry, hugging the shadows morning had left along the walls. *Hang on, Stas. I'm coming.*

In another quarter when the rains hadn't been so frequent and the overflow from the cisterns hadn't regularly washed through the drains, it would have been worse. Knowing that didn't help much. Pjerin tried not to think about what squashed beneath his boots or knees or hands, but he couldn't stop breathing and every breath told him unmistakably where he was. The complete lack of light helped and when he began to pass the privy holes, he looked up, not down.

Fortunately, he'd stopped gagging although his ribs burned and his stomach was a tightly knotted ache. Without a healer, the shoulder wound would have to be cauterized to prevent infection.

Nice to have something to look forward to, he mused darkly.

He'd never thought of himself as having an overly active imagination, but he couldn't banish the screams of soldiers from his mind—their scalded skin sloughing off their bodies as they drowned in boiling water. If they'd been seen as they freed the grille or Annice had been taken on her way back to Bohdan ... Even now fires could be burning under the huge kettles in the laundry, the water steaming gently, Olina waiting for just the right moment to pour an agonizing death into the drains.

Not fond of small, enclosed spaces at the best of times, which this most assuredly was not, he held a picture of Olina in his mind's eye, his hands crushing the ivory column of her perfect throat. The image pulled him forward, teeth gritted, muscles tight. She'd pay for what she'd done to him, and to Gerek, and to Ohrid.

The Ducal sword scraped along the stone as he crawled through a puddle less foul than the rest and smelling faintly of lye. He'd long since lost his bearings in the darkness and the stench but he was sure he'd passed the kitchens, so the laundry had to be close.

Had to be.

A strand of hair stuck to his cheek and he fought the urge to yank free his dagger and hack it off short rather than consider what agent plastered it to his skin.

Up ahead he could see the graying that meant another opening into the drain. Eyes streaming, he scuttled for the circle of dim light and thankfully sat back on his heels trying to work the painful kinks out of his back. The stone was damp and cold under his bruised and filthy legs, but that was all. When he stretched up his arm, he could touch the grate over the opening.

The laundry. The drain ended just beyond it at the cisterns. Moving as quietly as he could, Pjerin unbuckled his swordbelt and rehung the weapon around his waist. Up on one knee, he paused, head cocked to one side, straining to hear any sound from above. Nothing. Not that there would be if Olina waited, bow drawn, for his head to crest the stone.

Rising to a crouch, the steel grid pressed against his shoulders, he straightened bent legs.

Tried to straighten bent legs.

As far as he could remember, there were no bolts. The skin between his shoulder blades crawling with the thought of arrows trained on his back, he shifted position slightly and tried again.

The instant age and rust finally released their hold, he threw up his good arm, toppled the grate, and vaulted stiffly out of the drain. If this began the moment when Olina made her move, he'd have less than a heartbeat's grace to defend himself.

The laundry was empty, cool, and clean. A shuttered window laid only broken bands of light against the smooth stone floor, but he'd been in darkness so long the room seemed brilliant. Water dripped from a loose tap into the massive copper kettle, but no fire burned beneath it and the two huge cedar tubs standing beside it on the platform against the cistern wall were dry.

His sigh of relief nearly choked him with his own stink.

What good secrecy when they could smell him coming in Marienka?

Climbing into one of the tubs, he stripped off his shirt

and opened the cistern spout, ducking down under the gush of cold water.

"What are you doing?"

Heart pounding, feeling like an idiot, he stood in the laundry tub flourishing the Ducal sword, water slamming against his back and rapidly rising up around his feet. "What am *I* doing?" he snarled. "What are you doing *here?*"

Annice clutched at the wooden rim and glared up at him. "This is not the time to be ..." Then she gagged and turned away, hand clamped over her mouth. "You're covered in shit."

Somehow he resisted the urge to scream at her. Grabbing up a boarbristle brush, he scrubbed violently at skin, clothes, and hair until he felt flayed and blood dribbled from the edge of the purple scar in the hollow of his shoulder. With as much of the encrusted filth removed as quickly as possible, he slammed the spout closed and clambered out onto the floor.

"All right," he growled, water streaming from breeches and boots and hair and running for the open drain, "let's try this again. What are you doing here? I told you to go back to Bohdan's ..."

Her stomach still twisting, Annice sank down on the platform. He hadn't *told* her to do anything. *She'd* decided not to attempt the drains. "Stasya needs me."

Stasya. He might have known. "I told you I'd get her out."

"I know. But ..."

"But you couldn't wait. Didn't trust me."

"It's not that ..."

"What did you do? Just dance in through the gates?" When she nodded, Pjerin's eyes narrowed. "I'm crawling through shit and you just danced in through the gates!?"

"Well, they're not going to recognize me, are they? Not like this! You're the one who had to stay hidden."

"Really? Did you even once think that with you as a hostage Olina can dictate her own terms with the king?"

"Hostage?" Annice looked startled. "What are you talking about?"

"You're a princess, Annice. Even if you, and His Majesty, and the whole unenclosed country have pretended otherwise for the last ten years."

"I'm a bard!" Or was. She tried to swallow, but her throat was too tight.

"And you're the king's sister. And you're carrying my child. *Think* what Olina could do with that, Annice, *think*."

It started with her lower lip and then her whole body began to shake. She couldn't stop it. He was right and she was so tired. "I wanted to be there for Stasya."

"She's been down there for six days!" He closed his hands on her shoulders, too angry to hold back. "How long does it take to die of thirst?"

Annice stared up at him, every muscle suddenly rigid. "Shut up."

"No, I wo . . ."

"SHUT UP!" The words ripped past the constriction in her throat, force of will making up for the ruined delivery. "She's not dead. I know she's not dead. She has her pack. Gerek said she has her pack. Without you, I can't free her. I can't even find her." Tears streaming down her face, she closed her eyes and broke the Command. "You just get her out like you promised, and then you leave us alone."

Cursing his temper, Pjerin reached out and lightly touched her cheek. When she slapped his hand aside, he walked a few steps away and tried to find an apology. If someone he loved were down in that pit, he'd have done the same thing, taken the same stupid risks, refused to believe the worst.

"Annice? I'm sorry."

She shrugged and wiped her nose on her wrist. "I don't care."

He wanted to hold her. He didn't know where the desire came from, but he knew better than to give in to it. "Come on. Let's go rescue Stasya."

Sobbing in frustration, Gerek fought to free his quiver from a tangle of thornbush, his struggles dumping the arrows out onto the ground where they slid further down the steep slope. A deep bleeding scratch across one cheek and several smaller ones up both arms were a painful testimony to the battle, but he refused to give up. His papa would never give up.

*   *   *

Sarline ground her teeth and kicked at an uneven edge of cobblestone in the outer court of the keep. Lukas hadn't been in his chamber, or the kitchens, or the stables and she didn't know where to look next in this great, echoing pile of stone. None of the servers hurrying about their early morning duties had seen him and she trusted none of them enough for a message. The servers in the keep had a personal loyalty to the duc that would overcome common sense about the kigh.

Rozyte would have missed her by now, the kids would be up, the cow would be bawling. *In another minute, he's on his own with this.*

Then she saw him, coming around the corner by the stable yard, hitching up his breeches. Her clogs ringing against the stone, she ran toward him.

"Where have you been?"

Lukas gaped at his cousin in astonishment. Partnered as she was to the old steward's daughter, he hadn't even thought of approaching her with the Lady Olina's plan. "I was having a shit. Why?"

"Pjerin a'Stasiek was in my house last night."

"The duc?" Lukas traced the sign of the Circle on his breast. "His spirit came to you?"

"Not his spirit, you idiot, he's alive!" Sarlote grabbed up two handfuls of tunic and shook him, hard. "And he's with a bard! And they're both in the keep right now! If you want the kigh out of Ohrid, you've got to stop them!"

She's alive. Stasya's alive. Annice repeated the litany over and over as Pjerin lit a torch and led the way into the cellars. *She hasn't died. I'd know it if she died.* How long did it take to die of thirst? Six days? *No. She's alive.*

"Here," Pjerin began, but Annice had seen the grille and the shadow below it and dove forward.

"Stasya!" Searing pain shot through both hips as she strained to lift the steel. "Stasya! Can you hear me?" She fought Pjerin's grip as he tried to move her out of his way. "Stasya!"

"Hold the torch!" He pushed her back and forced her fingers around the butt. This was the third grille he'd had to remove since dawn and he threw his anger—

or whatever emotion that Annice had evoked in him—
against it.

"Stasya!" Annice leaned dangerously far forward,
torch shoved out over the hole. Shadowed holes in a
gleaming ivory skull stared up at her. Her throat closed
around a disbelieving moan. A giant's fist wrapped
around her heart and squeezed. Pjerin caught the torch
as it dropped from slack fingers and then caught her as
she began to fall.

Stasya knew that voice. Even hoarse and desperate,
there could be no mistaking it. It spoke to her in her
dreams every time exhaustion overcame the cold and
she slept. Slowly she unwrapped herself from her fetal
curl and shoved the stable blanket back. Eyes shut
tightly against the light, she lifted her head and tried
to answer.

Days of cold and damp and thirst held her voice. No
sound emerged.

The light burned through her lids and she raised a
trembling hand to shield her face.

"N . . . Nees?"

"Pjerin is alive."

Lukas wet his lips. Standing well out of her reach, his
tongue occasionally outrunning the story, he'd told her
everything Sarline had told him. "Yes, Lady." Her calm
soothed him. He could feel his heart begin to beat a
little less erratically.

Olina pushed the last pin into the ebony crown of her
hair and stood. She'd dismissed her dresser the moment
she'd seen Lukas' expression as he stood quivering at
her bedchamber door. "It seems you did well to take
down that bard, after all," she mused. "She's given us
time we wouldn't otherwise have had."

When she turned her ice-blue gaze on him, Lukas
shivered.

"I am curious though, as to why you added delay in
coming to me rather than sending your cousin while you
dealt with my nephew."

"Myself?" His eyes darted from side to side, searching
for a way out. "Lady, His Grace is a swordsman. I could
never defeat him. But you . . ."

"Indeed. Well, you've told me. Now go and leave me to deal with him."

"Yes, Lady." Lukas bowed himself back out the door and scurried off. There were things he wanted from his chambers and then he had no intention of remaining in the keep. Not until he knew who won.

Olina picked up a beautifully carved horn comb, stared at it for a moment, then snapped it in half.

"Pjerin is alive," she repeated, throwing the pieces to the floor. It was the one thing she had not planned for. Albek had assured her it would not be necessary.

Eventually, Albek would pay for that error.

Striding across the room, she pulled a padded surcoat from a trunk and slipped it on. Mouth pinched white at the corners, she lifted her sword from where it rested on curved pegs over the bed and buckled the belt around her waist. It dragged at her hip, an unaccustomed weight.

Pjerin was a swordsman. And she was the only other person in the keep trained to fight with the sword.

Not that she had any intention of doing so.

Pjerin knew she had betrayed him. He was larger, younger, stronger and the moment he saw her would be consumed with a blinding rage—she knew her nephew too well to doubt the last. Had Lukas done the intelligent thing and run to the village for all twenty of their committed people, there might have been a chance of stopping him.

But she face him in single combat?

She laughed bitterly and ran for the stables.

Pjerin was alive.

If she wanted to remain alive, she had only one chance.

The Cemandian army.

Let Pjerin and King Theron have the keep; they'd find the pass not so easy to defend as they assumed. Especially in the midst of trying to explain the situation to confused and angry villagers.

Lukas could save himself by crawling back under the rock where she'd found him.

"Nees?"

"Yes. Oh, yes. Stasya, I've got you. Hold onto me.

Everything's going to be all right. You're safe." Annice breathed the last two words into a blood-encrusted cap of dark hair as she shoved the torch at Pjerin and tumbled Stasya onto her lap.

Without a rope, Pjerin had lain on the floor, his arms stretching into the hole. Stasya, harp case slung on her back, had crawled erect up the curved wall of her prison and, with the stone supporting her, lifted her arms over her head.

His hands had closed around her wrists and inch by inch he'd dragged her out of the mountain.

"S'cold, Nees." Her lips were cracked and bleeding, and every word ground shards of pain into her throat.

"C–can't . . . stop . . shaking."

"I know. We'll go into the sun. You'll be fine." Lips pressed against the clammy skin of Stasya's face, Annice repeated, "You'll be fine," as if defying her not to be.

"My voice . . ." Her voice had lost all the highs and lows; all the music. Even Pjerin, who had heard Annice reduced twice to a rough whisper, could tell the difference.

"You're just cold. It'll come back."

"No." Stasya clutched at Annice as hard as numb fingers allowed. "Too c–cold, too long. I'm afraid. Oh Nees. No K–Kigh. No K–kigh for so long. I can't Sing anymore. I c–can't Sing."

Urmi stared at Olina in astonishment, wiping sausage grease from around her mouth before she spoke. "You want Fortune saddled *now*, Lady?"

"Now, Stablemaster."

Under her tan, Urmi paled. Her gaze dropped to the sword hanging at Olina's hip. "Yes, Lady. But he's in the paddock, it'll take me a moment."

"A moment and no more, Stablemaster."

"No, Lady. I mean, yes, Lady."

"Can you manage from here?"

Annice nodded, Stasya supported in the circle of her arms.

Pjerin jabbed the torch at the floor, then took off at a dead run. Olina had escaped her fate for as long as she was going to. He pounded across one end of the

Great Hall, down a short flight of stairs, and through the kitchen, ignoring the crash of breaking crockery as he was recognized by the cook's helper. Shoving the slack-jawed youth aside, he exploded out into the inner court. The fastest way to Olina's rooms was around—not through—the building.

He raced past his woodpile, heard a shout of disbelief from the direction of the stables, and turned in time to see Olina swing up into the saddle. Her lips pulled off her teeth in a feral smile as she drove her spurs into the stallion's flanks and tried to ride him down. At the last instant, he dove aside. A hoof slammed into the packed earth a prayer away from his hip. Another grazed his calf as he rolled, the glancing impact still enough to drive a cry of pain through clenched teeth. Then he was scrambling back onto his feet, rage blocking everything but his desire for revenge.

Roaring Olina's name, Pjerin broke from between the buildings into the outer court just in time to see Fortune's glossy hindquarters disappear out the gate.

"NO!"

Satchel clutched in a white-knuckled grip, Lukas tottered a disbelieving step forward. "Lady?" She was abandoning him. How could she abandon him? "Lady!"

Behind him, he heard a bellow of fury. Unable to stop himself, he turned.

Lukas did not consider himself an imaginative man, but what he saw standing at the edge of the court was not the taciturn lord who allowed the kigh such license within Ohrid nor even the huge, soot-covered figure who had struck him down in Fourth Quarter. His bare and heaving chest streaked with blood, his hair a tangled mass of darkness about his shoulders, his face contorted with rage, Pjerin a'Stasiek looked like one of the old gods broke free of the Circle.

The sudden realization that with Lady Olina gone, the duc would deal instead with him, brought a rush of cold sweat dribbling down his sides.

The same realization came to the duc.

"LUKAS!"

The satchel fell from limp fingers. Fear froze him to the spot. Lukas watched his death approach, unable to move, unable to protest. Then some instinct of self-preservation broke through the paralysis, and with a shriek of terror he started to run.

He didn't know where he was running to. He just knew he had to escape. Plunging into the dark recesses at the base of the inner tower, he searched for sanctuary and found only the narrow, spiral stairs leading up four stories to the roof. A mistake. He should never have come inside.

Too late to go back.

Whimpering, all he could do was climb.

His face tear-streaked, his tunic tattered, Gerek came through the gate in time to see Lukas run into the tower with his papa following close behind. Hitching his quiver and the one arrow he'd saved over his shoulder, he darted forward.

"Gerek!"

"I'm okay, Jany," he yelled toward the edge of the court and his suddenly hysterical nurse. He could hear her crying and babbling his name, and it made him feel bad, but he had to help his papa.

From the top of the tower, there was nowhere to run. On the one side, the mountain fell away from the tower's base, adding even greater distance to the ground. On the other, there was only the court with its border of upturned faces.

From the stairwell came the sound of leather slapping stone. The duc was nearly on him. Lukas cringed back against the battlements.

Annice pushed past a babbling group of servers, too astounded by the return of their duc—of both their ducs—to notice a pair of exhausted bards. Supporting much of Stasya's weight, as well as her own, she sank gratefully into a sunny doorway where the wood and dark stone had collected all the heat of the morning.

"S'cold, Nees," Stasya murmured, red-rimmed eyes still squinted nearly shut after so long in darkness. "Still no k–kigh."

"That's because you're with me. Remember?" Annice settled the other woman more comfortably in the bend of her elbow and with her free hand worked the stopper out of a jug she'd picked up as they made their way through the deserted kitchens. "Here, drink some more of this." Glancing up at the tower where Lukas had become momentarily visible as he looked down into the court, she added softly, "When this is settled, I'll go far enough away that the kigh will come and you can Sing the news to the captain."

"No." Stasya shoved her face into the curve of Annice's neck. Too long with the dark and the cold. Too long with no kigh. If she tried to Sing, and failed, she'd know for sure her voice was gone. Better not to know. Better not to Sing.

Annice heard the subtext under Stasya's denial and tightened her hold. With her own voice uncertain, it was the only comfort she had to give.

Too angry to remember that cornered rats would fight, Pjerin charged out onto the top of the tower and was slammed sideways to the stone.

Lukas cursed and stumbled back. The duc had been moving too fast and a kick intended to smash into his temple had hit only the solid flesh of his upper arm. It wouldn't be enough. It wouldn't be nearly enough. His advantage gone, Lukas began to babble. "Your Grace, I can explain. It wasn't me, it was . . ."

Pjerin shook off the blow, lurched to his feet, and lunged, growling wordlessly. The two men crashed back against the battlements and Pjerin's hands closed around the steward's throat.

Crouched at the top of the stairs, Gerek readied his bow and his single arrow.

Gasping for breath, unable to break the duc's hold, Lukas jabbed his knuckles again and again into the bleeding scar below Pjerin's left shoulder.

Muscles began to spasm and howling with as much frustration as pain, Pjerin stumbled back, his left arm falling useless to his side.

For an instant, Lukas stood alone, silhouetted against the sky. Gerek took a deep breath, held it as he'd been taught, and released the string. The arrow flew wide, rang against the stone, and rumbled over the edge, falling end over end into the court below.

Both men wheeled to track its path.

Lukas saw one final chance to survive. Diving for the stairs, he grabbed up the boy and held him, kicking and shrieking against his chest as he scuffled back to the edge of the roof.

The sight and sound of Gerek's danger pulled Pjerin from his frenzy and gasping for breath he took a step forward.

"No farther," Lukas warned, shifting his grip and swinging the child out over the drop.

Gerek screamed and fought harder to be free.

"Gerek, be still!" Pjerin commanded, muscles knotting with the effort to remain where he was.

Twisting his small body around to face his father, Gerek hiccuped and went limp.

"Good boy."

"Papa . . ."

"Shh, everything's going to be all right." Pjerin lifted his gaze to Lukas' face. "Lukas knows that if he drops you, he'll go off right after you. That if he hurts you, he'll wish he'd never been born."

The steward's lips twitched up in a hideous parody of a smile. "What difference would that make? You're going to kill me anyway."

"Let him go, Lukas."

"Grant me safe passage out of the keep. Give me your word I can go free."

Pjerin nodded and although every instinct said to rush forward, he stepped back. "Without Olina," he said quietly, "you're nothing."

Nothing. When he'd been so close to having it all. It wasn't fair. It wasn't fair that Pjerin a'Stasiek should have everything and Lukas a'Tynek nothing. Not power, not wealth, not even a child. His only daughter had been taken from him, destroyed by the kigh. No second chance for his child. No one to pull her to safety. Blinded by tears of self-pity, Lukas heaved Gerek roughly up onto the stone and let go.

"PAPA!" With too much of his body still dangling over the court, Gerek slipped backward.

"GEREK!" Pjerin dove, right arm desperately reaching, but he arrived at the edge half a heartbeat too late.

Below, a dozen voices shrieked and a dozen people surged uselessly toward the tower.

Surrounded by stone, with no earth to hear her Song, Annice heaved her body around, threw open the door, and plunged inside. "Sing, Stasya!" she cried as she put thick walls between her influence and Gerek's only chance.

Eyes locked on the falling child, Stasya staggered to her feet. No time to think of what she was doing. No time for fear.

She Sang.

And the kigh answered.

Long pale fingers clutched at Gerek's arms and legs until the child was hidden to bardic sight behind a surging mass of slender bodies. As he continued to plunge screaming toward the stones of the court, the air below him grew translucent, then opaque.

A handbreadth from the ground he stopped, held by Stasya's Song. Tears streaming down her face, she Sang a gratitude just in time for the kigh to loose the sobbing boy into the comfort of his nurse's embrace.

The wind howled about the walls of the keep as each of the kigh swirled joyously around Stasya's head. They pulled her hair and tugged at her clothes and one even went so far as to poke an ethereal finger up her nose. Then, en masse, they rose to circle the tower.

His heart having stopped as Gerek fell and started again as he was saved, Pjerin leaned into the rush of air and breathed a prayer of thanks to every god the Circle contained. He couldn't see the kigh, but he'd heard Stasya's Song and understood what had to have happened. His son was safe. Nothing else mattered.

"No! Get away! Help me!" Whites wreathing his eyes, Lukas frantically worked his right hand in the sign against the kigh. The wind roared around him. His left arm flailed at the air and he stumbled from one side of the roof to the other in an attempt to escape the invisible demons he knew were there. He lurched against the battlements, overbalanced, and began to topple. "Your Grace! Save me!"

Eyes nearly closed by the force of the wind, Pjerin fought his way along the crenellations. Bits of loose mortar, sand, and dirt, stung bare skin. His reaching fingers

grazed a bit of rough, homespun cloth, a wrist ...
nothing.

All at once, the silence became absolute.

Pjerin stared down into the court. Lukas lay face up,
staring at the sky, a dark stain slowly spreading out from
under his flattened skull. The fingers of his right hand
remained bent halfway through the sign against the kigh.

Sagging against the stone, Pjerin half turned to meet
Stasya's gaze. Even over that distance, he could see her
measuring him. *You didn't Sing,* he thought. *Although
you found time and strength both to save Gerek. Are you
wondering how hard I tried?*

*Had it been anyone other than Lukas, would I have
reached him in time?*

CHAPTER EIGHTEEN

"Did you hear that?"

Theron swiveled to face the bard. On the road since dawn, they'd just broke out from under the cover of the trees and he'd been squinting up the length of the valley at the brooding bulk of Ohrid's keep backlit by the morning sun. "Hear what?" he asked. "I didn't hear anything."

"Stasya. She's Singing the kigh."

"Is she all right?"

A sudden gust of wind rocked Tadeus back in his saddle. "As near as I can tell." He raised a hand, fingers stroking information from the air. "But someone else is dead."

"Who?" Theron demanded. If Annice was at the keep and Stasya was Singing and someone was dead . . .

"A man." Tadeus Sang a short series of notes, his hair whipping around his head even while the pennants on the lances hung limp. After a moment, he slammed his fist down onto the saddle horn. His horse sidestepped nervously. The king reached over, grabbed the reins, and pulled it up short. "Stasya's gone again! And the kigh won't go back into the keep."

"Annice?"

"Probably."

Theron nodded grimly. "That's it. Captain!"

"Sire?"

"Form up the guard to advance on the keep."

"Sire!"

"Tadeus, I want everyone to hear this."

"Yes, Majesty."

Wheeling his horse around in a tight circle, Theron's gaze swept over the company stretched back along the narrow track, somehow seeming to include even those he couldn't see. "There's trouble up ahead," he said as the bard's quiet Song lifted his voice, carrying it over the noise of the guard leaving their positions and moving to the fore. The faces of the four nobles lit up, but then, they'd been chosen because they thrived on trouble. "Servers and pack animals will follow as they can." The noncombatants knew who they were. "The rest of us are needed at the keep." When he unhooked the crowned helm from behind his saddle and slipped it on, a murmur of excitement rose from the ranks. Even the horses seemed to catch it.

"You forget how incredibly dull State Visits are," he'd told the Bardic Captain the day the company had left Elbasan. *"Even truncated ones. We're talking days of tedious travel interspersed with tasteless banquets and endless posturing. By the time we reach Orchid, if I'm any judge, this lot will consider taking on the entire Cemandian army a welcome relief."*

At the time, the words had been for the most part the only sort of bravado kings were permitted. Now, Theron hoped they held an element of truth.

"What do you think you're doing?" he barked a moment later as Tadeus brought his horse into line.

Ebony brows flicked above the tolled leather mask the bard wore over his eyes. "Preparing to gallop to the rescue, Majesty."

"You're blind!"

Tadeus flashed him a brilliant smile completely free of compromise. "The horse isn't."

"Vencel!" Braid flying, the boy raced across the field, leaping the rows of young corn. "Vencel! The king is coming! He has soldiers and he's galloping!"

"Soldiers?" Vencel grabbed his little brother and gave him a shake. "What are you talking about?"

Too familiar with this form of interrogation to be bothered by it, the boy grinned and explained. "They're in two lines and they're on horses and they're galloping and they have flags and helms and everything just like in the stories."

"How far from the forest?"

"Not far. I was down by the creek with Miki and . . ."

"Never mind that. Where's Tas?"

The child shrugged. "Sheep pen, I guess."

"Find her. Tell her what you told me, then tell her I said to get the others and to go right to the keep."

"I want to watch the King!"

"Do it!"

Ducking his brother's fist, the boy bounded away, throwing a jaunty, "And what did your last slave die of?" back over his shoulder.

"Come to the keep in ones and twos," Lukas had told them. *"You'll have lots of time."*

Something had gone wrong. Vencel didn't know what, but he did know they no longer had the time they'd been promised. If he ever wanted to be more than what he was at this moment, he had to change the rules. Dropping his hoe, he ran for the village. At least two people were in the forest and wouldn't be able to beat a galloping horse back to the keep. There'd be less than the full twenty archers on the walls but still enough to give the King of Shkoder a welcome he wouldn't forget.

The stablemaster stood, wiping her fingers on her breeches as she turned away from Lukas' corpse. "He's dead," she said flatly.

As though they were only waiting for that confirmation, a hundred questions rose to beat at the air.

"Stasya didn't take me nowhere!" Gerek's piping voice pierced through the chaos in the court, offering the only answer. "Lukas and Aunty Olina put her in a hole, so I went to get Papa."

"But how did you know he was alive, little one?" Jany demanded, scrubbing at the tear streaks on his face with the hem of her shift. Her own eyes continued to well and spill, but the action seemed to calm her.

Gerek shoved her hand away. "Stasya *told* me."

Heads swiveled to stare at the two bards huddled in the open doorway, holding each other and paying little attention to the world outside their embrace. Several hands rose to flick out the sign against the kigh, but only a couple completed the motion. Most stopped at the point where they realized their fingers were folded in the same position as the stiffening fingers of Lukas a'Tynek.

"Papa!" Tearing himself out of his nurse's grip, Gerek raced to the base of the tower and threw himself into his father's arms.

Pjerin winced at the impact but gathered the small body up against his right side and rested his head on the dark cap of hair, breathing in the clean child scent. He had a thousand things he wanted to say, from "Don't ever do that again!" to "Thank every god in the Circle you're alive!", but none of them meant as much as just absorbing the presence of his son and he knew he'd only be allowed an instant of it.

"Your Grace . . ."

"They sent a messenger! He said you were dead!"

"There was a Death Judgment . . ."

". . . guilty, Your Grace, we heard you under Command!"

"You were dead . . ."

". . . alive . . ."

"Enough!" One by one the voices stilled. Pjerin shifted Gerek's weight on his hip. "The Cemandians have a way to subvert Bardic Command. Olina used it to remove me and gain control of the pass."

"But you're her blood," someone protested.

Pjerin's eyes grew darker. "So is my son. That didn't seem to matter. She made Lukas a'Tynek her tool, although how much she told him . . ." His glance flicked down to the corpse and up again. ". . . we'll never know. Right now, we've . . ."

A dozen villagers—most showing some indication of tasks hurriedly left—pounded through the gate, into the court, and rocked to a stop. Pjerin a'Stasiek was alive! The duc was alive! They jostled about for a moment as those in the rear pushed forward, then a heavyset man with a full, curling beard broke into the clear and threw himself down beside Lukas' body.

A heartbeat later, he sat back on his heels and looked up at Pjerin, eyes wide. "You're alive and my brother is dead. How did this happen?" One hand made the sign against the kigh, the other hovered over the hilt of the skinning knife he had shoved through the wrapped ties of his bloodstained, bullhide apron.

Gaze locked on Nikulas a'Tynek, Pjerin set Gerek on

the ground and turned him to face across the court. "Go to Annice," he said shortly.

"But ..."

"Just go."

Gerek sighed deeply but trotted across to where the two bards still stood in the open doorway.

"Gerek, are you all right?" one of the new arrivals called as Annice drew the child in against her legs.

" 'Course I am." The weary indignation in his voice clearly added, *how many times do I have to tell you.* "I just went to find Papa."

"We thought the bard took you ..."

"And murdered you!"

"My brother is dead and a dead man is alive!" Nikulas roared, rising to his feet. "Tell me what is going on!"

Tersely, Pjerin explained again how Olina had made him appear an oathbreaker in order to gain control of the pass. How she'd used Lukas and, finally, how Lukas had died.

"He fell?" Nikulas snorted. "And am I to believe you didn't push him?"

"Shame, Nikulas! Shame!"

"... saw His Grace fight to save your brother with every right to let him fall!"

"Lukas would have dropped the boy ..."

"... accident ..."

"... shame!"

Breathing heavily, Nikulas backed away a step. With no one supporting his accusation, not even those members of the family scattered amid the group still standing just inside the gate, the last thing he wanted was a one on one confrontation with the duc. "Still more questions than answers," he muttered.

"I have a question!" Vencel pushed his way forward. "Now that you've returned, Your Grace, where do you stand? Are we in Ohrid to continue as forgotten vassals of the King of Shkoder, valued only for our willingness to stupidly throw our live between him and conquest? Or will you lead us to victory?"

"Articulate farmers in these parts," Stasya murmured for Annice's hearing alone.

Annice nodded. "He's going to lose his tongue if Pjerin loses his temper."

"Lead you to what victory?" Pjerin demanded.

"In throwing off the yoke of Shkoder!"

"And replacing it with the yoke of Cemandia?" His voice had taken on a dangerous edge.

Vencel ignored it. "We were promised change!" he declared, punching the air. "A chance to be more!"

Several people muttered in agreement and a wave of movement traced a restless shift in position.

"You believed those promises?" The edge in Pjerin's voice had become a sneer.

"Cemandia gave us trade!"

"It was what you wanted, Your Grace."

"It was what Olina wanted," Pjerin bellowed, his grip on his temper slipping. "Those were not my words! The Cemandians will grind you under their boot heels! Take away your freedoms!"

"We want our chance!" Vencel yelled.

The court erupted in a cacophony of shouting.

"Let it be." Stasya grabbed Gerek with one hand and Annice with the other. "Olina has played these people against themselves, fears against desires for nearly two quarters. Their duc was dead. Now he's alive. Cemandia's bad. Cemandia's good. Cemandia's bad again. No one knows *what* or *who* to believe. Can't you feel it? This storm *has* to break."

"Someone's going to get hurt, Stas."

Still holding Gerek, Stasya let Annice go and gestured at the seething mass. It was no longer possible to determine who had been originally at the keep and who had come up from the village. "How," she asked, "do you suggest we stop it?"

"Lukas a'Tynek was a superstitious fool!" Pjerin's voice rose above the din. "Olina used him! She used you!"

"Kigh lover!"

The first blow occurred simultaneously in a number of places.

Gerek clutched at Annice's shift. "Is my papa gong to get hurt?"

"I don't think so, sweetheart." Annice added her grip to Stasya's. The last thing they wanted was for Gerek to plunge into the fray. "No one's hitting him. He's trying to stop the fighting."

"Why doesn't he just tell them to stop?"

"Nobody's listening."

It was one thing to agree to capture a foreign king, convinced he was the overlord who kept Ohrid isolated and poor, but it was another thing entirely to physically strike the hereditary duc—the man who was Ohrid. The blows Pjerin took were accidental as he waded into the battle pulling men and women apart.

A knife flashed in an upraised fist. Pjerin smashed his forearm into the snarling face below it. The knife went flying, clattered against the cobblestones, and was lost amidst the dance of scuffling feet.

Flesh pounded against flesh. Urmi, her nose streaming blood, kicked the legs out from under a cursing villager and followed him to the ground. A pair of cousins rolled and spat obscenities as they struggled for a hold. Vencel sucked air past a split lip as an elbow caught him in the stomach, but he recovered in time to block the next blow and return a quick flurry of his own. Someone screamed as teeth clamped down on a fold of skin. Pressed against the base of the tower near his brother's body, Nikulas, skinning knife in his hand, watched and waited for a clear shot at the Duc of Ohrid's back.

His brother was dead. The duc was alive. That wasn't the way it was supposed to be. Lukas'd had plans. Big plans. Now he was dead.

Pjerin grunted as a flailing arm slammed into his wounded shoulder. He staggered back, yanked two villagers off the keep's scullion, helped the boy to his feet, and ducked a swinging fist.

Nikulas crept out from the wall. Not even the demon kigh would be able to follow the strike in this confusion. He fixed his eyes on the dirt-streaked skin just below the tangled mass of the duc's hair, where the heavy muscle bulk over the ribs gave way to softer tissue. Up and under. Then away. No one would ever know. His brother would be avenged.

Only Annice and Stasya saw the first pair of guards gallop into the keep. The second and third were harder to ignore. By the time the fourth and fifth were taking their positions, the fighting had begun to stop as people were pushed into an increasingly smaller area in the center of the court.

Recognizing his last and best chance, Nikulas lunged forward. A lance cracked down on his wrist. Crying out, he dropped the knife and cradled the swelling arm against his belly. When he tried to hide himself, he found the lance blocking his way and a smiling guard shaking her head. She might not know exactly what was going on, but the laws were clear concerning back-stabbing. Nikulas could only stand and watch as horses plunged past struggling combatants and the people of Ohrid staggered to their feet to face this new threat together.

By the time the king, his standard bearer, Tadeus, and the four nobles rode into the court, the guards were ranged around the perimeter in what became a closed circle the moment the last rider cleared the gate. Pjerin and his people stood, differences forgotten, shoulder to shoulder, wiping away blood and glaring about them at this show of force.

"Nees! I can't see!" Gerek bounced up and down on the doorstep and scowled at the pair of dusty haunches that blocked his view.

Trying very hard not to break into hysterical giggles, Annice took his hand and pushed between the two horses. "Excuse me, Corporal Agniya." She tapped the guard lightly just above her greave. "If you wouldn't mind shuffling your mount to the left just a bit."

Corporal Agniya looked down and her jaw dropped. "You're ... I mean, you ..." The orders she'd been given didn't begin to cover this. Wondering just what in the Circle was going on, she did the only thing she could. She moved her horse.

"Pjerin a'Stasiek, Duc of Ohrid." The sunlight blazed on each point of the crown encircling Theron's helm and threw the stern lines of his face into burnished relief. "I am pleased to see you got safely home." Although he spoke the local dialect with a strong accent, astonishment that he spoke it at all showed on most faces in the court, including Pjerin's.

As the tall man, bare torso streaked with blood, stepped forward to bow before the king, Tadeus translated Theron's words into Shkoden for the benefit of the guard and nobles. Several of the guard broke discipline enough to exchange astonished glances. The last they'd heard, Pjerin a'Stasiek, Duc of Ohrid had been executed for treason.

"Although it seems," Theron continued, "that your welcome was not all you might have hoped." He scanned the crowd behind the duc, noting those who moved closer to their lord and those who backed away. Finally, his gaze rested on the broken body lying a little apart. "I came to Ohrid to find the traitor who thought to sell our country out to the Cemandian horde. It appears I've come too late."

There was enough of a question in his last words that Pjerin, as confused as everyone else, opened his mouth to reply. Before he got the chance, Vencel shook off the hands holding him and stomped forward.

"What treason is it to want a better life?" he demanded.

Theron bent his head to meet the young man's angry eyes. "None at all," he said. "But what kind of life can be gained by the betrayal of an innocent man? Not a better one."

Vencel dabbed at his mouth with the back of his hand and shot a glance at Pjerin. "But *you* killed ..." His voice trailed into uncertainty as he realized what he was saying.

"Killed him?" Theron asked gently. He very much doubted the boy was even as old as Onele. An easy age to lead with confusion and anger.

"What about the kigh?" Beneath the king's steady gaze, Vencel fell back on the one thing everyone kept shouting about. "You listen to the kigh!"

"No." Theron shook his head an Annice was surprised to hear an undertone of disappointment in his voice. "I cannot hear the kigh. But I do listen to those who can. Don't you think it's important that we're aware of the world around us?"

"But the kigh are outside the Circle!"

"All things are within the Circle. That is the very Center of what we believe. If all things are not enclosed, then there is no Circle."

"But the Cemandians believe ..."

"The Cemandians are afraid."

Vencel stiffened, resenting the implication. *I'm not afraid of anything,* his posture declared and others around the court mirrored it. "We were promised that the world would come to Ohrid."

"Who promised this?"

The only sound came from the horses as Vencel turned toward the corpse of Lukas a'Tynek.

Theron straightened and his voice filled the court. "I am Theron, King of Shkoder, High Captain of the Broken Islands, Lord over the Mountain Principalities of Sibiu, Ohrid, Adjud, Bicaz, and Somes." Above his head, a breeze spread the royal standard so that the crowned ship sailed over the keep. "Acknowledging the claims of your duc, *I* have come to you to see that the promises made to Ohrid by the crown are kept. *I* will bring the world to Ohrid if you but let me."

Shaking her head, Annice couldn't help but admire how Theron had taken control through sheer force of personality. He was king. Without doubt. Without question. And by speaking in the local dialect he'd explicitly said, *I am king* here. Even Vencel was beginning to look impressed.

Tucked in behind her shoulder, Stasya murmured, "Practically bardic."

Annice smiled but concentrated on separating out individual statements from the muttering of the crowd.

". . . means something coming from the actual king . . ."

". . . kings can break promises as easily as traders . . ."

". . . here, isn't he?"

"We mean enough to him, that he came here . . ."

Brows drawn into a dark vee, Pjerin raised his hand and gradually silence returned. Obviously, there were layers upon layers upon layers of understanding involved here but this was not the time to find out who knew what and when. The king no longer believed him forsworn and that would do for now. "Majesty, I regret to inform you that we have not actually dealt with the treason in Ohrid."

Around him, faces paled, as people remembered suddenly that they had agreed to turn this king over to a Cemandian army.

"Lukas a'Tynek . . ." Pjerin gestured at the body, ". . . was only a tool for my father's sister, Olina i'Katica."

"And where is your father's sister now?" Theron asked.

A muscle jumped in Pjerin's jaw. "Probably Cemandia. When she discovered I was alive, she ran."

"Let her run." Theron smiled and his voice rang against the stones. "And let the Cemandian army come. The keep of Ohrid holds the pass!"

As the bruised and bleeding people in the court began to cheer and Tadeus had to practically Sing his translation in order to be heard, Annice had to admit she'd never really appreciated her brother's power as king before.

When the cheer died, Theron spoke again. "There is, however, still a treason that must be dealt with." Then he turned his head and looked straight at Annice.

Annice felt her heart stop. *How could I have forgotten.* She tried to back up, but Stasya blocked the way.

"He's seen you, Nees. You've got to face him."

"But ..."

"Nees." Stasya laid a gentle kiss on the top of the other woman's ear. "If you can't trust him, trust me. Go. I'll be right behind you."

Gerek squirmed out of her hands. "Nees, why is everyone staring at you?"

Stasya reached forward, grabbed his shoulder and pushed him toward his nurse. "I'll explain everything later, Gerek."

"Promise?"

"I promise."

He looked mutinous, but he went.

Annice thought she was used to people staring at her. She was a bard. People always stared at bards. But the weight of speculation, concern, astonishment, pity dragged at her, and she wouldn't have made the last few feet had Pjerin not reached out and pulled her to his side.

"Your Majesty," he began, switching to Shkoden.

"Your Grace." Theron cut him off in the same language. "Be quiet." He sighed, and pulled off his helm, resting it in front of him on the saddle. "Did you honestly believe," he asked sadly, running one hand through sweat-flattened curls, "that I would have you put to death for bearing a child?"

Annice blinked. This was not the king who had just gathered the hearts of Ohrid into his hand. This was not the man who had first threatened her with Cemandia's heir, then used his power like a sledge against her. This was the brother she thought existed only in memory. Did she honestly believe that he would have her put to death for bearing a child? And if she didn't, why hadn't she gone to him, told him what she suspected about Pjerin?

Was she so petty as to risk the life of her baby, to risk Shkoder itself just because ten years ago a king, newly crowned, had lashed out in pain. She bit the inside of her lip as, for the first time, she realized that if Theron had rejected her, she had equally rejected him and he'd very likely been as hurt as she had been.

"Answer him, Annice," Stasya whispered.

Did she honestly believe. . .?

She closed her eyes. "I don't know." How far would he let that mix of pain and pride take him? She couldn't know—not when hers had insisted he remain the villain for ten long years.

When she opened her eyes again, Theron had dismounted and was standing in front of her, only slightly more than an arm's length away. He still looked majestic. He still looked like the brother she remembered. Both Pjerin and Stasya fell back.

"Your captain tells me that the king's word must be perceived as law, but bad laws should be changed." He took a deep breath. "I, Theron, King of Shkoder, High Captain of the Broken Islands, Lord over the Mountain Principalities of Sibiu, Ohrid, Adjud, Bicaz, and Somes do on this day remove all conditions on the bard known as Annice who was my sister and I hope will be again."

"Witnessed." Tadeus declared as he finished the translation. Still in the saddle, he smiled over the king's head at Annice who couldn't seem to find a reaction to Theron's words. "Don't be a gob, Nees. He loves you, and there's never enough of that to go around."

Theron rolled his eyes. "Shut up, Tadeus."

Tears spilling down her cheeks, Annice covered her mouth with both hands but couldn't prevent a ragged giggle from escaping. She rubbed the back of her wrist over her nose and shook her head. "Long trip?" she asked her brother, shooting a glance up at the bard behind him.

Theron opened his arms. "Too long," he said softly. "Come home, Annice."

One step. Two. He met her halfway.

She burst into sobs against his shoulder. "I'm sorry," she murmured for his ears alone. "I'm sorry I humiliated you in front of Father. I'm sorry I was too self-absorbed to recognize a peace offering when you made it. I'm sorry that even for a moment I believed you might actually hurt my baby." She felt him sigh, felt warm moisture seeping through her hair where his cheek lay against her head.

"I'm sorry, too," Theron said softly. "My anger at your betrayal hid the fact that I betrayed you first—it wasn't you I couldn't forgive, it was me. I didn't want to think of myself as the kind of king who could use someone who loved him in such a way. I'm sorry that I allowed my pride to dictate the distance between us for so long."

"I was just so afraid that if I gave you the chance, you'd hurt me again."

Theron remembered how once she had trusted him more than anyone alive. "You have no idea," he told her, throat closing around the words, "how sorry I am for that."

After a moment, he kissed her and pushed her gently away. "We'll have much to speak about later, but right now, we've one unenclosed mess to straighten out."

Annice nodded. It felt as though knots had been untied all through her body. She wiped at her face with her palms. "I understand. You've got an army to get ready for."

"The army's not likely to be the problem now that His Grace is back in control of the keep," Theron said with a smile, changing back to the local dialect and raising his voice enough to be heard by everyone in the court. "But there are a number of explanations, long overdue."

"Begging your pardon, Majesty." Stasya stepped forward. Her voice still sounded as though she'd been storing it in brine and her eyes were half shut against the light, but the gray had begun to leave her skin and she stood unassisted. "Explanations will have to wait. The pass can't be closed. The palisade has been emptied and partially dismantled."

"What!" Pjerin spun around, grabbed a handful of Vencel's tunic and nearly hauled him off his feet. "What do you know about this?"

With the full force of his lord's temper not a hand-breadth from his face, Vencel blanched and stammered defensively, "The palisade needed repairs! A crosspiece at the bottom needed to be replaced. We took it out, but—I mean—it wasn't finished because there's been field work to do, and, well, other things kept coming up. . . ."

"Other things?" Pjerin's tone dripped disbelief.

Vencel stiffened. "Yes, Your Grace, other things."

"And who kept you busy with these other things?"

"It's still First Quarter, Your Grace," someone called from the crowd. "There's always things that need doing."

"It was First Quarter when you emptied it," Pjerin growled, cutting off the murmur of agreement.

"But Lukas said," someone else began, then stopped, realizing that anything Lukas said would not now help their case.

"Said what? That there was no need to hurry?" At Vencel's nod, Pjerin overcame the urge to shake the boy until his teeth rattled and, jaw set, released him with only one, near involuntary, jerk. He was beginning to regret that Lukas had died so easily although he took some small comfort in knowing that Olina had undoubtedly given the actual orders. "Lukas was in no hurry because he needed the pass open for a Cemandian army. Something—" his angry gaze raked the crowd, "—that I'm sure crossed a number of minds considering what's been going on around here. Whatever else you may be, *I* know you're not stupid." Unable to raise his left arm, he clutched at the ornate hilt of the Ducal sword and snarled, "Anyone who'd rather be with the Cemandians, can leave now."

No one moved.

"You?"

Vencel looked mulish, but he shook his head.

"Good. Where's the crosspiece you took out?"

No one spoke.

"Well?"

Urmi pushed forward, her face streaked with drying blood. "It, uh, was cut up for the kitchen fires, your Grace." She swallowed and squared her shoulders. "The palisade hasn't been repaired for some time, Your Grace. It was an easy lie to believe and things were, well, unsettled while you were, uh, dead."

Pjerin could feel them waiting for his response, could feel his bond with his people teetering in the balance. Glancing at Annice and Theron, he thought of how much holding onto the past had denied them. What was done, was done. He snorted and some of the stiffness went out of his posture. "Well, it was unsettling *being* dead." As an echo of his easing rippled through the crowd, he turned to the king who'd been standing quietly watching Ohrid pull itself back together. "We have a problem," he said shortly. "We won't have time to repair and refill the palisade. We'll have to rely on a wooden barricade, well soaked to keep it from burning."

The king nodded. "How long will that take to build?"

"We'll need some big timber to anchor it."

"Your Grace?" Vencel twitched his tunic straight but did not allow anxious hands to pull him back into the crowd. He lifted his chin defiantly. "We could use the logs in the palisade."

At Theron's raised brow, Pjerin nodded. "We'd have to go at least a day's travel to find trees that size." Turning to Vencel, he smiled approvingly. "Good idea."

The duc's praise was as overwhelming as his temper. Vencel colored and looked away, ears red.

"Before we get to work, I do have one explanation I need to make." Stepping away from Pjerin, Theron let his gaze sweep over the guard and the four nobles who had accompanied him, unaware that they probably rode to war. Obviously, they now knew differently and deserved to be told the whole. *No, not the whole,* he decided. *Cemandia would be at the sea before I started to untangle it.*

He spoke Shkoden this time and finished the severely edited chain of events leading up to this moment with,

". . . now we must stand side by side with the people of Ohrid to defend our land from Cemandian invasion!"

There's something about being a king, Annice decided as the guards, caught up in the appeal, cheered, *that lends a certain grandeur even to overblown rhetoric. From anyone else, that ending would've been over the edge.* Even as Tadeus repeated it, it had lost a little of its majesty.

She glanced up at Pjerin, trying to gauge his reaction. If they hadn't run, then Olina would never have believed him dead, and they wouldn't have been able to regain the keep, and they wouldn't all be preparing to stand off a Cemandian invasion. *If only Olina hadn't emptied out that palisade. . . .*

The two younger nobles—as Theron had known they would—looked thrilled at a chance to prove themselves against such overwhelming odds. One hated the Cemandians for personal reasons and had spent the entire trip wishing for much this situation. The fourth merely smiled.

"You're not surprised, Lady Jura."

The scarred and grizzled veteran of the Broken Islands campaign inclined her head. "Sire, I am many things, but I am not a diplomat, nor a courtier, nor a friend who might keep you company on the trip. Now I understand why I was chosen. How long have we to prepare?"

Even the horses seemed to hold their breath waiting for the answer.

Theron spread his hands. "Two days, maybe three. No more."

"Rider in the pass!"

All heads turned toward the high watchtower. Some things needed no translation.

"Maybe less," the king amended dryly.

"Surrender?" Theron folded his hands over the saddlehorn and looked calmly out at the Cemandian herald. Although the herald had addressed him in fluent Shkoden, he continued to speak the local dialect. "I don't think so."

The herald shot an anxious glance at Tadeus who was Singing softly so that all those gathered on the battlements above could hear the conversation. A muscle twitched along the side of his face, but holding both lance and reins he had no way to make the sign against the kigh. "Majesty, Prince Rajmund wishes me to point out that you are vastly outnumbered and unable to close the pass. You may be able to hold the keep, but you cannot keep us out of Ohrid. It will only be a matter of time."

"Then it will be that matter of time."

"Majesty, there will be many deaths for no reason . . ."

"There may be many deaths, but they will all be for a reason. To keep this land free of Cemandian rule."

"My prince says that he believes the people of Ohrid have no wish to die for such a reason."

"Your prince is wrong." Pjerin's voice barely needed bardic assistance to fill the pass. "You can tell him I said so. And you can tell my aunt that if she had a heart, I'd cut it out and feed it to her."

"I will tell them both, Your Grace." The herald turned his attention back to the king. "Majesty, my prince suggests that it is not yet too late for a joining between himself and your heir to unite these kingdoms in peace."

"Tell your prince that I do not wish these kingdoms to be united and I, and my heir, will fight to our last breath to prevent it." Theron's voice changed slightly. "And herald, tell your prince that it is not too late for him to take his army home before he spills the blood of Cemandia to no avail."

The herald, who recognized a dismissal when he heard one, bowed, wheeled his horse, and galloped back over the border, flesh crawling with the certain knowledge that his every move was watched by the kigh.

"I should be on the barricades!" Pjerin tossed his hair back off his face. "This can wait."

"No, it can't, Your Grace." Elica put her hand on his good shoulder and pushed him back into the chair. "Unless you want to lose the use of that arm, it has to be healed. Now. You haven't exactly taken care of it."

"I haven't exactly been in a position to," Pjerin growled.

"Let her work," Theron said quietly coming into the

room. "We'll need you whole come morning. But if you have a moment, Healer, I was wondering about Annice."

"Well, she's exhausted and perhaps a little thinner than I'd like, but, all things being enclosed, I don't think there's anything to worry about. The blood ..."

"Blood?" both men exclaimed.

"The blood," Elica repeated, once again pushing Pjerin back into the chair, "is perfectly normal for this time in her pregnancy given that it's been only pink or brown spotting. I wouldn't have even mentioned it had I realized she hadn't told you."

"What else hasn't she told me?" Pjerin wondered, shifting irritably. "She said she was fine."

"She is fine. After a little sleep, she'll be in much better shape than you are if I don't take care of that wound. In fact," Elica sighed, "she'll be in better shape than I am after half a Quarter in the saddle." The rest of the king's party had arrived in the late afternoon to find the keep on a war footing and explanations more confusing than enlightening. Elica had taken one look at Annice and ordered her to bed; had taken a second look at Stasya and ordered her to follow. During the examinations, she'd heard the complete story.

Annice's healing of Gerek—if that's what had actually happened—would have to be investigated by the Healers' Hall. Before she left, she'd take a look at the boy herself. At the moment, with a war imminent and no other healers closer than Marienka, Elica was willing to acknowledge that the Circle held many wondrous things and leave it lie.

"Stasya," she continued, anticipating the king's next question, "may need healing to help her body overcome the effects of that pit. I'll know in the morning. His Grace," she added pointedly, "needs healing now because when I'm finished, he's going to want to sleep."

"When you're finished," Pjerin declared, "I'm going back to the barricades."

The healer rolled her eyes. "Was there anything else, Majesty?"

"No, nothing else." Theron nodded at the duc and Elica and left the room. When a healer used that tone of voice, even kings gave way.

Elica turned to Pjerin and studied the angry red lines radiating out from the torn scar tissue. "This is going to hurt," she began.

Pjerin's mouth twisted up into what might have been a weary smile. "I've been healed before. Let's get this over with."

"You're not going back to the barricades."

The smile showed more teeth. "You're not going to be able to stop me."

Some time later, Elica picked up the lamp and gently patted the hand of the sleeping duc. "I'll see you in the morning, Your Grace," she told him and quietly left the room.

"What can you see?"

Heart pounding, Pjerin jumped and spun around. "Annice! Are you supposed to be up here?"

"What do you mean?" She smiled at the sentry, then leaned against the battlements of the high watchtower and stared out into the pass. "Stasya and Tadeus want to see how far away I have to be in order for them to Sing. This is as far away as I can get and still be in the keep. If it comes to it," she added distastefully, "I may have to lock myself away in an interior room for the duration. Someplace with a heavy door and no windows."

"I meant, should you be up *here* in your condition?"

She wasn't going to tell him that she'd had to rest four times on the way up the narrow stairs or that she'd thought more than once she wasn't going to make it. "We walked across the country with me in this condition. How's your arm?"

"Better." He'd been furious to discover he'd fallen asleep and more furious still to have His Majesty tell him not to use it until he had to.

Annice smiled, correctly interpreting the undertones, then suddenly sobered. "I don't think you should have just let Nikulas go free. I mean, he tried to kill you."

"His brother was dead and he believed I was responsible. It was a perfectly natural response."

She couldn't believe him sometimes. "Of course it was. And suppose he tries it again?"

"He won't."

"Pjerin . . ."

"I know my people, Annice. One way or another, he'll be convinced."

"And Sarline?"

"Rozyte's not even speaking to her. She has enough personal problems right now without me adding to them."

Annice sighed. "Pjerin, it's all very well to be a compassionate lord, but don't you think . . ."

"I think we're about to have a war," he interrupted, his expression grim. "And I think I've had enough of death already."

Even she couldn't argue with that, so she carefully swung her bulk around and gestured toward Cemandia. "I don't see anything."

Pjerin turned to follow her hand. "Sun's been up on the other side of the mountains for a while. They're moving, count on it. We should be able to see them any . . . there!"

The sentry shook her head. "Just the sun flashing on a bit of shiny rock, Your Grace. Happens every morning there's enough light. We won't spot them until they're actually in the pass. Plenty of time to ready bows."

The battlements overlooking the pass would bristle with archers, many using crossbows and quarrels supplied from Albek's packs.

"Nice of him to leave them," Theron had said. *"Gives the whole situation a certain circular nature I'd like to consider a good omen."*

Pjerin squinted into the east a while longer, then twisted to face Annice. "You're very quiet," he said. Noting her confused expression and the way she was staring down at her legs, he asked, "Anything wrong?"

"I'm having a baby."

"I *know* that."

"You don't understand." She clutched his arm, conscious only of warm fluid dribbling down the inside of her thighs. "I'm having a baby *now*."

"Now?"

"Your Grace! There! Did you see it?"

"Now?"

She shook him. "Yes, now."

"But you're not due until Second Quarter! That's . . ."

He tried to count, but numbers failed him. "... days away."

"You think I don't know that?"

"Riders in the pass!"

"Annice, this isn't a good time."

"What are you talking about!"

"We're about to be attacked by the Cemandian army!"

"Fine!" She glared up at him. "You can tell *them* to wait!"

CHAPTER NINETEEN

". . . because you've probably been in labor for the last few hours."

"But I've had worse cramping during my flows," Annice protested as Elica sat her down on the end of the bed.

"Good." The healer turned to a bowl of warm water a curious server had just brought in and began washing her hands. "You may breeze right through this. We'll get you cleaned up and into a smock and then we'll find the rhythm of the contractions." She shot a grin over her shoulder at Annice. "You can put it to music if you like."

Annice felt some of her apprehension fade and took a deep breath, unlacing tightly clasped fingers.

"What should *I* do?" Pjerin hadn't realized how small Annice actually was until he'd carried her down from the top of the tower—all the way from Elbasan, even before at the keep, she'd given the impression of being much larger. She'd convinced him to let her walk once they reached level ground, by the volume of her arguments if nothing else, but he'd kept her arm tucked in his while he sent the first person he saw running to find the healer. He paced to her side, then back to the door, then to her side again. "Should I boil water? Rip up sheets? Rub her back?"

"Ow! Pjerin!"

Elica sighed. "Don't you have a war to fight, Your Grace?"

"A war?" For a moment Pjerin's face went blank. "Center it!" Three long strides and he was almost out of the room, three more and he returned to gently hold her face cupped between his hands. "I can't stay, Annice. I'm sorry. But I've got to . . ."

"I understand." She pushed her hands up under his. "I'm fine."

He snorted. "You keep *saying* that."

"Then keep believing it."

Bending forward, he kissed her lightly, then, as the sound of someone shouting for him drifted in through the shuttered window, almost ran from the room.

"Did you want him with you?" Elica asked, helping Annice to her feet and pulling the damp shift up over her head.

Emerging from a fold of fabric, Annice winced at a sudden contraction more powerful than the rest. "No." Her tone dressed the words in a multitude of meaning. "He got me here. I think he's done enough."

"Are they still holding back?"

Tadeus cocked his head into the breeze. "Yes, Majesty. Just out of bow shot."

Theron grunted and pulled on his gloves. "Stasya ready on the battlements?" The bards would not only use the kigh to carry orders beyond the range of his voice, but would see to it that everyone, regardless of what language they spoke would understand what was happening.

"She's there, but she's not happy. She'd much rather be with Annice."

"I know. I wish I could allow it, but we need her too badly out here. What about you?"

"Me, Majesty?" Tadeus grinned. "No, thank you. I've been with Annice when she's not having a good time, so all things being enclosed, I'd much rather stay here, be shot full of arrows, galloped over by heavy cavalry, have my throat slit by a camp follower, and my broken body left to rot under a merciless sun."

"Idiot," Theron muttered. "Are you sure my message got through to the captain in Elbasan?"

"Perfectly sure, Majesty."

"Then all we can do is wait." He squinted up at the sun. "Still, there's no question that waiting beats dying."

"How much longer is this going to go on?" Pjerin growled, stomping up from the barricades and yanking off his helm. With his hair clubbed back tightly into a wire-bound braid, the angles of his face enhanced an irritated expression. A knee-length vest of scale added a certain barbaric splendor compared to the simple breast-and-back of the king's company. Although he wore greaves, they were boiled leather rather than metal and both arms were covered wrist to elbow in laced leather guards. Waving his huge mountain bow at the keep, he snarled, "I thought the healer was going to tell us when something happened!"

Theron covered a smile. "Then nothing has happened."

"But it's been hours!"

"Pjerin, I sat with Her Majesty through the birth of each of our three children and I've learned from the experience—babies come in their own good time and there's nothing in the Circle you, as a father, can do to change that."

"Gerek was easier," Pjerin muttered, cramming his helm back on. "No one told me when it started, just when it was over. Handed me my son and that was that."

As the duc stomped back to the barricade, Theron shook his head. "With any luck, the baby will get his looks, her voice, and someone else's temperament."

"Is he very beautiful?" Tadeus asked, sounding just a little wistful.

"I heard you sing *'Darkling Lover'* just outside Caciz," Theron reminded the bard. "It contains some pretty explicit description, don't you think?"

"Explicit, Majesty, is not always accurate."

"Well, allowing for the passage of time, it's accurate enough."

Tadeus sighed. "Lucky Annice."

"How long does this usually go on?" Annice panted, right hand gripping the crook of Elica's elbow and her left pressed flat against the wall to support her weight. She'd lost track of how many times they'd walked up and down the hall, bare feet shuffling against the smooth stone. Although the contractions were definitely coming closer together and with greater intensity, as far as she could tell, nothing much seemed to be happening.

Elica shifted position slightly so that they both fit through the doorway. "It isn't over until it's over, Annice. Every woman is different. Every baby is unique."

"That's *not* very reassuring."

The village midwife stood as they came back into the room. She was a plump, grandmotherly sort of woman with tiny hands and a perpetual smile Annice was beginning to find extremely annoying. "So, how are we doing?" she asked.

"We," Annice began, but a contraction cut her off. She hadn't been able to talk through them for some time, and when it finally ended, she'd forgotten what she meant to say.

"Fifty-six," the midwife said. They'd established early on that her pulse would be used for timing.

"Good." Elica lowered Annice onto the clean sheet that draped the end of the bed. "I need to have a look and see how far dilated you are."

"A look?" Annice's eyes widened. "Are you talking about what I think you're talking about?"

"Probably." They had a small fire going in the fireplace and a kettle sitting over it on a tripod. Elica poured some of the hot water into a basin and washed her hands.

Fingers twisting the sheet into two sweaty bundles, Annice reclined against the pile of pillows and tried to relax. "How come nobody warned me about all this?" she asked the top of the healer's head.

"Well, possibly because you decided to take a Walk to Ohrid before anyone got the chance." Elica's tone made it quite clear what she thought of that particular choice.

"You're the one who told me pregnancy wasn't a disease."

"I'm also the one who told you there'd have to be some changes in your lifestyle."

"There were. Rescuing beautiful, arrogant men from execution and then waddling across the country with them was not something I'd previously made a habit of."

Elica looked up and smiled. "If you still have enough energy to be witty, you're doing all right."

As compared to what? Annice thought as another contraction hit.

The half-dozen horsemen, lances fixed, galloped wildly at the barricade under a rain of arrows. A horse screamed and stumbled as a feathered mountain-shaft penetrated a boiled leather crupper but managed to keep its feet.

"Hold your fire!" Lady Jura bellowed.

Tadeus Sang the command over the pass.

Behind one of the arrow slits built into the barricade, Pjerin stood, string at ear, triangular arrowhead centered unwaveringly on an approaching breastplate. He'd killed Otik with no time to think, no time to consider what he was doing. He'd tried to save Lukas; perhaps not as hard as he might have, but he'd tried. This was different. This was cold-blooded killing. Not a stag, not a boar, not a bear. A person. With a name and a family.

Who would destroy his name and his family if they could.

He'd told Annice he was tired of death. And he was. And it didn't matter.

Just before they reached the planted spikes, when the Cemandian pulled his horse's head around to wheel back the way he'd come, Pjerin loosed the string. At such close range, the arrow easily pierced the breastplate, the force of the impact lifting the Cemandian out of the saddle.

The body hit the ground, rolled, and lay still.

"Center it! I said hold your fire!" Lady Jura bellowed again. The guard had obeyed, but the people of Ohrid, following the example of their duc and less than willing to take orders from a Shkoder noble, continued to fill the pass with little effect.

The riderless horse wheeled and raced away with its companions. One of the remaining Cemandians swayed in the saddle and another carried a crossbow quarrel spiked through stirrup and leg.

One final flight struck sparks, metal against the stone, before the enemy was obviously out of range.

Glaring at the waste, Jura stomped to Theron's side. "Sing this," she snarled at Tadeus. "The next person who shoots after I've told them to stop is in more danger from me than from the Cemandians! And that," she added, twisting around to face Pjerin as Tadeus began to Sing, dropping her voice so as not to be overheard "includes you, Your Grace."

Pjerin stiffened. "Lady Jura, this is *my* land."

"And *your* liege has given *me* battle command."

Under the edge of her helm, her pale eyes glittered dangerously. "If there're Cemandians in that pass and I tell Your Grace to hold your fire, it would be in your best interest if you listened." As he ground his teeth together, she caught his gaze and held it. "We haven't time to turn your people and my people into one unit, but if we want to save *your* land and *my* land, we all have to be very clear on who's in charge."

"Your pardon." He inclined his head, the motion in no way a surrender, at best a grudging acknowledgment of the truth. "It won't happen again."

"Thank you, Your Grace." Point made, she nodded and looked away first, making it seem as though he had released her.

"What did Prince Rajmund hope to accomplish with that?" Theron asked, pleased with the way Jura had handled the duc. They had too few people to worry about inherited rank over ability, but it was equally important that the leadership they had not be undermined. *And she says she's no diplomat.*

"He was testing us, Majesty," she snapped. "Drawing our fire to build an idea of our strength and we gave him exactly what he wanted."

"Testing us with the bodies of his own people?"

"Every army has a few hotheads who don't believe they can be killed."

"Well, now he has one less," Pjerin said quietly.

"Shallow breaths, Annice. You don't want to push yet."

". . . why . . . not . . ."

"Because your body isn't ready."

". . . tired . . ."

"I know."

". . . hurts . . ."

Jazep shoved his way through the underbrush and out into the west end of the valley. The keep of Ohrid brooded in the distance.

By avoiding the kigh and tracking by more mundane methods, he'd managed to very nearly catch up with Annice and her companion. He only hoped he was in time. He hadn't been able to Sing up a kigh since just after dawn. It wasn't that they weren't listening. There weren't any around.

Breathing heavily, he wiped the sweat off his forehead with the back of one grimy hand and let his pack slide to the ground. Then he blinked as a low wave ran the length of the distant fields; north to south and back again.

"This isn't good."

Dropping to one knee, he pressed both palms hard against the earth and Sang.

The wave paused, then slowly continued, the swell growing larger with each pass.

"What the. . . ?"

Thanking all the gods in the Circle that the sun had shifted enough to stop blinding them, Jura peered up the pass. "It's called a tortoise. One of His Highness' commanders probably picked it up from the Empire."

Pjerin glared at the advancing square of overlapped shields and knew that the view from the battlements would be the same. "We can't get arrows through that!"

Jura snorted. "That's the idea, Your Grace."

At that moment, the front rank parted slightly in three places and a trio of flaming arrows thudded into the barricade, splattering hot pitch against the wood.

Then three more.

Then three more.

"Leave them," Jura barked. "Show yourself to put them out and they'll put one in you. Tadeus, stones."

Tadeus Sang and up on the battlements, Stasya turned and waved her fist in the air. Grinning broadly, Vencel set his bow aside, balanced a head-sized rock on one hand, then heaved. It arced up and over and slammed down onto the top of the shields.

A dozen followed, some smaller, a couple larger.

For a greater part of the night, those not building the barricade had loaded the battlements.

Under the second onslaught, the shield wall broke.

Jura nodded. "Now, fire."

Four more bodies littered the pass.

Elica forced her concentration back to Annice. There was someone hurt, dying. She could feel it even through

Annice's labor. Feel the loss of a life she could have
saved.

The rich topsoil of the fields began to heave.

Bagpipes in one hand, tambour in the other, Jazep ran
toward the pass, head down, short legs churning. With
all her abilities thrown to earth, Annice was stronger
than he thought. He didn't know what was going to happen, but he was afraid he was going to be too late to
stop it.

"Stasya says there's something going on. She can see
a lot of activity all grouped in one place but can't make
out what's happening."

"What about the kigh?" Theron asked.

Tadeus shook his head. "I can't make any sense out
of what they're telling me. His Highness seems to be
building something."

"Catapult?" the king wondered.

"Too complicated," Jura growled. "He doesn't care
about the keep, he just wants us out of his way."

"Battering ram."

King and commander turned toward Pjerin. Jura nodded grimly. "Odds are good."

There was a rhythm to the pain and that was all that
made it endurable. Her body Sang a scale, up and down
then up again, never so high she couldn't hit that top
note, but every time it trembled just at the edge of her
range.

During the high notes, her whole world narrowed to
Elica's voice soothing, supporting, keeping her focused
on what she had to do.

Which was nothing.

Except ride the pain.

Sing the scale.

Endure.

During the low notes, when she could think a little,
all she could think of was how totally her body had
moved out of her control. All her personal boundaries
had been breached. She felt as though she were being
physically invaded.

And she didn't like it.

* * *

The valley stirred in answer to her Song. A hillock
began to form in the cornfield, shoots growing out of
it at odd angles as more and more earth moved into
the shape.

A head.

Shoulders.

Two more bodies lay sprawled in the pass. One had
managed to crawl back far enough to be dragged to
safety.

"What's he doing?" Pjerin demanded, wiping his eyes
as smoke and steam rose off the barricade. "He knows
we can break up those unclosed turtles of his before the
fire really catches. He's wasting lives!"

"He also knows how long we had to prepare, that we
have a limited number of missiles on the battlements,
and a limited number of people to get more." Jura explained without taking her gaze off the pass. "My guess
is his ram's nearly done and he wants to disarm us as
much as possible before he brings it out. He's forming
up another square."

"Then we'll let it come!"

"We can't risk a lucky shot actually burning down the
barricade, Your Grace."

"There has to be another way we can stop him then."
Pjerin spat the words out like a challenge. "Ohrid will
not fall."

"What about the kigh?" Theron asked, turning to Tadeus. "The Cemandians are terrified of the kigh.
Couldn't you Sing something at them?"

Tadeus shook his head, dark curls lifting slightly in
breeze only he could feel. "We're not allowed to use the
kigh that way, Majesty. We've taken vows."

"And if I release you from them?"

"Begging your Majesty's pardon, but we didn't make
them to you." All at once, Tadeus smiled. "But that
does give me an idea. Captain!"

The troop captain, one leg straddling the top layer of
logs, crossbow trained down the pass to cover the four
guards attempting to put out the latest fires, grunted
without turning.

"Does your troop know 'Shkoder's Glory'?"

He snorted and a couple of the guards glanced up at the bard with surprised expressions. "Of course they do. Why?"

Tadeus twitched his heavily embroidered, turquoise silk collar into place. "The next time that shield wall approaches, we're going to give a little concert, your troop and I." Turning the brilliance of his smile on Theron, he explained. "The Cemandians are so terrified of Singing the kigh that they have very little vocal music. A chorus of 'Shkoder's Glory' by an entire troop of guard in this enclosed space ought to give them something to think about."

Jura nodded approvingly. "Think about anything other than what you're doing and a tortoise falls apart; not enough room in there for mistakes. Might work."

"Sire?" The troop captain came off the barricade and stared up at the king.

"Best decide, Majesty," Pjerin called. "Here they come again."

Theron nodded. "Do it."

Tadeus straightened and took a deep breath. His clear tenor rose over the noise around him. "Seven hearts and seven hands and seven lives are all that stand . . ."

Lady Jura laid a surprisingly strong alto under the bard's voice.

". . . shall we yield such hard bought land . . ."

One by one the guard joined in.

". . . not while breath remains. Though no one lives to tell our story, we fight for greater gain than glory . . ."

The left arm pulled itself free.
And then the right.

"This is impossible." When Terezka had given birth, although the kigh had been very present, they'd been no larger than usual. "Trust Annice."

Eyes on the huge kigh forming between him and the keep, Jazep fell, somehow managing to avoid landing on either instrument. With one foot back under him, he paused. Over the sound of his breath scraping in and out of his lungs, he could hear singing.

The kigh cocked its massive head to listen as well.

*   *   *

Vencel clutched at Stasya's arm as the song echoed between the mountain and the keep. "What are they doing?"

The bard shrugged. "I'm not sure." She knew the song. It was one of those patriotic death before dishonor anthems sure to be requested if there were two or more guards in the same inn.

"Is it bardic?"

"Not the way you mean." She frowned down at the approaching Cemandians, tried just for a moment not to think about Annice, and almost understood.

"Why aren't we stopping them?" Vencel scooped up a melon-sized rock in each hand. When they were gone, he had only three remaining. Along the battlements, other villagers began shouting similar questions.

Stasya waved at them to be quiet. Even if the words were in another language, surely they could hear what was going on.

The guard seemed to be throwing the song at the enemy.

This square was not as solid as the others had been. Cracks were definitely showing.

The first flaming arrow hit the barricade, but the second plowed into the dirt a body length away.

An answering arrow flashed from the barricade and into the space between two shields.

The song gained in defiant volume.

The square fell apart as those at the rear, without the press of bodies to drive them forward, broke and ran.

"Bows!" Stasya yelled. "Your duc's quite a shot," she added a moment later as a second Cemandian fell. Pjerin was the only one at ground level using a mountain bow.

Vencel grinned and notched an arrow. "We eat a lot of venison."

"All right, Annice, on this next contraction, I want you to push."

Annice forced her eyes open for the first time in what seemed like days. "Push ... what?" she croaked. She'd always thought that when it came to it, her body would know instinctively what to do. Her body didn't have the faintest idea.

*   *   *

The legs under the great curve of belly were short and took very little time to form.

"I don't expect that'll work twice," Theron pronounced as the song fragmented into insults and jeers hurled at the retreating foe. "Prince Rajmund has proven himself too well prepared to invade without someone around who knows how things actually work."

"Albek," Pjerin snarled.

Theron nodded. "Very likely. Tadeus, what's wrong?" The bard had gone pale and his hands had come up as though he were ... blind.

"The kigh. They're gone."

Up on the battlements, Stasya groped at the air. "Shit. Shit. Shit!"

"What?"

"They're coming with the battering ram!"

"So?"

She swallowed fear. *This isn't like it was in the hole. This isn't like it was in the hole.* "So we're on our own."

"That's it, Annice. Push."

Screaming would take more than she had left.

They'd had to cannibalize at least two wagons to hold the length and weight of the tree. A spiked metal cup hammered onto the head protected the men at the crosspieces from the archers behind the barricade while shields fixed to the ram covered them from above.

Iron-bound wheels struck sparks against the stone of the pass.

"We can't stop that," Theron yelled. "Clear the barricade! Get ready for what follows!"

"To horse!" Jura bellowed.

Pjerin fired one last arrow, then ran with the rest. It infuriated him that he had to turn his back on Cemandia if only for a moment.

The earth trembled.

Several of the guards were flung to their knees.

Someone on the battlements screamed.

Paying no attention to the tiny creatures around its

feet, the huge kigh reached the barricade an instant before the battering ram. As the metal head shattered the spikes, it ignored the shards of splintering wood that slammed into its legs and the lower curve of its belly and reached down, wrapping both hands around the massive trunk.

Over surrounding sounds of disbelief and terror, came a wet crackling, and the two Cemandian soldiers caught under its grip stopped moving. The rest, unable to see because of the shield protecting them and unable to hear over the impact, felt the ram lifted skyward. The lucky ones let go.

"What is it?" Theron demanded, shaking Tadeus by the arm.

"Majesty! I can't *see* it!"

The kigh held the ram for a moment, then threw it back over its shoulder.

"Take cover!"

Corporal Agniya dove for the side of the track and hit the ground shrieking as a piece of jagged metal as big around as her thumb went through her thigh.

"Push, Annice! I can see the top of the head!"

Pjerin threw himself flat as a wheel whistled over his head, then crawled to Theron's side.

"How do we stop it!"

"We can't!"

"Jazep?" Tadeus twisted around and grabbed at the panting bard. "What are you doing here?"

"Was following Annice's trail. She's doing this."

"Doing what?" Tadeus wailed.

"Near as I can figure, it's a giant, uh, well, earth kigh."

Pjerin rolled over and stared at the creature methodically stomping the barricade to kindling. He should have known. "I've got to get to her!"

"Hold it!" Theron snapped. "No one goes anywhere until we know what's going on!" He jabbed a finger toward Jazep. "Bard?"

"Yes, Majesty." Jazep swallowed, trying to catch his breath. "I Sing earth. Annice is ..." He broke off, searching for the words. "Annice *is* earth right now."

Theron gritted his teeth. "Very bardic. I thought the kigh were less ... physical."

"Usually they are, Majesty."

"Can you stop it?"

"I don't think so, Majesty. If I'd been here since the beginning, I might have been able to contain it, but ..."

"Try!"

"Yes, Majesty!"

"Would you stop that!" Stasya shrieked as Vencel and everyone else on the battlements frantically flicked their fingers out in the sign against the kigh. "It doesn't work! It never works! And it certainly won't work against this!"

Pushing people aside, she ran for the stairs in the inner tower. She had to get to Annice. If anything had gone wrong, she'd never forgive herself for not being there. She knew that if she closed her eyes, she'd see the crushed bodies of the two Cemandians etched into the lids, but the only thought she could hold onto was, *I warned her about this Mother-goddess shit.*

"Just a little more, Annice, and I can help. Deep breath. Hold it. Now *push*."

Jazep began to Sing. The kigh paused, one foot raised. It shivered, as though it were shaking off a fly, and then continued to shuffle forward.

"Keep Singing," Theron commanded.

Clear of the debris, Pjerin stood and began to run for the gates.

Exactly halfway between the two forces, the kigh stopped and suddenly swung one massive arm, the blow taking a huge chunk out of the mountain.

"Head's clear." Elica bent and sucked the tiny mouth and nose free of mucus.

A faint cry of protest seemed to fill the room.

Annice tried to track the sound and failed. "What. . . ?"

"It's your baby, Annice. Give me one more push and we'll get the shoulders ..."

"My baby ..." Staring down over the bulge of her body, Annice found herself responding to her first glimpse of an oddly shaped crescent of wet hair with a sudden surge of energy. She didn't know whether it was caused by rapture or relief. She used it without caring.

The kigh began to rock back and forth, shifting its weight from one leg to the other.

Jazep fought to Sing to another rhythm.

The mountain began to tremble.

The walls of the keep began to shake.

"It's a girl, Annice."

Annice lay back against the pillows, the midwife's arm supporting her shoulders. Very gently, she touched the grayish-pink and bloody bundle still connected to the faintly pulsing cord that Elica laid on her stomach. "A girl?"

"Healthy in every way."

"You sure?" She'd never seen a baby that looked quite so . . . so . . .

"Trust me." Wrapping the umbilical cord around her finger, Elica kneaded Annice's abdomen with the other and began to work the afterbirth free. "I'm a healer. If there was something wrong, I'd know."

"She's beautiful, Annice."

The midwife's smile was no longer irritating. "She's slippery." Annice tried to cup an arm around her daughter's tiny back, but she was just too tired. "Are you sure she's not going to fall off?"

"As if in response, the baby squirmed and made another, louder, protest.

"She looks . . . annoyed."

"She's been through a lot." Elica tied off the cord, cut it, and wrapped the afterbirth in a piece of clean sheeting. "Let's get the two of you cleaned up and . . ."

The room shivered.

Loose rock careened down into the pass.

The hall rose up to meet her boot. Stasya staggered and kept running. *I should have been there. I should have been with her.*

* * *

The huge oak gates creaked on their hinges and the portcullis shook against its supports as Pjerin pounded into the court.

Elica threw out one hand to support the baby and another to support herself against the bed. "What in . . ."

"Annice!" Stasya exploded into the room. "Annice are you all . . . oh."

"It's a girl, Stas." Her voice was gone yet again. It didn't seem to matter.

"Oh, Nees." Stasya sank to her knees by the bed. "Are you all right?"

Annice reached out and touched the other woman's cheek, realizing now what had been missing all along. "I'm glad you're here."

Tears in her eyes, Stasya turned her head to softly plant a kiss on Annice's palm. "She's . . ."

The room shifted again. A crack ran down the outside wall.

Suddenly reminded of what was happening outside, Stasya rocked back onto her feet and darted to the window, wrestling the shutters out of their clamps. "You've got to sing a gratitude, Nees."

Annice looked up from investigating five perfect fingers. "A what?"

"A gratitude. Now."

Elica took the bard firmly by the arm. "Stasya, this is no time . . ."

Stasya shook herself free and returned to Annice's side. "Have you ever delivered a bardic baby before?"

"Well, no, but she's a baby like any other."

"Granted. But Annice Sings all four quarters and right now, the answer to the Song she's been Singing the last few hours is outside indiscriminately tearing the pass apart."

"She hasn't been Singing . . ."

Annice remembered the rhythm of the pain. High notes. Low notes. "I think," she said slowly, "I have." She looked at her daughter and smiled. It wouldn't be hard to Sing a gratitude.

The kigh fell apart so quickly it very nearly took Jazep

with it. He rocked back on his heels and would have fallen had Theron not flung up an arm in support.

He blinked at the pile of dirt nearly blocking the pass and let his Song trail off.

"Annice?" Theron demanded.

"She's fine," Tadeus was grinning broadly, his hair blowing around his head. "She had a girl. They're both fine. Stasya's with her."

Jazep gestured into the pass. "Shall I try to Sing it away, Majesty?" he asked.

Theron looked thoughtful. "No," he said after a moment. "I think we'll leave it there while Prince Rajmund and I discuss a new treaty as a reminder of what Shkoder can call to its defense."

"But, Majesty, we were in as much danger from it as the Cemandians were. We weren't controlling it. Annice wasn't even controlling it. And unless the circumstances were repeated exactly, I doubt anyone could ever call the kigh up like that again."

The king smiled. "I don't see any reason we have to tell Rajmund that."

"Annice!" Pjerin entered the room much the way Stasya had, only more heavily armored. "Are you . . ."

Smiling up at him from the circle of Stasya's arms, Annice stroked one finger over the soft cap of dark hair, dry now and feeling like nothing else in the world. "I told you it was a girl."

Pushing off his helm, Pjerin slowly crossed the room to the bed. "A girl? A daughter?"

Annice watched him stare down at the baby and thought, *I never believed in love at first sight before.*

"Have you decided what you're going to call her?" The king of Shkoder looked as besotted as everyone else as a tiny hand grabbed onto his finger.

Annice shifted the baby's weight a little and yawned. She hadn't slept in the last two days. Although Elica had taken care of much of the pain, it seemed that every time she closed her eyes, the baby started to cry. "Well, Stasya's pulling for Cecilie, Pjerin wants Evicka, and Gerek said something about naming her after a goat."

"That was before I knew she was a girl!" Gerek protested indignantly from the floor by the window.

Theron smiled and held out his arms. "May I?"

He has three children of his own, Annice reminded herself as she hesitated. *He's not going to drop her.* Lower lip held between her teeth, she passed the baby to her brother and attempted to relax.

"She looks like you did," Theron murmured, lightly kissing the tiny forehead. "Her hair's darker, but she has the same way of screwing up her face and turning red."

Annice felt her own ears grow hot. "Uh, Theron, that means she's ..."

"I know."

As he didn't seem to mind, she tried not to.

"Have you decided what you want to do about raising her?" He looked over at her, his expression serious. "She needs a family."

"I know." Annice glanced over at Gerek, who was, he said, building a palace for his sister out of wooden blocks. "I know," she repeated. "But I'm a bard."

Theron shook his head and sighed. "I thought we were past that."

"I can't give it up."

"No one's asking you to."

"Then what?" She picked at the hem of her borrowed robe. "Stasya and I can walk together for a while, and, well, we're used to planning our lives around what we do, but what about Pjerin? I can't ask him to come to Elbasan, or the Bardic Hall in Vidor even if the captain would agree to base us there. Which she probably wouldn't because it's tiny and they've already got someone who Sings all four quarters. And it could be years before I Walk this way again." Reaching out, she stroked the perfect curve of her daughter's ear. "I'm babbling."

"If there's anything I can do ..." He laid the fussing baby back in Annice's arms. "... will you ask me?"

Would she? "I don't know."

He nodded, as aware of the ten years as she was.

"Nees, she's beautiful."

Annice grinned and tweaked a long dark curl. "How can you tell?"

His smile more brilliant than she'd ever seen it, Tadeus bent forward and kissed her cheek. "I'm blind," he said softly. "I'm not stupid."

Jazep, the baby held securely in the cradle of his hands, stared down at her, his eyes wide with wonder. "A new life," he murmured through the catch in his voice. "A new beginning"

"You are such a suck," Tadeus declared fondly. He reached over and with one finger lightly traced the moisture on Jazep's face. "I just got the best idea for a song . . ."

The terms of the new treaty were thrashed out much as Theron dictated.

"The world is changing," he told a glowering Duc of Ohrid as they walked back to the keep from the huge tent that had been set up at the midpoint in the pass. "We can not close ourselves off from it because if we do it's not only trade we prevent, but the spread of knowledge and new ideas. Ignorance breeds intolerance. Intolerance breeds war."

Pjerin snorted. Kings and princes both he'd discovered over the last few days, were much given to that type of pronouncement. "I don't trust the Cemandians, Majesty. Suppose they suddenly decide to start developing the kigh as weapons."

"It isn't that easy for an entire people to change their beliefs, Your Grace." *Or,* Theron added silently, *for one stubborn duc to change his.*

"Will he give us what we want?"

"We're negotiating from a position of strength. There's no reason why he shouldn't."

"Will he give *me* what *I* want?"

"I think so. He has no reason to protect her and every reason to distrust her. There's an old Riverfolk saying: 'A snake on the left bank is still a snake on the right.' "

"And Albek."

"No. By Cemandian standards, Albek is a patriot. Prince Rajmund is no fool. He'll let it be seen that he protects his own people." Theron raised a hand to cut off a growled protest. "You'd do the same. Don't push on this, Your Grace. You won't win."

"What about Adelka?"

Stasya shook her head. "Nees, she doesn't look like an Adelka. What about Cecilija?"

"That's almost the same as Cecilie," Annice protested, wincing as the baby nursed. No one had told her that it was going to hurt—although everyone was telling her now that it would soon stop, she'd decided not to believe them. "What do you think, Pjerin?"

Pjerin turned from the window, brows drawn in. "I don't trust the Cemandians," he said. "Prince Rajmund still hasn't agreed to all the terms of the treaty."

The two bards exchanged identical expressions.

"We know that," Stasya sighed. "But what do you think about Cecilija as a name for the baby?"

"Even when he does, I don't think they're going to stop trying." His hands curled into fists. "They need to be watched."

"Fine. Watch them." Stasya used just enough Voice that she was sure of gaining his attention. "But first, tell us what you think about Cecilija before your daughter reaches her first name-day without a name."

"Cecilija?" Frown lifting, he crossed the room to sit on Annice's other side. "I don't think so." He enclosed a flailing hand in his. "What about Kornelia?"

"Yuk!" Stasya made a face. "I had an Aunt Kornelia. She smelled like seaweed all the time."

"The Cemandians need to be watched ..." Annice stared at nothing, her attention distracted from the ache in her breasts.

"Nees, don't you start. He's bad enough. What about Tasenka?"

Pjerin snorted. "Forget it. What about Milena?"

The Cemandians need to be watched. Annice smiled. She had an idea.

"Theron? Can I talk to you?"

"Of course." He gestured his valet from the room and closed the door behind him. "What is it?" he asked. "Does my niece finally have name?"

"Well, yes." Annice settled gingerly into a chair. "I pulled rank as her mother and we settled on Magda."

"Magda," Theron repeated, pleasantly surprised. "Grandmother's name. Magda i'Annice a'Pjerin. Maggi. I like it." He perched on the edge of a parchment covered table. "But that's not why you've come?"

She took a deep breath and released it slowly. "No.

Did you mean it when you said, if there was anything you could do?"

"Shall I have it Witnessed?"

Half-smiling, she wiped her palms against her shift. "In a way, I suppose you already did." *Ten years. Will he understand?* "I've thought of something you can do."

"A Bardic Hall here? In Ohrid? In the keep?"

Theron hid a smile at the tone of Pjerin's voice. "You have plenty of room, Your Grace.

"Yes, Majesty, but . . ."

"A Bardic Hall here will serve a number of purposes. The Cemandians need to be watched. Ohrid has been promised closer ties with the rest of Shkoder. Your people need to learn that the kigh are no threat. And I would just as soon not have our next war with Cemandia be a religious crusade. The more contact the Cemandians have with the kigh and with bards the better—this way, every Cemandian through the pass will have contact."

"Ignorance breeds intolerance," Pjerin murmured, a little stunned. "Intolerance breeds war."

This time, Theron allowed the smile to blossom. "Well said, Your Grace." He sat back in the chair and fingered his collar button. "It will, of necessity, be a minimal Hall, with one bard who Sings all four quarters and one other, strong in air, to Walk."

"Majesty?" Stasya stepped forward, suddenly understanding why all four Bards had been commanded to attend the king and why Jazep and Tadeus both had been told to recall. "If you're saying that Annice and I are going to form a new Bardic Hall here at the keep, would you please just say it."

"You and Annice are going to form a new Bardic Hall here at the keep," Theron said. He grew serious. "It won't be an easy task, half of Ohrid still believe the kigh to be outside the Circle. You'll have to work against that, against their fears. Convince them otherwise. Convince them that their future lies with Shkoder, not Cemandia."

"We can do that, Majesty."

Bards, Theron mused, *have found more than their share of self-confidence in the Circle.*

Pjerin glanced from the king to Annice, who was serenely contemplating the swaddled bundle in her arms, and back again. "Maggi will be raised here? As a bard?"

"By a bard," Theron corrected. "And by you. the child will discover for herself what the Circle holds for her."

"Begging Your Majesty's pardon." Stasya hated to bring this up, but someone had to. "But what about the captain?"

"What about her?"

"What if she doesn't agree?"

Theron stood. "I," he said, "am king in Shkoder."

Annice looked up and smiled. "Witnessed."

"Olina i'Katica, step forward."

A murmur ran around the court as the people of Ohrid, packed shoulder to shoulder on the ground and on the battlements tried to get a better view. Theron had intended the Judgment to be held in the Great Hall, but Pjerin had insisted that all the people of Ohrid had the right to attend.

Prince Rajmund had agreed to all the terms of the treaty.

Back straight, expression disdainful, Olina stepped away from her escort and stood alone in the only empty space in the court. Her cold gaze swept over Theron— seated in her favorite chair, she noted with bitter irony— past the bard standing beside him, and over the three bards off to one side. She stared for a moment at Annice, at the tiny bundle in her arms. No one had told her exactly how things had gone so impossibly wrong, but with the sister of the king bearing her nephew's child, it wasn't difficult to find the probable cause. If she hated anyone, she hated Annice.

"I heard," she said, turning at last to Pjerin, "that congratulations are in order. A daughter?"

Teeth clenched, Pjerin nodded.

Theron sat forward. "Olina i'Katica, do you know why you are here?"

She inclined her head graciously. "So that your bards can use the kigh to put words in my mouth and a foreign king can take my life."

The crowd stirred. The sound that followed the motion was tinted with doubt. Words had been put in the mouth of their duc. Who knew what was true anymore? Here and there, fingers flicked out in the sign against the kigh.

"You have been given no command save that of stepping forward," Theron told her evenly. "And I am king in Ohrid as in Shkoder by virtue of oaths sworn by your great-grandfather to mine."

Olina spread her hands. "I swore no oaths. You cannot accuse *me* of treason."

"I am not accusing you of treason. The Death Judgment is called for another crime. Do you deny that you arranged, with the help of Cemandia, to have your nephew killed?"

"I deny nothing. I admit nothing. To do either, would acknowledge your right to judge me, which I do not."

Pjerin stepped forward. "Do you deny that I am Duc of Ohrid?" he asked quietly.

The crowd stilled to hear him.

"Does your master allow you to speak, then?"

"Answer me, Olina. Do you deny that I am duc?"

"You are the duc," she answered. She knew where he was going with this and planned to meet him there. Over the last few days when Cemandian guards made it clear that Prince Rajmund would not protect her, she'd had little to do but plan.

With a hiss of steel, Pjerin pulled the Ducal sword free of the scabbard and held it out, point aimed at her heart. "The day I gave my blood to Ohrid with this sword, you swore to have me as your lord."

"Agreed." Her smile held no humor. "But if you wish to be a part of Shkoder, then you should know that only the king can sit in a Death Judgment. You have surrendered your right to judge me to someone who has no right." She turned and addressed the people. "The kigh rule the bards, the bards rule the king, the king rules your duc. Do you want the kigh to rule in Ohrid?"

"NO!"

The cry still echoed off the mountain when Vencel pushed his way into the open.

"The kigh," he declared, "are not the issue."

"Vencel . . ." Pjerin began, but Theron cut him off.

"Let him speak. If Lady Olina wishes the people to

decide whether I am to judge her, I will abide by their judgment."

Sweat darkened the pale sides of Vencel's tunic but he wet his lips and went on. "How anyone feels about the kigh doesn't change the fact that you arranged to have His Grace killed."

Ebony brows rose. "Who says I did?"

"Well, His Grace!"

"Who you also heard say that he broke his oaths and sold Ohrid out to Cemandia. Which time was he telling the truth?"

"You ran to Cemandia when he returned!"

"Have you seen my nephew in a rage?" Her voice was silken reason. "I had no wish to meet him until he calmed. You know what happened to Lukas."

The crowd fell silent, and she felt her chance slip free. She'd heard that Lukas had gone off the inner tower, that Pjerin had been up there with him. She knew his rages. How could he not have taken advantage of that opportunity?

Urmi slipped between two of her stablehands to stand at Vencel's side. "Lukas threatened to drop Gerek off the tower. Whatever was between you and His Grace, or Lukas and His Grace, Gerek wasn't a part of that. We," her gesture took in everyone in the court, "all heard you insist that Gerek had been taken away by a bard you knew was half-conscious in a pit . . ."

"Lukas," Olina began.

Gerek twisted out of his nurse's grasp and ran across the court to stare up at his aunt. Except for the sword, his stance was a copy of Pjerin's. "I saw you!" he told her. "I saw you put Stasya in the pit, and if you say you didn't, you're telling lies."

"You were willing to let a young child die!" Urmi spat. "And for what?"

"So all of Ohrid would have a chance to be more than it was," Olina snarled.

"Less!" Vencel shouted. "You can't be more if the cost is an innocent life!"

When the shouting died down, Theron stood. "People of Ohrid. Am I to judge?"

The response was deafening. It was one thing for ambition to remove a grown man and quite another for that same ambition to demand the life of a child. In all the confusion, that, at least, was certain.

Pjerin stared into Olina's eyes, the Ducal sword still pointed at her heart. "I promised that I'd nail you to the door of the keep with this," he growled.

Her smile was ice. "I wonder if you've found everything we put in your head," she purred. "You'll never know, will you?"

"It's *over*, Olina."

"Yes. It's over. But I said in the beginning that no one would take my head." Her face twisted and a trickle of blood ran down her chin as she bit through her lip.

Pjerin stared down at her grip on his wrist, too astounded to react.

She yanked herself a little closer and another handbreadth of the blade slid in under her breastbone.

Someone screamed as the point ripped out through her back.

Pjerin could still feel the heat of her fingers on his skin as they slid off to stiffen, once, twice, in the air. She stumbled. Fell to her knees, the blade pulling free with a rush of crimson. Eyes wide, her mouth worked as she tried one last time to speak. She tumbled forward.

An instant later, the sword rang on the cobblestones beside the body.

"What a waste," Theron said softly. "What a terrible waste."

"Are you sure about this, Annice?"

"I'm sure." Annice settled the baby more securely in her sling and carefully sat on the stool Stasya had carried out for her.

"His Grace won't like it," Jazep murmured, adjusting the tambour strap around his neck.

"His Grace doesn't have to like it," Annice pointed out tartly as Tadeus reached out and twitched Jazep's collar down. "This has nothing to do with Pjerin. It's bardic business."

Overhead, the stars seemed close enough to touch. Around them were the remains of Annice's kigh. Most of the earth had been returned to fields—as far as the people of Ohrid were concerned, fear of the kigh did not extend to starving to death over the winter. Newly planted crops were already nearly the height of the corn that had been destroyed. Luxuriant growth hid any crack or crevasse in the pass that hadn't been completely cleared.

"Are you sure you're strong enough for this, Nees?" Stasya squatted beside the stool. "You haven't really slept for more than an hour at a time since you had the baby and remember the captain's message—you're supposed to be resting your voice."

"Stas," Annice reached out and stroked the other woman's cheek. "Tadeus and Jazep are leaving tomorrow with the king. It has to be tonight."

Tadeus turned toward Cemandia. "He might not be anywhere he can hear us."

"He is."

"How can you be so certain?" Jazep asked softly.

Annice sighed. "I'm not."

Shaking her head, Stasya stood. "They've crippled him, Nees. He might not be able to come to us even if he hears."

"I know." She checked her sleeping daughter and when she looked up, her expression was grave. "But how could we live with ourselves if we don't try?"

The night came alive as Jazep stroked a heartbeat out of the drum. Eyes closed, he Sang. He wasn't calling the kigh, but he was calling, voice anchored to the earth and reaching into Cemandia.

Tadeus nodded in time and added a Song that burned along the path Jazep laid.

One hand resting lightly on Annice's shoulder, Stasya's Song rose to touch the stars.

Earth. Fire. Air.

"Annice, he's a spy, and a saboteur, and . . ."

"And in Shkoder, he would have been a bard."

Water.

Tears.

The other three faltered as Annice added her voice to theirs. For a moment, the longing, the pain, the loneliness overwhelmed everything but the steady beat of Jazep's drum.

Stasya recovered first. Then Tadeus wrapped his denial around hers. When Jazep gathered them all together, they stopping Singing and became the Song.

Slowly, they answered the longing, and eased the pain, and reached out to the loneliness.

Annice saw him first and fell silent.

The Song she'd been Singing carried on. The voice was untrained, rough, but it didn't matter because it was the heart that was Singing.

A moment later, he Sang alone, then the kigh, gathered thickly about him, spun away and carried the last note into the night.

His face twisted with terror, trembling so violently he could hardly stand, Albek stared at the four bards. "What have you done?" he whispered hoarsely.

Annice stood and reached out toward him. "Only told you that we understand."

He shook his head and took a step back. "No." Another step back. In moment he was going to bolt and run.

Then the baby began to cry.

Albek started at the sound.

Without thinking, Annice Sang comfort to her.

When she looked up, Albek was on his knees, sobbing in the circle of Tadeus' arms, the dark head bent close to the gold one, and Singing the same Song.

". . . *and* nursing my daughter on the Cemandian border in the middle of the night." Pjerin wanted desperately to yell—had wanted desperately to yell since he and Theron and half the inhabitants of the keep, who'd been roused weeping from their beds by Annice's song, had met the five of them coming back through the gates—but the baby was asleep and Annice wouldn't leave her. "What were you thinking?"

"I don't need to explain myself to you, Pjerin."

"You *know* who he is. *What* he is."

She reached into the cradle and touched the rosebud curl of her sleeping daughter's hand. "Better than you do."

Pjerin sucked in a deep breath and jabbed a finger at her. "Don't hand me some crap about bards being more sensitive, more all-seeing than the rest of us because I'm not in the mood. I heard what you Sang; you pulled out all the stops on telling him how pathetic his life was and then promised you'd make it better."

"That's not quite what happened, Your Grace." Stasya unfolded her legs and slid off the bed.

"Stay out of this, Stasya. This is between Annice and me."

"That wasn't his Song she was Singing, Pjerin. It was her own."

"What are you talking about?" He frowned down at Annice. "What's she talking about?"

"Don't even try," Stasya cautioned as Annice opened her mouth to deny the accusation. "Words might hide the truth, but a Song never lies. That was your pain. Not Albek's."

"Was," Annice admitted, refusing to look at either of them. "But I let go of it."

Stasya sighed and shook her head. "How am I supposed to believe that when you spent ten years telling me it didn't exist?"

Brow furrowed, Pjerin heard again the incredible loneliness, the heartbroken sense of betrayal that had pulled him out of a dream where he'd had Olina by the shoulders and was asking her over and over again, *"WHY?"*

"Your brother did that to you." His tone bordered on treason.

"No." This time she looked up. "I did it to myself. Or maybe we did it to each other, I'm still not sure how Theron feels. Albek had it done to him, but I don't have his excuse." She stroked the baby's cheek and smiled a little at the dark line of lashes so like Pjerin's. And so like Stasya's, too, for that matter. "If I'm going to be responsible for her life, I've got to take responsibility for my own."

"And everyone else's?" Pjerin wondered, thinking of how she'd thrown herself in front of Albek and Tadeus when he'd charged across the court demanding the Cemandian's heart. The edge had left his voice and it wasn't really a question as he already knew the answer.

"I'm someone's mother now, Pjerin. I'm no longer *that* extreme . . ."

Over her head, Stasya and Pjerin exchanged identical expressions of disbelief.

A Note from the publishers concerning:

NINE ABOVE!

Tanya Huff readers take note! "NINE ABOVE!" is a quarterly newsletter devoted to the work of Tanya Huff. Publication updates, appearances, interviews, correspondence section, and more! Please join us in our appreciation of Tanya's work and our enjoyment of each other.

For more information please send a business-size self-addressed stamped envelope to:

NINE ABOVE!
P.O. Box 204
Brattleboro, VT 05302

(This notice is inserted gratis as a service to readers. DAW Books is in no way connected with this organization professionally or commerically.)

Mickey Zucker Reichert

☐ **THE UNKNOWN SOLDIER**   UE2600—$4.99
☐ **THE LEGEND OF NIGHTFALL**   UE2587—$5.99

THE RENSHAI TRILOGY
☐ **THE LAST OF THE RENSHAI: Book 1**   UE2503—$5.99
☐ **THE WESTERN WIZARD: Book 2**   UE2520—$5.99
☐ **CHILD OF THUNDER: Book 3**   UE2549—$5.99

THE BIFROST GUARDIANS
☐ **GODSLAYER: Book 1**   UE2372—$4.99
☐ **SHADOW CLIMBER: Book 2**   UE2284—$3.99
☐ **DRAGONRANK MASTER: Book 3**   UE2366—$4.50
☐ **SHADOW'S REALM: Book 4**   UE2419—$4.50
☐ **BY CHAOS CURSED: Book 5**   UE2474—$4.50

Mercedes Lackey

The Novels of Valdemar

Don't Miss These Exciting DAW Anthologies